ALL THE LITTLE RAINDROPS

ALL THE LITTLE RAINDROPS

A NOVEL

MIA SHERIDAN

Ⓜ Montlake

Text copyright © 2023 by Terra Newman
All rights reserved.

Published by Montlake, Seattle

www.apub.com

Amazon, the Amazon logo, and Montlake are trademarks of Amazon.com, Inc., or its affiliates.

ISBN-13: 9781662514104 (paperback)
ISBN-13: 9781662508233 (digital)

Cover design by Caroline Teagle Johnson
Cover images: © Ellen Queiroz / 500px / Getty; © Midnight Blue / EyeEm / Getty; © Yasser Chalid / Getty

Printed in the United States of America

*To those who have crawled from wreckage and refused
to live a meek life in the aftermath*

PART ONE

Man is the cruelest animal.

—*Friedrich Nietzsche*

CHAPTER ONE

Noelle had tried to keep track of the days, but they were indistinguishable from the nights, both bathed in still silence and utter blackness. So finally, she'd given up. How could she have known how hard it was to measure an hour when that hour was spent in dark, quiet terror?

She'd become aware that there were places where time did not exist. Because even in the absence of a clock, its measurement was based on sensory input: the rising and setting of the sun, the sounds of traffic, a church bell in the distance . . . or a hundred other signals from the surrounding world. Not here in the cage she currently inhabited. And so instead of counting, the way she'd done once she'd gotten her bearings and forced herself to stay as calm as possible, she drifted. She tried not to let her imagination take over, tried not to picture herself in an airtight box deep under the sea. That only made her blood pressure spike and her breath come in ragged pants, as though her air were actually running out.

The only things that did give her any indication of the passing hours were the clues of her own body. She grew hungry and thirsty. But food and drink came at random intervals from some type of small door in the wall just beyond her barred enclosure. She would hear it being lifted, and then a small shaft of milky light would appear, causing her to turn her head away, even the very dim glow too much for her dark-adjusted eyes. Like a bat in an underground cave reacting to a slant of muted sunlight streaming through a crack. But even turned away, she could smell the yeasty bread within, and it compelled her to crawl toward it and reach mostly blindly toward the food, her fingertips just barely reaching the plain piece of bread or a few crackers and a paper cup of water. The first time, unaware of its presence, she'd accidentally tipped the water over, and later, she'd grown so parched, her tongue had swelled and her lips cracked. Now she knew to be more careful when reaching for both. And then, before she could force her eyes fully open, the slot rolled shut, leaving her only with the hazy picture of the shape of the opening.

Sometimes food and drink came when she was so famished and dehydrated that she shook as she reached for the nourishment, and sometimes they arrived when she still felt mostly full. It had to be by design. To confuse her. To torment her. At first, she'd yelled and begged when the food deliveries were made; after all, a human must be somewhere just beyond, but no one had ever answered. She'd thought she heard footsteps somewhere far above. But other than that? Nothing.

If she had to guess, she'd say her cage was about six feet by four feet, and there was a toilet in the corner. She'd found it when she'd finally worked up the nerve to feel around her surroundings after waking there, disoriented, petrified, and alone. She'd felt its shape, determined it was made of metal like one of those prison toilets. Apt. After all, she was a captive. Whose, she did not know. She could not guess. The toilet flushed the same way an airplane toilet did, with a loud sucking sound followed by the soft closing of a flap. At least it offered some dignity. But it wouldn't save her from dying of thirst.

When she'd realized her predicament and that she'd been kidnapped, Noelle had cried and rocked, imagining how terrified her father must be. He would have been raising hell with the police to find her. Recently, they only saw each other in passing, or not at all, but he would have called her or grown worried if she hadn't called him back. He was working a night job right now, and because it was currently

4

spring break and school was out, she was working her waitressing job during the day. But they spoke by phone at least every other day or sent quick texts. *I love you. There are leftovers in the fridge. Don't forget to put the trash out tonight.* And it'd been at least a week. *Right?* But maybe she was wrong. Maybe it'd only been a few days. At this point, maybe her job hadn't even called to see why she hadn't shown. Eventually she had to stop thinking about her dad because it made her panic ratchet higher, made her want to wail for him. Made her feel like she had when she was a little girl and had woken from a nightmare, screaming for her savior. Her father had always shown up then and taken her in his arms. "Hush," he'd said. "Daddy's here. You're safe."

The depth of longing for that now almost made her hyperventilate. And she wondered how long it would be before she began losing her sanity. Part of her reached for the reprieve of a broken mind, one that could not think, one that could not fear. Or imagine things that lay in wait in the surrounding dark. But the stronger part of her rejected giving up one of the few things she currently possessed: her will to live.

~

Noelle rolled away from the sudden burst of light, clenching her eyes more tightly shut and letting out a pained gasp. She sat up, holding her hand in front of herself defensively as she scooted back as far as possible, her spine hitting the bars of her enclosure. Through squinted lids, she saw alien-like moving shapes. She heard a grunt and then some clanging. Someone was, or a couple of *someones* were, in the room with her. "Hello?" Her heart raced, breath bursting harshly from her lips as she tried desperately to open her eyes all the way. But she'd been in the pitch black for so long that her eyes would not yet cooperate. "Please? Hello? Let me out. Please," she begged, hope giving her the courage to pull herself to her knees and crawl forward to the front of her cage. More clanking, some type of door closing to her right, and then footsteps as whoever had been in the room with her walked toward what looked like an open door on the wall to her left. "Please, no!" she screamed. "Don't go! Please! Let me out!"

The door slid shut, and the room went dark once more, the gaps where the door was not even emitting a small trickle of light. The soft sounds of footsteps moved away, and Noelle fell backward, tears coursing down her cheeks as she gave in to hopelessness.

There had been two people in the room, and they'd ignored her pleas. Her shoulders shook with her sobs, the ones she couldn't afford as they were depleting her body of moisture. And who knew when the next drink of water would come. Maybe there wouldn't be another.

Maybe that would be better.

Stop it, Noelle. You're stronger than that, aren't you?

She'd thought she was. At least . . . she'd hoped she *could* be. But how did anyone prepare themselves to be captured and caged in the dark for no discernible reason? And the biggest question she'd agonized over? Why? Why had she been taken? *Why me?*

Noelle startled, letting out a squeak when she heard a small groan from her right. She froze; her ears perked up as she listened. Another groan. Movement. Terror ripped down her spine. *Oh God.* Something was in here with her. An irrational vision filled her head: a scaly lizard-like being with jagged teeth that would tear her apart. She remained still, suddenly grateful for the protection of the bars surrounding her, the ones she'd gone over with her fingertips, every inch.

"Help." The word was barely whispered, more like the release of breath than an actual pronunciation. Noelle remained frozen, every cell in her body, every tiny hair on her skin, focused on the direction of the sounds coming from her right. A slide, another groan, what sounded like the slap of skin on metal. "Help." A definite word this time, stronger, clearer, and in a man's voice. Not an alien, then.

Probably.

Noelle remained still.

More movement, a louder grunt as though the . . . man might be pulling himself upright from a lying-down position.

"Is anyone here? Help."

Noelle's shoulders lowered infinitesimally, her hand releasing the death grip she'd had on the bar of her cage as she'd held herself completely rigid. "Y-yes. I'm here," she whispered.

There was a beat of silence, and then, "Who are you? Where are we?" He still sounded pained, but there was panic in his voice too. Fear.

"My name is Noelle. I don't know where we are. I don't know what day it is. The last thing I remember is leaving my job. I think . . . I think someone put a cloth over my mouth." A taste came back to her. Sharp. Medicinal. She thought she remembered flailing, being lifted . . . but nothing more. "I woke up here. In the darkness."

Other than a harsh exhale, the man was quiet.

"Who are you?" she finally asked.

"Evan. My name's Evan. I think something similar happened to me." He let out a sigh, a slight groan. "Someone attacked me from behind as I was leaving the gym. I've been kept in darkness somewhere else. I'm not sure what day it is."

Her mind spun. She didn't know what was happening, or why, and terror still sat heavy on her chest, but she almost wept with the sudden relief of having another human with her. Of no longer being alone.

"Are you hurt?" she asked when again she heard the sounds of movement, and he let out another soft, pained groan.

"A little. I fought whoever came for me earlier. They obviously had the upper hand. I think the person was wearing goggles to see in the dark."

She'd turned in his direction, though it was too dark in the room to even make out his outline, and she wrapped both hands around the bars, her face pressed between them as they spoke. *Goggles to see in the dark.* What the *hell* was going on? "Who? Who brought us here? And why?"

7

"I don't know. I have no idea."

"For what *reason*, then? Why are they doing this?"

There was a brief pause. "My family has money. They could have taken me for a ransom."

She licked her dry lips, her tongue probing at one of the cracks. "My dad . . . he doesn't have any money." Her father worked as an electrician. He did fine . . . now, after many years of struggle. Even during those hard years, she'd never lacked for food or shelter, even if they couldn't afford designer brands. Nowhere close. But he certainly didn't have any large sum of money stashed away that might be used to ransom her. Or small sums, either, for that matter. No stocks or bonds. No jewelry. All that had been sold, even the sentimental items. If that's what her abductors—whoever they were—were hoping for, *money*, they'd be sorely disappointed. Then again . . . "If they chose me at random, they must know that by now," she said. She'd been wearing a purse over her shoulder when she was taken. They would've looked at her ID, and with the barest amount of research, they would have discovered that her family had no money. Also, she was snatched leaving a *waitressing* job. Wouldn't that alone tell them she had little in the way of riches?

"You mentioned your dad. What about your mom?"

She let out a quiet sigh. "My mom died when I was twelve. She was a homemaker. And my parents had never bought life insurance." In fact, for many years after her mother had died, they'd struggled to pay off all the lawyer fees that had come in the aftermath as her father had tried—and failed—to enact some justice for his wife's death, which was ultimately ruled an accident. The fight had wiped out his savings, and his business had suffered. He was still her father, and she loved him dearly, but in many ways, he'd become a shell of the man he once was.

"Sorry," he murmured.

She didn't respond. He had nothing to be sorry for, and the grief of her mother's death had long faded. It still pierced her sometimes, randomly, but more so for her father than for herself. But not now.

Now, her problems were far greater than any heartache she still carried over the loss of one of her parents. Now, she longed for her father, the parent she still had. The one who might save her, who *would* save her if he had any chance to do so.

Her mind returned to the man in here with her. He'd said his family *did* have money. "If they took you for a ransom, wouldn't you know that by now? Wouldn't they have had you send a proof of life or something?" she asked.

"I really have no idea. No one's said a goddamned word to me." Now that he was talking more, his voice clearer, she could tell he was young. Maybe even close to her age.

"How old are you, Evan?"

"Eighteen. You?"

"Same." A strange fluttering took up in her chest. She heard him move, sensed him turning toward her, and his voice—even a few inches closer—confirmed it. There was a heavy pause that she felt as much as heard.

"Do you go to Northland High?" he finally asked.

She let out a breath. "Yes." *It can't be. Oh my God, it can't be.*

"Is your name Noelle Meyer?"

She swallowed. "Yes." The word was as thick as her parched tongue. And she suddenly knew exactly who he was too. "Evan Sinclair," she all but whispered. "Your father is Leonard Sinclair. He killed my mother."

CHAPTER TWO

The Collector leaned forward, his face only inches from the screen. *They've realized they know each other.* His father had killed her mother. They'd discuss it further, of course, which would clue the other players in. It definitely added another layer to the situation at hand, did it not? The picture flickered minutely, the green cast giving it an otherworldly glow. But it was remarkably clear for a room being televised through a night vision lens.

The man (a boy to be more precise, still a teen) sat with his back pressed to the bars of his cage, while the girl was on her knees, her hands gripping the bars of her own container. The audio was good. The Collector could hear every whisper, every breath, every pained sigh.

My, but you bastards enjoy your entertainment.

One of the boy's eyes was swollen, and he had what looked like caked blood on his lip. He kept bringing his fingers to his cheek and pressing, his expression contorting each time as though if he did it enough, he'd soon encounter a different result. Despite the injuries to his face, it was obvious that he was an extremely good-looking kid. Tall. Muscular. A square jawline and even features. An all-American golden boy. Good breeding, one might say. The thought made him chuckle. But it was a laugh laced with acid.

The boy must be having an especially difficult time relinquishing control. Life was typically quite easy and very good for boys like him.

How many allowances had already been made for the kid? Ones he didn't deserve and hadn't earned? *Many,* the Collector surmised. Perhaps far too many. It tended to be a disservice when tragedy struck. And tragedy had definitely struck this particular golden boy, currently sitting in a metal cage like a dog.

Perhaps he should dislike the boy, considering that . . . good breeding. And yet, he rather found that, instead of feeling any loathing, he . . . related to him. In some ways, at least.

His gaze moved to the right, where the girl had sunk down and turned to the side so she was now sitting on her hip, her knees still bent, long legs drawn up, cheek resting on what had to be cold steel. Slender. Fine boned. Straight, dark hair. Pretty in a plain-Jane sort of way. In a cheesy made-for-TV movie, she'd be the girl her friends would perform a makeover on because they could see the potential lying just beneath the surface. That only happened in movies, however. In real life, teenage girls were typically too jealous to purposely create a swan when having an ugly duckling beside you made *you* the pretty one.

Women. What petty creatures they could be. So ruled by emotion.

It could be their strength, too, of course. But most often, it controlled them, rather than the other way around. Pity.

He reeled in his thoughts. He didn't want to make too many assumptions and miss something that might tell him otherwise. *Watch. Listen. Learn.* It was what he did best.

A light in the room flashed, and both the boy and the girl made sounds of surprised fear, moving backward to the corners of their respective cells, away from the bulb. The girl brought her arm over her eyes, her face screwed up in pain. The light must be torturous after so long in the dark. The boy sat still, though his face was contorted similarly, one arm held out in front of him like he expected an attack. He couldn't do much about it, but he wanted to feel it coming. His left eye was swollen shut, but he blinked the other repeatedly, trying desperately to see.

"What's happening?" she asked, voice breathless and filled with fear.

11

"I don't know," he answered, his arm moving one way and then the other, warding off whatever invisible threat his mind was conjuring. There was nothing in front of him, though. Only light had entered his cage.

The Collector watched, waiting along with the captives to see what would happen next. His eyes slid to his cell phone on the desk next to him. One of his options was to call the authorities. But he didn't think that was the best choice. At least not yet.

He had ended up here, this voyeur, through a series of well-strategized liaisons but also a twist of auspicious events. When he'd realized what this was, he hadn't anticipated having any interest in watching. He would play, yes, but he'd intended to skate the perimeter. After all, he had a different form of winning in mind. But now, he couldn't look away. People thought they watched reality TV, but there was very little reality to it. It was scripted and edited to lead the watcher toward predetermined conclusions. This, though—it was riveting. He understood the draw.

God help him, he did.

CHAPTER THREE

Evan flinched, trying to see but helpless against the painful pinpricks of sudden light that jabbed his eyes. Blindly, he swept his arm from side to side. If he was attacked before he managed to crack his lids—or *lid*, rather—open, he wanted to feel it coming. Not like the first time when he'd been roughly woken from sleep and hauled from the first cage he'd been kept in for what felt like weeks. He'd been taken off guard then, but he wouldn't let it happen again. At least not while he was awake.

He took in flashes of the room through the slit of his eye, holding it open for a millisecond at a time.

His own splayed hand held out in front of him.

Gray metal bars.

A hazy counter-like structure beyond his cage.

He heard Noelle gasp, heard her movement, and turned his head in her direction. He saw her blur as she crawled to the front of her own cage, situated several feet away from his own.

Concrete floor between them.

"What do you see?" he asked, as she'd obviously managed to open her eyes before him. Likely because she was working with two.

"There's a table. Or a counter," she said, and he lowered his hand. He could see enough now to know he was the only one in his cage. He moved forward, too, crawling toward the front of his enclosure. There was a door on the front of his tiny cell, and when he tilted his head, he could see a black keypad lock toward the top holding it closed. He'd look at that more closely in a minute.

He felt a surge of hope, small but energizing. If he could *see*, his chances of working his way out of this improved dramatically.

He held on to the bars as he looked over at Noelle. Yes, it was definitely her. He didn't know why or how they'd ended up here together, but he had to believe it had been by some sick design. They'd been chosen purposefully. Why, he couldn't guess, but their connection wasn't a coincidence. He was all but sure of that.

Your father is Leonard Sinclair. He killed my mother.

What the fuck? Who is behind this?

She looked over at him, eyes still partially squinted, skin pale. She was wearing black leggings and an oversize pale-pink sweatshirt. Her feet were bare like his. His heartbeat quickened. He could feel his pulse thrumming in his neck. As they'd first spoken in the dark, even after she'd told him who she was, he'd half believed he'd made her up. He'd finally cracked after so many days and nights alone in the pitch black, and she was nothing but a figment of his deranged imagination. It even seemed appropriate somehow that it was *her* he'd summoned to torment himself as he descended into all-out crazy.

She'd turned her head as he stared, and leaned forward, studying what was in front of them. He faced forward, too, toward the counter against the wall. It was about six feet away from them, out of reach, but there were several items on it. He couldn't see the things on the back of the counter from his position, but he could see one that was slightly toward the front. "There's an ice pick," Noelle said breathlessly. Her eyes were wider now as she glanced quickly at him and then away. He craned his neck, blinking his one eye rapidly as the room came into sharper focus. Yes, yes, he saw the ice pick among the things that were farther back. It *looked* like an ice pick anyway. But all he saw was a *weapon*.

He turned around, looking desperately around his cage for something he might use to retrieve it, but the enclosure was empty except for the metal toilet in the far corner. He reached his arms wide, gripping the bars on either side of his metal prison and throwing his body forward in an effort to move the entire structure with the force of his weight. The cage trembled, causing his teeth to vibrate, but it didn't budge. It felt like it was bolted to the floor. He let out a grunt of frustration, returning to the front and peering at the counter.

"One of the things near the back has a cord attached to it . . . I think," Noelle murmured, her head touching the top of her cage as she attempted to peruse the elevated table. "It's hard to tell." She looked his way.

He could only see out of one eye, and so her account was going to be better than his. His gaze hung on the weapon he could see clearly for a moment before he huffed out a breath, sitting down and leaning against the bars before drawing his knees up and planting his feet on the ground. He raked his hand through his greasy, unwashed hair. "Fuck!" he yelled. "What the fuck good is a goddamn machine gun, much less an ice pick, when it's halfway across the room and we're caged like fucking animals!"

"If we can retrieve it, maybe we can jimmy that thing somehow," she said, glancing up at the identical lock at the top of her own cage.

"Jimmy it?" he asked. "Do you know how to jimmy a keypad lock with an ice pick? If you even had a way to *get* the ice pick? Jesus, even if you managed that, you couldn't fit your hand through these bars to grab hold of the lock anyway," he said as he jerked his head toward the bars of the door portion of the cage, skinnier and closer together than the bars that made up the rest of their enclosures and going in two directions so they formed a grid.

"Do you have a better idea?" she spit out.

"Someone turned on the lights," he said, ignoring the derision in her tone. "Maybe that someone will make an appearance."

She let out a thin laugh. "Is that your plan, then? To charm your way out of here? Flash them that megawatt smile? Maybe you can promise them a few bars of gold if they don't already know who your daddy is."

So it had come to that very quickly. How could it not? Even in this unimaginable situation—trapped and traumatized.

He felt himself spiraling, disbelief and horror fighting to take control of any rationality or calm he might try to hold on to in an attempt to figure his way out of this.

He gripped the bars again, shaking them with all his strength and letting out a feral roar. For a few minutes, he allowed himself to rage, to fight, even though he knew it would be fruitless when what he fought was steel and circumstance. Some ghastly plan, the meaning of which—so far—was beyond his understanding. Evan yelled and bellowed and shook the bars of his prison until his muscles weakened and his throat was raw. And still, no one came. Finally, depleted, he fell back against the bars, gripping his hair in his hand as his head dropped forward.

"Didn't you already try that?" Noelle asked, her calm a contrast to his wildness.

Evan worked to catch his breath, a trickle of sweat moving slowly down his cheek. Yes. Yes, he had. He'd done the same thing when he'd woken the first time in the dark. He'd even fought when the faceless man had come into his cage to retrieve him and bring him here to this second cage. He'd flailed around like a drunk seal as the man had easily sidestepped him and swung his fists at Evan at each opportune moment. He'd knocked him out and then somehow transported him here to this room.

"Maybe your dad's behind this," he finally said. What other reason for *this* than some skewed sense of revenge?

"You asshole," she hissed. "How dare you?" He still didn't look up. He didn't want to see her expression. "*My* father's not the murderer." She tossed the statement at him, and as though it were a spike, he felt it lodge in his flesh.

"He didn't murder her. It was an accident."

"Was ruining my mother's name an accident too? Devastating my father? And me?"

He did raise his head then, his gaze meeting hers. She looked upset but defiant. The sight made his thoughts blur. A caged girl, eyes blazing. And for just a second, he was glad he'd brought that out in her, regardless of the cause. Because for this one moment, at *least*, her will had been too big to be contained. It didn't last. She deflated against the bars, and they both sat facing each other in silence. He'd had this impression that she was meek. The way she walked, head down, arms always loaded with books. But there was fire inside her. Maybe it would help their cause.

"Why haven't you ever asked me these questions before? Or any questions, for that matter. You've never even spoken to me, and we walk past each other almost every day," he said. Maybe *he* should have spoken to her. But what would he say? And she'd always studiously avoided him, and so he let her be. He'd watched her without her knowing, though. He'd been . . . curious about her. Was that the right word? They hung out with completely different crowds. Not that she had a *crowd* around her, not like he did. As far as he could tell, she only had one friend, a mousy redhead. Both she and Noelle were from public schools and had been chosen for academic scholarships to attend the exclusive private academy. There were four scholarship recipients at Northland, and they were all treated like the outsiders they were.

"Talk to you?" She asked it as though he'd suggested she eat dirt. "There was never a point. I knew the answers then, and I know them now. I only brought it up because emotions are high. Understandably." She waved her arm around her prison as though she needed to explain the cause of her current mental state.

"What, then? What are the answers?"

She let out a gust of breath. "Maybe you should be asking what the *questions* are, Evan. Why did your father have to ruin our lives rather than take responsibility for what he did?" She gave a small shrug. "Privilege. Entitlement. Opportunity."

"Your mother was trespassing, Noelle," he said softly. "Stalking him."

That fire again as her eyes flared. She directed it to the wall, chewing at the inside of her cheek. "She wouldn't have done that. And there was no evidence she was stalking him," she bit out. "I've always thought he invited her over and then lied about it to cover up his own crime."

"The jury thought otherwise."

She stared at him for a minute, and he sensed something churning in her. But whatever it was, she held it back, obviously deciding that it didn't matter or this was not the time. "Listen," she said, "if we have any hope of getting out of here, we'll need to work together. Anything else is pointless."

He gave a nod, acknowledging that that was probably easier for him. She clearly held deep animosity toward his family, whereas he'd mostly been curious about her. To be perfectly honest, the thing that had decimated her life had been more of a tragic blip on the radar for him, an extremely unfortunate accident that his father had had to manage. He hadn't even been at home that summer. He'd been staying with his mother in the Hamptons. And in any case, from his perspective, before the . . . tragedy, both her mother and his father had been at fault. Perhaps Noelle was right about privilege. He'd moved on, while she had not. *Her mother died, though.* "You're right. We need to work together."

Unfortunately, at that particular moment, there was no "work" to be done. No tools within their grasp. No person to appeal to. For the time being, all they could do was wait. For what, he had no idea.

CHAPTER FOUR

She was running along a path, following it as it twisted and turned, someone hot and heavy on her heels. Vegetation surrounded her. Not a forest, but a garden, full of bushes trimmed into monstrous shapes. She had the vague notion that they were watching her, whispering her whereabouts to whoever was chasing. She'd never get away. Not here, where there were eyes everywhere. Suddenly, something hot tore into her chest, agonizing pain ripping through her, and she was falling, falling—

"Noelle!"

She sat up with a jolt, a scream on her lips, looking around wildly as she attempted to get her bearings. Bars surrounded her. She lay back down, letting her head hit the cement floor. *Oh God. This is real. I'm still here.*

The horror that swept through her each time she woke would never diminish. How could it? Tears threatened. For a moment she considered praying to die. She'd had the thought several times since she'd first woken in darkness but stopped herself each time.

"Food delivery," Evan said from beside her.

She sat up again, smoothing her hair back. She'd been dreaming of her mother. Of the night she died. She'd *been* her mother, a bullet tearing through her flesh. She pulled herself to her knees, looking at the tray sitting inside the small compartment on the wall behind her cage. The sound of the door opening had been what woke her from her dream. A quick glance told her Evan had a compartment just within his reach as well.

She crawled toward hers. This was the first time she'd been able to *see* her food, and unlike all the other times, when she'd reached for the bread and water, this "meal" came served on a tray made of soft plastic. A yellow children's tray. She reached, grasping it with her fingertips, and then carefully pulled it forward, her hands confirming what her eyes had already told her. It had rounded corners, nothing that might be filed into a weapon, even if she broke it into pieces.

There was a slice of plain white bread, a paper cup half-filled with water in the corner, and sliced peaches in the portion of the tray that curved into a small bowl. Her eyes widened, and she put her other hand through the bars, dipping her finger into the pale-yellow peach juice and licking it off. She moaned, picking up one of the four pieces of soft, syrupy fruit and bringing it to her mouth. The sweet taste burst on her tongue, and she took a moment to savor it. It was the first thing she'd been served that contained any real flavor in what felt like years. She reached for another one, eyeing the white fabric napkin on the side of the tray. Her first peripheral glance had made her think it was unfolded and just sort of crumpled in a messy pile. But upon closer inspection, it appeared to be sloppily wrapped around something.

"What'd you get?" Evan asked.

She glanced over at Evan, who was holding his own piece of white bread. He brought it to his mouth, practically inhaling the whole thing in one bite. "Peaches," she murmured.

He stopped chewing. "I didn't get any peaches."

"And I think there's something under my napkin."

"Napkin?"

He crawled toward where she was in the back of her cage and placed his head between two bars to get a closer look. And now that he mentioned it, she'd never gotten a napkin before. Why would a jailer, keeping her in a cage and feeding her bread and water, add the nicety of a napkin? She eyed it for a moment, almost expecting it to *move*. It didn't, but still, fear filled her, and she reached out tentatively while holding her body as far away as possible.

Noelle grabbed the edge of the napkin, and with a sharp intake of air, she pulled the piece of fabric off the . . . *thing* beneath, immediately yanking her hand back and flinging the white cloth.

"It's a rope," she said.

"What the hell?" Evan asked.

She reached out, picking up the white nylon rope. It felt silky between her fingers.

"Let me see that," he said excitedly.

Noelle hesitated. She'd been given this rope, not him, and she wasn't going to give it up so quickly. "No," she murmured, frowning down at it. Had someone *smuggled* this to her under the napkin? Or was it given to her on purpose? And if so, for what reason?

Evan made a sound of frustration in the back of his throat. "Fine, but try to use it to lasso that ice pick. Hurry up."

Noelle glanced at the ice pick and back to the rope. She didn't know if she had any lassoing skills, but she might be able to fling the rope at the tool and somehow knock it off? Evan was at least onto something. It was worth a try.

She crawled to the front of her crate, and instead of attempting a lasso on the end of her rope, she tied a double knot, something she hoped would provide enough targeted force to knock the ice pick off. "Tie a lasso," Evan instructed again. He'd crawled to the front of his own crate too.

"Anything other than a knot will shorten this rope too much," she said. She could already see that even completely unknotted, it was likely too short to reach the counter. She looked over at Evan, at the eager expression on his face. He had marks on his cheek from the rough cement floor where he'd slept. "And it's been a while since I ran down a heifer. I'm out of practice."

"Funny. Okay, try your method."

Noelle stuck both hands through the bars at the bottom of the front of the cage. The door, the bars of which were too small for her hand to fit through, took up the rest of it, and so going low was her only choice. She could feel Evan's eyes on her, feel his tension mixing with her own. As best as she could from the awkward position, she tossed the rope up and out, but it flopped uselessly on the floor, a good foot away from the counter and nowhere near as high as it would have needed to be to reach the surface. "Damn," she muttered.

She gave it a few more tries, just to prove to herself the fruitlessness of that plan, but then pulled her hands back through the bars, tossing the rope aside.

"Yeah, damn," Evan muttered. To his credit, he didn't ask her to pass the rope to him so he could try what was clearly impossible. He'd seen as well as her. "Any other plan?" he asked instead.

She sighed, heading back to the tray of food and reaching for the bread. Next to her, she heard Evan moving too. "Trade you half a pat of butter for two peach slices," he said.

She whipped her head in his direction. "You got a pat of butter?"

He nodded, holding up the small rose-imprinted square, a tiny piece of plastic covering it.

She stared longingly at that miniature package of creamy goodness. When was the last time she'd eaten any fat? Didn't you need fat to live? She was pretty sure she'd read once that fat was what carried vitamins and minerals to your brain. But they also needed vitamin C. How long until scurvy set in anyway? "Deal," she said, scooping up the two remaining slices of peach and holding out her cupped palm to him.

Evan eyed her hand. "Some of the juice too," he commanded.

She narrowed her eyes but pulled her hand back through, turning to the tray. *Why does he think he has any right to make demands?* Evan

Sinclair was simply used to getting his own way, and right now, while trapped in cages, it was in their best interest to cooperate. *Even with someone I loathe.* She drank all the water in her cup in three big gulps and then scooped half the peach juice up before again reaching both hands through her bars and offering the cup and the fruit.

While she'd been turned away, he'd begun to cut the pat of butter in half using the small piece of plastic that had covered it. He finished just as she shoved her hands through the bars. For a few beats, they both locked distrusting eyes, each obviously trying to figure out the best way to exchange their items. Someone would have to let go first. Evan thinned his lips as he placed the half pat of butter still on the paper bottom on the floor, using his finger to push it toward her. It slid to the edge of her cage. For the breath of a moment, she was the one in possession of all the goods, and by the look on his face, he had bet on her integrity, at least in this matter, but wasn't at all sure if it would pay off. Noelle leaned forward, placing the cup on the ground so he could reach it, and held her palm open.

Their eyes met and locked as he took the fruit from her, brought his hand back, and popped the peaches in his mouth. He closed his eyes as he chewed, letting out a small moan of delight.

Noelle looked away, picking up the butter and licking it off the paper. She wanted to cry as the rich, salty cream melted on her tongue. She closed her eyes, savoring each delicious swallow, sucking at the inside of her cheeks so she tasted every last bit.

"How long do you think we've been held hostage?" he asked.

She opened her eyes just as he tore the paper cup to give himself access to the inside. He brought it to his mouth, licking the paper clean of the juice that had been in it. She didn't blame him. If she could manage to turn it and slip it through the bars without spilling the last drips, she was going to pick up her tray in a minute and lick any remnants of juice on it too. She just wanted to enjoy the buttery taste on her tongue a few minutes longer.

Noelle licked the small piece of paper the butter had been on. "I don't know. I tried to keep track at first, but—"

"They didn't do anything on any particular schedule," he finished.

She nodded. "And the darkness was discombobulating."

"If that means it made me feel mixed up, then yeah."

Her lips curved into the ghost of a smile. She rubbed the small piece of paper on her shirt, drying it. She supposed she was free to keep it. What would they do to her if she didn't give it back? Come and get it? *Good.* At least then there'd be someone to fight. Though if there was something to do with a small square of paper that would turn the tide in her favor somehow, she didn't know what that might be.

"What would be the point of mixing us up about how long we've been here?" he asked.

She considered that. "I don't know. But it could be positive. It could mean they plan to release us at some point but they don't want us to be able to give the police any information."

"Others will be aware that we disappeared, though," Evan said. "They'll know how long we've been missing."

She drummed lightly on the bars. "Probably." She'd left work with three days off in front of her when she was taken. Her father certainly would have realized after a few days that something was wrong when she didn't answer one of his usual calls or texts. But even so, the exact timing of her disappearance might be unclear. Then again, it also could probably be investigated using cameras from the area.

She glanced to the corner of the cage where she'd stacked her empty water cups. There were sixteen. But that didn't help determine the exact amount of time she'd been there, because they'd been delivered randomly, sometimes with only a few sips of water and sometimes almost full so that she rationed what she'd been given. "I don't know," she finally answered. "Maybe us being left in the dark was simply to torment us."

He let out a chuffing sound. "Mission accomplished."

She acknowledged his statement with an agreeable sound in the back of her throat. "Why do you think they finally turned the lights on?"

Evan was quiet for a moment, obviously trying to work that out. "I think we can assume that they want us to see the things in this room. You were given a rope for a reason too. They expect something."

A shiver snaked down her spine. Funny that she could still be chilled by anything, all things considered. Could it really get creepier and more horrifying than this? She shoved the thought aside violently, refusing to think about that question lest she work herself up into a terror cyclone. It would be so easy, so easy. She'd been skating the edge of that storm since she'd first woken here, and she refused to let her mind do to her what *they* had not.

Yet.

"But what? What could they possibly want from us? And why don't they tell us what it is?"

"Look at me," Evan said, and she did, turning her body and leaning the side of her forehead against a bar as she peered through them over to where he sat in a similar position. "Let's try to put our emotions and our fear aside so we can think as rationally as possible, okay? We don't have a positive view of the other person. Is that fair?"

"Sure."

"And we have a connection that makes us natural . . . enemies, I guess."

She tipped her chin in agreement.

"So here's what I've got. Let's assume that connection is no coincidence. Who benefits from this?" He gestured his arm around the small space. "Is it an exercise to get us to work together somehow? Sharing our food? Trying to figure out how to get out of here?"

She wrinkled her brow. His theory sounded far fetched. "Who would do something like that, though? We've been terrorized and half starved so far. Our *parents* wouldn't do this to us, at least I know my dad wouldn't. And if not them, who?"

"That redheaded friend of yours who always gives me the death stare when I pass her in the hall?"

She felt a sliver of indignation lodge under her skin. Of course he was assuming it was one of *her* people. "Paula?" She let out a short, humorless laugh. "Paula didn't do this."

"How do you know?"

"This isn't the work of a shy eighteen-year-old girl who cries at sad commercials and dreams of working in the publishing industry because books bring her such joy." Plus, Paula was smart and kind and loyal. She had to be scared to death right now by Noelle's disappearance.

"Why not? Still waters run deep."

"Oh, shut up." She turned her body more fully. "You know nothing about us."

"Okay, then. Why'd you accept that scholarship anyway?" he asked.

"Why shouldn't I?" She'd *earned* that scholarship, and because of it, she might get another scholarship to any number of good colleges. It was her ticket to a life where she could not only support herself but help her dad, too, after his life had been decimated.

"Because I'm there," he said.

"I ignore you," she retorted.

"No kidding."

She gritted her teeth. "What about you?" she asked. "Who do you know sick and twisted enough to set up something like this? I'll bet there's a list. Someone totally soulless, with plenty of money to pay enough people off to go along with this? To aid and abet? What about your gang of purposeless androids always looking for the next thrill?"

"You're getting emotional, Noelle."

Fuck off. She didn't say it, but she wanted to. Instead, she turned away with a huff because she was well aware that he'd be more than happy to fuck off if he could. He was right. She was letting her emotions take over when they were supposed to be thinking rationally in order to *solve* this. To come up with *something* that might help their situation.

She took a deep breath, exhaling slowly. "Someone put us in these cages. *Someone* benefits from this. What types of benefits are there?"

"Financial."

"Yes, but this is not a ransom situation. That makes no sense as far as me, and like you said, if they were interested in ransoming you, you'd know. Your father would have asked for proof of life, and they'd have put you on the phone or taken a photo or something."

"Okay. Revenge. But it would have to be someone who hates us both and is looking to punish us *both* for something."

"Or punish our families, those who care for us."

"That's still a type of ransom, though. Wouldn't your father and my parents ask for proof that that person has us?"

"I mean, we're missing. If the point is to scare them, that would be enough. Whether we're alive or dead is sort of immaterial to that, right? Either way, they're suffering. The not knowing might make it worse." She pushed away the vision of her father, walking the floor until all hours of the night, gripping a handful of hair the way he'd done after her mother had been found shot dead. She couldn't let herself imagine what he was experiencing now. She would lose it if she did.

Evan blew out a breath, bringing his hands up and massaging his temples. "Who hates both of our families that much? As far as I know, they haven't had any contact since the trial, and that was six years ago."

Yes, six years had passed. Seven years and three months since Noelle's mom had died. And yet, in some ways, it seemed like yesterday. It'd taken that long for her father to get a handle on the lawyer fees he still owed. Six years where every day his eyes seemed to dull just a little bit more. He'd gone from thirty-seven to forty-three during that time, and yet he looked far older than that. Noelle sighed, massaging her head as she stretched her mind, trying to come up with anyone who might be connected to them both who also might hold some sort of grudge, rational or not.

The sudden squeak of a speaker made Noelle jump, and Evan jerked his head in her direction. "Deposit your trays and refuse in the dumb-waiters." The voice was robotic, the cadence odd, and Noelle froze, fear climbing as the doors their food had been delivered through slid open. There was nothing on the back or sides of hers. It appeared to be a silver metal box. A *dumbwaiter* that would be pulled up to some unknown place above.

"What the fuck?" Evan asked as he stared into his. The message repeated, the rhythm identical to the first time it had played. It was obviously some system, not a disguised human voice.

"Where is it coming from?" Noelle asked, scooting to the end of her cage and peering out between the bars. She couldn't see a speaker, and it was difficult to tell which direction the recording was coming from. It repeated again.

"Hey!" Evan called. "Hey, whoever's playing that! What do you want with us? What do we need to do to get out of here? Hey! Help us!"

The recording repeated. Evan shook the bars the way he'd done the day before. "Fucking talk to us! Tell us what you want!" The recording repeated yet again. It seemed that was the only instruction they were going to get. Noelle picked up her tray and extended her arm as far as possible, giving the tray a small toss so it landed in the tiny elevator behind her, then picked up the stack of cups she'd collected and tossed those inside too.

Next to her, Evan followed suit.

The doors shut with a slide and a click, and whatever system was used to pull the boxes upward was well oiled, because no other sound came from within. The recording ceased, and Noelle turned toward Evan. His one uninjured eye was wide and wary, and she could only imagine she wore a similar expression. Her heart slammed against her ribs. She had this strange sense that something was *starting*. That the second part of whatever this was had just been set in motion, something that she couldn't yet define or understand.

As if in response to her thoughts, a portion of the wall to her left slid open, and a man walked through. Noelle braced, pressing herself backward. Next to her, Evan hurled himself forward. "Let us out," he demanded. He shook the bars. "Tell us what you want. My father has money. Lots of it. He'll pay you." His words came out in a panted rush, tumbling over one another as he attempted to bargain with the emotionless stranger who had practically appeared out of nowhere.

The man, wearing black pants, a black button-up shirt, black coat, and red shoes, his hair parted and combed to one side, ignored Evan. Noelle watched him, tense and afraid, as he came toward the door to her cage. His outfit reminded her of some sort of uniform, and for reasons she couldn't explain, this alarmed her. Evan continued to appeal to the man, but the man seemed completely unaffected by his begging. But when he reached Noelle's cage and she met his near-black-eyed gaze, she could see the barely contained excitement in his beady eyes. Light reflected off his wide silver tie clip, and she slunk back farther.

"You've been rented," he said.

Terror shot through her, and for a moment, she felt like she couldn't breathe. *Nonononono.* Her breath released in a harsh gust. "Rented?" she squeaked. Next to her, Evan had grown quiet. "For what?" She knew. On the perimeter of her thoughts, she knew, but she refused to acknowledge it.

"Do you like cars?" Evan asked, and she heard the panic in his voice too. "My dad has a sweet Ferrari. Man, it's an icon. You could have it. No questions asked."

His voice was choked, desperate, and for the beat of a moment, Noelle wanted to laugh. He was bargaining for her. But it was also ridiculous because the promise of money hadn't worked, and so neither would a car.

A drumbeat of fear pounded in her bloodstream. *Rented.*

She couldn't think of another word that had ever inspired so much terror as that one, in this particular situation.

The man reached for the electronic lock and inputted a series of numbers. Noelle shrank back farther. "No! Please, no. I'm . . . I'm a virgin." That made the man pause, but only briefly. Her heart sank to see that his eyes had only grown brighter with her declaration. She'd fight him, then. She'd kick him in the nuts. She'd kick anyone in the nuts who tried to touch her.

He pulled the handle just as he took something from his pocket. A stun gun. The door swung open. "You have a choice," he said, his voice high pitched and nasal. "Here, you always have a choice." *Here? Where is here?*

Her breath came in pants as she shook her head. "Then no. I say no. I will not cooperate."

He smiled. His teeth were small and square. "That is not the choice. You may choose to come with me. Or you may stay here, sitting safely in your cage, and we'll take his fingers."

Her mind went blank. She worked to make sense of what the man had just said. "His . . . fingers?"

The man's smile had not slipped or grown. It remained oddly still. "Correct. I will stun him and remove two of his fingers."

Remove. The world around her seemed to have slowed as though she'd entered a nonsensical nightmare. One that was awful but that she would wake from, shaking her head in bewilderment at what disturbing scenarios the mind could manufacture when left to roam.

She looked over at Evan, whose skin had drained of color. Even the angry, reddish-purple bruise surrounding his eye looked suddenly pastel. He brought his hands slowly from the bars he'd been holding on to, as though unconsciously drawing back the part of him that had been threatened.

Come with me or we'll take his fingers.
We'll.

"Who is *we*?" she asked, her voice soft and shaky.

"I couldn't answer that," he said. "Even if I wanted to."

He was just a type of servant, then? A henchman? Hired muscle? He looked more soft than solid, a roll of flab at his waistline obvious even under the dark shirt, but she supposed a Taser made brute strength unnecessary. She also was pretty sure she saw the outline of a weapon beneath his coat. He was going to deliver her somewhere. And he was prepared should she decide to fight him.

But that was if she agreed to the terms.

Come with me or we'll take his fingers.

And if she didn't go with him? She didn't need that answer spelled out for her. He'd given her a choice. There wasn't a third option, not really. Save yourself from whatever unknown fate being rented meant, or save Evan's fingers. She felt like she was underwater, trying desperately to surface, to shrug out of her own skin rather than face this reality.

Rented.

She turned her head, meeting Evan's one wide eye. He stared back at her. She saw fear there, yes. Horror. Sympathy. Confusion and disorientation. His lips parted as though he wanted to say something but couldn't figure out exactly what. Instead, he waited. Waited for her to make her choice. He did not attempt an appeal. He did not give her the permission she might have been waiting for. *Let them take my fingers. It's a sacrifice I'm willing to suffer.*

She didn't want that, though. Her choice was already made.

CHAPTER FIVE

The Collector eased back in his chair, the wood creaking softly beneath his weight, as he watched the guardian step back, making room for Noelle to exit her container. He sighed. *Stupid Noelle. Brave Noelle.* Did she even know why she'd made the choice she had? He thought not. Perhaps she'd puzzle that out later. If later existed for her. For *them.* The boy, Evan, remained silent, his face turned slightly as he watched Noelle stand and wobble toward the door the guardian had nodded toward.

Evan. Noelle. He knew their names. All those watching did because they all had access to their conversation. But on the screen, they were still referred to as Dodger and Midori. Like horses at the track. They'd been given names. The Collector didn't know how or why the chosen monikers had been picked or if they were random, and he didn't care. He referred to them only as Evan and Noelle. He wanted to *know* them.

He'd viewed the entire exchange with the guardian with breathless interest. When the man had first entered, the Collector had watched as Noelle shrank back as though preparing for an attack. And Evan had raced toward what Noelle perceived as a sudden threat. His response was to meet the danger head on, whereas Noelle's was to run. Interesting. He tucked it away. Everything meant something. Everything might be valuable . . . later.

Whatever he decided that *later* might entail.

On the screen, the door slid shut with a resounding thud, and Evan pitched himself forward, his knuckles white on the bars of his cage, head hung as his shoulders rose and fell. The Collector watched his body language, taking in the curl of his spine and the press of his skull against the metal. Then Evan raised his head and pushed himself back very slightly. For a moment the Collector had thought the boy was crying. But he wasn't. He was enraged. *Ah, good.* The Collector tapped his fingers lightly on the arms of his chair.

The numbers at the top of his screen refreshed, showing the current odds. His eyes moved over the categories quickly. Those who had bet on Midori going willingly toward the unknown of being *rented,* had just made a pretty penny. Those who had wagered she'd give permission for the guardian to remove Dodger's fingers had lost. Interesting that she hadn't asked how his fingers might be removed. She'd still been in her cage when she'd made the choice, unable to see the array of tools on the high table directly under one of the hidden cameras. Apparently, it didn't matter whether a hacksaw would be taken to his hand or whether anesthesia and surgery would be utilized. Evidently the method mattered less to her decision than the outcome.

This was all good information to have if he was going to lay some money on the line. If he was going to become personally involved. There might very well be more risk to that than merit, however.

He pulled the report lying at the edge of his desk forward, flipping it open. There were printouts of the court docket, a few news articles, and any other publicly available references.

He had paid a private detective for this information. Perhaps it was frowned upon that the players have inside information, but how would the organizers know? He doubted most players bothered to look up specifics about the contestants. He doubted players would see any advantage in something like that. But the Collector knew better. The Collector understood the value of information.

His eyes skimmed the report he'd already read thoroughly. The tragedy occurred close to midnight on a humid summer night seven years prior. Noelle's mother, Megan, who had been engaging in an extramarital affair with Evan's father, a shipping tycoon who was twice divorced and recently remarried to a twentysomething lingerie model, was shot to death on his property. *Stupid Megan. Naughty Megan.*

Bennett Meyer, Megan's husband, an electrician by trade, sued for wrongful death. According to court proceedings, the defense claimed that Leonard Sinclair had broken it off with Mrs. Meyer earlier that day, and, scorned and obsessed, she had driven to his residence and gained access to his property through unknown means. Mr. Sinclair, armed and under the assumption that an intruder intending harm was outside his office door, shot Mrs. Meyer in the chest when she lunged at him from the dark. She died before an ambulance could even be summoned.

Mr. Meyer didn't believe Mr. Sinclair's story, and though it was proved in court via the existence of an intimate photo found on a camera in her purse that Mrs. Meyer was indeed having an affair with the multimillionaire, her husband continued to claim that the shooting was no accident. He lost his lawsuit.

The Collector knew very well how that whole scenario played out. Mr. Sinclair hired the slickest attorneys money could buy, while Mr. Meyer mortgaged his house and his business and used every cent of his savings to pay for a lawyer who didn't even have half the team or a tenth of the resources as the firm he went up against. The Collector knew other legal benefits had been paid for by Mr. Sinclair as well. Money could buy you your own brand of justice. The Collector had grown up in that world; he understood the inner workings.

In the end, Mr. Meyer wasn't only a widower. He'd lost his home and his business, drained his bank accounts, and gone into deep debt.

Whether or not his wife deserved justice for her untimely death would never be known. She'd been placed under six feet of dirt, and Mr. Sinclair had walked free, making a statement to the media waiting outside the courtroom that he was grateful to the jury who had seen the truth and that he wished Mr. Meyer well.

How that moment must have burned.

Of course, the Collector knew very well that it had.

A smaller screen within a screen blinked to life. As the viewer, he could decide which picture to enlarge. On the smaller screen, Noelle had entered a room upstairs and was sitting on a bed, waiting. Her hands twisted in her lap. Whoever had rented her had not yet arrived.

I'm a virgin.

Not for long.

The Collector focused back on Evan, who now sat back slowly, bringing his legs up and resting his forearms on his knees. He let his head fall back against the bars and sat staring straight ahead, one eye open wide, the other barely cracked. The Collector watched him for a moment before bringing his gaze to the various odds at the top of the screen once more.

They were constantly changing, based on shifting circumstances.

Just like life, he supposed.

You had to be quick to keep up, or others moved ahead.

There was one bet that remained constant for each of them, however. *Escape.* Highly unlikely. There were betting rules that made such a thing virtually impossible. No, if Dodger or Midori got free, it would be because they themselves had come up with something that the creators hadn't thought of. And then whoever had put money on that outcome would be a very, very rich man. Or woman. Though he didn't think there were any of those. Some sports were meant solely for men. The Collector didn't need, or want, the money. He had enough of that. And it wasn't what drove him. But still . . . his gaze kept returning to those odds, the number causing something hot to simmer in him.

Mia Sheridan

He knew why, of course. He was not a stupid man. His finger hovered over the keyboard momentarily before directing the cursor away from that bet. He'd decide later if it was one worth making. Or if it was foolhardy. Could he figure out a way to *help* them get free? The idea intrigued him beyond . . . everything. Was it possible? Maybe. It wasn't going to be easy, though. He'd need a strategy. On several levels.

The boy sat motionless in his cage, staring straight ahead. "What are you thinking?" the Collector whispered, his gaze hanging on the boy's bruised cheek. The Collector glanced at the rope they'd discarded near the back of Noelle's empty cage. Interesting that neither of them had considered using it to hang themselves. Of course, only one could do that. It couldn't be shared. He wondered if suicide had been the intent of the sender. A kindness, maybe. *Interesting.* Neither Evan nor Noelle had even mentioned the possibility, though. It hadn't occurred to them. At least not yet. Which meant they still had fight left.

On the small screen, a man had entered the room where Noelle sat. He was old and at least twice her weight, if not three times. The Collector zoomed in, focusing on her face. Her expression was blank, but hatred burned in her eyes.

Good. Hold on to it. It will help you survive this. Anger sharpens the mind. Fear clouds it.

He clicked off that screen. He wasn't interested in watching an old man grunt and rut as he tore into a young virgin. Many were, though. He could practically feel the excitement of all those faceless strangers emanating through the monitor.

Yes, perhaps he'd assist them in getting free after all. If he could. In the meantime, however, if they were going to stay alive, they'd need to eat more than bread and water.

He assumed the man who'd rented Noelle had sent the treats of peaches and butter earlier. A preemptive thank-you for whatever entertainment they were about to offer.

How generous.

Perhaps he was also hoping the peach juice would still be on Noelle's skin, making her that much sweeter.

The Collector clicked on a series of keys, spending what would equate to someone else's mortgage payment to order them each something special.

And this time, the gift came without strings. For now anyway.

CHAPTER SIX

The door slid open with a soft thud. Evan startled, moving toward the side of his cage closest to Noelle's. The same man, dressed all in black and wearing red shoes, who had taken Noelle out of this room now accompanied her back in. Evan's eyes were glued to her as she was walked to her cage and roughly pushed inside. The man locked the door and left without a word.

His breath emerged in a gusty tremor. He'd sat there alone for what felt like a hundred years, wondering if they'd bring her back at all. She'd been *rented*, and though he was pretty sure he could figure out what that meant, he couldn't be positive.

I'm a virgin, she'd said, telling him her assumption about what was about to happen to her was the same as his.

He'd sat there, stretching his fingers wide and then curling them into a fist, wondering what she'd paid for the fact that he currently possessed each one of them. He wouldn't disrespect her with a thank-you. God, she'd hate him even more if he did.

Noelle slumped down on the opposite side of her container, facing him. Her expression had been blank when she reentered the room, but now it crumpled into a grimace.

He didn't know what to say. *Are you okay?* hung on his lips, but he could see she was not. "What did they do to you, Noelle?" he asked softly. He had to know. They were in this together now, whether they liked it or not.

Her eyes opened, jarring him. The pain he saw there was raw. Palpable. "He . . . some man, whoever he was . . . raped me. He wore a mask. I couldn't see his face."

Fuck. While I just sat here, she was . . . He pressed his forehead on the bars, taking a deep breath and letting it out slowly. She was clearly distressed, but he was grateful that she'd been straightforward. "I'm sorry," he said. "I'm so sorry. I should have—"

"No," she said. "Don't." Her voice was raspy, and it made him wonder if she'd screamed, which made him want to do the same. He felt it rising in his chest like a tidal wave, and he swallowed it back with effort. He would not make this about him. He watched her. That fire he'd seen in her eyes the day before hadn't returned, but he saw a spark. Tiny but there. Flickering. For just a moment. "I survived it. I'm here. And now, I need you to turn around and make some noise so I can clean myself up."

Noise. She wanted noise for privacy. Maybe to disguise the sound of whatever she was doing to clean herself, maybe so she could cry. He turned, looking for something to create noise with, but his cage contained nothing. Okay, his voice, then. What did he know by heart that he could recite? His heart beat swiftly. She had asked for something simple, and he was quickly failing. For the life of him, he couldn't think of the lyrics to one song, which was interesting considering he liked music and always had something playing in his car. But in that moment of stress, the only songs that crowded his mind were the children's songs his mother had once sung to him, still imprinted on his brain all these long years later. What a strange thing, considering his mom had lost interest in him years ago.

"If all the little raindrops were lemon drops and lollipops," he sang. Behind him he heard her doing something, but he couldn't tell what over the sound of his own voice. But she'd started moving, he knew that.

"Oh, if all the little raindrops were lemon drops and lollipops. Oh, what a rain that would be." He tapped his foot to the tune to provide her more cover. "Standing outside with my mouth open wide, singing la la la la, la la la, la la la, la la la, la la la la, la la la, la la la, la."

Finally, after several stanzas, he sensed her lack of movement, and his voice quieted. "Decent?" he asked, and when he got no answer, he turned slowly. She was curled up on the floor of her cage, eyes closed. He released a sigh, lying down in his own crate and staring at her as a tear rolled slowly down her face. His chest tightened, and he turned his hand, sliding it through the bars and reaching for her. At the sound, her eyes came open, and she stared at his open palm. For a moment he was sure she wouldn't reach back. Why should she? She hated him. But then she brought her hand from beneath her head and fit it between the bars. They weren't close enough to hold hands comfortably but close enough that he could wrap his index and middle fingers around hers, forming a link. She tightened her grip, joining him in the silent statement he'd made by offering his hand: We need each other now. Nothing else matters.

Noelle sighed, closing her eyes, her tears ceasing. The room went dark as the lights switched off. The vision of their linked fingers still burned in his mind. She'd saved those fingers of his; he'd never forget that. But she'd paid dearly for it.

～

The lights came on what seemed like mere moments later, but he knew it'd been longer than that. His fingers were still linked with Noelle's, but his muscles ached from being held in the same position over time. And he'd dreamed, even if he could only remember fragments and pieces. Nothing he recalled made sense, his brain obviously in anxiety-ridden free fall, latching on to anything and everything in a desperate attempt to retain some sanity.

Or at least, that's what it felt like to Evan.

Noelle groaned softly, her fingers slipping free of his as she rolled onto her back, stretching and opening her eyes. Her expression barely changed, but he swore he could see the moment reality set in, even though his only view was of her profile. It was like he'd witnessed a slap to her soul, some form of deflating that he sensed as much as saw. Would there be a "morning" they'd wake here when it wouldn't be a traumatic shock? And should he wish for that? He didn't think so.

She ran her fingers through her hair, sitting up slowly. "So that's it then," she said after a moment. Her voice was bland, listless.

He frowned, running his hand through his own hair. "What?"

"The motive. The one we were trying to figure out. We're being rented out to sickos and perverts. It's as simple as that."

He rolled the words over in his mind. She was right. As far as motives went, it was a simple one. They'd been trafficked. And now they were being bought and sold. *How much?* he wondered. What was their going rate?

"Did he hurt you?" he asked softly.

He felt suddenly zapped of any and all energy, and maybe she did, too, because she lay down again, facing him, and he lay down as well so they were looking at each other through their bars.

"Of course he hurt me."

He closed his eyes, blew out a breath. *I'm a virgin.* "I mean—"

"Was it more than sex? No."

He felt a smidgeon of relief, not much, but something. She'd been raped, but she hadn't been brutalized. In a turbulent sea of horrible, it was a small life raft. Something to hold on to. Of course, that experience might have been an outlier. Who knew what was in store for them? Who knew what type of monster might rent one of them next?

He was here too. And he wondered if they were up on some dark marketplace. The very thought made him want to fall willingly into the abyss of madness.

"The items on that counter, the ones behind the ice pick?" she said.

"Yes?" He asked the word hesitantly. He almost didn't want to know.

"They're power tools. Smaller ones."

Power tools. An ice pick. Fear coagulated in his throat. He wouldn't think about them. He wouldn't.

He couldn't help it, though.

Come with me or we'll take his fingers.

He knew very well what the tools were for.

They turned in unison when they heard the dumbwaiters on the wall slide open, both crawling toward their deliveries.

He reached, pulling the corner of the tray toward himself and gazing down at it. Bread and water, their current staples, were there, but so was a handful of peanuts. *Oh, hot damn.*

Protein.

He picked a singular peanut up gingerly and placed it on his tongue, crushing it on the roof of his mouth and moving it from side to side to extract the small amount of oil. *Oh, that's good. Oil. Salt.* He'd never known how much pleasure could be contained in one peanut.

"What did you get?" Noelle asked.

"Peanuts," he answered. "What about you?"

She plucked something from her tray and held it up. "A chocolate-covered strawberry." She glanced down. "On a bed of artificial rose petals."

"Romantic."

"That's what I'm afraid of," she murmured, and if she'd attempted to add some levity to her tone, she'd failed.

He'd scooped up the peanuts and begun counting them but now paused. "Yesterday you were given peaches, and then . . . you . . ." He paused, and she nodded. *Thank God.* He hadn't wanted to say that out loud. "Is there a connection between these deliveries and what was done to you?"

"Like what?"

He couldn't think of anything that made sense. "I don't know," he said as he continued to try to understand the situation they were in based on the new information.

"Did the man who . . . do you think he's the one who took us?" he asked her after a moment.

"I don't know," she said. "But I don't think so. He wasn't very . . . he wasn't strong."

"How do you think he knew about you, then? About us? Where did he *rent* you?"

She met his eyes. "A marketplace where you can buy and sell . . . people. I . . . I don't know."

Yes, he'd had the same dark suspicion. He'd even come up with the same word—*marketplace*. "Okay, yes, I agree. So then maybe these are . . . gifts . . . and are from the people who rent . . . us?"

"Gifts?" she asked and then shrugged. "It's possible."

"Why, though? I don't think wooing is necessary. We're sort of a sure thing."

"Not funny."

"I wasn't trying to be."

She stared morosely down at her strawberry for a moment before using her fingernail to score the middle and then pull it apart. She reached through the bars, giving him half. "It doesn't matter. Rejecting this food won't get us anywhere. We need it."

He took the strawberry and set it on his tray, quickly counting the peanuts and handing her half plus one on account of the one he'd already eaten.

They ate in silence, allowing the other to savor the food, especially the chocolate, which he continued to suck from his teeth long after it was gone. He knew she was as aware as him that it would be the only small pleasure they'd receive that day.

When they were done, they pushed their trays back in the dumb-waiters without being directed to, and the doors slid shut, the internal cart lifting to some unknown location above.

They sat there in silence for several minutes before she picked up the conversation they'd been having before their food arrived. "We're being sold. But I keep coming back to . . . why us? Why us in particular? Our connection . . . it still . . . it has to mean something."

He couldn't answer that. But like her, his mind kept returning to the same question. And if he could figure out what, maybe they would be able to appeal in some way to whoever was keeping them captive.

It wasn't random. They'd been taken from two separate locations. It must be someone who knew them both, but he couldn't fathom who. Maybe it was simply some sicko who'd followed the court case and had developed some strange fascination with them or their families or who knew what aspect of the case.

It had to be an operation, though. This wasn't some singular deranged madman. There were at least a few more people involved, one being the lackey who'd escorted Noelle to the room upstairs. The man who'd threatened to take his fingers and appeared excited at the possibility. Another being the man who'd rented her. If they were being "rented," then they were being advertised. On some black market, like she'd said. But where? He had no comprehension of that kind of thing.

He couldn't even fathom the depth of evil he was pondering.

The kind of evil they were living.

"I think there were cameras up there," she said after a few minutes. "I saw this tiny red light on the upper portion of the wall near the ceiling. I focused on it."

"Cameras," he repeated. "People watching as this man—"

"Yes."

Someone watched? God. This is insane. He sat up slightly, leaning on his forearm. "Do you think there are cameras down here too?" He whispered the words as though speaking quietly might help make him invisible. "Do you think someone is watching . . . and listening?" It was like he could suddenly feel their eyes. The unknown predators behind all . . . this.

She leaned up, too, looking around. He hadn't seen any small light, though. If it was here in this room, it was hidden well. Or perhaps the equipment was different. "I think we should assume there are," she answered. "Otherwise, how did someone rent me? Based only on a description?" She shook her head. "No, I'd think they'd want to see what they were getting for the money." She fell back on the floor, rolling onto her back and throwing her arm over her eyes.

For a minute he thought she was crying, and he began to put his hand through the bars to reach for her. But then she lowered her arm, turning her head toward him. "My father stopped taking me to church when my mother died," she said.

Evan's forehead met the cold bars, and he watched her as she spoke. "She'd been the more religious one." She let out a small laugh that didn't hold much humor, if any at all. "Ironic, I guess. I don't know. She was committing adultery, after all." He hid the grimace that threatened. "I think my father thought maybe it was all just BS. A building to go to on a Sunday morning. Words that went in one ear and out the other. I wonder if that's what church became for him, because obviously that's what it'd been for her." She gave a fleeting smile and a small shrug. "Or maybe he just couldn't bring himself to be around so many people. I really don't know."

Evan hung on her words, wondering where in the world she was taking this. "When I first woke in the dark, I thought about praying to die. But each time the words began to form, even in my mind, I stopped myself from saying them."

"Why, Noelle?" Because he thought maybe there'd come a time when he said that very prayer. Wouldn't it be better to fade into nothing than to live in untold suffering for who knew how long? How long could a person endure being caged the way they were before their mind slowly rotted anyway?

"Because a prayer like that felt like an affront to God," she said, her eyes moving around the room, maybe searching for the cameras they'd just been wondering about. "And if there's any chance God exists, we need him now more than ever."

He looked up at the top of his cage, gripping a handful of hair and giving it a gentle tug. It already felt longer than it'd been when he'd left the gym that night . . . "God put us here," he finally said.

She breathed out a laugh. "God didn't put us here. Some person did."

"God didn't stop them. He didn't intervene."

"No, I guess not." He turned his head and met her eyes and saw that tiny spark again. "But I can't seem to give up on the hope that maybe he still will."

He was amazed by her. She was in a cage after having just been raped, with unknown tortures in front of them, no possible way to get free, and there was still the flickering ember of hope in her eyes. And if she could manage it, so could he. "We can use all the help we can get." He smiled. "But God helps those who help themselves."

She smiled over at him, and for a moment he was able to linger in that tiny light of hope. It was abruptly interrupted when the door clanged open. Evan jerked, sitting up, and Noelle did as well, pushing her hair back from her face.

The same man in the black suit with red shoes entered the room. A spike of adrenaline speared through Evan's system, his breath suddenly growing shallow. The man headed directly to Evan's cage. "You've been rented," he said, bringing the Taser from his pocket and holding it in one hand as he keyed a code into his lock with the other. Evan's throat swelled, and for a moment, he had trouble catching his breath.

"For what?" he demanded.

The man laughed. The sound was squeaky and mean. "I don't possess that information. All requests are unique. You'll have to wait to find out." He leaned his head on the top of the open door. "The choice, of course, is yours. You may opt out for the small price of her ear."

Shock radiated through him, and he glanced over at Noelle, who was holding herself completely still. "Her . . . ear?"

The man grinned, nodded. "She has two, after all."

He looked over at Noelle again, who had brought one hand to her ear. She blinked, her hand dropping away. Their gazes lingered; her lips parted, though she did not speak. She did not ask him to spare her ear, just as he had not asked her to spare his fingers. She didn't need to. "No," he said, his eyes held to hers, "we stay whole. We leave here whole." And then he crawled toward the man at the front of the cage, who stood back to let him exit.

Noelle crawled forward hurriedly, gripping the bars on the front of her crate as he stumbled by, his legs already weak from constant sitting. He couldn't look at her right then. His body vibrated with fear. *We stay whole* repeated in his mind, a mantra to give him courage.

But distantly it occurred to him that they'd already begun to be carved up. Noelle was no longer whole. She'd already had something taken from her. And he was all but certain that's what awaited him too.

CHAPTER SEVEN

The Collector watched Evan double over as the paunchy man's fist connected with his midsection. No rape. This time anyway. The predators on the other side of the screens had so many reasons for renting the prey. The short man with a curved spine and toothpick legs swung again, hitting Evan in the jaw as Evan's head whipped back, spittle spraying in the air.

Yes, the motivations could be varied, but some—like the one he was watching—were so predictable, so boringly trite.

Despite the older man's success (and he had to be successful to afford *this* sport), inside he was still the ugly, gawky kid who'd once been pushed into lockers. And he'd never moved on. He likely wore a three-piece suit most days, commanded some boardroom in a luxury zip code, and dined in the finest restaurants. In that life, he didn't need a mask to hide his face. The Collector would bet he had a penchant for young prostitutes and especially enjoyed hurting and humiliating them. Because now that he'd amassed power, he was bent on revenge.

Hungry for it.

And he'd take his fill wherever and whenever he could. He'd seek it out if he had to. Like now.

The Collector supposed this was especially satisfying given that the kid who was tied up and being beaten by him was handsome and strong, everything all those long-ago bullies had been. The ones he'd wanted to be. Maybe even the ones he'd wanted to fuck, though that might be going out on a limb.

The Collector zoomed in on Evan's face, watching carefully. He could obviously take pain. He appeared completely zoned out. Interesting. It took some practice to achieve that. He'd bet the boy was used to being hit. Maybe not often, but enough that he knew how to take it without flinching. The Collector tucked that away. He'd use it at the right moment. He'd know when—and if—that was.

He glanced down at the picture reduced in size near the bottom. The girl lay curled on her side in the cage, her eyes closed, hands tucked between her knees. She'd rolled into a small ball, and though it almost appeared she was sleeping, the Collector knew very well she was not. He was quickly learning her tells, each and every one—the ones she was aware of and the ones she was not. Her hair streamed over one shoulder, and he could see one delicate ear. The picture above showed the boy taking a strong blow to his gut, paying the price for the fact that her pretty little ear was currently still attached to her head.

The Collector had entered a chat room connected to the sport a few days before. He hadn't participated in the conversation, but he'd listened in. He'd heard chatter about past games, the players reminiscing about other contestants who had opted to see each other chopped to bits. Apparently, once it got started, it was gory indeed, each unwilling to have mercy on the other. The Collector wasn't surprised in the least by this information. Even the most civilized could become savage under the right circumstances. And sometimes, like now, the most unlikely contestants—two people with a bone to pick with the other, enemies, one might say—took pain on themselves rather than hand it off to the other. *Fascinating.*

He rubbed his thumb over the chocolate-brown wristband of his watch. It was a Patek Philippe Reference 530 time-only watch. He'd found it at an auction house a year ago for close to a half million dollars. He supposed, now that he thought about it, he was no stranger to making bets, after all. But he'd never bet before when his chances of winning weren't all but guaranteed. This situation . . . it most definitely added an edge. Did it mean he was one of them? No. His motives were different. Very different. He glanced down at his prized possession. He loved it because it was deceptively simplistic. All the best things were, to his mind. He wasn't a man who appreciated bells and whistles. Showy. Unnecessary. He'd heard the watch he was wearing called a wolf in sheep's clothing. He liked that. Yes, he liked that very much.

The skinny beak-nosed man was done beating on the boy. He looked exhilarated as he pumped his sticklike arms in the air in triumph. The boy's head hung limply as blood dripped from his lip and a cut on his cheek. He'd receive no medical care, the same way he'd have received no medical care had his fingers been sawed off. Things that might bring medical relief were off the table of items that players could gift the contestants, as was outright weaponry and a short list of other objects. There was nothing anyone could do to ease his pain. He'd have to live with his injuries, at least as long as he lasted.

The Collector wondered if he'd look at that rope differently when he was thrown back in his cage. But even as he thought it, his lips curved in a smile. Something told him the boy would not.

CHAPTER EIGHT

"How do you feel?" Noelle asked softly, her face pressed between the bars.

His eyes flickered, and he became aware of the pain, first the screaming of his ribs, then the ache in his eye, the one that had just begun healing and was now swollen shut once again. His other eye hadn't fared much better, but at least he could open it a slit. His head pounded, and his jaw hurt. He brought his hand to his mouth, assessing his teeth. "Like I was tied up and beaten half to death," he finally rasped.

Her face was blurry, and he blinked to bring it into focus, sorry he had once he saw her bleak expression. She looked like she'd been crying. Neither of them could afford that. It was a waste of bodily fluids. Of course it didn't help that he'd lost what looked like a pint of blood. "I don't think my ribs are broken, though," he said, as much to her as to himself, pulling his body up and grimacing as he leaned against the bars, scooting over so his spine was between two of them rather than being supported by one. "The guy who did this weighed all of ninety pounds soaking wet. It's probably why I'm not worse off than I am," he said, attempting to make her smile. His effort failed. Just like the asshole who'd used Noelle, his guy had donned a mask, so the top of his face was unrecognizable. *Coward. All fucking cowards.*

"Listen, I need to mop up some of this blood, and about all I've got to do that with is my underwear, so . . ."

She stared at him for a moment as if waiting for him to go on before her face registered understanding. "Oh," she said, pushing herself away and turning around. "Right. That's a good idea."

He groaned as he sat up, and he saw her shoulders rise right before she started singing.

"You are my sunshine, my only sunshine. You make me happy when skies are gray."

Evan removed his pants with effort, attempting to hold in his groans of pain, but damn, he hurt. He hurt everywhere. He didn't think he had any broken bones, but he had at least two lacerations that probably needed stitches, one on his cheekbone, and one he felt gaping open along his jaw. He pressed the flap of skin closed, grimacing against the sting, doing what he could to get himself back in order. His body would have to do the rest.

His father had hit him over the years when he'd been displeased with him. And he'd often been displeased with Evan. They were so different. Evan had this sense that his father considered him weak, and the physical abuse was his way of "toughening him up." But he'd been careful not to leave marks, careful not to hit his face. Evan almost laughed. Maybe his father had done him a favor after all, because he'd learned how to take some hits.

"You'll never know, dear, how much I love you. Please don't take my sunshine away. Hey!"

As he began removing his underwear, he paused for a heartbeat at her overly exuberant added lyric, smiling slightly despite his present state, then continued undressing.

"The other night, dear. As we lay sleeping, I dreamed I needed you in my arms. When I awoke, dear, I was mistaken. So I hung my head and a plan."

He let out a small huff of breath, what would have been a chuckle if it hadn't been swallowed up by a grunt of agony as he dabbed at the cuts on his bruised ribs, wiping the mostly dried blood away. Noelle obviously didn't know all the lyrics to that song, even though it was simple.

She sang softly as he completed his cleanup tasks to the best of his ability. The song died away, and she turned, sitting across from where he was. "Better?" she asked.

"A little, yeah. Do I *look* better?"

Her eyes washed over his face, and she gave him a sad smile. "Not much."

He let out a pained laugh, squinting over at her.

She gave a slight wince. "I don't know that my ear was worth all that."

"I meant what I said, Noelle. We leave here whole. It's a promise. It belongs to us."

She bit at her lip, and he had the idea that she was thinking what he'd thought earlier: that appearing "whole" from the outside could be misleading.

"Can I tell you about my mom?" she asked.

He tilted his head, surprised. Her mom was the very last topic of conversation he'd expected Noelle to bring up. They'd agreed to leave all that aside so they could work together. Why was she willing to talk about this now? Was it because she felt indebted to him for taking a beating rather than allowing her to be physically hurt again? She shouldn't. She'd endured a rape, for Christ's sake, so that his fingers remained attached to his hand. She'd had her virginity stolen by a disgusting predator.

"Noelle, you don't have to—"

"I want to," she said, flaring her eyes slightly as though communicating some message. "I want you to hear who she was from me. Not from your father, or some court transcripts, or a news story, or whatever else you might have read about her. I want you to know who she was to me."

"Okay."

She pulled in a breath and let it out slowly. "My mom . . . she was a really great listener. She had this ability to read between the lines." That slight eye flare again, there and gone, and followed by a casual shrug. "And then after she listened, really *listened*, she gave great advice. She had this way of sprinkling just the right words in to get her point across in the simplest way. It was like music, the way she did that. Her message always felt so perfectly strung together." She looked away on a sigh as though picturing her mom. The skin on the back of Evan's neck tingled. What she was saying . . . it sounded reminiscent, but there was something else mixed in there. Was she sending him a message? Saying something secretive under the guise of sharing memories of her mother? "I miss her," Noelle said. "I still talk to her in my head. These private conversations." She let out a small embarrassed laugh. "I guess that's hard to understand."

She read between the lines . . . sprinkling just the right words in . . . like music . . . perfectly strung together.

Evan stilled, understanding dawning.

The song. He'd thought she had forgotten words and was inserting the wrong ones to make up for what she didn't remember. But no. She'd been inserting words for him to pick out and string together. A secret way of speaking that would be just between them. Because she believed, as did he, that they were being watched and listened to. "No," he said, meeting her eyes. "I do understand. Perfectly."

Their gazes held, his head tilted so he could see her clearly out of his one good eye. "I'm so glad," she said, her voice slightly choked and a tempered excitement shining in her eyes.

He searched his mind to recall the words that had stood out as wrong to him, the ones he'd chuckled at as she'd sung. He couldn't remember them now because he really hadn't paid much attention. Songs became such background noise. It was why he'd started singing when she'd asked him to create noise. The mind naturally drifted into its own thoughts, in essence tuning out the specific words of the music.

She was fucking brilliant, and despite his aching body, he felt momentarily elated. And he suddenly remembered one word he'd picked out as she'd murmured the song he knew well. It was another one his own mother had once hummed to him as he fell into dreams. A *plan*. Noelle had put the word *plan* into the song.

She'd been telling him they needed to come up with a plan.

He had no idea what remote options they might have, but he did understand that if they were going to implement anything at all, they needed to be able to strategize discreetly.

And though he had no access to pain medication or soothing salve, for the moment at least, his discomfort faded to the background as his thoughts took flight.

CHAPTER NINE

It'd been a week since the Collector had logged on and checked on the contestants. The boy. The girl. Evan. Noelle. He'd had a work commitment that couldn't be delayed and, because of it, had been away from the computer in his home office where he watched the game. He felt a small buzz of excitement but tamped it down. He never allowed his emotions to control him. He'd had many long years of practice, and he used it still. He'd found that, in all matters, both consequential and not, a much cooler head prevailed when one could remove their own feelings and sympathies. Not everyone could master the ability, but it came naturally to him. It always had.

He sat down, turning on the monitor and going through the many steps necessary to join them where they were, locked in a building, in some room that had been prepared just for them. From what he understood, the locations were chosen months in advance and set up not only for the purposes of the game but in such a way that if it became necessary to disassemble them, it could be done in record time. In this business, he supposed, all sorts of contingency plans were necessary. The point of the game was that *anything* might happen. The more unlikely, the better, as that's where players stood to make the most money.

The Collector steepled his fingers, bringing them to his chin as the live feed spread across the screen. They lay in their cages, arms stretched toward each other, two fingers linked as they—he leaned in and turned up the volume slightly. Ah, they were singing those same children's songs they sang to give the other privacy. Silly, stupid jingles that they half murmured sometimes. Some of them he recognized; some of them he did not. It was a comfort for them, he supposed. A coping mechanism. They'd found something else to share. Always helpful in the case of dwindling optimism. How many times had they been rented since he'd been away, he wondered. He regretted that he hadn't been there to take note of the details.

When Noelle ceased singing, Evan picked up where she'd left off. The boy looked better. His swelling was down, and both his eyes were open, though his bruises had darkened, much of his face mottled in deep red and dark purple.

The Collector turned the volume down again, lightly tapping his fingertips together. He wondered if they realized that the stakes of the game were bound to increase. This was the first time the Collector had played, but he knew very well the gamers would become bored if the contestants were allowed to go on enduring rapes and beatings indefinitely just to save some fingers or an ear . . . an eyeball maybe.

He'd be sure to listen in on a few more chats and see if he could glean more specifics about where this might go. But he was pretty sure he already had an idea. They'd made a vow to *leave here whole*, and so the creators would strive to break them of that notion. Silly of them to say that out loud, really. They'd freely doled out ammunition, and they didn't even realize it. Pity. It'd make things less interesting, and he'd had high hopes that these two would be interesting indeed.

He paused, watching them, noting their body language, assessing their mental states, listening to her softly murmured singing voice. She had a lovely singing voice, and surprisingly, his wasn't half bad either. At least not when it came to nursery rhymes. And the way they concentrated so intently as the other person sang . . .

His brow dipped, and he turned up the volume, leaning in closer to ascertain if he was right about what he thought he'd just heard.

"Twinkle, twinkle, little star. How I wonder what fit bars."

They sounded like two little kids in their playpen babbling. It reminded the Collector of the secret language of twins. He felt a small pang in his chest but ignored it, leaning forward and listening to a few more bars. No, they *weren't* merely singing. He let out a small incredulous laugh. They were speaking in code, inserting words into the songs to form messages. She'd lowered the volume of the parts she'd changed, barely enunciating the words, and moved hurriedly through them, both to signal to Evan what to pay attention to and to make it more difficult for anyone listening to be able to note what she'd said. Even if they did hear it, it would be easy to assume she simply didn't know all the words to that particular song and was throwing anything in there, as people often did with forgotten lyrics.

Yes, similar to twin language, indeed. No wonder he'd caught on.

He laughed again, delighted and intrigued. People rarely caught him off guard, but these two had. They'd been doing this for at least the entire time he'd been away, if not before. And even he, who considered himself a master at seeing things others did not, hadn't noticed the subterfuge, simple as it was. But that's why it worked. No one suspected it. *Clever.* "Well, color me impressed," he murmured.

How much had they already conveyed in secret that none of the viewers had realized? What had they already said? How many had turned the volume down as they began singing so as not to get annoying preschool tunes stuck in their heads? Or because it was plain boring? He wished there were a way to rewind the video, but of course, there was not. Not for him, a mere player, anyway. It was a live feed, after all.

His gaze hooked on Noelle. She'd come up with it; he knew she had. He'd had this vague notion that she was mixing up the lyrics to whatever song she was singing the week before, not because he knew all the lyrics to that song but because of Evan's bemused reaction as she sang. He wondered how long it had taken her to clue him in. Well, either way, they were clued in now. Secret languages moved quickly once both people understood the rules. Secret languages morphed and quickened and became more and more difficult for outsiders to understand. Smart. Very, very smart. Songs. A well-known language that could be easily and discreetly altered if the listener was paying attention.

His gaze stopped on Noelle once more, the outline of an idea unfolding. It was a long shot. A very long shot, indeed. But he knew now that her mind operated the same way his did. He knew now what a worthy contestant she actually was.

And the boy. Well, he didn't think she would leave the boy unless she had to. Like secret languages, bonds formed extremely quickly, as well, if they were nurtured even the barest bit. He knew that personally. Regardless of his thoughts on the boy, however, it would require a team effort to make this work. And yet, even still, there was so much room for error, so much that might fail or go wrong.

And perhaps that was what made the choice for him.

Long shots were his specialty; he was here, after all. He logged on to another screen and spent an exorbitant amount of money for what he wanted. Then the Collector logged off, heading to his bedroom, where he opened his closet and began to pack another suitcase after he'd just unpacked the one he'd taken on his business trip. He packed a variety of items for different types of weather, since this time he had no idea where his destination would be.

CHAPTER TEN

They'd blindfolded her, and she didn't know why. She'd been brought to the same room, told to undress and lie down on the same bed as the first two times she'd been here. The same beefy man holding a gun stood at the door, looking stoically ahead. The only difference so far was the silky blindfold the man in the black suit and red shoes had tied around her head.

"Why?" she had asked.

"Rental request," he had said, right before she heard him exit the room.

Rental request. She was nothing more than a *rental* now. Like a car, or a bike, or a hotel room. A thing to *use* temporarily.

And so now Noelle lay on the bed, shivering, trying her best to prepare mentally for what she was about to endure, but distracted by every small sound, her vision gone, her other senses hyperaware.

There was no preparing for what she'd have to endure physically. She was not in control of that. Others currently possessed her body. But she was determined to keep her soul if she could.

She heard a soft knock at the door. Her muscles tensed. *God, I hate this. I hate it. Make it fast. At least make it fast.* She heard the man with the gun move aside and the soft footsteps of someone else enter the room. *Light on his feet. No shuffling.*

"Hello, Noelle." His voice was deep and somehow melodic. He sounded older, but perhaps not as old as the other two men who had entered this room the last two times. She hadn't been able to identify all their features under the masks they wore, but she'd been able to ascertain their age by their bodies and their sagging necks, veiny hands, and balding heads. She had only this man's voice. So far. "You do not greet me. Why?"

His phrasing. It was different.

"Should the rabbit caught in the trap greet the hunter?" she bit out. Her voice shook, but her anger and hatred gave her courage. They were the only things she had in which to clothe herself.

He chuckled, and she felt the bed depress. He'd sat down directly to her right. Instinctively, she drew away. "If the rabbit wants to get free," he answered smoothly.

That confused her. "You're going to . . . help me get free?"

He made a tsking sound. "That's against the rules, little rabbit. Would I . . . *break* . . . the rules?" He'd emphasized the word, though subtly, and she had no idea why. He dragged a finger down her arm, and she tensed and pulled away.

Still, this was the first man who'd offered any conversation at all, and she'd take advantage of it if she could. The other ones had laughed and grunted and made lewd commands and taken every liberty with her body, but they hadn't spoken more than a handful of words, and they definitely hadn't required any from her. One of them had enjoyed her tears, and so she'd cried harder to hurry it along. "Who makes the rules?" she asked him. "Who's doing this? Is there anything I can do to get out of here?"

"You know I can't answer those questions," he said, using two fingers now to feather down her arm. She wanted to lift it and slap him. She fisted her hand to resist the impulse.

There was an accent she couldn't place that floated around the edges of his words. It was slight. Very slight. She might not have even noticed it if she hadn't been blindfolded. Maybe he was trying to hide it, or maybe it'd been a very long time since he'd spoken the language that gave his English that particular lilt, and only on certain words.

His scent wafted toward her. Expensive. But also clean and understated. The other men had smelled expensive, too, but she'd smelled them the moment they'd entered the room, their cologne preceding them. Some overpowering fragrance that barely hid the scent of sweat and dry-cleaning chemicals and whatever else they'd carried on them. She had a very good sense of smell. She wished she didn't. Only one of them had chosen to get fully undressed, and then she'd been exposed to a whole new slew of smells she had tried to hold her breath against.

This man, though—she didn't have the desire to draw away from inhaling his air. He smelled good; she'd give him that. And she'd take it as a very small mercy.

"Can I take off this blindfold?" she asked. She'd felt exposed before, but this was a whole other level of bared. To be naked and blind, while the other untrustworthy person was not, was awful and unnerving. He might hurt her, and she'd never see it coming.

"No," he said. "I believe you've already been advised that the rules of this room were established beforehand. If you break them, the large man by the door will not hesitate to put a bullet in your brain." He opened her palm and ran his fingers across it. "Some would enjoy that. Some would benefit from that. I, however, would do neither."

"So others are watching then? That's all this is?" She didn't know why she was being so brazen with this man. He was just like the others. Vile. Taking advantage of a helpless girl without consent. But she felt she had a chance to speak her mind, and she had no idea if she'd ever get that again. The way he was running his fingers down her skin made her want to scream, although she bet he thought she'd find it relaxing. In this way, she was actually *glad* for the blindfold. It was like being hidden behind the windshield of a car and feeling more comfortable road raging. She wanted to attack him with violence, but she also wanted to appeal to him for help. She didn't know why or what or how. All she knew was that since she'd arrived here, she'd been operating mostly on instinct and gut survival, and this man was somehow different from the others she'd so far come into contact with. Was it his refined voice? That gentle accent that almost seemed to ebb and flow? The clean, elegant scent of him? *Forget all that. He's no different than the others.* All those things were falsehoods, a costume so to speak, meant to put others at ease. *He's a monster. He rented me.*

"Roll over, little rabbit," he said, and she heard the command in his tone. This was someone used to being listened to. It had been the same with the others. The difference was, they'd said it meanly. And they'd added insults to the orders. *Roll over.* Her heart thumped in preparation of being hurt in a new and different way. She wanted to scream, but that would only prolong things. She did as he asked, bracing. She felt his heat above her and was surprised when his hands came to her shoulders and he began kneading, his thumbs pressing into her sore muscles. *Oh God.* She clamped her lips shut as she sucked the sound of pleasure that had threatened back into her mouth. She wouldn't give him that. She would not.

He chuckled as if he saw her struggle and it amused him. "Do you want me to tell you a story, little rabbit?"

"No." She held herself still, willing her body not to respond to the manipulation of her muscles. But, oh God, it felt good. She'd been in a cage for weeks, sleeping on hard cement, hunched over, and contending with stress that most other people had never come close to experiencing.

She hurt everywhere. She'd stopped addressing it, but his hands on her muscles made her extremely aware.

"I believe I will anyway," he said.

"I'm shocked."

He laughed softly, and she heard genuine appreciation in the sound.

Her mind was going slightly fuzzy in response to the combination of his melodic voice and kneading hands. That, too, was a pleasure, and one she hadn't allowed herself since she'd been taken. By necessity, she'd been on high alert, her mind constantly churning with a way she—*they*—might escape. "Go on then," she said, and he again produced a deep chuckle that rolled over her skin. "Tell me your story."

"Did I say it was my story, Noelle? It was relayed to me recently, and it's one I find vastly interesting."

"What's the point of you telling it to me?"

"Does there have to be a point? I'm simply trying to put you at ease."

"Why?"

"Because it satisfies me. I find pleasure in yours. Some men find fulfillment in hurting others, and some do not."

"But you're using me, just like they did, so what's the difference?"

"I'll leave that to you to decide," he said.

That confused her, but she didn't press it. And maybe he was lying. Maybe his kink was to lure her into relaxation and then spring something terrible on her. She would try to be ready. Or maybe she wouldn't. Maybe she'd take what she could, too, while she could. Maybe a back massage would better prepare her to fight.

He paused in his machinations, as if expecting something, but then continued, her body sinking into the mattress beneath her. "There was once a man who collected things, very fine things," he said. "Jewels. Rubies. Emeralds. Diamonds. And he draped them on the women he stole."

"Stole? What do you mean?"

"He took them, Noelle. Much like you've been taken. He took them and he used them."

"Used them for what?"

"Sex. Violence. But mostly, he took them for power. All those half-drugged girls, naked and draped in gems. They made him feel like a king."

"If he could afford all those gems, it sounds like he already was a king."

"Peculiar, isn't it? Or maybe a better word is *gluttonous*."

Gluttonous? What did he mean by that? Her mind defined it for her before she'd even decided to try. *Greedy. To want more and more and more. Never enough.*

His hands moved down the backs of her arms, kneading and then feathering lightly. She pretended to be merely enduring his touch. How would he know if she wasn't? Why not take what comfort she could? Wasn't this the same as the nourishment she was provided each day in the form of bread and water and small treats? Who would she be punishing if she turned away the food? *I need it if I'm going to find a way of escape.* "Are you a second tier of torture?" she asked. "Here to bore me to death?" He couldn't read her mind. In this moment, it was one of the only things that was hers.

"On the contrary," he said, his hands moving over her buttocks, lingering, squeezing gently. She came out of the half trance she'd allowed herself to be lulled into. Of course this wasn't just a massage. But she'd known that. "Others have told me I'm quite interesting."

"That's not exactly the word I would use, considering the circumstances," she said. *Pervert* and *sicko* came to mind.

He only hummed in response, his hands continuing to run over her skin. She distracted herself by going over the plan she and Evan had been discussing for . . . a week? She thought it'd been about a week, though who really knew? Time was somewhat irrelevant where they were. They spoke in staggered strings of words inserted "incorrectly" into simple jingles, leaving out any that were obvious and therefore unnecessary. *The, and, if, or.*

"Man tie clip. Reflect," she'd told Evan, meaning the man in the black suit who escorted them to and from their cages wore a silver tie clip that might reflect the keypad at the top of their cages. As she'd sung, she'd pretended to rub a sore spot on her chest where the man wore the clip. Thank God Evan was quick. Thank God he got almost everything she conveyed the very first time. Of course, a little earlier, when the man had come to escort her to the room she was in now, she'd not only been too far back in her cage but he'd been turned slightly so she couldn't make out the numbers he pressed on her lock, not even one. The rub was that with each chance they had to read the numbers, it meant one of them was being removed and taken here to be further victimized. And yet, it was an outcome they had to hope for nonetheless.

The man was running his short fingernails up and down the backs of her legs, and without her permission, her mind began to drift again, a moan rising in her throat. She swallowed it down as he went on, blathering on probably just to hear himself speak. "Anyway, this man was well equipped to ensure none of his girls got pregnant, but, well, nature is quite adept at asserting her superiority where she can." One hand kept stroking her leg while the other parted her thighs. "Children were born. Twins. A boy and a girl," he said, leaning in close to her ear. "They grew up in the house of gems as well. The king had a court, other men with interests such as himself and their offspring. Generations of gluttons raised with the knowledge that they should take as they wanted from those with less and that every whim be satisfied." He leaned in closer, exhaling the next line on a murmured breath. "But the boy and the girl? They had only each other."

She clenched her eyes shut, turning her head to the mattress as his fingers moved delicately along the inside of her thigh. He leaned in close to her, and even though her face was pressed to the mattress and she was barely able to breathe, she could still smell him, and though she was loath to admit it, it was another pleasure she wanted to take comfort in. He smelled expensive, yes, but he also brought to mind dim, secret, wooded places where sunlight streamed in muted beams of light and wild sage grew. She'd smelled only her own funk for so long that the clean scent of him felt like a luxury. How could a scent convey all that? She didn't know, and yet it did. His scent had . . . layers.

She felt like she was losing her mind. In a sense maybe she was, her brain doing cartwheels as her thoughts merged with the relaxation of her body, as she both enjoyed it and hated it. She tried desperately to suppress her pleasure. She despised this man. Whoever he was, she hated him even more than the others. She hated herself for her body's betrayal. Hated herself for wanting more of what he was giving her.

He kneaded the backs of her thighs and then dragged the pads of his fingers down them, making her toes curl. He let out a soft chuckle. He'd seen her reaction; the laugh had told her so. "Is this wrong, little rabbit? I suppose it is. But when so much is wrong, sometimes you must find what rightness you can."

He came over top of her. She felt his heat, and she braced for some sort of invasion, but then he applied both hands to her shoulders, massaging deeply, his thumb moving up the back of her sore neck, releasing the tightness and tension she'd held there for so long. *Oh God, yes.* Despite her attempt to bite it back, a deep moan came up her throat, breaking free of her mouth as she pressed her face more firmly into the bedding so that her air was all but cut off. *No, no, no.*

"That's it," she heard him say through the fog of pleasure. "Let it make you angry, Noelle. You're so *hot* when you're mad." After a moment, she turned her face, gulping in a breath, warm tears soaking her blindfold. He'd broken her. That moan meant he'd won.

Somehow, of all the shames she'd endured, this one was the worst. She'd let a monster give her pleasure. She'd all but admitted to him that he had.

"It all ended," he murmured, continuing on with whatever story he'd decided to tell her for reasons unknown, "the night of the king's annual ball—his version of one anyway, even if the scheduled merriment was unusual for a ball. That's when the massacre happened."

She attempted not to move, not to let him know in any way that, even now, she wanted his hands to start stroking her flesh again. Instead, she focused in on his story to distract herself from her painful desire.

Massacre? What was the point of this? "One of the women displeased the king, and he slit her throat right in the middle of the ballroom. The others, fueled by drugs and the sight of blood, went just a little wild, and the killings began. It didn't stop until the eleven women they'd stolen and three members of the household staff were dead. And still, little rabbit, the music played on."

He removed his hands from her skin and got off her, and God help her, she suddenly missed his warmth. When he spoke, his voice was casual. "Like the man I told you about, and yet very different, I collect things as well, little rabbit," he said. "As you have nothing to offer that I might take with me, I should like you to create something. A poem. A note. A drawing, perhaps. Something personal to frame and hang in my gallery. Something to make me smile and remember this interlude."

Interlude? What a sick joke. What the fuck was he talking about?

The mattress lifted as he stood. "The paper and pencil are on the desk. I paid a king's ransom for both. Please make it worthwhile. You'll be asked to leave both behind. The powers that be determined that writing utensils were against the rules once out of view. Secret messages and all. It wouldn't be fair now, would it? Once I leave, you may remove the blindfold. It's been a pleasure, little rabbit. I hope you take something of our time together with you as well."

She waited, her breath hitching as she heard the door open and then softly close. Noelle ripped the silk blindfold from her eyes, simultaneously rolling over and sitting up. She tossed the small piece of silken fabric aside and blinked at the empty space before her, sure she could see the *outline* of the man in the air before her as though he'd disturbed the atmosphere and it was taking a moment to fill back in the space he'd just occupied. *Stupid.*

You're so hot *when you're mad.* The words hung in her head similar to the imagined outline of him. Even in her haze, they'd seemed odd. Or maybe it was because he'd said them at the precise moment he had—on the heels of her unbidden and oh-so-telling moan—that they'd imprinted on her brain that way. But also . . . they hadn't fit the persona she'd assigned to him. They sounded more like some current teen than a sophisticated man who wore cologne that probably cost more than the rinky-dink car she drove.

The man by the door remained still, staring straight ahead, his firearm held by his side. Noelle brought her hands to her naked breasts, jumping off the bed and quickly dressing in her filthy clothes. She took a minute to pull herself together as best as possible, eyeing the singular piece of white paper on the table, a pencil sitting beside it.

She took the few steps to the desk, then picked up the pencil and tapped it lightly as she assessed the sharpness of the point. She considered using it to lunge at the man with the gun behind her, but he'd likely shoot her before she had a chance to turn and make it across the room. Would Evan hear the shot from below? Would he realize right away that he was now completely alone?

No.

She leaned over the desk, writing out a short poem, and then she took several minutes to sketch an accompanying piece of art. It was juvenile both in content and in lack of talent, but it gave her a small burst of satisfaction all the same. *I hope you take something of our time together with you as well.* She paused, something occurring to her as the words he'd emphasized pricked at her mind.

Would I . . . break *. . . the rules?*

You're so hot *when you're mad.*

She left the paper on the desk, gripping the pencil and turning slowly toward the tiny eye of the camera peeking from high up on the wall. Why hadn't *they* hidden this one? Did they want them to know they were being watched up here? Was it meant to add to their humiliation? She stared, wondering how many sets of predatorial eyes stared right back at her. It made the hair on the nape of her neck stand up.

Noelle raised the pencil held in both hands, hesitating only a moment before snapping it in two. She narrowed her eyes, gritting her teeth as she pictured her hatred like a ball of flame flowing from her eyes and leaping through the lens of that tiny eye, straight to whomever was on the other side as they burst into flames.

Her chest rose and fell as she took in swallows of air, lowering her hands and then tossing the broken pencil to the floor. She waited a beat, then two, but no repercussions came in response to her mini temper tantrum. Perhaps *they* had enjoyed it.

The man by the door remained still, staring straight ahead, his firearm held by his side. A moment later, the man in black arrived to return her to her cage.

CHAPTER ELEVEN

Evan's muscles burned, his arms shaking as he grunted and struggled to push his body up one more time. He growled with the effort, straightening his straining arms, then dropped down to the floor with a whoosh of released breath, pressing his cheek to the cold cement floor. He had to stay strong. He had to push through the pain. And even though he wasn't getting nearly enough calories to do this, he refused to lose all muscle tone. Refused to grow weaker. Because someday . . . someday, he was going to be the one doing the beating. "If it's the last thing I do," he murmured beneath his breath.

The door opened, and he came quickly to his knees, waiting as Noelle was returned, eyes cast away as they always were. A scream of rage rose in his chest. How much more of this could they take? The door slid closed behind the henchman, and Noelle sat down, though not as gingerly as she had the past couple of times. He wished he didn't notice that kind of thing. He wished he didn't realize what it meant.

She seemed different, though, her eyes alight despite the slackness of her features. And this time, she didn't lie down immediately and close her eyes. Was she in shock? Oh God, whatever had been done to her must have been worse.

"It was only my teeth, Noelle," he said. They'd said they'd leave here whole. They'd made a silent pact the moment he'd followed her lead and refused to hand to her what was to be his own suffering. But some sufferings were greater than others, and they should recognize that too.

"We leave here whole," she murmured.

"Yes, but—"

"No buts," she said. "None."

He sank down to the ground, turning his back without being asked so she could use the toilet or do what she could to wipe away the evidence of the man who'd rented her.

And then he waited for her to sing, tapping lightly on the bars as though accompanying her with percussion. He didn't expect that she would utter a word about what had happened upstairs. They had an unspoken rule about that, developed over time. Neither asked anymore, and neither offered. Of course, they were in the same predicament, which meant neither was completely in the dark about what the other was enduring.

Instead, they planned and discussed possibilities for escape, few of which they'd come up with so far. Sometimes they spoke out loud, too, after they'd sung the most secret part of their conversation. They'd pretend they were talking about another topic, when they were actually discussing the secret they'd just shared. He hoped that anyone listening in, even if they were suspicious about some part or another of their spoken conversation, would have no frame of reference from which to make any assumptions.

So far, they'd worked out that they needed the codes to their cages, and they might have a way. By watching in the henchman's tie pin, which, so far, he'd worn each time he'd shown up. But that presented a few problems. Number one, he only entered the code when they'd moved away from the door to their cage. Number two, sometimes he was turned slightly away. And number three, they weren't even sure the code could be seen clearly in such a small accessory. The theory hadn't been tested.

Evan kept tapping, and Noelle finally began to sing.

"Stole a song of sixpence, a something full of rye," Noelle murmur-sang, raising her voice on the correct words so *those* were the ones that stood out.

Stole. Something.

His pulse gave a sharp leap. No wonder she'd looked like she was vibrating in some strange way. He'd assumed it was shock, but no; was it nervous energy she'd been trying to contain since she'd swiped some object from the room? But what? He'd done a full visual inspection of the space, and even when he wasn't tied up, there was nothing small enough to swipe and hide. He stretched his neck, giving a small questioning shrug in response, knowing she was watching him from behind. *What?*

"Four and twenty pencils baked in a pie. When the part was opened, the birds began to sing."

Pencil. Part.

That confused him. He knew that sometimes it was too difficult to say a specific word because it either didn't blend into the song or it gave too much away, should it be overheard. He assumed that was the case now, so he considered the parts of the pencil and what purpose they might serve but couldn't come up with anything other than maybe a sharp piece of wood. But that would be so tiny that even if they managed to sharpen it into a blade, it would break upon contact with even the softest target. Another stretch, another shrug. *Why?*

"Oh, wasn't that a dainty plug, to fire before the king?"

Plug. Fire.

He'd been rubbing his shoulder, sore from the push-ups he'd done while she was gone, and now he paused, his breath catching. He gave a small cough to cover his reaction.

"I'm done," she said.

Evan turned, lying down on the floor of his cage and facing her where she was now doing the same across from him. "You were telling me about that kitten you found when you were a kid," he said, picking up the topic they'd been using to converse about their plan earlier. He assumed that, like him, she made up some of what she told him to fit within the framework of the secrets they told but that she also inserted some truth.

"Right," she said. "Yes. So, I adopted this kitten, but he was a little troublemaker who was always causing havoc in places he shouldn't." She yawned, and her eyes slid upward and slightly to the back before her gaze quickly returned to him. Evan stretched his neck, his glance going to the place behind her that she'd signaled toward. There was only the small square of the dumbwaiter directly behind her cage. Was that what she meant? "Even the smallest, seemingly inconsequential places," she said.

So not the dumbwaiter. His gaze slid backward on another stretch, his eyes moving over the outlet off to the right of the dumbwaiter and low on the wall. Was that what she was talking about? Her chin tipped downward. *Yes.*

Yes. Okay. So . . . she was proposing using the piece of pencil she'd stolen to start a fire in the outlet somehow? That seemed . . . highly unlikely. Then again, he actually had no idea if that could even be accomplished, but she seemed to think otherwise. He could do nothing except trust she knew something he didn't.

Something occurred to him. Wasn't her father an electrician? Maybe she'd picked up some knowledge on electrical from him. His hope soared.

He blinked once. *I understand.* Enough, anyway.

He saw her lip curve slightly before she turned it against the arm her head was resting on. They were both very precise now with their movements and signals. This second language they'd created had been built on fear and necessity and therefore honed in a way Evan didn't think he'd be able to teach someone if he had months to do it. They had no idea where the cameras were in this room, so they had to assume they were everywhere.

He quickly filtered through what they had as the outline of a plan. So far they had two maybes. Maybe they could unknowingly gain access to the codes to their locks. And maybe they could start a fire that would . . . what? Provide a distraction while they attempted to input those codes and escape?

Yeah, that, or burn them alive.

The hope that had blossomed a moment before deflated. Several problems still remained. Even if they were able to obtain the codes to their cages, the bars at the front crossed both vertically and horizontally near the top, making up small squares. It wasn't as if they were made of wire. The bars would not bend, even under the greatest of pressure. He'd have to shrink his hand to the size of a child's to force it through. Or use a tool of some sort that could fit through the smaller section of bars and then bend to reach the keypad. Given that it was impossible to collapse his hand, they'd need to find or steal the perfect item.

The problems were stacked up far higher than any potential solutions.

They spoke about the possibly made-up or possibly real troublesome kitten for a while, brainstorming on the things he'd just considered, finally running out of ideas. All they could do now was wait for more opportunities. He reached his arm out, and she did the same, their eyes meeting as their fingers linked.

"We leave here whole," he said to her, not caring who heard that, figuring they imagined it to be an empty promise anyway, something they said in a useless effort to keep their spirits up during hopeless circumstances.

"And we leave here together," she added as they were both pulled in to sleep.

They slept; they woke. They ate bread and they drank water. There were no extras, and there hadn't been for days. He felt weaker, and he could see by her movements and the listlessness in her speech that she did too.

Still, they sang, they discussed possibilities that seemed unachievable, and they fell asleep, fingers linked.

Their hands fell apart as the man in red shoes woke them three days later as he walked toward Evan's cage. He blinked with sleep, his head foggy, and yet, he knew what he had to do. *Now. This is your chance.* He threw himself forward, grabbing the bars at the front of his cage and shaking them just as the man raised his hand to enter the code. He had ceased announcing that either of them had been rented, assuming correctly that Evan and Noelle knew the drill. "Please," he begged. "I can't take it!"

The man blew out a breath, appearing bored. "Move back."

"Please help," Evan begged. "It's not too late to let us out of here. It's not too late to do the right thing."

"Move back now, or I'm going to tase you," the man said, pulling the Taser from his outside coat pocket.

Evan threw his body on the floor of the cage, his face turned and pressed against the front grate as he kicked the top with his feet, rattling the bars and sending waves of pain through his legs but causing no damage whatsoever to the enclosure he was in. The man's mouth set, and even through his fear and the performance he was putting on, Evan saw the look of excitement in the man's eyes. Finally, he was going to be allowed to inflict pain. Still, he gave Evan one last warning, and Evan put his hands flat on the floor as he braced for the jolt.

When it came, it felt like hot lightning flowing through his veins and rendering him incapable of movement. He gritted his teeth and rode through the agony, his eyes locked on the man's tie pin, the small blurry reflection revealing the man's finger as it stabbed at the keypad. 9906.

Evan let out a sound that was something between a sob of victory and a growl of pain and anger and horror at what he had to suffer before he could use what he'd just obtained. Because they didn't yet have Noelle's code, and he wouldn't even attempt to leave without her.

He'd made a promise, and one thing Evan had learned as he'd sat in the bowels of hell was that he could be stripped of everything and still keep his word. It was his. No one had been able to steal it, and he wouldn't allow them to now.

The man with the red shoes grabbed Evan's arm and yanked him back before Evan could even attempt to force his limbs to work. The man slammed the door of his cage and then stepped back, allowing Evan to slowly pull himself to his feet. "Enjoy that, meathead?" the man sneered.

Evan let out a feigned whimper as he followed the man toward the door, hanging his head but shooting Noelle the smallest of covert winks as he passed, a movement that, if seen, would be construed as nothing more than a blink. She was at the front of her cage, her hands gripping the bars, her eyes following him as he moved by. At his signal, her lips parted, eyes widening slightly. She knew.

She knew he'd been successful. One step down, about ten more to go.

But they'd moved one space forward.

Both he and Noelle were so much weaker, physically and emotionally, and he had no idea how long they could remain hopeful on so little. What he did know was that if breaking free was possible, they were very quickly running out of time.

CHAPTER TWELVE

The Collector swirled his drink, tipping it back and closing his eyes as the liquid burned down his throat. He rarely drank alcohol. He didn't enjoy a dulling of his sharpness, and he didn't require being anesthetized, either physically or mentally.

But some things required a special celebration, and so the Collector toasted Noelle with one shot of Old Fitzgerald Bourbon, a specialty liquor of which only a finite stock was still available to those bourbon enthusiasts who could afford the $6K price tag.

The Collector set the empty shot glass on the bar cart in his office and then opened the french doors to the patio. He took the bottle with him, smashing it against the outside stone wall of the house and watching as the amber liquid pooled on the flagstone floor.

There was much more where that came from.

The Collector's lips tipped, and he brushed his hands, reentering the house and then sitting down at his desk. He'd been delivered back to his home that morning after a day of travel. Somewhere south, he thought, based on the few clues he was able to pick up, even in his drugged state. The organizers insisted on it, and though the Collector was loath to put his narcotized body under someone else's control—someone else's ownership—he'd made an exception.

He hoped the girl and the boy appreciated it, but he could see why they might not. Even if they knew what he had sacrificed.

He pulled the envelope forward that they had left with him, the souvenir he'd paid for. If others enjoyed mementos of their time spent with a contestant, he imagined they chose a piece of clothing or perhaps a lock of hair. Soiled underwear no doubt went for a pretty penny. But he'd chosen what he had for a reason, and she'd already impressed him greatly by committing the theft he'd hoped she would. He'd watched from a screen on the wall outside the room as she'd stared at the camera defiantly, breaking the pencil in two, and—he thought at least—slipping the piece of graphite under the wristband of her filthy sweatshirt.

He hoped she'd managed to steal a long enough piece.

Only time would tell. Time that was slowly filtering away, the grains of their survival dwindling.

He pictured her lying on the bed, her naked skin dry and dirty. Cracked and bloody in spots. She'd looked malnourished and broken. Completely vulnerable. But ah, looks could be deceiving. Who knew that better than him?

He thought back to the way she'd fought against the pleasure of his kneading hands. He almost regretted causing her such humiliation. And he knew well that it *was* a humiliation to submit in such a way to your subjugator. She might as well have called him *master* with that moan, and she'd obviously known it by the tears that followed, staining her blindfold. But the men watching only understood two things when it came to a rental: violence and degradation. He had to *blend* if he was going to win. Perhaps, initially, they'd thought his form of manipulation weak, but then, he'd earned her tears, while they had not.

Should it trouble him that manipulation came so easily? Or did it? Because his time spent with Noelle had held truth too. He'd uttered a few chosen words using the accent of his native tongue and then mixed it with a subtle rendition of the other accents that were a result of the various languages he spoke. He hadn't used the accent of his youth in a long time, though he did move between the others, depending on whom he was conversing with and which aspect of his life. He'd been so many versions of himself and found it easy to slip on each persona. A skill honed over decades. Allowing his original accent to be heard—even briefly, even murmured—had been a small risk, he supposed, but the part of him that was still the boy he'd once been had wanted her to know him. Or at least to hear him.

He'd also given her information about who *they* were. He'd waited for the flashing light on the wall that would warn him he was broaching subjects that were off limits. He'd only get one chance. But no such warning came. He assumed, though he had no proof, as this was his first game, that if he didn't heed the warning, he would not be making his flight back home.

They hadn't stopped him from repeating the story, the one his game sponsor had shared with the Collector, bragging about his past exploits. Perhaps it even amused them. What could one little rabbit do with a tidbit of vague information he'd presented as some tall tale? But certainly they'd recognized themselves as the king and his court that he spoke of and believed him to be giving them a nod of appreciation.

Perhaps the fact that he hadn't worn a mask gave him leeway. They had him on video now.

Regardless, here he was.

The Collector broke the envelope seal, sliding the paper from within. She'd written the poem he'd asked for, and his smile grew as he read it.

> Werewolves have fangs
> But they also have pelts
> I hate your guts
> Go fuck yourself

His gaze moved to the rendering next to it, a poorly drawn sketch of a werewolf, saliva dripping from his fangs and looming over a tiny rabbit in a trap. He looked closer and laughed out loud. Ah, yes, that tiny rabbit held a knife in its paw hidden behind its back. It was hoping to skin that hunter. Somehow. Against all odds.

He laughed again. She was divine.

The Collector went through the steps of logging in, his fingers flying over the keys as the screen within a screen blinked to life. There was Noelle, his little rabbit sitting alone in her cage. The boy was in the room upstairs.

The Collector sighed as he took in the scene in that room where rental contracts played out. He could see that he'd been right about the spindly man with the beak nose. He *had* wanted to beat those boys who'd pushed him into lockers and called him names. But he'd also very much wanted to fuck them. There he was again, having obviously made the trip once more, his head between the boy's legs as the boy gritted his teeth and covered his own eyes, in essence blindfolding himself, shutting out what was happening to him in the one way he could. He wondered if Evan was picturing Noelle. If such a bet could have been made, the Collector would have made it, and he believed he'd have won. Evan would experience emotional consequences for that later. If there was a later.

The Collector clicked off that screen, zooming in on Noelle and steepling his fingers as he assessed what they already had in their possession. The things the others had sent them had been consumed. The Collector had sent them treasures to keep. To use. And he'd send them something more. Each item had to follow the rules of the organization that wrote them. But he had his own criteria. Each item had to serve a purpose. And speak to them, as though he himself were there.

He pulled the drawing she'd done for him forward again, running a finger over the rabbit, stroking it much the way he'd stroked her. He'd planned it. What he'd say, what he'd leave; and she'd understood. She'd risen to the occasion, just as he'd hoped she would. He was still riding the high, and now that the small amount of liquor he'd consumed was taking effect, he couldn't help closing his eyes as he replayed the scene in his mind. What had she felt the moment she realized what he'd left for her? Hope? Excitement? Fear? Yes, certainly all those.

Her heart had certainly been beating triple time as she'd surreptitiously slipped the small piece of the graphite from its broken casing. She'd hid her fear behind her hatred. *Please don't notice,* she must have prayed. The piece of graphite had to have been small, but if whoever cleaned up the room reconstructed the pencil, they'd surely notice a small piece was missing.

But they hadn't. She'd have lost something if they did. Something vital. Something that would negate that vow to leave whole. The contestants had rules, too, though they didn't know what they were. He opened his eyes. And there she was, looking completely intact. He watched her for a moment, recalling how angry she'd been when he'd elicited that moan of pleasure. He understood. He'd been angry once too.

He took in a deep breath. He needed to *think. What to send?* It might be their last chance before the rules of the game changed. The longer the contestants held out, the longer the devils had to use them and the more money could be made. But eventually, that wouldn't be enough for them. He sensed their restlessness.

He smiled as the possibility of something specific to send the boy came to him. If he understood how to use it . . . what perfect poetry. Beautiful.

Violent. But beautiful.

The door to the room Noelle was in slid open, and the boy was shoved back through it and returned to his cage, the metal door slamming shut.

"Hey, limp dick," Noelle yelled at the man in the red shoes. The man hesitated, turning, and the Collector leaned closer to the screen as he watched this interesting turn of events. "Why'd you get this job? Do you know what your position is called? Lackey. Because you obviously lack balls. You must lack money, too, or you'd have one of us up there, wouldn't you, lacking balls?"

The Collector let out a soft chuckle. *Smart. Very smart.* Make the man angry. Prod him into doing something unwise, and take advantage of it. But how? *What do you have up your sleeve, little rabbit?* What had she and the boy discussed that he had missed, either because he hadn't been watching or because he didn't know the songs they sang well enough to discern their secret language?

The man with the red shoes walked to her cage, then stood in front of it, and Noelle stared defiantly up at him. "Hi, limp dick," Noelle said, and the Collector saw by the set of his chin, even in profile, that Noelle had already infuriated him. The task was made much easier now that she and the boy had stuck to their guns in regard to sacrificing the other. The man with the red shoes had bid on the position because he expected to carve two people up. He'd expected to *use* those electric tools sitting on the counter, and yet there the devices sat, nary a drop of blood or tissue on their sharp, shiny blades. How disappointed he must be that his job had come down to merely escorting the captives to and from their cages for others to enjoy. For *others* to abuse and draw blood from. And Noelle was picking that wound. The Collector made a tsking sound, but he didn't take his eyes from the screen. He was riveted. "What are you, the local eunuch?" she asked.

The Collector chuckled again as *the eunuch* removed the Taser from his jacket pocket. Noelle's knuckles turned white as she gripped the bars to the cage, not cowering, not moving back an inch. "I'm surprised you can even shoot that straight," she said. "Are you sure you can? Maybe hitting Evan was a one-off, eunuch."

She wanted him to tase her. Why? What was she hoping to achieve? It only took her spitting at him and calling him a eunuch again for him to take the bait. He shot the barb, and Noelle dodged, going in the other direction. The man let out an enraged grunt and shot the barb again, and Noelle went down, the side of her face slamming against the bars and then the floor. "Eunuch," she slurred, even as her muscles twitched, her body rigid with what must be indescribable pain. And yet . . . she seemed to be trying so hard to keep her head lifted . . . focused on the man's chest.

The man with the red shoes punched in the code to her cage and opened the door, grabbing a still-immobile Noelle by the hair and punching her square in the face. The boy yelled and rattled the bars in his cage, looking like a wild animal. A nice show. The players must be enjoying it. He knew he was. *The eunuch* tossed Noelle back inside as though she were a rag doll and slammed the door. "A new phase starts in the morning," he growled. "The choices get *bloodier*." The Collector could have turned on the camera behind Noelle's cage so as to see the man's face, but there was no need. Even from behind, he could tell *the eunuch* was sneering, eyes shining with malice. Ah, yes, the stakes would rise in the morning. He supposed the man wasn't supposed to let the boy and the girl in on that little secret. But he was clearly too excited to stop himself. After all, finally, they'd be given a choice that would lead to him slicing off a piece of them either way.

The man turned to exit the room. It was then that the Collector noticed the silver pin on his tie. He hadn't paid that any mind before. He was getting far too comfortable from this chair in his office far away. He'd have to do better at channeling the girl and the boy. Comfort had slackened him. The tie pin flashed once more as *the eunuch* turned out of the room. The Collector rocked once in his chair, letting out a surprised chuckle. Well.

Well, well, well. His little rabbit was even smarter than he'd thought she was. His gaze moved to the boy. He appeared concerned about her condition, but also . . . hopeful. He knew very well what she'd been doing. The boy had surprised the Collector too.

And the Collector was very rarely surprised. His gaze moved to Evan. Good breeding, indeed. The Collector grinned, standing and heading to his home gym, where he'd push himself until his muscles burned. He'd think about exactly what to send them as he worked his body to the point of exhaustion. Things that would arrive in the next few hours while they still had time to use them. Something special for each of them. Either they'd understand, or they would not.

CHAPTER THIRTEEN

"How's your face?" Evan asked.

"The least of my problems." Noelle sucked in a breath as her fingertips found the open cut on her cheek. She lifted the hem of her sweatshirt and dabbed it lightly, but it had mostly stopped bleeding. Yes, her body hurt like hell, but there was also a current of victory running through her.

Mixed with frustration. 330?

She'd only gotten three out of four numbers. She'd have to bait the man with the red shoes again and hope for the best. But her chances got slimmer and slimmer. Perhaps he'd be counseled about his lack of discipline in allowing them to rile him the way she had. Perhaps someone watching would catch on to what they were actually doing and quickly put an end to any delusions they might have about breaking free.

She'd told Evan she'd only seen three of the numbers by tapping at her wounds with three of her fingers. He'd given a quick nod, then turned away, his mouth set.

Three was better than zero. And if they found an appropriate tool that would allow them to input the codes into their locks, they could attempt to find the last one by going through all ten digits if they were given time.

And if the keypad allowed for unlimited tries.

Which it might not.

A new phase starts in the morning. The choices get . . . bloodier.

She didn't want to think about what that meant.

Hopelessness began to swirl, but she forcefully pushed it aside. There was no point to that. Because once you turned down that road, it was very difficult to turn back around. Giving up meant certain defeat.

She lay down on the floor, and Evan did the same, their hands reaching for each other, fingers linking, a movement that now felt as natural as breathing air. She exhaled, and for a moment, they simply stared into each other's eyes. His eyes were an oasis to her now, an island in a deep, dark sea. Something to cling to. A reason to hold on. The knowledge that she was not alone.

She thought of the man with the voice like velvet who had given her pleasure that made her moan. *Let it make you angry, Noelle. You're so* hot *when you're mad. Would I . . .* break . . . *the rules?* And then he'd left a pencil for her to write him a note. A pencil that could be broken to extract something that could be used to create fire. Was he helping her? Them? It couldn't be, could it? He was using her. Playing with her. Some confounding game within a game. But she—they—had no choice but to play along.

And tomorrow, the stakes would rise.

Fear shimmered inside, a nuclear blast in the distance rocking her world and making her want to shut her eyes, hit the ground, and never look up. Instead, she stared into his eyes.

Evan's expression was more desolate now, even though they'd been—mostly—successful in getting the codes to their cages. Noelle didn't know if it was because they were closer than they'd been but still so damn far away, or perhaps, like her, he was considering that the level of horror was about to rise in the morning. Or maybe it was because of something that had happened to him upstairs. She wouldn't ask. They'd come to an understanding, and she didn't want to talk to him about what happened to her up there, either, the way her body had been used, her soul disregarded.

Like the road to hopelessness, if she started to go to that dark place inside, she wouldn't return.

She was already standing at the intersection of so many bleak crossroads.

She tightened her fingers on his, creating what felt like an unbreakable link.

We leave here whole.

We leave here together.

Much later, their dumbwaiters dropped, and the doors opened. They both dragged themselves upright and then crawled to the backs of their cages. Noelle pulled out her tray. There was only one slice of white bread and one cup of water to eat and drink, respectively. But she stared down at what was on the other side of the tray, picking them up gingerly and turning them this way and that.

A tiny pair of nail scissors, dull and slightly bent at the end.

A grooming tool?

She turned to Evan, who held something of his own.

"Nail scissors," she said, holding up the small tool and looking with confusion at what he was holding.

A hammer with a rubber head? "What is that?"

"It says on the side it's a chime mallet," he told her. "Like, an instrument or something." He turned it over, staring down at it for a few seconds, and then tapped it on his open palm. It looked light, less than two pounds. The head was rubber, solid but unlikely to hurt anyone. And it would definitely lose against a Taser and a gun. Disappointing.

Evan raised it uncertainly and paused before dragging it along his bars. He let out a small huff that might have been a laugh. "Ah," he said, "accompaniment for our songs. Someone enjoys our singing."

Or is mocking us for it.

She looked down at the scissors. They were small and flimsy. They wouldn't successfully go up against a Taser either. Even if she managed to hide them and bring them out at an opportune moment, they'd probably break when they struck something solid. Not that the guard ever got close enough for them to do something like that anyway. They were useless. Except . . .

Noelle sat down, inspecting her long, dirty fingernails. She'd chewed a few off, and another couple had broken. But those ones were jagged and bothersome. Yes, she had aches and pains and had suffered in ways great and small, but her instinct was to groom herself, and the fact that she could not had stolen a bit of her humanity. She took a few minutes to trim them all while Evan experimented with the sounds the chime mallet made on the different bars of his cage.

She turned toward him. "Here," she said, sliding the small pair of scissors across the floor. "Clean yourself up."

He scoffed. "Not exactly running for prom king here."

God. The thought of school or dances hadn't been something Noelle had thought about for what seemed like forever. *Prom.* Ha. How ridiculously simple. Maybe she'd even have worried about it in her old life. Would someone invite her? Or would she pretend not to care and make plans for a girls' night with Paula? She'd never even considered being prom queen. But Evan . . . Evan had been a shoo-in for prom king.

King.

All those half-drugged girls, naked and draped in gems. They made him feel like a king.

His voice. Unbidden. She pushed it aside and mustered a chuckle. Evan put the mallet on the floor and sat down to trim his own nails. She watched as he did it, seeing that the small grooming errand was making him feel, if not like a king, at least a tad more human too. That was good. Perhaps whoever had sent them had done so understanding the small pleasure. Or maybe it was worse than that. Maybe whoever had sent them had been given some advanced notice that their fingernails would be torn from their fingers in the morning, and this was a sick inside joke. She swallowed, refusing to let her mind go there. In any case, she had a specific use for them in mind, and it wasn't just to trim her nails.

Evan started singing low and slow, mostly under his breath, as he focused on his chore. She turned away from him and pretended to pick at a scab on her arm but listened intently to what he said.

Her heart raced as he sang and then plummeted as he explained what he was going to do.

Evan . . . no.

Yes, he insisted. *Yes.*

Oh God, oh the sacrifice. She clenched her eyes shut, picturing what he'd described in fewer than five words. She couldn't allow herself to grimace, in case they were watching closely and her expression tipped them off that they weren't merely mumbling nursery rhymes. She lifted her shoulders and let them fall. *Okay.* They had no choice.

She turned and he looked up, their eyes meeting. He picked up the mallet and dragged it over the bars, certainty in his gaze.

Oh, Evan.

On a silent exhaled breath, she turned away. He was right. The plan must be enacted now, before things got bloodier. Before they were each missing parts of themselves that would make an escape attempt impossible. These two new tools had made the decision for them. They had what they needed to try.

It was now.

Or never.

Noelle came to her knees, and so did he as she joined him in song. They sang loudly, belting out their certainty, Evan dragging the mallet along the bars. They sang on and on until their voices were hoarse, laying out their plan, the entirety of it.

This was it. Things would only get worse from here. They would break free—or not—after the lights had gone out.

There would be cameras on them, just as there were now. They had to act quickly and without hesitation.

Exhausted, they sank down on the floor, reaching for each other, fingers linking, gazes locked as they waited for the darkness.

CHAPTER FOURTEEN

It seemed forever until the darkness came. And even longer that they lay still and silent, feigning sleep. A small squeeze of her fingers, and then Evan sat up and crawled to the front of his cage, and she watched as he reached for the mallet.

Oh God. She was so scared she was shaking, her heart in her throat for him, for herself, for the risk they were about to take and the possibility of failure—when failure was not an option. *Go time.*

Evan's deep yell broke the silence, and he picked up the mallet, pounding on the bars and grabbing hold, shaking them as much as possible.

If you're watching, you sickos, watch Evan.

Just long enough . . . just long enough . . .

She pulled herself to the back of her cage, cringing and letting out a small whimper when Evan placed his hand flat on the cement floor and slammed the mallet down on his knuckle, howling with pain. The benign-looking instrument wouldn't pose too much threat to another person, but oh, the damage it could do to one singular hand . . . all those tiny bones.

Noelle took the small hidden piece of graphite from her pocket, the one she'd extracted from the pencil, willing her hands to stop shaking. She heard the hard smacks of the mallet and the wet sounds that told her Evan was pulverizing his own hand. He was *screaming*, but he wasn't stopping. She wanted to cry for him, but there was no time for that.

You're up, Noelle.

Watch him, creeps. Don't you want to see his pain? Doesn't it excite you, you sick fucks?

She pressed her body to the bars of the cage, her heart galloping and a bead of sweat rolling down her cheek as she brought out the tiny pair of scissors as well, and the handful of rose petals. *Gifts.* Tools. The lights came on, and though she squinted, she did not pause.

The countdown had begun.

She had counted each time she was taken from her cage and brought to one of the men upstairs who had rented her. It had taken four minutes to make the walk down the long hallway and up the metal steps to another series of hallways above. If someone was in a similarly placed room upstairs, watching them, sending food down through the dumbwaiters, if they ran, it would take them a third of the time it'd taken her. One minute. Maybe a few seconds more. That was it. If they got very lucky, whoever was upstairs was in a room that was farther away—maybe even sleeping—and it would take them even more time. But they couldn't count on that. They had no real idea of the layout. They only knew of the one room where they'd been taken.

She reached, reached, turning her head so she could press her face against the cold metal and shifting her eye so she could see the small outlet off to the side of the dumbwaiter. Her fingers barely brushed it, and she let out an exhale. She hadn't been positive until now that she could reach it at all, though she'd attempted to measure it using her vision alone and hoped she was right in her calculations. She used the small pair of scissors to unscrew the outlet plate, each screw coming off easily and falling to the floor. She dropped the scissors and reached back through the bars for the small piece of graphite she'd set down, her breath coming shallow. *Breathe, breathe, stay calm. One step at a time.*

"Fuck," she murmured when she dropped the piece of graphite, picking it up, letting those two precious seconds go. They were gone, she couldn't get them back. *Breathe, breathe, breathe.*

Behind her, Evan had ceased pounding the bones of his hand to mush, only his small grunts and whimpers meeting her ears. *You've got this, Evan. I know you do.* She couldn't look, though. She had her part, and he had his. They couldn't afford to pay attention to anything except their own assigned tasks.

Noelle retrieved the graphite and the handful of fabric petals, reaching out with both hands now, her face pressed between the bars so hard her cheekbones hurt. One hand was poised to stick the graphite in the socket; the other held a rose petal as far toward the back of the outlet as she could manage in order to catch the spark.

Please please please.

Evan let out a roar of agony, and then she heard the beep of a button being pushed. He'd forced his collapsed hand through the smaller bars of the door. He was accessing the panel with his broken fingers. She held her hands steady as she jabbed the piece of graphite into the socket. Nothing. *Oh God, oh God.* She did it again, a little harder, but not hard enough to break the small tool, and a tiny spark shot off the back. She heard three more beeps behind her and then the sound of Evan's cage door opening. A sob welled up inside her. But it was far too soon to celebrate. *Stay calm. Keep going.* She pressed the rose petal closer and then stuck the graphite in again. A bigger spark this time, that jumped to the edge of the petal, catching and glowing red. *Yes yes yes yes.*

Evan's agonized yell as he pulled his hand back through the bars made her stomach cramp, and then she heard his footsteps and a loud kick, wood splintering, but she tuned all that out as best she could as she held the petal steady, the edge barely burning, bringing it from the outlet and touching it to another petal. The small fire transferred, and now two petals were burning, a thin trail of smoke rising in the air.

She heard the pounding of footsteps overhead now, but toward the rear of the building. Someone was, or a few someones were, on their way. But they weren't coming from the direction of the only room she'd been in upstairs. They'd been in a different room farther away. *Thank God, thank God.*

And then Evan was there, going down on his knees next to the tiny fire she was keeping burning by adding one rose petal after another. His hand dripped blood, creating a small puddle on the floor. He stuck a splintered piece of wood—a portion of the counter holding the power tools that he'd kicked apart—into the fire, holding it steady until it caught fire; then he stood carefully, walking the short distance to where there was a hole in the plywood wall. She watched, breathless, panting with fear, heart beating out of her chest.

He held the stick to the edge of the jagged wood, waiting as the splinters turned orange, and then the fire began spreading and growing rapidly. Noelle let out a surprised gasp when the flames leaped up the wall with a whoosh. She leaned away, the heat finding her even from several feet away.

Shouting now. More pounding from above.

Distract with fire. But she hadn't expected it to work quite this well. She heard an explosion in the wall and then the pause of their feet as they changed direction. Whatever was in the walls wasn't fire-retardant insulation. No codes had been followed here. From the way the fire was spreading, it seemed like there was paper and kindling between the studs. The men above were obviously confused by the sounds of the traveling flames. Noelle and Evan were getting lucky. *Good good good. Please hold out.*

Noelle's breath came short, her limbs shaking.

Evan opened the dumbwaiter and used the burning stick to light the walls inside there as well. He closed the door, and through the cracks, she could see the red glow of the flame and hear as it began climbing the walls, moving upward as well. There were sounds everywhere now. The men's footsteps went one way and then another. Their shouts were full of confusion.

"Let me out, let me out," she chanted, smoke billowing into her cage as Evan ran around to the front, and she crawled quickly on her hands and knees. She kept chanting, and her voice sounded very far away. She worked to breathe, to stay calm. She couldn't lose it now. They still had so far to go.

"I'm going to get you out," Evan said, his hand creating another puddle on the floor as he used his good one to punch in the three numbers she'd been able to see: 330.

"I think the last one was on the right," she said, her words stumbling over each other. The man with the tie pin had moved his hand to the right . . . she thought.

"Okay." He punched in a number. She thought he'd tried *3306* but couldn't be totally sure, as she couldn't see. And there was nothing reflecting what he was doing. She had to wait. She had to trust.

She went lower to the ground, coughing as the smoke made it to the front of her cage.

"Shit, shit, shit," Evan chanted, punching in a second code that didn't work.

Oh God, oh God. What if it only gave him a certain number of chances? What if it reset? She would burn to death. The fire was raging behind her, smoke billowing into the room. The heat was already intense, and she could feel it getting closer. Evan's chest rose and fell, blood splashing in the puddle at his feet from his limply hanging, ravaged hand. Noelle went low, staring at the puddle of blood, drawing her feet in as the heat came closer, clenching her eyes closed. Maybe they shouldn't have planned to light the walls on fire first. But they'd discussed and calculated, and it had seemed wiser to buy time, to hope the men above went for a fire extinguisher, or to potentially set off an alarm, *something*, considering they only had three of the numbers to her code. She hadn't expected the fire to spread so quickly. But now . . . oh God, she was scared.

"I won't leave, no matter what," Evan said, his voice strangely calm. "We leave here together."

"No, Evan," she whispered. "No. One more try and then you run. Bring back help." She was okay, even if she burned to death in this cage.

It would be better because she'd chosen it, rather than giving her death to the monsters who'd put her here.

A strange peace came over her, and tears pricked her eyes. They'd given it their all; they'd made it farther than she had dared hope they would. She'd give him the final tool and tell him what to do. He still had time to make it out.

She heard the beeps as he tried a third code. The door unlatched, and Noelle fell forward as it opened. For a beat, she didn't understand what had happened. Then Evan was yanking her to her feet and they were running unsteadily together toward the door.

Another code.

She reached in her pocket for the small pair of scissors, almost unable to say whether she'd put them back there per the plan, letting out a gust of relief as her fingers found them.

The heat was almost unbearable now, the smoke thick. She brought her sweatshirt over her mouth, and beside her, Evan was using his shirt in the same way.

Tears ran down her face, and she blinked away the burning smoke, prying the cover off the electronic panel on the wall that held the wiring for the door. She prayed the system was simple. Why wouldn't it be? They'd been in locked cages. There was no need for anything more than simple security to access the room.

The fire had spread quickly through the walls, and it had already made it to the inner portion of the one that held the door. It was still far enough away—she hoped—that the electric system hadn't melted.

The fire roared and crackled, and they could hear random crashes behind them as things collapsed, but she thought she heard two male voices and the pounding of feet descending the metal stairs. Then they'd be at the long hallway that led to this room. Noelle and Evan would be cornered. A gun in front of them. A raging fire behind them.

"You've got this, Noelle," Evan said from beside her, his voice hoarse. "You've got this."

Deep breath. *Okay. Okay. Yes.*

She blinked at the wires, using her fingers to separate them, clipping the one she hoped operated the door. It remained shut. She let out a grunt of frustration and fear, refocused, and clipped the one beside it.

The door groaned open.

Noelle and Evan shot out into the hallway, coughing and gulping in lungfuls of fresh air as they ran.

"There! They went that way!" a man yelled. "Holy shit. Watch out." Something exploded behind them, a portion of wall falling into the hallway, or so she thought. Her lungs burned, chest heaving as they ran, no idea where to go except away from those in pursuit.

"Up there, turn," Evan panted as they approached a turn in the hallway. She followed him, ducking around the bend and then skidding to a stop as he yanked hard at her sweatshirt, plastering himself against the wall and signaling that she do the same. Evan pushed her behind himself and then reached in his back pocket, handing her the rope he'd tucked there. She took it, confused and terrified. What was he doing? She wanted to scream and pull at him, make him run with her. Away from the pounding feet that were approaching quickly. They had guns. They had weapons. They'd throw them back in cages.

Nonononono. I'll die first.

Evan planted his feet and raised something in his good hand. The ice pick. He'd taken the ice pick when he'd kicked the one piece of furniture in the room to pieces for the wood.

She wished they had the power tools now. They'd be no good, of course, for full usage. They'd nixed the idea of taking one as they'd planned their unlikely escape. They'd only slow them down. They were too awkward and cumbersome to stab with. But she wished she had one now, just to swing at the man running toward them. Just to hurl at his head.

Crashes could be heard all around them, from up above and somehow down below. The building was quickly being consumed, smoke billowing past them in the hallway that led from the room where they'd started the blaze.

The footsteps were almost upon them. Evan raised his hand higher, and Noelle swore that for a moment the world stilled, then froze, then sped up, racing toward her in living color. She swayed, her fingers touching the wall next to her as Evan gave a mighty yell, bringing his hand down in an arcing motion at the same moment the man who had stood guard in the room upstairs while she was brutalized appeared at the turn where they were waiting, his head whipping toward them as Evan planted the ice pick in his neck. The man screamed, going down on his knees as he grabbed for the pick with two hands, a geyser of blood spurting from the wound.

He went down hard, his face hitting the ground with a crack. He did not move.

Evan pulled the ice pick from his neck, and she barely registered the squelching sound over the noise of the fire and her pounding heart.

They heard the other man's running footsteps. He'd taken a different route, but he was close. And coming closer. He called a name that sounded like *Mo* or *Joe*, but the fire was roaring loud; the sounds of beams falling made it all but impossible to hear.

"Yeah!" Evan answered, deepening his voice as he pretended to be the guard he'd just killed responding to his friend's call. Then he took the dead man by one arm, and Noelle took the other. Together they pulled him around the corner so he couldn't be seen from the main hallway. Then they waited again, their panting breath loud but mixing with the other noises as the footsteps drew closer, the man with the red shoes coming around the bend and stopping just as the first man had done. Noelle saw the hatred in his expression, and then it morphed into shock. And fear. Evan brought the ice pick down again, the sharp end going directly in the man's eye. He screamed, bringing his hand up and firing the gun he held. Noelle felt the bullet whiz by her cheek, and she screamed, too, throwing herself against the wall.

It all happened so fast. Evan knocked the gun out of the wounded man's hand, but the man succeeded in getting his hands around Evan's neck, and they both went down, Evan underneath the man with the pick in his eye, blood flying into the air around them.

Noelle screamed, circling behind the man and using the rope to wrap around his neck. She pulled with every ounce of strength in her body, his head bending backward but his hands remaining on Evan's neck, whose face was a ghastly shade of crimson.

It was not going to end this way, and especially not with *this* man who had led them upstairs over and over to be used and degraded. She gritted her teeth and let out a yell, pulling once and then again, the man making hideous wet grunting noises as blood spurted from his eye socket.

He almost took her with him when he fell, toppling over and landing on his back. Evan scrabbled from beneath him, his good hand going to his throat as he coughed and wheezed and worked to regain his breath.

Was the man dead? She had no idea, but she hoped so. *Rest in hell. No time. There's no time.*

Who knew how many more were behind those two?

She pulled on Evan, and he stumbled along with her back to the main hallway, where a piece of falling ceiling barely missed them. They jumped over it and then dodged a fiery section of wall as it popped and crackled and burned.

A loading dock. There was some sort of loading dock ahead, a pulley next to the garage-type door. Noelle dropped the rope and used both her hands to pull on the chain. The door rose with a creak and a groan, and when it was open enough that they could scoot under, they both did, rising to their feet on the other side, standing on the edge of a dock.

Outside. They were outside, and it was night.

"This way," she said to Evan, pulling his shirt as she bolted to the concrete steps that led to the ground. They practically flew down them.

And then they ran.

She had no idea where they were headed. All she knew was that it was away. And they were *free*.

Behind them, the building was a wild inferno. She glanced back, just once. The building appeared to be a giant factory or some old warehouse, and the entire thing was going up in flames, sparks shooting into the nighttime sky like fireworks. If she weren't so petrified, fighting for each breath that came into her burning lungs, she might have thought it beautiful. It might have looked like victory.

Instead, she sobbed with fear and pain, grabbing Evan's uninjured hand as they raced into the night.

They ran until they couldn't run anymore. The terrain was desert-like, the earth hard packed and cracked from the sun. The light from the fire faded, but the moon shone down, lighting their way.

Her legs gave out, and she crumpled to the ground. Her body had done all it could for her after being virtually immobile for weeks, if not months, brutalized, half starved. It would not go on.

"Noelle," Evan wheezed. "We have to keep going."

"I can't," she said. "I'm sorry. I just need to rest. Just for a little while."

He looked like he might argue, but then he sat down beside her, lying back, both of them staring up at the twinkling stars.

She heard only movements of the night, a soft breeze that stirred the brambly bushes dotted here and there, the faint scurrying of some small animal. She had no idea where they were. Had there only been two henchmen in that building with them? Had the men who had raped her traveled to be there? *You've been rented.*

She pushed that from her mind. It was too much. She had all she could handle not to fall to pieces.

"Do you think there are others coming to look for us?" Evan rasped. His thoughts had obviously traveled along a similar path.

"Maybe," she said. Who were *they*? Did they have sweeping helicopters or all-terrain vehicles? Would they find them where they lay in this unknown desert under the stars, the burning building where they'd been held prisoner too far away to see?

It felt like they'd emerged onto the wasteland of some other planet. She knew that wasn't true because the same stars she'd known all her life were overhead. There was Ursa Major, and her star sign, Gemini. The twins.

They lay there, still and silent for several more minutes, her lungs filling with air and the acrid smoke clearing from her sinuses. She felt his arm brush hers, and then his hand, his two fingers linking with her own and squeezing.

Oh God. Oh God.

They were holding hands the same way they had for so long, but now their shoulders were touching and they were free. She let out a gasping sob, turning to him and weeping against his side. He raised his arm and put it around her, and she thought she heard him crying softly, too, but she wasn't sure.

Her sobs dwindled to soft cries, and then her tears dried. Wordlessly, they sat up and then stood. They had to keep moving. Soon, morning would come and they would lose the cover of darkness.

They walked this time, Noelle leading as Evan followed behind. She glanced at him now and again, his broken hand cradled against his chest. It wasn't bleeding, though, which was good. But the damage, she knew, was contained within, the mayhem of which had allowed him to collapse his knuckle so that it could fit through the small opening of the bars of his cage.

His cage.

Horror rose within her at the vision of where they'd been such a short time ago.

It didn't seem real. Her mind was spinning, hysteria seeping into the cracks of her thoughts.

Don't think. Not now.

They weren't safe, not yet. And so they traveled on.

CHAPTER FIFTEEN

Evan's hand throbbed mercilessly. He hurt everywhere, but his hand was where the pain radiated so harshly he felt like he might throw up.

Still they walked, Noelle shuffling over the cracked ground in front of him. He followed because he didn't feel capable of leading and he didn't want to let her down. But he wouldn't leave her, not even to sit for a minute, and so if she kept moving, so did he.

Don't stop. You're the only reason I'm upright.

They were in the middle of fucking nowhere. How far had they been transported? And who the fuck took them to be locked in steel cages and forced to make horrendous choices? *Rented?* And why them?

We leave here whole.

We leave here together.

And they had, they *had*, against all odds. So far anyway.

A wild roar stirred in his chest, and he wanted to sink to his knees and scream at the sky. He wasn't even sure what that sound would contain if he allowed it to emerge. Tempered triumph? Rage? Agony?

Yes. Yes to all of that.

And Evan sensed that emotions that enormous and all encompassing would not lie dormant for long.

But for now, the agony of his hand overtook the thrashing emotions inside, and strangely, he was grateful for that.

A slip of pale gray met his eyes, peeking into the dark sky.

Morning had come.

Fear leaped inside. Noelle glanced back at him, and he saw the concern in her face that he felt too. The darkness had seemed like protection, like cover from those who might be hunting for them, though they hadn't heard any sounds, near or far, that might have suggested that, not even fire trucks to extinguish the inferno they'd left behind.

And so they walked on, the shadows of the desert becoming sage-green and brown plants, shiny, yellow-topped cacti covered in white spines, and red-hued dirt beneath their feet.

The sky moved from pearl to pale pink, and then all at once seemed to explode in streaks of purple and orange.

Noelle stopped in front of him, sucking in a breath as she met his eyes. He stopped, too, realizing that the sound of a vehicle could be heard moving in their direction. He'd zoned out, synchronizing his steps to the pulsating of his hand, and almost missed it. Adrenaline surged, and he pointed to a hedge of dry bushes to their right, and both of them limped as quickly as possible for the cover they provided.

The vehicle was driving slowly, and Evan realized there was a road ahead of them. He heard the tires rolling over the gravelly ground, but also the sounds of . . . laughter and . . . singing?

"It's Spanish," Noelle said under her breath, her eyes wide as they met his. Were they in . . . *Mexico*?

They held themselves still as the vehicle passed slowly by, coming to a squeaky stop a hundred feet from where they hid. More Spanish, an adult saying something and a child responding. Evan moved a piece of brush aside, peering out. It was a truck, and six or seven people sat in the open cab at the back, a few of them children. A little boy about nine or ten jumped down from the flatbed and ran into the desert, stepping behind a cactus and unzipping his pants. Evan heard the sound of him urinating.

He turned his head and met Noelle's eyes. Did they dare? Did they dare ask for help? There was nothing as far as the eye could see, and he was so parched he felt like passing out. He could see she was at least as bad off as he was. They wouldn't make it much farther on their feet. And that would mean they escaped hell simply to die in a desert alone. That'd be better, but not by much.

"There are *children*," she whispered.

He gave a nod. They looked like farmers or laborers of some type, headed to a day of work along with their sons. If they were there as part of whatever Noelle and Evan had been dragged into, would they have their children with them? And—he looked closer—one old lady, sitting at the back of the flatbed, a scarf tied around her hair?

No, these were locals, whatever *local* meant. Evan looked at Noelle, giving a tip of his chin. Then he took her hand, and they stood, stepping from the bushes.

The man standing at the back of the truck waiting for the boy startled, letting out what sounded like an epithet in Spanish. The little boy came running from behind the cactus and joined his father. The other people on the truck were staring at them, eyes wide, expressions incredulous.

Noelle and Evan approached slowly. It was all they could manage anyway. "We need help," Evan said. "Can you help us?"

The man standing at the back of the truck with the boy stared, then said something in Spanish to them. Evan shook his head. "I'm sorry, we only speak English."

"English," the man said with a heavy accent. He turned to the rest of the people in the truck, speaking several strings of words.

Next to him, Noelle swayed, and he put his arm around her, holding her up.

The old woman stood and said something, and then one of the men jumped down, and he and the father came toward Evan and Noelle, each taking one of their arms and helping them over to the truck and then up to the open bed, where they sat on built-in wooden seats.

A man leaned through the open back window of the cab and said something to the driver, and the truck began moving slowly again, dust and gravel kicking up in its wake.

A different man offered them a jug of water, and they both drank greedily, thanking him and returning it mostly empty. He handed over something wrapped in a cloth, and Noelle opened it. Food. She broke it in half and gave part to Evan. They both ate it. Evan couldn't have said what it was or how it tasted. He only knew they were half starved and needed to eat if they were going to make it any further.

"Where are we?" Evan asked the father and son, who were sitting across from them, staring suspiciously.

The little boy said something to his father and then turned back to Evan. *Sobreviviente,* he thought the little boy had said. Evan nodded. He had no idea if he'd heard the word correctly or if it was the name of where they were or not.

The old woman said something and gestured for Evan to come join her where she sat. When he hesitated, she pointed to his hand and then removed a piece of cloth and a small jar from the bag next to her. When he hesitated again, she repeated the same line, but this time with more command, clucking and tsking. "I think she wants to wrap your hand," Noelle said.

He glanced at her and then stood, mostly crouched over, shuffling the few steps in the swaying truck and then sitting next to the woman. She took his hand gently in hers, and when he hissed in pain, she said something low and under her breath. He sensed sympathy, and so he didn't pull away. His hand had swollen and was twice its normal size, the skin angry red and cracking in places where it stretched tight. His fingers looked like five fat sausages.

He watched Noelle as the old woman put some kind of clear salve onto his skin, clucking some more and muttering under her breath. He felt like he was floating out of his body and had the strange urge to laugh suddenly as he and Noelle stared at each other from a few feet away, knees bouncing along with the other riders'. A man had taken out a very small guitar and begun to sing, and it was just all so surreal and hilarious. Evan's lips trembled, and he looked away, out to the brightening horizon. He knew that if he started laughing, he wouldn't stop, and would eventually end up a howling, writhing nutcase on the floor of this truck.

The woman said something else, patting his hand very lightly. He caught the word *médico* and figured she was telling him to see a doctor.

He nodded. "Gracias." It was about the only word he knew in Spanish. He was taking German in school, of all things. That suddenly seemed hilarious, too, but he couldn't for the life of him explain why.

The truck came to a stop, and Evan turned. He could see the roofs of buildings. It looked like a small town. His heart quickened, but it felt far away. He was numb, and half out of both his body and his head.

The little boy pointed to the town and said something, and then the man jumped from the truck, reaching his hand up to help Noelle down. Clearly, they were dropping them off at the edge of whatever town this was. The man pointed. "*Vamos,*" he said.

Evan stood and followed Noelle as she sat on the edge of the truck and hopped down. They both turned around. "Gracias," Evan said again. "Uh, police?" he asked.

They all looked at each other, their expressions filled with wariness. He heard one of them say the word *policía*.

"*No,*" the little boy said. "*No policía, no bueno.*"

The police are no good?

Before either of them could try to communicate any more, the truck began moving, leaving them in a cloud of dust.

They walked again, skirting the streets, moving behind buildings. Evan didn't know if the people in the truck didn't trust the police in this town just on general principle, or what. Maybe they were involved in organized crime of some type. He'd heard stories about corrupt departments in foreign countries. Who knew if they were true. They wouldn't risk it.

"Look," Noelle said, her voice slurring. She was pointing at a building with a sign on the front. He recognized a word: MOTEL. It wasn't like any motel he'd ever seen, but it looked like it might rent rooms. She stumbled, and he grabbed her arm, practically dragging her there. If they didn't make it somewhere, she was going to fall down in the street.

A young girl sitting behind a desk stared when they walked in the door. A ceiling fan turned above, rattling slightly with each rotation. Evan blinked, working to keep himself upright. A small TV set played behind her, the picture zigzagged with static. The young woman greeted them in Spanish.

"Do you speak English?" Evan asked.

She stared again. "A little," she finally said.

He let out a long breath. "We need a room," he said. "A room with a phone. We've been robbed. My father will pay double for the room, but I need to get a hold of him first. He'll call the front desk with his credit card if you could show us to a room. Please." He didn't know if he could trust her with the truth, but he had to tell her something. They desperately needed her help.

She stared again, her eyes darting to Noelle and then back to him. "Please," he said. "Double. Quadruple. Anything."

She stared for another beat but then turned, taking a key from a pegboard behind her and handing it over along with a business card. "This number," she said, tapping the card.

"Thank you," he breathed. "Thank you so much. My father, he'll call."

She nodded, pointing to a side door, and Evan led Noelle back outside to a walkway that led to the three rooms along the side. The key had a two on it, and Evan began moving toward that door when Noelle stumbled, almost going down. He grabbed her before she hit the ground and then picked her up and walked with her toward their room.

He could hardly feel his left hand anymore. It'd gone numb, maybe from whatever the woman had applied to it but more likely because he was going into shock.

His hand shook as he finally got the key in the lock on the third attempt and then entered the room and placed Noelle on the bed, less than gently. She didn't seem to notice, though. He shut the door behind them, locked it, and closed the curtain on the one window before sitting down on the bed himself and picking up the receiver of the old-fashioned phone on the bedside table. It took him a minute to figure out how to place a collect call to the US. Later, he couldn't have said how he did it. His body was shutting down. His brain was foggy, thoughts disjointed. His voice shook as he gave his father's cell phone number to the international operator, and he started to fall forward but caught himself as the phone began to ring.

"Hello?"

"Dad?" His voice cracked.

There was the briefest of pauses. "Evan? Holy shit, Evan?"

His voice must have woken Noelle, because she sat up groggily, dragging herself from the bed and shuffling into the bathroom. How, he did not know. He realized also that he'd never known a stronger person than Noelle Meyer.

"Yes, Dad, it's me."

"Where are you?" His dad's voice cracked now too. He sounded desperate.

"Mexico." He read the address from the card he'd been given by the woman at the front desk. "I don't know if we should go to the police. I don't know if it's safe."

He heard the shower turn on and then the sound of the clips sliding on the bar as she pulled the curtain aside.

His dad swore, and there was much movement in the background, as though his dad was hurrying somewhere as he spoke. "Stay there," his dad said. "I'll pay for the room, so no one should come knocking. Lock the door and stay put. Don't let anyone in. I can be there in four hours."

"Four *hours*?" It seemed like a lifetime. Too long to endure. But what other choice did they have? Were the people who'd taken them looking? Hunting them down? Evan's eyes flew around the room, looking for potential weapons. An iron on the shelf in the open closet, a chair leg . . .

"Thank you, Dad." His voice was fading.

"I love you, son. I love you. I'll be there soon. Don't let anyone in. Not anyone, you hear?"

Evan dropped the phone back in the base on the nightstand and then pulled himself to his feet. He began dragging the larger items of furniture in front of the door, grunting with the effort. He heard the squeak of the pipes as the water turned off in the bathroom.

A moment later, Noelle emerged, a towel wrapped around her body and her hair hanging, partially wet. She'd been slender before, but now there was nothing to her. She looked dead on her feet, but he understood why she'd stayed conscious long enough to cleanse her body. "Help is coming," he said.

"I need to call my dad," she slurred.

He picked up the receiver, going through the same process he'd just gone through to call his own father. She gave him her father's number, and when it began to ring, he handed her the receiver. She held it to her ear, a small sob emerging as he heard it go to voice mail, and the call was disconnected.

"You can call him from my dad's cell phone as soon as he gets here," Evan said. There was pain on her face, but she gave a woozy nod, shuffled to the bed, brought the quilt back, and got under it, still wearing nothing but her towel.

Evan opened his mouth to ask her if she was okay, but before he could, he realized she'd fallen asleep the moment her head hit the pillow.

He watched her for a second, her chest rising and falling, mouth open as she slept.

He looked at the mountain of furniture he'd somehow piled in front of the door, then he checked the lock on the window again, peering out quickly onto the sunlit street. People ambled by; a woman with a baby strapped to her back called out to a toddler running ahead, and a skinny dog lay in the shade of a building.

Evan turned, wanting nothing more than to fall into bed and sleep for an hour, just one, but before he did that, he turned to the bathroom, headed inside, and shed the clothes he'd first put on in another life entirely.

CHAPTER SIXTEEN

Noelle woke to the light streaming around the edges of a curtain. For the briefest of moments, she thought she'd awoken in her own home, having fallen asleep on the couch. She'd had a terrible, traumatic dream. The boy from school, handsome, popular Evan Sinclair, had been in it. How odd. How vivid.

But then she smelled the smoke. Her eyes opened wider, and she blinked around, everything coming back to her in a horrid rush.

The cage.

The hunger.

The dreadful loneliness and fear.

The men, their breath hot on her face as they tore at her body from the inside. Taking.

Evan, smashing the bones of his hand.

The escape.

The fire.

The chase.

The ice pick.

The desert.

Oh God, oh God, oh God.

It felt like a crushing weight, bearing down. She didn't trust her freedom. She was flailing inside. She couldn't accept it. It would be taken from her. This was a dream or a wish or a prayer, and in a moment, it would burst and she'd wake behind bars. Trapped like an animal.

A sound met her ears. It was her. Moaning. The whimpers were coming from her. She couldn't stop them.

A hand, reaching, fingers linking with her own. Her breath released in a whoosh, her lungs expanding with air. She could breathe. *In. Out.* She took in gulping breaths until her heart slowed.

"You're okay," he said. His voice was groggy. "We're free. It's real."

A sob was welling in her chest. She clutched his fingers with one hand and gripped the sheet beneath her with the other, holding on. He was solid, and the sheet was soft, so very soft. Outside she heard the distant sounds of children playing, a dog barking. Life. People. The world moving around them. They were part of it again. They'd risen from the depths of hell.

She turned her body toward him. He was already on his side, his broken hand resting on his hip. His chest was bare, and she saw the top of a towel wrapped around his waist. She could see his ribs. He'd lost so much weight. He'd showered as well. Washed as much of the filth and smoke and horror from his skin as he could.

And yet she knew, like her, it still remained embedded inside. She'd never feel clean again. She'd never feel free.

Their eyes met, and she saw the same desperation in his that must be in her own. The vital need to feel alive. To grasp control. To prove that they hadn't been irreparably broken. To freely consent to another person's touch. She came up on her knees, dropping her towel as he rolled to his back. Then they were clutching at each other, both making animalistic sounds that might be sobs or grunts or pleas for help. Maybe all that and so much more. Unspeakable things that must be expelled. He ran his hand over her breast, and she wrapped her palm around his penis, which was already hard. She moved it downward, cupping his balls, and he hissed, pressing against her hand.

She had the vague sense that choosing Evan, choosing anyone, truth be told, would erase the memories of those others. And so when the sob burst free, the words that rushed from her mouth were "I can't forget. I want to."

He sat up, turning her so he was on top. She didn't mind, but she kept herself propped on her elbows so they were both in control. Her eyes were open, because it was essential she see what they both chose to do with each other. For each other.

"Forget with me. Make new memories. We'll only think of this. This is all we'll let ourselves remember."

"Yes," she breathed as he entered her. "Yes." She wasn't wet, but she didn't care. It wasn't about pleasure. It was about much more than that. It was about survival, a form she hadn't even known existed. She was trying to save her soul, and she looked in his eyes and knew he was too.

He began moving, plunging into her. He wasn't gentle, but she didn't want gentle. She wanted hard and pounding. She wanted it scored into her flesh. She wanted it to smash and beat out the smells and the sounds and the feelings she'd experienced against her will. "Harder," she breathed. He complied. He didn't have to tell her he needed this too. They couldn't have explained it to anyone else in all the world so that it sounded right or good, or even sane. But they had been there, and they were here now, and they knew.

They knew.

She wrapped her legs around his hips, and then she did fall back, landing on the pillow. He followed her down, still thrusting, and she chanted in his ear, "Yes, yes, yes, yes." The word was healing. It was medicine. It was the beginning of knitting some terrible gash closed, tiny stitch by tiny stitch.

It wouldn't close the wound, but in that moment, it felt like a start. One so desperately needed.

When he came, he came with a growl and a sob mixed up into one. She tightened her legs around him, and she held him there, breathing in the scent of his skin. She realized she was crying, hot tears that leaked from her eyes and dripped into her ears.

Their breath evened, muscles loosening as she lowered her legs to the bed and he pulled himself away from her. There were no words, no eye contact as they sat up. Evan brought the discarded towel around his waist, and Noelle covered herself with the one she'd slept in.

"Three hours," he murmured, looking at the bedside clock. "We slept three hours."

"I feel like I could sleep for eternity," she said as he stood.

He glanced back at her, a small sad smile playing on his lips. He didn't say anything, but she knew what he was thinking. *We avoided that. You will sleep for eternity someday, but not yet.*

Not yet.

She stood, too, smoothing her hair.

Evan held up his bandaged hand. "Do you think you might . . ." He nodded to the bathroom, and it took her a moment to understand, but then she did.

"Of course," she said.

Evan turned on the shower, and they both dropped their towels. She supposed it was odd that they weren't embarrassed by their nudity, but in some ways, she felt that she'd spent the last however long with him, completely stripped bare. What was naked flesh when a person had seen your soul?

They'd had sex, and yet it almost hadn't been sexual, in a way she was too cloudy headed and close up to make sense of. Maybe later she'd be able to articulate the meaning of it, but now she neither wanted nor needed to.

They stepped beneath the hot spray, and Noelle used the bar of soap to wash his body. She poured a generous amount of shampoo into her hands and scrubbed his hair and the beard that had grown on his face, and then she repeated the process.

When she was done, she washed herself again, including her hair this time. A few hours ago, she'd wanted a shower more than anything in the world, but she had been too exhausted to do more than the minimum. Now she was thorough about it, leisurely.

She turned, and wordlessly Evan used his good hand to lather the entirety of her back. "I'm sorry," he murmured as he rubbed the soap in circles on her skin. "I'm so damn sorry."

She hung her head and closed her eyes. She knew what he was apologizing for, and she supposed she felt the same, or she should. Their sex had been necessary, but in some way, they'd used each other. They'd used each other's bodies to relieve their pain. She wouldn't take it back, and she didn't think he would, either, but still. Surely the regret would come later, and she'd be glad she'd said the words. "No, I'm sorry," she told him.

He put his forehead on her shoulder, and she felt his breath on her skin. "I'm sorrier," he said. "Seriously, Noelle—"

"I'm the sorriest," she said. She turned, taking him in her arms.

He released a breath, mixed with the smallest of laughs. "Stop. I'm—" He lifted his head, his eyes widening, and that's when she heard it too. The approach of vehicles.

Evan turned off the water, jumping from the shower and grabbing a towel as he raced for the window. "It's my dad," he called, panic and elation and a hundred other emotions in his voice.

Noelle grabbed a towel and dried herself hastily and then reached for the only clothes she had—items that were now all but oily, bloody, disintegrating rags—and began to put them on as what sounded like a fleet of vehicles arrived outside their room.

Evan had pulled on his clothing and was now moving the items of furniture he'd piled in front of the door. How he'd done that with one hand and half dead from exhaustion, she wasn't sure, but he had. She ran to him, beginning to help, when a loud knock came at the door.

"Evan!"

"Dad, hold on, I'm moving things. Hold on!"

"Jesus Christ, hurry, Evan!" There was the sound of heavy commotion outside, as though Evan's father had brought a hundred men.

She and Evan huffed and puffed and pulled until there was room for the door to be wedged open, and then Evan turned the two locks and a man—his father—came pushing through the door. He let out a sob as he took his son in his arms, shaking as he held him. Then he stood back and took Evan's face in his hands and searched it as though looking for the injuries he might have imagined. Where his cheek had been ripped open just above his patchy beard, there was the start of a nasty scar. Apart from that, and his terribly broken hand, Evan looked like Evan, though.

Skinnier, bearded, but still himself.

And so utterly, completely different. There were far too many scars beneath the surface that no one would ever see. Only she would fully know.

Her thoughts tripped clumsily over themselves. She felt out of it, unable to believe this was real. That they'd been rescued. They were going home.

"Thank God," Evan's father said. "Thank God." Mr. Sinclair dropped his hands and stepped back, his eyes moving over Evan. "We'll get your hand fixed," he said. "I'll find the best surgeons. For your face and for your hand."

"It's fine," Evan said.

His father blew out a breath and nodded, his relief obvious. That's when he noticed Noelle standing off to the side. For the briefest of moments, she swore she saw raw hatred on his face, but then it was gone, and he nodded at her. "You've both been through a lot. But you're whole. You're here. We'll get you back to the US, and then you'll receive the medical care you need. Let's go."

They exited the motel, and Noelle saw that, rather than one hundred men, there were only three other black SUVs. Mr. Sinclair said something to one of the men he passed, and that man stepped toward Noelle, touching her arm. "You can come with me, ma'am."

Evan had stopped and now began walking back toward Noelle. "No, she'll ride with us."

"Son," his father said, gripping his shoulder.

"It's okay," Noelle said before his father had to say anything more. She could imagine that he wanted time with his son. She had no love for the man, even now, when in essence he was rescuing them, but she could only imagine the fear and grief he'd been experiencing while his only child had been missing. "I need to call my father. Can I use your phone?" she asked the man standing next to the vehicle.

"Yes, ma'am. Let's get on the road and you can make your call. That way we'll have an ETA."

She nodded and turned back to Evan. "I'll be okay," she said.

Evan hesitated, not looking happy but accepting with a nod. The man opened the back door of the SUV for her, and she looked back at Evan, every muscle in her body telling her to run to him, to latch on, to never let go.

They'd depended on each other for so long. *We leave here whole. We leave here together.* They'd *done* that. So why, now, did it feel like they were breaking a promise? It felt like she was losing a piece of herself. It wasn't rational, she knew, but it was still true.

She turned and ducked into the vehicle, sliding over the supple leather seats and then lying down as the tears began to flow. It felt like she had a never-ending supply. It felt like she might cry forever.

The driver pointed to a bag on the floor behind his seat. "There's food for you, Ms. Meyer. Water too." She mumbled a thank-you. *Food. Water.* As much as she wanted. She should have been only relieved, but the thought brought mostly pain, and she wasn't even sure why.

She felt so intensely bereft. Bereft of the boy who'd held her fingers throughout her nightmare, who may never hold her fingers again.

The car she was in began backing up and then turning, driving away, leaving the small nowhere town where they'd found refuge for a few brief hours. Noelle didn't watch it out the window as they left. Instead, she continued to cry.

CHAPTER SEVENTEEN

Night came, the sun dipping below the desert horizon. Evan watched blankly as the clapboard houses along the highway whizzed by. He ate a sandwich and drank a bottle of water. Strangely, he wondered when he'd feel a sense of freedom even in eating. "Does Noelle have food?" he asked. His father gave him a thin-lipped look but nodded. Evan glanced back every few minutes to ensure that the car Noelle was in trailed close behind his own. His father only asked that he describe the building where they'd been kept and its location as best he could in reference to where they'd traveled. He did, speaking in a monotone. His emotions felt muted, and he was somewhat grateful and a little concerned. He sensed they were gathering, the way storm clouds did, and at some future time, the sky overhead would split.

He heard his father on the phone, talking to some form of law enforcement, relaying to them what Evan had described regarding the general direction of the building they'd been kept in and the fact that it was on fire. Whoever it was on the phone sounded displeased. "I wasn't going to trust anyone with my son's safety. You failed to find him," his father spit out.

Evan drifted off and then woke. His father was sitting stonily, his jaw set as he stared out the window. He turned his head and met Evan's eyes. "Do you have any ideas about who they were?" his father asked.

Evan shook his head. "None."

His father studied him for a moment but didn't ask any more questions, and for that, Evan was grateful. Perhaps his father didn't want to know the details of what had happened to him. Maybe he was scared to find out. That was fine. Evan didn't want to tell him anyway. He didn't want to tell anyone. He and Noelle knew. It was all that mattered.

Finally, too exhausted to keep his eyes open, he slept again, the car rocking him into a chaotic dream in which he relived their escape, only this time making different choices that resulted in terrible outcomes where he watched Noelle die in horrific ways over and over.

His father shook him now and again so that he came awake, choking back a scream. "Shh, son, it's okay," his father said. "You're safe."

He slept through most of the drive to the border and then across it. He realized that his father had Evan's passport, but how would they get Noelle across the border? He bolted upright in a panic and turned to look out the back window, breathing out a sigh of relief when he saw the three SUVs still trailing them.

However they'd worked it out, she was still with him, just a car away. He slept again.

It was almost morning when Evan opened his eyes, wiping the sleep from his face and sitting up. They were in the parking lot of a police station, the SUV still idling. He was alone. How long had he sat here sleeping?

His head swiveled, taking stock, looking for Noelle. The other cars were parked nearby, a bevy of news vans all around, the logos telling him they were in San Diego. What the hell was happening? His father was just outside the car, talking to a man in a suit. Evan opened the door. "Evan," his father said, moving forward and wrapping his arm around him as he got out. Cameras flashed, news anchors yelling questions at him, only disconnected words that didn't form full sentences making it to his ears.

"I'm sorry," his father gritted. "Someone from the police department leaked it to the media that we were on our way. Fucking vultures."

He rushed with his father and the other man into a side door of the building, the calls and clicks muting as the doors fell shut. "Noelle?" he asked. "Where's Noelle?"

"She's with a detective," his father said. "Don't worry about her right now."

Don't worry about her right now.

But Evan didn't know how to do that. Her well-being had been connected to his for so long. He didn't know how to separate himself.

He whipped his head around, looking for her, but a tall man in a blue suit stepped in front of him, extending his hand. "Evan, I'm Agent Crokin. If you'll come with me, we need to get a statement. Time is of the essence."

"Noelle!" he called, pushing past the man and turning his head one way and then the other.

"Evan!" his father said sternly. "Stop it. She's poison. Her family is poison. Whatever you experienced together, it's over. And thank God for that. Thank God."

His father didn't understand. All that old stuff, it'd ceased to matter. It wasn't even real.

Everything buzzed. The lights. The people walking by. His head. He couldn't get his bearings. And so he let the agent lead him down a hall and out into a wide area filled with desks. He saw Noelle sitting on a bench, her head in her hands, as a woman knelt beside her.

Evan broke free of the man guiding him and ran to Noelle, going down on his knees next to the woman. "Noelle, what's wrong? What happened?"

She raised her head, her eyes bloodshot, face wet with tears. Her expression crumbled as she leaned toward him, and he wrapped his arms around her. "My dad . . . he's dead," she said. "He died while I was missing."

"Died?" He didn't understand.

The woman who had been comforting Noelle had taken a seat next to her on the bench. "It was a heart attack," the woman told him, and Noelle sucked back a sob. "Right after Noelle went missing."

He felt a hand on his arm, and his father pulled him up, his arms falling as Noelle sat back. "They need your statement now, son. If we have any chance of catching the people who did this, you need to tell the agents everything you can remember. Then we'll get you to the hospital. Your mother is flying in. She'll be here in the morning. And then we'll fly home."

"All that can wait," he said, yanking his arm away and stepping back toward Noelle.

But she shook her head. "No, Evan, go. Tell them what you can. I will too." The sound of footsteps moving quickly made him turn, and there was Noelle's friend Paula, red ponytail bouncing as she rushed toward Noelle, two older people hurrying behind her. Paula's parents. Someone obviously called them to jump on a flight. Maybe his father. More likely the police. He'd slept through a lot.

Noelle stood and let out another sob as Paula took her in an embrace, both crying and shaking. Paula's parents were crying, too, as they wrapped their arms around the girls.

Evan stepped back. He felt lost without her hand in his. Stripped of his identity, the only one he knew now. Alone in a way too painful to describe. And Noelle was alone too. Fatherless now. No family. She was in the arms of her friend and her parents, though, wrapped in safety, at least for now. He allowed his father to guide him away, his arm, still reaching toward Noelle, finally dropping. He turned, then walked down the hall and into a room with a table in the middle surrounded by chairs.

The agent offered them drinks, and his father requested a coffee and Evan asked for a bottle of water. He was thirsty. He'd been thirsty for so long. But he didn't have to be thirsty anymore. Or hungry. Or petrified.

He was no longer caged. But he didn't know how to stop feeling like he was. He started shaking. He sank down into a chair, and his father sat next to him. "Who did this, Dad?" he asked, his voice a mere croak.

His father stared at him for a moment, his eyes murderous. He looked like he was barely containing his rage. "I don't know," he gritted. "But let me work on figuring that out. You need to try to forget."

Forget? He was tempted to laugh. But if he did that, he knew he would cry. And he would not cry in front of his father because, even now, Evan knew his father would consider him weak.

~

Three days. Three days had passed. In some ways it felt like three years since he'd seen her, and in some ways, mere minutes. He'd never known before how tangled his emotions were with the passage of time. He stood for a moment, staring up at her house, the place where she was, somewhere just beyond those walls. The yearning spurred him forward.

The home was older, the white shingles clearly in need of a coat of paint. Evan let the short white picket gate swing closed behind him and then walked up the path to the hunter-green front door. The lawn had been recently cut, but the flowers in the beds under the front window had died, as had the ones in the pots on the front porch.

A fly bumped into the bulb of the porch light, giving off a tiny buzz. Evan raised his fist and knocked.

Footsteps approached, and then the door swung open. "Hi, Paula," Evan said, putting his good hand in the pocket of his jeans, his left hand across his chest in a sling. He felt strangely like he was doing something wrong to be there, at this house he'd never visited before and never thought in a million years he'd have reason to.

The house where his so-called enemy lived. At least on paper.

What a joke. It was laughable now. That had been a different life.

Paula hesitated, clearly torn about how to respond to his presence. "She's resting upstairs," she finally said, obviously knowing full well why he was there. As if to illustrate the point that he wasn't welcome in the house, Paula stepped to the side, her body blocking the entrance. *Jesus.* She was looking at him the way she always had in school. With distrust. Contempt. Did she still hold a grudge against him for what his father had done to her friend's family? Hadn't Noelle explained to her how they'd worked together? How they'd bonded? Or was it that, like him, she'd been unable to put their experience into more than a handful of words?

"Let him in, Paula." He leaned in slightly as Paula turned around, both of them peering up at Noelle, who stood on the stairs, hair mussed, eyes a little swollen but not like they'd been at the police station days before.

He felt momentarily disoriented seeing her in a gray sweatshirt and jeans after having seen her in the same outfit for so long. For a moment he thought he'd leaped backward, to the time before. To the time when they'd been different people. But he hadn't. He was here. And she was only a few feet away. He nudged past Paula, who made a tiny gasping sound as he rushed up the stairs. As soon as he reached Noelle, he pulled her into his chest, carefully avoiding where his damaged hand lay. He held her, not just her two lone fingers, but her, all of her, nothing between them at all. He held her, and he could finally breathe. Finally.

She pulled back and shot a glance over his shoulder. By the look on Noelle's face, he imagined Paula still there, staring disapprovingly up at them. But she simply turned and led him to her room.

"She's staying with you?" he asked once she'd closed and locked the door to her bedroom.

Noelle nodded, sitting down on the bed. He was glad Noelle wasn't alone. He'd pictured her that way, standing in an empty house, grieving her father who she'd never gotten to say goodbye to. Another parent lost suddenly. And his family was entwined in that loss, too, though in a completely different way. He didn't want to think about it. He couldn't, not right then.

He'd passed by the officer sitting in front of her house and was glad she had that security, at least temporarily. When that was no longer the case . . . maybe he could convince her to stay with him. She pulled the cuffs of her sweatshirt over her hands, fidgeting. He hadn't known her to fidget before, not when he'd watched her in school and not when she'd occupied the cage next to him.

"How's your hand?" she asked, nodding to his sling.

"It's okay. I have surgery scheduled on Friday. My doctor thinks he can fix it. The plastic surgeon has high hopes, too," he said, gesturing to the cuts on his face. "I'll be good as new."

She let out a small breathy laugh. They both knew that was an impossibility. For his hand and anything else. If only.

He looked around her room briefly, noting the shabby white furniture that he'd bet anything she'd had since she was a kid. The unicorn stickers half peeled off the side of the desk confirmed his thought.

Her bookshelf was loaded down with books, not just in rows but with singular copies wedged in along the top. He wanted to take a minute to glance through them, but not now. It occurred to him, though, that he knew her as well as a person could know anyone, and also barely knew her at all. "What's your favorite color?" he asked.

She looked briefly confused but then smiled. "Blue."

"That's pretty broad."

"Turquoise, then. The color of that Easter egg dye that comes in those little kits from the grocery store."

Well, that was very specific. What a luxury to talk about things like favorite colors and Easter egg dye. The realization made his mind spin. And it made him sad. He smiled again, but it felt sort of odd. For the last few days, he'd felt like his face was underwater and all his expressions came out sort of wrong and distorted, like they were being pulled in several different directions by an unseen current.

"Did they find anything?" she asked, her finger playing idly with a thread on the throw blanket on the end of her bed.

He sighed. He knew what she was referring to, but he'd hoped to have a few more minutes to talk about mundane things. Sad things. Because it felt like they mattered too little now. And it felt like they were everything. Life had become a circle of conundrums, and he didn't know how to make it make sense. "No. The fire destroyed almost everything. By the time fire trucks got out there, it was a smoldering pile of ash. There were bits of human remains found, though, belonging to two individuals."

She worried her lip for a moment. "The men we killed," she said. "So they were the only ones there."

He nodded, taking a seat next to her on the bed and leaning his forearms on his knees before tilting his head to look at her. "Whoever else . . . visited . . . was only there temporarily." It'd only been a few days since they'd given what information they had to give to the authorities. Multiple agencies were still testing and investigating and whatever else they did with a case like theirs. The FBI was involved. Cyberteams and forensics experts and all the best of the best. Surely they'd find those responsible. Evan couldn't consider living in a world where the people who'd tortured them for almost a month and a half—it'd been five weeks and one day that he'd been gone, three fewer for her—weren't apprehended.

From what he'd been able to gather so far, when they'd first gone missing, it had seemed overly coincidental that two kids from the same school had disappeared within days of each other. In the beginning, the police had wondered if they were together—a secret romance, perhaps? But when their friends had insisted that that wasn't possible and there was no evidence he and Noelle had ever even spoken, much less were carrying on a secret relationship, that potential lead went dry. If they'd been taken by the same person, there was no evidence of that, either, despite that they did have a connection in their fathers' legal battle.

Seemingly, both of them had just disappeared into thin air for no discernible reason. Not much had been uncovered in their absence, so for all intents and purposes, the investigation was just beginning now.

Evan stood, bending a slat in the blind and peering out at the quiet street. The sun was lowering. It would be nighttime soon. Those hours when he was tormented by dreams that felt so real he woke clawing at nothing, his fists swiping at invisible shadows that existed only in his mind.

And reaching for her, his fingers stretching to link with Noelle's and then dropping when they met only emptiness.

"You have a weapon," she said, nodding to the hunting knife in his back pocket. It flipped open with the slide of a button and was hooked and sharp and could be deadly if used with enough force.

He'd use that force if he needed to.

"When I was grabbed," he told her, "there was a moment when I could have used a weapon if I had one. But I didn't. I only had my fists, and those ended up being mostly useless. I won't make that mistake again." He looked out the slat again at the black car parked just down the street. His driver waiting for him. It was supposed to make him feel safe. Whatever *safe* was.

"I know what you mean," she said softly. "I looked up how to register for a concealed carry yesterday. It's like . . . I'll never feel safe again, you know? I haven't even left the house."

He returned to where he'd been sitting on the bed next to her, taking her hand in his, running his thumb over her knuckle. They were still scraped, but they were healing. The bruise on her face looked better too. "Your dad . . . Noelle, how are you?" he asked. "Really?" Was she even able to grieve amid everything else she was trying to bear? The memories, the nightmares. He didn't have to ask if she was having nightmares too.

She let out a shaky breath. "I just keep thinking about him here in this house alone and so terrified. They say he died of a heart attack, but I think it broke. I think it just broke in two. He couldn't stand the torture of not knowing what was happening to me. He couldn't stand another sudden loss." Tears welled in her eyes, and he took her in his arms, rubbing circles over her back. He'd wanted to do this so many times over those long weeks when she'd come back from that upstairs room, the one that would be burned into his memories for all time, kept in the dungeon of his soul. He'd wanted to comfort her this way, but he hadn't been able to. He was able to now, though, and it soothed him as well.

He kept rubbing her back as she cried, and then he began whisper-singing. "If all the little snowflakes were candy bars and milkshakes, oh, if I the little snowflakes, were candy love and milkshakes, oh what a you that would be."

He felt her lips move into a smile, even though her tears were still wetting the crook of his neck. He leaned back so he could look at her and offer her a smile, too, as small as the one she wore, as pulled by that unseen current.

Their eyes held, and something shifted, some deeper need that each realized could be fulfilled with the other. His heart beat harder, and he saw her pulse pick up speed in her throat as she exhaled, her tears ceasing.

The sex was the same as that in the motel room in Mexico. Frantic, confusing, yet so desperately wanted. Like that day, he both rushed toward his orgasm and regretted it after it'd exploded through him. It wasn't the point of what they'd done, and yet maybe he should have tried to make it pleasurable for her. She hadn't seemed to want that, though, and truth be told, neither had he, necessarily. His body was different, however, and it simply couldn't be stopped.

Whatever need they were fulfilling in each other, it was like a drug, and like any good narcotic, it made him briefly numb.

"Noelle," he said, when he'd rolled away and they both lay staring up at the ceiling, "we didn't use anything, this time or the last—"

"They did a rape kit on me at the hospital," she said, her voice monotone. "They gave me a morning-after pill."

"Oh." He reached up, running his fingers through the front of his hair and clenching a handful in his fist. "But this time . . ." God, he hadn't even thought about that. Both times, he'd just become pure need, no thought. *Jesus.*

"I got an IUD put in at the hospital," she said. She sat up, bringing the bedspread with her and bending to retrieve her clothes. He hated the look on her face. She looked remorseful and confused, and just plain sad. This was hurting her. *He* was hurting her, and it was the last thing he wanted.

"We have to stop doing this," he said. He felt confused and upset. And he'd felt like he needed the release, or her touch, or just *her*, but he didn't know why, or if it was right or wrong anymore. Because it'd stopped the pain for a moment, but not longer than that.

"Yes," she agreed without turning. "We do. We need to stop this. It's not right."

That was the thing, though. It didn't feel wrong exactly either. It just felt like they were substituting sex for something else, and for the life of him, he didn't know what the fuck that was or how to get it. If he could have, he would have. He opened his mouth to say something just as loud banging met their ears from below.

Evan sprang off the bed, going to the window and pulling at the slat again. "My dad," he said, letting out a whoosh of breath. What the fuck was his dad doing there? They both dressed as rapidly as possible, he rehooking his sling and rushing from her room to the stairwell and looking over to where Paula was arguing with Evan's father in the doorway.

"Where the hell is my son—"

"Dad, what are you doing?"

His father pushed past Paula the way Evan had, yet with more force, and Paula jolted backward, giving his dad a death glare as he passed her.

"Let's go," he said to Evan, standing at the bottom of the steps.

"Let's go? How did you even know I was here?" *Oh.* He took his phone from his pocket, holding it up. "You put *tracking* on my phone?"

"Do you blame me?" his father practically yelled, face reddening. "Jesus! You were abducted. You don't get to just run off without telling me where you're going."

"I'm not a child, Dad," he said between clenched teeth.

"As long as you're under my roof, you're my responsibility. And you may. Not. Come. Here. Again." His father's jaw clenched like his own, and the older man was studiously refusing to even glance at Noelle standing behind his son. Evan felt her heat at his back. He felt her anxiety.

"She didn't do this!" Evan yelled, his frustration boiling over. His father wanted to blame someone, and she was the only option. He'd noticed how his father had quietly seethed over the past few days as he spoke with the police and the FBI and his own personal security, whenever Noelle's name was brought up. "She was there with me. She's a victim too! For the love of Christ—"

"Evan." Noelle put a hand on his shoulder, and he sucked back the words he wanted to spew at his dad. This wasn't fair. None of it was. When he looked back at Noelle, he saw the hostility in her face too. "If my father knew this man was in his home," she said, glaring at his father, her words cutting off as she pulled in a breath. "Please leave."

"Noelle would like you to leave her home." He heard Paula's voice from behind him and turned to see her looking at his father. Her eyes moved to Evan. "And your father is right. You two probably need some time apart." She gave Noelle a look, and he saw the sympathy there, but it pissed him off too. "You went through something terrible together," she went on. "Give yourselves time to process it."

"No one asked you," he spit out. "You don't know a goddamn thing."

Her nostrils flared, and Noelle let out a quiet cry. He hated that stupid girl, but she was protecting Noelle too. A part of him was glad to know she had someone else on her side. He turned back to Noelle, and the sorrow on her face broke him. "Evan," she said. "I'm planning my dad's memorial service. Maybe Paula's right. Maybe your dad is too. Let's take some time. At least a few months."

"A few months? You don't mean that!"

"I do. I do mean it. I need that. And so do you."

"The girl has some sense. Let's go, Evan," his dad said. *The girl.* The way his father said it enraged him. *She* had been destroyed by the animals that had taken them too. *She* was the biggest part of why he was alive. Was his father so filled with hate that he couldn't see that?

He turned back to Noelle again, and she'd already taken a step backward, away from him. His chest felt like it was caving in, and he was having trouble catching his breath. "Evan," she said gently. "Both of us . . . our thoughts, our emotions, they're tangled. Conflicted. We both have to remember what it's like to live in the world again. To find new footing."

He stared at her. What she was saying made some sense. Yet it also made him want to scream and claw the same way he did when he woke from those night terrors. Alone. It made him feel alone.

"Noelle—"

"Please, Evan," she said. "I have to plan a service for my dad. I have to say goodbye. He deserves that." She looked behind him at his father. "The police, they'll find answers. I feel good knowing you're working with them and focusing on that so I can . . . so I can grieve. Please, let me grieve."

He felt like she was falling away from him, like he was standing on the edge of a cliff, watching her disappear, not because he'd let her go, but because she wasn't reaching back. "I—"

"Goodbye, Evan." And with that, she turned and jogged back up the stairs, turning the corner out of sight.

Evan waited only a moment, his heart in his throat, before he turned in the opposite direction, joining his thin-lipped father and walking past Paula without looking at her.

Outside, the sun was a mere slip on the horizon. Night was coming, the place where nightmares waited.

CHAPTER EIGHTEEN

The Collector sipped his cup of tea and then placed it down on the saucer, enjoying the small clatter of porcelain against porcelain. The liquid was piping hot, dosed liberally with sugar and a slice of lemon. A man he'd once known long ago had drunk this exact tea prepared in just this way, and now he did too.

Not because he had revered the man. But because he had hated him. Because he sought to keep that hatred alive. In his heart. In his soul. Even in his mouth. He took another sip. Despite the sugar, this one tasted bitter.

Good.

The Collector clicked on the news article about Evan and Noelle. Their pictures were at the top of the page, the same ones that had been used in each article posted during the time they were missing. Their senior pictures. Evan in a suit and tie with a megawatt smile. Ah, the boardrooms he'd thought he'd command one day.

Not that he couldn't still, if he chose to. But the Collector would bet his plans had shifted. Or they would.

Captivity changed a person, after all.

Priorities rotated.

And there was Noelle. His little rabbit. He felt a distant sort of flutter in his chest at the vision of her shy smile. If he didn't know himself better, he might describe it as a form of love. But he had long since become incapable of that emotion.

By choice.

No, not love, then, but pride.

Yes, he was so proud of her.

She'd been so strong. She'd done just as he'd hoped she would.

And he felt a connection. The strongest connection he'd felt in a long, long time.

How could he not?

He ran a finger over the screen, tracing her dark hair. She'd curled it that day. It fell over her shoulders in long waves. He wondered what she'd thought about as she'd run that curling iron through her hair. Certainly not that in just a few short months she'd find herself bait in a cage, the innocent pawn in the twisted grip of a hundred psychopaths.

Life was unpredictable, though. It could be anyway, if you didn't plan ahead for every possibility. And even then . . .

He opened a drawer, reached toward the back, and carefully removed a framed photograph. *Celesse.* His throat grew tight. He ran a finger over her delicate cheekbone, the same as he'd just done to Noelle's image. How beautiful she'd been. He could still recall the fragrance of her hair. But it was growing fainter by the year. Someday soon, would he forget it altogether? The Collector seldom felt fear, but that thought distressed him greatly. He gazed at her shy smile. She'd rarely spoken to anyone but him. He'd been her voice then, and he'd be her voice now.

His finger traced her necklace and then moved to the jewel sitting in the hollow below her throat. A red diamond. He owned the matching ring. He didn't wear it much anymore. It was too recognizable. "*Schatje,*" he whispered in his native Dutch before sliding the photograph back in the drawer. *Little treasure.*

He took a sip of tea. It had grown lukewarm as he'd sat and gazed at the photograph. He moved his mind back to Noelle as he again looked at the screen and began to scroll down through the article, but not because he wanted to read about the nightmare they'd survived. The press knew nothing, even if they thought they did. The police didn't either. Nor did the FBI. They'd try. They'd find a few leads perhaps, but by the time they followed them, the game would have been moved, new codes sent out, deeper hallways built within the dark basement of the internet. These people had unlimited cash to spend, and there was always a dirty cop ready to be bribed somewhere.

He imagined some of the players even worked in the three-letter agencies. A king's court required such men, after all, to operate outside the law.

No, he didn't care what the article said or what the investigative update might be. He wanted to look at the photograph of Noelle being led into the police station at dusk, the high streetlamps in the parking lot and the flash of a multitude of cameras lighting her pale and haunted face.

He'd thought her plain at first, but that was before he'd seen the fire that made her glow from the inside. The one that made her beautiful.

He'd touched her naked body with his hands, but he'd also entered her mind. And that was far, *far* more gratifying.

Fulfilling in a way even he hadn't thought it would be.

He stared at her for a few more minutes, his blood pumping swiftly through his veins, making him feel alive. Watching their escape, fueled by *him*, had been one of the greatest thrills of his life.

He'd never forget them. And while—by choice—Noelle might forget him for a while, she wouldn't forget him forever. No, he was quite certain she would not.

The knowledge was intoxicating.

A message appeared on the phone, and he used the code to log in to the site he'd been directed to.

A new game was beginning. He'd play, of course. And maybe once again, he'd play to win. Because why the fuck not?

CHAPTER NINETEEN

One Year Later

Noelle's knee bounced as she raised her head, glancing at the sidewalk just beyond where she sat on the umbrella-covered restaurant patio. Dappled morning sunlight sparkled off the water of the fountain nearby, and the soft splashing offered a sense of calm. Despite the still morning and the peaceful sound of flowing water, Noelle's heart beat swiftly, anxiety causing her to shift her legs repeatedly.

She knew it was him approaching from down the block even before she could register any discerning quality that told her so. The man walking toward the place where she sat was taller than she remembered Evan to be, his shoulders broader, and she'd never become very acquainted with his walk. After all, she'd regularly averted her eyes when she'd seen him at school. And then after that, they'd spent the majority of their time together on their knees.

Or their backs.

He was blocks away, but she recognized him all the same. Maybe she'd know he was near even with her eyes closed. She didn't necessarily like to think that was the case, but for a brief span of time, her emotional survival had been dependent on his presence. Perhaps they were fused in some inexplicable way, a tightly woven tether that stretched over seasons and distance. She'd felt the space between them this last year, and she felt his nearness now. A reeling. A buzzing inside. An internal meter emblazoned with his name.

Noelle stood, smoothing her hands over her jean-clad hips and then fluttering her hands, unsure of what to do with her arms.

God, she was nervous.

He came closer . . . closer. He didn't glance around the open space. His eyes were focused directly on her. Perhaps he felt her too. He smiled, and her breath released, her lips curving in response. He was wearing low-slung jeans and a black T-shirt with some logo she was too preoccupied to attempt to discern. He was as staggeringly handsome, as breathtakingly *golden*, as he'd always been. Even more so. Something about that made her rejoice, and simultaneously made her want to cry. Truth be told, something about it hurt. She didn't understand why, and maybe she'd think about it later, and maybe she wouldn't.

Evan walked through the short black gate, let it swing closed behind him, and then made his way to where she stood at the small bistro table. His smile grew. "Hey," he said. His voice. It washed over her. A ray of light. A hand in the dark. Fingers linking with hers. *You're not alone.*

"Hey," she greeted him, and she couldn't help the way her smile widened too. It felt good. Effortless when so much in her life had felt forced this past year. Slow and lonely.

"You look good," he said. "Damn good."

"So do you."

"Your hair," he said. "It's lighter."

"Oh." She ran a hand over it, shrugging in a girlish way, surprising herself with how much she liked that he'd noticed. "Highlights," she explained, feeling ridiculous for her response. As if they were nothing more than old classmates who'd run into each other unexpectedly. Next they'd speak about the weather.

It'd been a *year* since that day he'd left her house after his father had shown up to fetch him. All but dragged him away. It was still so hard to believe. She'd told him they both needed time to process, and that had been true, though the further truth was probably that they'd both be doing that in some way or another for the rest of their lives.

They stood there for a minute, the air thick with all the words she knew they wouldn't say. All the things for which no words existed, really. And that was okay, she supposed. They both knew. She guessed they always would. She gestured to the table where a thermos of coffee and two white mugs sat. "I wasn't sure if you'd want to eat or just have a coffee."

"Just a coffee," he said. "I ate earlier." They both sat, and the waitress approached them, her eyes hanging on Evan. Noelle took a sip from her cup as he told her no menu was necessary.

"I'm so glad you called me," Evan said. "This is . . . wow, this is great."

She almost hadn't. She'd hemmed and hawed for weeks after making arrangements to be in San Francisco for Paula's grandmother's funeral. She hadn't known the woman well at all, but Paula had asked if Noelle would accompany her for support, and she'd been happy to do so. "So tell me how you've been," she said.

Evan poured himself a cup of coffee, took a sip, and then sat back in his chair. She could see what having the money to hire the best plastic surgeons could do. His face held no trace of the beatings he'd taken. His left hand came to rest on the table, and her heart clutched as she saw that that part of him, at least, still held the faint physical proof of his trauma. Her gaze traced the white hairline scars before she raised her eyes to his. He was watching her as she studied the surgical scars. "I've been good," he said. "Pretty good anyway. Stanford is . . ."—his brows moved in two different directions before he decided on the word—"intense." He smiled, but it appeared tight.

She tilted her head, studying the clench of his jaw, the way one shoulder had inched up. "You don't like Stanford?"

Evan laughed, his shoulder dropping. "I can't hide anything from you, can I?"

Noelle's lips tilted, but she kept her eyes on her coffee as she stirred in another packet of sugar, only raising her gaze when Evan cleared his throat. He squinted out to the street where a woman was going by with a dog almost as tall as her. The woman struggled and yanked on the leash, and it was unclear who was walking whom.

"No, the truth is, I . . . well . . . I hate it." He let out a breath. "There it is. That's the first time I've said that even to myself. I hate it," he repeated, as if confirming it for himself.

"Why do you hate it?"

Evan sighed. "It feels pointless. You know, I sit in these classes, and they're all talking about corporate governance and executive leadership, and I just keep thinking how fucking useless it all seems. It's like I feel myself careening toward the exact life my father leads, and it . . . fuck, it feels like a death sentence, Noelle."

The exact life my father leads. His father was a mogul with every luxury money could buy. And yet . . . Noelle understood exactly what Evan meant. "I think it's fair to say we see the world differently now than most people do. For better or worse."

Their eyes met, understanding passing between them. He tapped the knuckle of his unscarred hand on the table for a moment. "Yes, but I still don't know exactly what that means or . . ." He let out a frustrated breath. "How to apply it to my life."

"I think it'll take time."

He gave a small nod. "In some ways, it feels like I started over last year. Like I had to learn to do everything all over again because everything was different. New. A . . . rebirth, only without the innocence." He gave a short laugh that dissolved into a grimace.

She smiled, too, though. "I relate," she said.

"And you? How are you?"

"I'm okay. Better." Except for the nights, but he'd know that. She didn't think she needed to mention the nights.

He was watching her closely, his expression worried. Knowing. Yes, he understood the things she wasn't saying. But she was telling the truth too. She *was* okay. In most ways, she was just fine. "And you're still in school?" he asked.

"No. I dropped out." She'd been taking classes at the local community college. She gave a short laugh. "I guess I found the classes useless too. At least for now." She stirred her coffee again. It'd grown cold, and she'd already had two cups anyway as she'd waited for him to arrive, the caffeine only working to intensify her anxiety. She felt calmer now, though. Her mind had worked her into an emotional tsunami. His presence had ended the internal storm. "I found I couldn't sit still, you know? Maybe someday that will change, or"—she shrugged—"I'll find the topic that keeps me there. But for now, I prefer to be on my feet. Moving. Working." *Thinking as little as possible.* "I'm waitressing at a sports bar. It pays the bills."

Evan nodded. "There's so much you could do. You'll figure it out."

She felt the ghost of a smile float across her lips.

"I didn't expect it to be this long not seeing you," he said.

"I know. I didn't either," she told him. "I guess . . . after I said goodbye to my father, and started the process of figuring out where to go from there, it almost . . ." She trailed off. She wasn't sure how to finish that sentence without hurting him.

"Focusing solely on your own emotions rather than both of ours was the easier option."

"The healthier one anyway."

"I get it." He took his full bottom lip under his teeth for a moment, obviously considering whatever he was about to say. "I went to your father's memorial."

She blinked. "You did? I didn't see you—"

"I didn't let you. I stood in the back. It was a nice service."

She wasn't sure what to say to that.

"I held myself back from going to you, so many days," he said. "But then . . . I started feeling a little bit more on solid ground. And then I was sort of . . ."

"Afraid to see me? To confront those feelings all over again?"

He gave a small smile, and it was sort of sad. "Yeah, I guess."

She nodded. It had been like that for her too. Seeing him every day would mean staying stuck. In a sense, walking away from Evan had been like another step away from that cage. Away from the person she'd been while she was there. The differences that existed between that girl and the one she'd become could only be understood with distance. And once she'd begun making strides, to even consider moving backward—where, in her mind anyway, he still remained—was unthinkable.

They were quiet for a moment. Perhaps he, too, was thinking about the push and pull of those early days. The spinning desperation. The despair. The longing to be with someone who understood everything. The anger, though that had come later, at least for her.

"And . . . are you dating anyone?" He'd been playing with the edge of a paper napkin, and his hands stilled now as he waited for her response.

She shook her head. "I went on a couple dates a few months ago . . ." Noelle bit at her lip. "But that's over." She'd ghosted the guy she'd agreed to go to coffee with, and then a movie. He'd tried to hold her hand, and she'd felt like her skin was crawling.

The air around them seemed to have stilled, the background blurring so that only he was clear and crisp. Her sole point of reference. "Why?" he asked, and his voice had grown soft. There was a scratchiness to it as though something had gotten caught in his throat. "I mean, is it . . ."

"Difficult for me?" She swallowed, her eyes sliding away. "Yes, I freeze up," she whispered. "I don't even seem to tolerate hand holding. And . . . I worry that I'm not capable of feeling pleasure. And eventually . . . you know, if things go further with someone, it will take so long . . ."

"He'll take it personally?" Evan asked.

"Yes. Yes, exactly. And then it's a vicious cycle. The more tense I become, the less likely it is that I'll get there." So why even try? Why do that to someone? Maybe she'd just accept that she was broken.

"You could explain that . . . to the right person," he said. Her face felt hot. Even with him, even with *him*, this was hard. And yet she'd offered the truth willingly. Because he'd asked, and she wouldn't lie to him. For whatever reason, doing so felt like lying to herself.

"I could," she agreed. "With the right person. Eventually." And yes, it felt good to be honest. There was so much she couldn't be honest about with anyone.

She saw a tick in his jaw. His hands remained utterly still. She had the sense that he was jealous, that he didn't like talking about her love life. And perhaps that was true. They were both damaged by what had happened. Like they'd already admitted, their emotions were not based on healthy things.

Their emotions were not based on anything *real.*

Or lasting.

Which was why their reunion would be brief and uncomplicated. Two old . . . friends? Were they friends? Sure. Two old friends, talking about their struggles regarding the thing they had in common. The things they'd endured that only they could talk about. She needed to move on. He needed to move on. He *should* move on.

And they both *had.* At least enough to live a mostly normal life. She'd learned to leave the house without constantly looking over her shoulder. She'd learned to laugh again. She'd learned not to burst into tears at the drop of a hat. He obviously had too. He seemed to be doing well, despite questioning his current path. But lots of twenty-year-old guys did that.

"And you?" she asked. "Are you . . . seeing anyone?"

"No."

He answered quickly, and she felt her muscles relax. She hadn't realized she'd been holding them taut. She was jealous too. That strange tether was twisted together with so many varying emotions. "Why not?"

He shrugged and lifted his hand before stretching his fingers. "I've been busy focusing on getting my strength back and . . . you know, hating my classes, wondering what the hell I should really be doing with my life." A breeze stirred, and a tree near the low gate shivered, its leaves rustling. He turned his head toward the soft noise, the smile that moved over his face fading. "And I haven't met anyone I'm interested in." He paused, and she waited. "I get stuck emotionally too. A lot." He tapped the table. He didn't like admitting that, she could tell. But he'd told her, and she was glad.

"Are you still seeing that therapist you mentioned in your last email?" she asked.

He let out a soft chuckle. "I sent that email six months ago."

"Sorry. I don't check it very often." She didn't like to go online. It felt like a field of virtual land mines. Everything was a trigger for one reason or another. The last time she'd gone on Instagram, a post appeared on her feed of a girl comparing two lip liners, and she'd cried for an hour. *Because you were robbed,* Paula had said later when she'd told her. Robbed of the possibility of being a girl who cared about which lip liner possessed the most lasting color. She'd laughed, but then she'd cried some more. She wanted to care about that. *Desperately.* She did feel robbed.

And so she rarely logged on to . . . anything. There were enough potential land mines involved in just leaving the house. But those ones were necessary. She had to work because she had to eat.

He was watching her as her brain tripped over the cascade of thoughts. "Maybe I should have been writing you letters on paper and sending them through the mail," he said after a moment.

She laughed. "Maybe."

"But, ah, to your question, yes, I am seeing the same therapist. Not as often, but . . . you know, when I need to."

"Does it help?"

He appeared to think about that. "Yeah, I think so. He's very smart. Very . . . soothing, I guess is a good word. And just knowing there's someone I can talk to who won't fall over with shock and horror when I disclose details is a relief. What about you?"

"No. I went to a therapist a few months ago. She was okay, but . . . I don't know, I guess I didn't really click with her. But I have Paula. Paula's been a rock for me." She didn't mention that she'd also stopped going to a professional because she couldn't afford one. But she meant what she said about Paula. And, of course, she had herself. She was getting by.

"That's good. I'm glad," Evan said.

"Can I get anything else for you?" the waitress asked.

"No, thank you, just the check," Noelle said. What else could they talk about? It'd only been a year. They were both still struggling, and both still doing just fine. She missed the hell out of him. And knew they weren't good for each other. It would simply take time to heal and to move on in any measurable way from what they'd experienced. But she was glad they'd checked in. She could picture him now as he was. Healthy. At least mostly happy. Moving forward.

"What do you have planned for today?" Evan asked, and his words came out in a rush.

She hesitated. "I hadn't really made any plans. Paula is helping her mother with some last-minute arrangements and greeting family who flew in for the funeral." She pointed across the street to the hotel where she was staying, and the reason she'd chosen this particular restaurant. She had a view from her room. "I was just going to hang out at the hotel pool for a few hours, or maybe see some sights. I don't know."

He nodded. "My day is pretty free too." Those rushed words again. The speed of her heart followed suit.

That old familiar clutching. The *need* she'd tried not to acknowledge since the moment her eyes had landed on him.

The waitress reappeared, placing their check on the table and then seeming to take an interminable amount of time clearing the few dishes and coffee accoutrements. Noelle's breath gusted out when the young woman turned away. Their gazes locked, and with effort she tore hers away. She wasn't going to ask him to hang out at the pool or to tour the city. She wouldn't even know how to do that. Not with him. They were strangers. Yes, they'd shared something unimaginably horrific, something that would change them forever. *Connect* them forever. But at the heart of the matter, they knew nothing significant about the other. It was better to simply say goodbye and allow him to get on with his life. It'd been too soon. They shouldn't have done this.

"Noelle—"

"Evan—"

Her eyes searched his. He didn't seem to know where to take this next either. He looked across the street toward the Hyatt, the bellman out front helping an elderly gentleman unload suitcases from his trunk. He met her eyes again. She knew what he was offering. Or asking. Maybe there were no words for that type of proposal. But she knew. And so did he.

She'd already decided she wouldn't. It was a bad idea.

"Yes," she said softly. She reached for her wallet, but he beat her to it, throwing a twenty on the table. They exited the small gate together and headed toward the hotel.

~

The room she'd checked in to the day before was nice, if basic. Noelle tossed her purse on the desk. Behind her, she heard the click of the door and a quiet rattle of chain as Evan engaged the lock. Her heart rate kicked up another notch. She was nervous, but now that she'd surrendered, now that she'd given herself permission even if it was wrong, she was also relieved. She'd made a choice. There would be consequences for both of them, but she wouldn't back out. Not now. She could see the certainty in his gaze as well. There would be no need for artifice here. There was only a goal in mind—and complete understanding. She kicked off her shoes and turned, watching as he approached her.

He tilted his head, smiling softly. He looked nervous, and it made tenderness sweep through her. This was different, then. She hadn't felt tenderness before, only raw need. "We've never kissed," he noted.

She couldn't help the laugh that bubbled up from her chest. It seemed ridiculous. "Haven't we?"

"I'd remember."

She supposed she would too. Sometimes she pictured the two and only times they'd had sex, the grasping, the feel of his skin as it slid over hers, the hot press of his flesh as he'd entered her body. She closed her eyes, and she saw him come over her, again and again, to shut out the other visions that threatened. And she was grateful she had those memories. She clutched them the way she'd clutched him all those months ago. They felt like a weapon, a torch among shadows.

"Let's do it differently this time," he said. "We'll go slow. As slow as you need. There's no rush. No time frame. Okay?" It was as if he'd read her mind. Yes, she had those old memories, but these ones would be sharper, brighter.

"Yes," she breathed. "Yes, okay."

He brought a finger to her chin, tipping her face and leaning in. He was sweet. He really was. She'd been so wrong about him for so long. It'd only taken a month and a cage and a fiery escape to bind her to her mortal enemy. A small laugh escaped her lips, and he pulled back for a second, a smile floating over his lips as well. He didn't ask what was funny.

Her eyes fluttered closed just as his lips touched hers. She knew his taste. Maybe that was because she knew the scent of his breath.

Despite the newness of this, their first kiss, in some ways, it felt like coming home. A home where a hundred ghosts dwelled, maybe there to live in peace, but maybe there to rattle their chains deep in the dead of night. He dragged his tongue slowly along the seam of her lips, and she opened, pressing closer.

His arms came around her, and he wove the fingers of his scarred hand through her hair, cradling the base of her skull. That felt good. She'd never been touched that way. She sighed into his mouth and met his tongue with her own.

Before that second-floor room, she'd only kissed three other boys. She barely remembered any of them except that they hadn't been very good at it. Evan was good. He was very good.

Their kiss was slow. Deep. Divinely passionate. She could *do* this. He was going to give her all the time in the world, all night if that's what it took. She was certain of that. And because of it, her confidence grew, and so did her enjoyment.

She melted. Her arms encircled him, and she pressed even closer, running her palms up his biceps to his shoulders and moving her fingers so that his pulse beat beneath them. She felt the bulge in his pants and the heat of his skin. He was turned on, but he did not make a sound. He was attempting to hold back his excitement so that he didn't rush too far ahead of her.

Their lips broke, and he stepped back, his cheeks flushed and his lips wet from her mouth. He was so beautiful, not just because of his features or his hair but because of the intense concentration on his face as he stared at her and made her heart nearly stop. He gripped the hem of his T-shirt and brought it over his head. He'd obviously been working out. He was strong and sleek. She allowed herself a moment to drink him in before she, too, pulled her shirt over her head.

This was different too. New memories to replace the others. Ones where they weren't haggard versions of themselves—exhausted, hungry, thirsty, fearful, *desperate*.

They both undressed, gazes heated as each piece of clothing was removed. She felt the first buzz of anxiety when his erection sprang free, but she breathed through it, toeing her clothes aside and sitting down on the edge of the bed. She lay back, and instead of coming over her, he lay next to her, turning toward her. Evan reached out, moving a piece of hair off her cheek. She felt shy, but excited, intensely *present* in a way she hadn't felt in any other part of her life recently. She had the fleeting thought that this was what it would have been like if Evan had taken her virginity rather than the disgusting old man wearing a strange, silver, expressionless mask who'd had onion on his breath and grunted as he'd raped her.

As if sensing her sudden mental distress, Evan pulled her to himself, running his fingers gently over her spine. "It's hard for me, too, sometimes," he said at her ear. "To think about touching anyone else. I think about you, Noelle. I can't help wonder . . ."

She brought her lips back to his, quieting him. She didn't want him to speak of anything other than *now*. No promises. No plans. She knew at least part of him still carried misplaced guilt for what had been done to her, and it wasn't necessary. It had been done to him too. If this helped alleviate that false concept, then she was glad because this wasn't only for her. But it shouldn't be more.

She turned toward him as they kissed, sliding her leg over his hip and bringing their cores together. His breath hitched, and he pulled back slightly, looking in her eyes, reading her. His left hand splayed on her skin, over her heart.

She moved her arms, cupping his hand between hers and bringing it to her lips. He sighed as she kissed his fingertips, slowly, one by one. "How is it?" she whispered. "Really?"

"Stiff. Sore. But it works," he said on a small breath-filled laugh. "Physical therapy helps. The doctors think that in time, it will be mostly normal."

"Sort of like the rest of us?" she asked on a smile. She'd said it jokingly. But really, it was true. Or so she hoped.

"Exactly," he said, a smile flitting over his lips. "Mostly normal. In time. It's a pretty good prognosis, don't you think?"

She shrugged. Talking to him like this, so close, their skin bare, was causing her blood to move faster in her veins. She felt warm, hopeful. "As far as prognoses go, yes. It could be worse."

He laughed softly, and it fell over her like a piece of velvet caressing her skin. She shivered slightly, nipples growing hard. She could feel undone with a throaty laugh. What a nice thing to know.

He leaned in and kissed her neck, his breath hot against her skin. His thumb moved in lazy circles over her nipple. "Good?" he asked.

"Yes," she breathed. "Yes, good."

She kept her eyes open. She wanted to feel him, but even more so, she wanted the sight of him emblazoned in her mind, available to retrieve at a moment's notice. Was it sickness that ensured she'd have the memory of Evan to pull forth whenever she was intimate with another man? Perhaps. Perhaps it was terribly unfair to that unknown future partner. But the alternate visions were far worse. The alternate visions would make any future intimacy an impossibility.

Eventually, you'll hang on to the feeling of Evan, but his face will blur. Someday. And then she'd be truly free.

She wanted that for him, too, if he needed it. And maybe he didn't. But she was fairly certain that giving her pleasure was healing him in some small way.

"It definitely works," she murmured as his hand did magical things to her breast, and his lips curved in a smile.

His hand skimmed her stomach, and tentatively, he used his fingers to part her thighs. She stilled, her instincts telling her to pull away. To run.

"Breathe," he said, redirecting her thoughts. "And look at me."

Her breath gusted out, eyes locked with his. They were so blue. As clear as the still morning sky after a long night of rain. He smiled, and it was kind of silly and unexpected, and so she smiled, too, just as his fingers dipped inside her. "Oh," she whispered. And then she was sensation, anchored to his stroking hand, yet floating into that clear, blue sky, letting herself drift away. God, it was nice to drift. A drug. A beautiful escape. Evan dipped his head, taking a nipple in his mouth, and she cried out, threading her fingers through his soft hair. She could feel him against her leg, hot and hard, but she knew he would spend as long as it took, until she told him she was ready.

She didn't want it to take too long, though, didn't want to chance the possibility that she would mentally spiral when her body was responding so well. It was a balance, a delicate one. That goofy smile had helped. Only he would know that.

He moved his finger slowly in and out of her, using his thumb to circle lightly in the spot that made her press toward his hand, seeking more. She parted her legs so he had more access. His scent surrounded her, mixed with a masculine-smelling deodorant and nothing more. She'd know the smell of his skin anywhere. She knew the flavor of his fear, too, and the tang of his blood. But she wouldn't think about that now. She refused to see his face as it'd been when they were dragged down to hell. She realized she'd closed her eyes with pleasure, and they flew open now. He was watching her. "You're fine," he reassured. "Everything's good. You're so wet, Noelle. Everything about you is perfect."

She *was* wet. She could feel it, feel the way his fingers were gliding in and out, using the slippery evidence of the desire he'd stoked. Her body was still her own. No one had committed her to a life of sexual aversion. She could heal. She was doing it now.

"Now," she said, pulling gently on his shoulders. She didn't want to allow the shadows to collect, didn't want to take that chance.

"I can do it this way," he said, his fingers continuing that slow glide.

But she shook her head. She needed him to come over her, needed him to enter her with more than his finger. She needed to surrender, to know she could.

He looked briefly unsure, but did as she asked, removing his hand and kissing her as he leaned over, bringing his body on top of hers and supporting himself with his knees. "Guide me in," he said. Noelle reached down, grasping his hard length, surprised by the silkiness of his skin. She marveled at it, using her hand to slide over it, mesmerized by the way the skin moved so easily, up, down. She might want to investigate that further later, with her hand and maybe even her mouth. The thought made her giddy.

Evan let out a pained laugh. "If you don't stop that, this is going to be over in a minute."

She smiled. What he was saying was that there was a goal, and his pleasure wasn't the whole of it. *Sweet Evan.* She looked in his eyes, and she knew she loved him. In that very moment, she realized she did. And it might be sick and twisted, based on things love should never be based upon. But regardless, she loved him, and that love was right there, warming her heart as she guided him into her body.

I love you, and it's why, when this is over, I'll let you go.

Again.

His eyes went slightly hazy, and she watched the pleasure that contorted his features. *That look.* God. It was beautiful. She drank it in and found more pleasure of her own, just in witnessing his.

That was a wonderful realization, too, to know that she could find her own pleasure but also that she took satisfaction from witnessing that of the man she was with.

He felt different. Much different from the two times he'd been inside her before. Being this turned on made it feel natural. *Right.* She'd almost thought he didn't quite fit before, but no, he was perfect. She lifted her leg, experimented with different positions as he moved leisurely, sweat breaking out on his brow. The skin of his back was damp, and she caressed him, enjoying the feel of him inside her and beneath her palms, loving his mouth on her breast and the way he trembled when she squeezed her internal muscles. There was so *much* about sex that she'd never even known.

He seemed to sense the moment she began the slow climb, bringing his hand between her legs and massaging her gently so that her blood flowed faster as her stomach muscles began to tighten.

Evan was breathing hard, his head hung, muscles so tense. He was holding on.

Then everything tightened as a wave of pure bliss crashed over her, and she gripped his shoulders, digging her fingernails into his skin and crying out his name.

She could tell he was coming, too, and for a moment they hung suspended together before floating back down to earth. She felt blissful one moment and bereft the next, tears flowing from her eyes as she laughed. Her laughter turned to weeping, and still she gripped him. He was fine with both her joy and her sorrow. He didn't need to question either. He simply held her through it. In that moment, Noelle didn't care if it was right or wrong. It just was.

CHAPTER TWENTY

Evan was relieved that she let him stay. He almost thought she wouldn't. They'd hurt each other this way before. And though he thought they had a clearer picture of what they were offering each other this time, he couldn't really be sure. He'd meant what he'd said about feeling a sort of rebirth when they'd escaped those cages. He was relearning everything. His boundaries, his emotions, his comfort level. His identity. His place in the world. His view of humanity. He was constantly spinning. Reeling. And being with her, spending the night with her in his arms, was the first time in so long that he'd felt grounded.

They ordered room service and ate in bed. Then they made love again. And again. He took such immense pleasure in watching her explore her limits, both physical and emotional. And he found healing too. He'd been victimized as well. He'd worried that he'd carry visions with him that would haunt him during intimacy. But that wasn't the case. She was all that he saw. He lived that night only in the present, and it helped patch together his wounded soul.

The third time they had sex, she didn't cry. "No tears," he said, rolling over and bringing her with him.

She laughed down at him, her face going serious. "No tears," she confirmed.

"You're better now."

"That easy?"

He nodded. "Should I send my bill?"

She laughed and socked him lightly on the shoulder.

In the deep of night, they woke, fingers hooked, eyes fluttering open as they stared at each other. He didn't know where he was, only that his hand was stretched and she was holding him the way she once had. The memory fell over him like an oily rain. The cage. The cold. The fear. The feelings of that place, that time, all came pouring in. Noelle gasped, pulling her hand away and sitting up, her back to him. Evan swallowed, leaping up and reaching for the lamp on the bedside table. He was unsteady, and in his flailing, the lamp clattered off the table and onto the floor, the bulb smashing.

The room remained dark. So dark. Too dark.

Am I still there? Was I dreaming that I was free?

Evan heard Noelle's quiet keening and felt his way along a wall, his fingers encountering a switch. He flicked it upward, and the room was bathed in blessed light. He was sweating. So hot. Breathing hard.

Just a rented room, the bedsheets rumpled. But it wasn't *that* rented room, the one where he'd piled furniture in front of the door. The one where he'd peeked through the curtains expecting to see a man in red shoes walking down the dusty street, a caricature of a smile stretched across his hate-filled face. That nightmare had haunted him once, but he hadn't dreamed it in a while. Hadn't even thought of it for so many months. Until now.

Noelle sat on the edge of the bed, her arms crossed over her bare breasts, eyes wide as they darted around the room. He could see on her face that her mind had taken her to that cage, or that motel, or even perhaps that room on the second floor that he'd tried so hard to wipe from his brain.

He went to her, going down on his knees on the floor and taking her hands in his. She lowered her arms, gazing at him. She was so beautiful. He'd thought it when he'd seen her standing in the courtyard of the coffee shop in her striped blue shirt and white pants, hair pulled away from her face. She'd looked fresh then. Young, but also older than she'd been. She looked so vulnerable now, and he wanted to take the haunted look from her eyes, but even though he hadn't meant it, it was there because of him.

They were like wounded warriors who had been through the bloodiest of battles together. They found refuge in each other's understanding because in many ways their experience was unspeakable. Together, they required no words. But being in each other's presence also brought with it visions and memories that were easier to bury when that person wasn't there.

If he hadn't known that before, he knew it now.

And it broke his heart. It did, and for the same reason it had the first time. He craved her. He needed the solace only she offered. But she also triggered him in a way no one else could. It had been easier to be away from her. And it ripped him in two.

He kissed her knuckles. He opened her hand and put his mouth on her palm. When he looked back up at her, she still wore that vulnerable look, but warmth had entered her eyes.

"We're still a mess," she said.

He sighed. "In some ways."

"I'll never regret this," she said.

"You're cutting me off," he said. *Again.*

"It's what we both need, Evan." She lifted their entwined hands and kissed his scars one by one. He wanted to argue, but he really couldn't. It hurt, but he knew she was right.

"I guess so. How do we know?"

"We know by living our lives."

A fissure formed in his heart, fibers ripping. He felt it. No one could ever convince him those words didn't alter his physical self in some measurable way.

He put his head on her knees, and she stroked his hair. "I feel empty when I'm away from you," he said. "This last year, I've thought about it a lot."

"Me too. But the emptiness is . . . important in a way too."

"Yes," he admitted. "But it also hurts."

"That will fade."

He felt that tearing again, his heart being stretched in two directions. He knew she was right, though. For now. Maybe forever. No future could be built on a foundation of trauma and nothing more.

But there is more. Was there? How could they know?

How would they *ever* really know?

Noelle lay back, and Evan crawled in bed beside her, spooning. They'd healed each other, and they'd hurt each other. They couldn't do anything different. Fate had determined what their impact on the other would be.

As he lay there with her, he had the strange urge to cry when he couldn't remember the last time he'd wept. Not even in that cage, not even in that upstairs room of horrors. He pulled her closer, holding on while he still could.

In the morning when he woke, Noelle was gone. Just as he'd known she would be.

PART TWO

He who fights with monsters should look to it that he himself does not become a monster.

—*Friedrich Nietzsche*

CHAPTER TWENTY-ONE

Seven Years Later

Evan's phone rang as he got out of his car. He clicked the lock on his key fob as he pulled the phone from his pocket and glanced at the screen. *Dad.*

He declined the call and returned the phone to his pocket as he headed out of the garage and turned in the direction of the Italian restaurant where he was meeting Aria.

He'd call his dad back later. These days, he ignored his call more often than not. He didn't want another lecture on how disappointed he was that Evan was *squandering his opportunities*. He was a twenty-seven-year-old man, and his dad *still* couldn't let go of the fact that he'd dropped out of Stanford's business program seven years before and opted instead to study criminal justice. His father had refused to pay for it, which was fine. His mother had come back with her simple platitude of *whatever makes you happy is fine with me*. Which really meant, *I'm busy living my life with my new husband and stepchildren, and I don't really care*. So Evan had applied to a couple of state schools and then gotten a job and supported himself through all four years.

A year after he'd graduated, he opened his own private investigation firm and had not one regret.

It wasn't glamorous. It wasn't even always interesting. But it fed that part of him that had gone without justice, to find closure for a client. Even a cheating spouse, though he rarely took those types of jobs anymore, the ones that he hadn't had the luxury of turning down in the beginning. They were mostly thankless and always depressing, and in his experience, if a spouse suspected their partner of cheating, they were.

And of course, he had his pet project, too, if that was even the right term.

He'd made several contacts at the Reno PD, who he worked with on a regular basis, and he was meeting one of them now, an officer named Aria Dixon.

The hostess smiled as he entered the small homey-feeling restaurant, but before he could let her know he was meeting someone, he saw Aria stand and wave at him from a table near the back. He raised his hand, letting Aria know he saw her, and then nodded to the hostess, who'd watched the exchange.

"Have a nice meal, sir," the hostess said.

"Thanks."

"Hey," Aria said when he'd made it to the table, standing and giving him a quick hug. "It's great to see you."

"You too." He took off the light coat he was wearing, hanging it on the back of the restaurant chair. "How are you?" he asked when he'd taken a seat.

Aria shrugged, her honey-blonde hair brushing her shoulders. He was more used to seeing her with her hair up and in a uniform, and it was always a little strange to see her as a civilian. Aria was about his age, with deep-green eyes and a smattering of freckles across her nose. She looked more like a pretty midwestern farm girl than a hardened cop. "You know, living the dream, as always."

He let out a chuckle as Aria shot him a smile. He could tell by the way she looked at him sometimes that she hoped to revisit the short affair they'd had about a year ago. It'd started when they'd gone out for drinks as a group and he'd ended up back at her place. They'd hooked up a handful of times, but it'd always been casual, and eventually he'd suggested they stop because he didn't want to further jeopardize their working relationship, and regardless, he wasn't in a place to focus on a romance. It wasn't that he didn't find her attractive and interesting. But he was busy building his career. She'd seemed to take it well, but he'd also noticed the quick flash of hurt in her eyes and regretted that he'd crossed that line in the first place and created tension with someone he valued as a work associate.

Because he was at a peaceful place. It'd taken a long time. Years. But he was good. He was damn good. He only woke from nightmares very occasionally. He could think about what had happened to him without breaking out in a cold sweat. He still experienced emotions relating to his victimhood, of course, but he was okay with that. He figured that should be the case. What had happened had altered him. How could it be any different? What he was finding, though, the more time passed, was that not all the change that had occurred was negative.

It had taken seven long years of healing, of on-and-off therapy, and of following the path that felt right inside his gut, to arrive at the place he was at. To risk that? In the slightest way? Well, Evan supposed he'd know when and if something, or *someone*, came along that made the risk worthwhile.

Aria had taken a sip of water and now set it down. "Thanks for meeting me here. I feel like I haven't had a day off in weeks. There's not a lick of food in my house."

"Still working the task force?"

"Yeah. Gang activity has been off the charts lately. A four-year-old boy was shot in a drive-by on Saturday."

He grimaced. "How is he?"

"It's touch and go right now. Say a prayer if it's your thing."

He nodded. It wasn't necessarily his "thing" on any regular basis, but he wasn't averse to reaching out to God on behalf of a four-year-old little boy who'd been shot by some piece of shit looking to prove his allegiance to a group of criminals.

Aria had been assigned to the gang unit a month or so before. It was an issue that was becoming a bigger and bigger problem in Reno. And, of course, with gangs came more drugs and therefore more crime, not only committed by the gang members but by the citizens who ended up hooked on something that required money to keep up. And there was always the more serious issue of human trafficking.

The waitress approached and took their drink order, a glass of wine for Aria and a beer for him. It was technically off-hours after all. "So it sounded like you might have something for me," he said.

Aria nodded. "Maybe. I'm not sure. I figured I'd let you decide." She reached into her purse beside her chair and handed him a folder. Evan laid it on the table and flicked it open, his brow creasing as he glanced over the details.

He'd been looking into abductions during his free time and asked Aria to pull aside anything that caught her eye that met his criteria. Naturally, he'd first had to tell her about his past, but she'd already known. She'd blushed when she'd admitted it, but she hadn't needed to. He wasn't surprised she'd remembered his name, considering the news coverage his and Noelle's story had gotten in the year after their escape. No one knew the whole truth. Certainly not the media, something both he and Noelle had ensured with their refusal to speak with them. The last thing he wanted was for someone to look at him and immediately associate rape and violence.

Of course, the Feds had swooped in and taken over the case almost immediately. It was a kidnapping, after all. Not just across state lines but into another country. But Aria had access to some information, and anyway, what he had requested from her was of a more general nature.

He flipped the page in the file, understanding why she'd flagged this one. "He told police he was kept in a cage," Evan murmured, the hair on the back of his neck standing up.

He almost startled when the waitress placed their drinks down on the table, closing the file that had photographs of a skinny man with multiple lacerations on his arms. He was surprised to see that he was an old man. He looked pale and wide eyed. *Shock.*

"Are you ready to order?" the chipper young girl asked.

"Do you want a minute?" he asked Aria.

"I'm ready if you are."

He wasn't, but he usually got the same thing when he ate at an Italian restaurant. He waited as Aria ordered a pasta dish and then put in his order for chicken parmesan. When the waitress turned away, he opened the file again. "He was kept in the basement of a warehouse in . . . Texas." Texas. That wasn't even close.

"I know," Aria said. "That was the only thing that seemed off. Unless whoever abducted you moved or works with a large network."

Whoever abducted you. He was tempted to correct her, to make sure Noelle was included in that sentence. It hadn't been just *him* who was abducted. They'd been a team, and it felt wrong—even now—not to acknowledge her. He pushed thoughts of Noelle aside, though. Of all the things that still caused those old scars to pull and stretch uncomfortably, it was the thought of Noelle.

Noelle, who he hadn't seen since that spring day in San Francisco.

He forced his mind back on the file in front of him and what Aria had just said about a large network. "I've always thought it was possible," he said. "We were on camera constantly. People were watching. They could have been stretched all over the globe, as far as I know." Some of them anyway. He figured the ones who had paid money to rape them or beat them had been closer to where they were kept in Mexico, in a dirt-poor town a few hours across the border.

Aria sipped her wine, her gaze stuck on him, eyes sad. She seemed to adopt that look any time he talked about the crime committed against him, or even alluded to the things he'd suffered. Her sadness said something given that the work she did on a daily basis was tragic as hell. "And yet, in all this time, there haven't been any reports of a similar abduction," she said as she set her glass down.

"Maybe whoever they abducted died in their cages."

Her mouth set. "They would have been found eventually, though, right? I mean, especially if this was a trafficking network. It wouldn't have just stopped with you. Things as lucrative as selling humans seldom do."

He sighed. It was a horrifying fact. "No, you're right. I just can't believe it . . . ended. That after we escaped, whoever was behind what happened to us packed their bags and called it a day. This was sophisticated stuff. Cameras. Potentially flying people in who had rented us from behind a computer somewhere. This was a big operation."

"The problem is, it was conducted from a random abandoned factory in Mexico."

Yes, yes, he knew that very well. The FBI had looked at the owner of what had once been a textiles business. The business had set up shop on the outskirts of several low-income towns, hoping to not only attract a workforce but help address the poverty of the area. Evan wasn't sure where that plan had gone awry, but the business owner had moved back to the States less than five years after construction was complete and the doors were opened. It had remained abandoned for three years before Evan and Noelle found themselves caged in what had once been a large workshop teeming with seamstresses creating apparel. "And an abandoned factory that burned down at that," he muttered. Maybe there would have been more forensics to find had the entire place not gone up in flames. For a second he smelled the smoke, felt the burn of his lungs as he pulled in a breath. He let out a long exhale, taking a deep swallow of his beer.

"I appreciate this," he said, tapping the folder. "It might be something."

She nodded. "Or he might be batshit crazy," she said on a small laugh. "The guy is seventy years old and has been in and out of rehab. Also, he's currently in the slammer for breaking and entering, so if you want his story, you'll have to go visit FCI Beaumont in Beaumont, Texas."

Jeez. That was a trek.

"Thanks, Aria," he said, closing the folder. He would read it more thoroughly later when he was alone. And if his gut said it was worthwhile, maybe he'd pay the guy a visit. If the FBI hadn't made headway with Evan's case, he wasn't likely to, either, especially almost a decade later. But trying, at the very least, was a burning need inside him. And so he wouldn't give up.

"One other thing," Aria said, removing another folder. "You asked me to dig up anything not in public databases about Noelle's father."

"Did you find something?" The FBI had looked into their fathers' connection, including the two men's personal and legal history, but hadn't found that it led anywhere as far as Evan and Noelle's abduction. That part was still odd and unsolved, but Evan still believed that that was no coincidence. If not, though, how did it factor in? If he could figure that out, he had a feeling it would lead to more. Much more.

"There wasn't anything else regarding their legal case than what you'd already told me. The shooting of Megan Meyer was rehashed in court. And you have those records."

Evan nodded. He'd already been somewhat familiar with the case, as he'd been living with his father when it'd been litigated. Still, he'd read through every word and learned all the details of exactly what had happened that fateful day his father shot the scorned woman he'd been having an affair with.

A mistake. A tragedy. One his father was deemed *not guilty* for by a jury of his peers.

"If it's not relating to the court case, what is it?"

Aria pulled a folded piece of paper from her purse and handed it to him, speaking as he opened it. "He filed a police report on behalf of a friend right before Noelle was reported missing."

Evan frowned. "Really?"

Aria nodded. "It might not be related to Noelle's abduction in any way, but I thought it was a bit coincidental that his daughter went missing within a couple days of a friend of his going missing too."

He scanned the document. Had the FBI discovered this? If they did, he didn't know about it. Either they'd missed it or investigated and found it to be unrelated. Maybe the FBI didn't even know about it, because the person who filed the police report on Noelle was her friend Paula Hathaway. Apparently, according to Paula, she was the one who'd first felt an internal alarm after days of not hearing back from Noelle. She'd called Noelle's father, who had informed her he hadn't seen her in person either. He'd hung up after telling Paula he was going to check her room and other areas of the house to determine if she'd been home. When Paula didn't immediately hear back from him, she called the police. What she hadn't known was sometime between that phone call and the police arriving at his home to take his statement regarding Noelle, he had died of a heart attack. "Dow Maginn," he muttered, bringing himself back to what Aria had just said about Mr. Meyer's missing friend. "Was he found?"

"He was." She pulled yet another file from her magic purse of information and handed it over. "He was the victim of a mugging, apparently. His body was found at the back of an alley, behind a dumpster. Mr. Meyer found out about his friend, and then was informed his daughter was missing two days later."

Tough week. Evan flipped open the file, scanning it. Yes, Mr. Meyer had had a tough week. But all his hardships ended with a major heart attack that killed him almost instantly. For his daughter, however, things were about to turn a corner into the realm of nightmares. "A mugging," he repeated. "They didn't catch the perp, huh?"

"No, but the guy was known to be a drinker and a fighter, and he'd gotten into scuffles before in that same area. He owned a computer repair shop nearby and would go drinking after work. Or sometimes during work, from the few statements the investigators got at the time. It's a high-crime area. Muggings are not unusual. His wallet and his watch were missing, so the police didn't have much reason to believe it was more than what it looked like."

Evan closed the folder, setting it with the other things Aria had given him. "Hmm."

"Yeah, it set my bells off too," Aria said. "Anyway, I hope there's something more for you to dig in to from all that."

"There definitely is." He held up his beer, smiling as he clinked it to Aria's wineglass. "To the possibility of a break. And to you for finding it. I can't thank you enough for this, Aria."

Her lips tipped, her gaze hanging on him as she took a sip of her wine. "Anything you need, Evan," she said. "I'm always here."

CHAPTER TWENTY-TWO

Evan took in a big swallow of air as the gate clanked closed behind him, and he followed the guard to the visiting room along with three other people. One was a young woman sporting a serpentine neck tattoo and pushing an infant in a baby stroller, another an old woman who hadn't bothered to take the curlers out of her hair, and the third, a man who appeared to be a lawyer. His ill-fitting suit and general look of apathy told Evan he was likely court appointed and had little interest, if any, in whatever client he was there to see.

Evan fell in line with the small crew of misfits, entering a barracks-type building on the grounds of FCI Beaumont. He took a seat at one of the small tables, and the other people did the same, spreading out from each other. The young woman closest to him took a bottle from her bag and stuck it in the infant's mouth, bouncing the stroller with her foot as she shot him a wink and wiggled her tongue suggestively. He gave her an uncomfortable smile as if she might be making a weird joke that didn't exactly land, lacing his hands on the table in front of him and training his eyes on the door at the back where he assumed the prisoners would enter.

He'd gotten to Texas a few hours before, stopped and had lunch, and then headed straight here. The plan was to meet with the man named Lars Knauer and jump back on a flight later that evening. He only hoped this trip was worth his while and the seven hundred bucks he'd put on his credit card.

The door opened, and a guard came through, four men shuffling behind him. He knew what the man looked like from his case file, and when he saw him, Evan stood, lifting his hand to get the old man's attention.

Lars approached slowly, obviously sizing Evan up. Evan did the same. In the photo he'd seen, the man had looked skinny and sunken in. Of course, the photo had only been from the neck up, and benders could do a number on a person's face. He hadn't been able to tell that the man was still so fit for a seventy-year-old. His shoulders were broad, and he didn't appear to have an inch of extra fat on him. He'd heard the term "built like a brick shithouse" somewhere, and that term came to mind now, though to be honest, he wasn't entirely sure what it meant or if it actually applied. Lars had a buzz cut, and though it was cropped close to his head and completely white, it was all still there.

Evan held out his hand, and Lars looked at it for a moment as if deciding whether or not to take it, but then he did, clasping it and giving it one somewhat rough shake before letting go.

"Mr. Knauer, thank you for seeing me."

They both sat down, and Lars Knauer set his hands on the table, palms down. He gave a chin tip. "Call me Lars. You said on the phone you experienced a crime that might be similar to what I reported to the police?"

"Yes, that's right. Although what happened to me happened eight years ago, so it's been a while."

"What was it that happened to you exactly?"

Evan took a deep breath and gave Lars the basics of what he'd experienced, ending with their escape through the desert. He wanted to gain the man's trust, but he held back on details, also mindful not to sway Lars's story in any way. Lars had watched him as he spoke, but now he looked out the window to his right, staring at the chain-link fence, which was the only view.

"Similar," he said, and Evan was almost taken aback by the way his voice had changed, the tone suddenly fearful.

"Will you tell me about what happened to you?"

Lars rubbed a hand over his short-cropped hair, still staring out that window. He sighed, training his eyes back on Evan. "Yeah, I'll tell you. I was nabbed coming out of a bar at two a.m. They musta struck me from behind, or maybe put a shot in my arm. Hell, someone coulda slipped something in my beer, for all I know. I was pretty wasted, so I have no memory of what exactly happened. All I know is that I woke up in the dark, in a cage."

"Shit," Evan swore.

"Yeah," Lars said. "Shit is right." He paused for a moment. "I freaked, yelled, screamed, but it became real clear that no one was gonna answer. So I calmed down and went Zen. You know what Zen means?"

"Uh . . . like Buddha Zen?"

"That's right. Zen is all about transcendent virtues. Moral training. Patient endurance. Meditation. Wisdom. I was a POW in Nam, and a guy I met there taught me about it. Kept me sane until my guys got me out."

Damn. This man had been a prisoner not once but twice? Three times, as a matter of fact, if you counted his present circumstances, and Evan had to figure he absolutely did.

"So anyway," he went on, "I remembered those teachings. Funniest thing, because I'd been through some shit since I got back to the States, and never once had I thought to practice some Zen. I guess I associated it with war, and waking in that cage definitely applied." He shook his head as though clearing it. "When the lights came on, there was another cage in the cellar with me, and there was a guy in it."

All the hair was standing up on Evan's arms. This was it. Exactly what he'd experienced. It had to be connected. *All these years later.* Evan's head was spinning. "Who was he? The guy?"

"Hanh. I don't know his last name. Don't even know how to spell his first name, so in my head I pictured it h-a-n-h."

Evan picked up his phone and opened the notes app, typing in the name. "Have you seen him? Do you know where he is?"

"Not a clue. We got separated during the escape, and I don't even know if he went to the police. He wasn't a legal citizen, for one thing, so he might not have for fear of being deported." He gave a low chuckle that held little humor. "Like that would be worse. I'd *want* to get the hell out of Dodge after that, but . . . evil shit happens everywhere. I told all of this to the cops, by the way," Lars said. "As for me, the police thought I was having a psychotic episode. I'd spent some time in the mental ward, diagnosed with PTSD. A few times, I even wondered myself if I'd imagined it all."

"I don't think you did," Evan said. "Although whether that's a comfort or not . . ."

Lars gave a distracted smile. "No, I know I didn't. Those memories have edges, just like the ones from Nam."

"You don't have to go through every specific, obviously," Evan said. "But if you could sum up what they did to you and Hanh, I'd really appreciate it."

"Sick mind games is what they did. They tried to make us sell each other out to avoid something worse. Just like you, it sounds like."

Words failed him for a moment. A nod sufficed.

"See, but I wasn't gonna do that," Lars went on. "I saw enough sick shit in that jungle over there, and I knew what giving in to the monster inside would do to you. Maybe not right away, but later."

"Were you . . . rented?"

"Rented? You mean like sex trafficked?"

Evan nodded.

"Not me. Maybe Hanh. We didn't talk about what had happened to us when they took us out of our cages. Hanh was . . . prettier, though, let's say. And definitely younger. If any of that even makes a difference to sick fucks who do stuff like that."

Evan swallowed. He figured there was a market for everything. But, yeah, youth and attractiveness were always going to be hot commodities in the trafficking business. Some people simply had less of a likelihood of being victimized in that specific way. Case in point: a seventy-year-old man. And yet . . .

"So what'd they do to you to try to get you to betray Hanh?"

"Betray," he said, as though testing the word. "Huh, yeah, I guess that's what it would have been, right?" He paused. "Scare tactics, mostly. They put me in a locked room with three hungry pit bulls. Told me I had to stay in there for an hour, and if I wasn't mauled, I could change my mind at any point before the time was up and they'd take Hanh's hand or a leg or something."

"Fuck," Evan said. He felt sick. "Zen?" he asked, and his voice croaked slightly.

Lars smiled. His teeth were strong, just like the rest of him. "Zen," he confirmed. God, this big dude, a Vietnam veteran who'd spent time in the mental ward, had *meditated* his way through an hour in a room with three hungry pit bulls. People surprised the hell out of him sometimes.

"Did you see any cameras in any of the rooms you were in?"

Lars shook his head. "No, but I knew someone was watching. The guy who came to get us out of our cage and toss us back in said things he could only know if he'd been watching us."

He pictured the guy who had played the same role with him and Noelle. Red shoes. He'd worn red shoes. He wondered if that had been part of some uniform as it was very distinct. "Did anything stand out about that man?" he asked. "Anything specific that he wore that you remember?"

Lars shrugged. "Ugly son of a bitch. Face like a pug dog. But other than that? No."

"No red shoes then?" Evan hadn't wanted to lead him, but he had to make sure mentioning it wouldn't jog a memory.

"Red shoes? No. He wore black boots."

Evan nodded. "Will you tell me about your escape?"

"Yeah." He scratched at his jaw, thinking. "We started getting things delivered with our meals—items and weird little riddles. We were told they were gifts, and they were, because they're the things that helped us get free."

Evan had broken out in a cold sweat, excitement and dread coursing through his blood. He felt sick and slightly feverish, and he now knew without a single doubt that the same people who were responsible for abducting him and Noelle had abducted this man and his "partner," Hanh.

"It was like—"

A guard sitting at the front of the room at a desk suddenly announced, "Ten minutes, and visiting time is up."

"It was like we were both sent things that only we would know how to use or that seemed meant for us in some specific way." He was speaking more quickly now, obviously aware of the time constraint. His forehead wrinkles became deeper as he frowned. "It's hard to explain."

"It's as if they knew your strengths and how you could use them."

"Yeah, exactly." He looked surprised to be understood. *Believed.* "Like, Hanh didn't speak much English, but he knew numbers. We had to gesture quite a bit to get something across to each other. But I'm good at that. Do you know how much time you spend in the jungle communicating with the other guys without ever saying a word? Maybe it worked in our favor, because if people were watching us, they couldn't figure out everything we were communicating. Hanh was—*is*, I guess— some kind of genius with numbers. He figured out the code being inputted into our cage locks somehow from the way the guy typed the numbers in before opening the door. It took hearing it many times before he knew for sure he had both. But once we had the codes—or thought we did anyway—it was a matter of figuring out how to make it out of the room. But it was like, the things we were given were tools only we might know how to apply to our circumstance." He scratched his head as though the idea still baffled him.

But it piqued Evan's interest. It was familiar. Someone had left Noelle a piece of graphite that she'd used to start a fire. How had someone guessed she'd know how to do that? And not only that, but they'd known she'd take the risk of being burned alive to be free.

When he thought back on it, some of it almost seemed *planned*. But not by them. Was that even possible? A chill snaked down his spine.

"We knew it would take both of us, and it did," Lars said. "One of us escaping would have never worked."

Yes. Again, the same with him and Noelle. Exactly the same. *We leave here whole, and we leave here together.* "Once you got free of your cages, did anyone try to stop you?" Evan asked.

"Yeah. I heard them coming after us, but it was weird because when we left the building, we weren't pursued. We were in the middle of fuckin' nowhere, so we had to make our way to the closest town."

"Where in the middle of nowhere?"

"Here. In Texas, but way out in the desert. It took us six hours to walk to civilization. But as far as I could tell, they just let us go."

That was similar to their situation too. He only saw that looking back, though. At the time, he'd been terrified and paranoid that they'd be found, that some sort of posse was hot on their heels and eager to put them back in cages. But in actuality, no one had come after them, even years and years later. And for a while, he'd been worried about that. So Evan had gotten a concealed carry. He worked out regularly and ran long distances whenever he had the time. He kept in fighting shape. Because maybe in the back of his mind, he thought there'd be a time when he'd be forced to fight again.

But maybe . . . maybe no one was interested in him anymore. Or the man across the table. Maybe once they'd escaped, they were no longer of any importance to their once captors.

Because they'd won.

They'd won some sick, twisted *game*.

Just like the gladiators of old, who won their freedom when they won the battle.

Another chill joined the others moving fast and furious down his neck and over his back, like cold, bony fingers trailing along his skin.

"I appreciate you listening to me. After I got out, my PTSD came back real bad. I had a few breakdowns, picked up a bottle. The police said I was crazy. There was no Hanh. He'd never existed except in my mind. Some holdover from Nam. The police humored me and went to the building I'd escaped from. It was empty. Not even a footprint could be seen in the dust. There was a pile of recent empty liquor bottles, though. I could see what they thought." He ran a hand over his head. "I got to drinking real heavily one night and walked back to my apartment. Only, it wasn't mine. It belonged to some old lady, and I scared her into having a heart attack right on her kitchen floor. Her husband called the police, and when they got there, we were both passed out, me from drink, her from cardiac arrest." He shook his head, regret and clear pain passing over his rough features. He sighed. "I'll be out in another year. It hasn't been bad, though. Being in here helped me remember that *life* can be war and I don't need to wait to be shot at in a foreign jungle or caged by sickos to find that peace-filled space. I vowed never to forget. Forgetting helps for a while, but then it doesn't." He paused. "I don't enjoy being caged again, but funny enough, I almost feel safer here than out in the world. I know what to expect within these bars." He sat back in his chair. "They say this is where the monsters are housed, but I know that's not true. The true monsters? They're out there." He jerked his head toward the window. "And they run in packs. They always run in packs."

~

Evan stepped out of the gray brick building and walked to his car. When he got behind the wheel, he rolled down the windows, taking a deep breath. It was a hot day, but he'd found a space beneath a tree, and the shade helped with the heat. He didn't care about the temperature, though. He wanted the air.

He thought about what Lars had told him, so many thoughts and questions streaming through his mind. The police hadn't included nearly the level of detail Lars had been able to give him in their report.

Because they hadn't believed him.

They'd thought he was a kooky, alcohol-drenched vet on some psychotic spree. There were some differences in particulars as far as what Lars had experienced, but if they both were involved in some sick game, wouldn't that naturally be the case? If they were going for ultimate interest, not every "event" could be the same.

He ran his hand through his hair, the mild queasiness he'd felt while talking to Lars about his experience increasing. A game. An event.

Christ.

Was that really what it was? An ongoing game, still being played to this day? He'd thought about gladiators earlier, and the vision came to mind now of the once-grand Roman Colosseum, where those slaves fought bears and lions. And most notably each other.

His head swam. Was that what this was about? Not sex or money . . . at least not at its core. Instead . . . was the main point . . . entertainment?

The idea wove through his mind like a venomous snake, fangs dripping.

Throughout history, some humans had always had a sick fascination with blood sport. Maybe it wasn't as ancient as it seemed.

For a moment he stared, unseeing, out the side window of his car. If that was the case, then the most important question remained: Who was in the "stands," watching and cheering? Hungry for the sight of blood and gore. Greedy to view others' pain and suffering. Humiliation.

And willing to pay to see it. Because he knew money had to be involved. Where there was evil, there was always money.

CHAPTER
TWENTY-THREE

Evan let out a frustrated breath, sitting back in his chair. There was no one named Hanh missing currently in the United States of America. And no one reported missing with that name in the last ten years. Not that that necessarily meant anything. Lars had said he was pretty sure he was an undocumented immigrant. Which made things exceedingly tricky. So it could be that he had come from a different country and his family didn't even know he'd gone missing. Or it could be that no one had reported his absence for fear of the authorities.

But damn. To have two more people telling a similar story to his and Noelle's . . . it might help put just enough pressure on the police and the Feds that they would start actively investigating again.

Even if the FBI had found nil eight years before, technically the case was still open. They'd just run out of leads. But Evan couldn't let it lie. Not only because he craved justice but because if this was ongoing, as his interview with Lars led him to believe, people were being horrifically victimized, perhaps even right that minute.

God, it made his hair stand on end.

He stood, his chair screeching backward on the wood floor, and he paced for a moment before grabbing his phone off his desk and dialing. "Officer Dixon," she answered on the first ring.

"Hey, Aria. It's Evan."

"How was Texas?"

"Hot."

She gave a soft chuckle. "I hear that."

"Good thing we're used to it," he said on a smile. Reno, Nevada, was not known for its cool summers. He gave her a quick rundown on his meeting with Lars Knauer, and when he was done, she let out a harsh gust of air. "Wow. The police didn't believe him."

"No. Which was why his statement was bare bones. They didn't want to hear what they thought were the ramblings of a drunk with mental health problems."

"Well. I can't say I blame them. We get a lot of that, and usually, it's exactly what it seems."

"I bet." Plus, it was in a different state entirely and a long damn time after what he and Noelle had experienced, despite that theirs was a high-profile case at the time. "It was a great find on your part, Aria. I'm really appreciative. Seriously. If I can just find a thread between our cases to follow . . . I might be able to break this open. Even after all this time."

"I'm rooting for you, Evan. Always."

"I know." He cleared his throat. "So, ah, the reason I'm calling is that I have another request, and it's a little gory."

"Oh. Intriguing."

He chuckled softly. He'd been considering different ways of coming at this case—his own—and if he couldn't find any victims that were alive, maybe he could find a few who were dead.

"I'm looking for bodies found with missing parts."

"Missing parts?"

"Yeah. You know, fingers, or ears, or limbs. Anything, really."

She paused for a moment. "I see why you're taking this angle, but remember, gangs have an affinity for that level of fucked up too. We have an informant who used to be part of the Diablos who's missing his pinkie finger and an eye. Some sick initiation gone wrong. Or maybe gone right, according to some people. It's hard to say. Anyway, my point is, there might be more bodies—alive and dead—in the system than you want to hear about."

"Point taken. Still, if you come upon something that raises your hackles, give me a call?"

"My hackles are all yours," she said with a soft laugh.

There was a slightly awkward pause. He could feel her waiting for him to walk through the door she'd opened, but he just couldn't bring himself to do that.

Not a good idea.

"Have I told you lately that I—"

"Appreciate me? Yeah, I know. Bye, Evan."

"Bye, Aria."

Evan sat back down in his chair, drumming his fingers. Lars and this unknown Hanh, maybe living in this country illegally and maybe returned home, wherever that was. They had been strangers. They hadn't known each other before waking up in those cages.

But he and Noelle had known each other. And they'd been from the same town. More than that, they'd had a connection. A negative one. That was different. So . . . why? Did it add some sort of sick interest? What would two people who hated each other do when asked to take on pain so the other didn't have to?

He drummed some more.

It was an interesting question. If only it'd been rhetorical.

One of those dreamed-up moral dilemmas asked in a board game where the answer didn't really matter because it was all for fun.

No, they'd lived it. They'd arrived at the answer.

Just like Lars and Hanh. Unwilling to throw the other under the bus. Or hacksaw, as it were. He shook off the creepy-crawlies that fell onto the back of his neck.

Lars, a Vietnam vet who had already decided he'd seen too much carnage before he even arrived there. And Hanh, a stranger in a strange land, seeing Lars as the first person who stood up for him. Who saw him not as an illegal alien but as a human being. Of course that was speculation, but it seemed to make some sense, if there was any sense to be made from what they'd all experienced. Or rather, how they'd reacted to the experience.

He sat back, gripping his head. He didn't know where to go from here. So back to square one. Except now he was certain that what had been done to him and Noelle had been done to others.

He sighed. *Noelle.*

He tried not to think about Noelle too often, because thoughts of her totally threw him off. Still.

All those years ago, they'd said goodbye to each other and gone their separate ways because their feelings were too convoluted. It was like they'd both survived a shipwreck and were floating on a dark sea, each clutching to their own small piece of wreckage, barely hanging on. To come together, to try to survive on a tiny, insufficient piece of flotation would mean that they'd both drown.

Intuitively they'd known it, even if he hadn't had the words to describe what they were psychologically experiencing at the time.

All he'd known was that he both wanted to run away from her and the feelings she stirred up in him, and simultaneously couldn't bear the thought of letting her go.

Noelle had been asked to sacrifice his fingers and his teeth and various other body parts, and she'd refused each time. Ironic how much he felt like he'd lost a limb when he'd woken in an empty bed that day so long ago.

And truth be told, for many years after.

Even now. Sometimes.

Like right that minute. He missed her. Jesus. He did.

They hadn't even kept in touch. Because at the time, he didn't think that would have worked. It had to be a clean cut, no matter how much it hurt.

Had Noelle regretted it sometimes, or had she known they'd done the right thing? He wondered if she wished so much time hadn't passed, to where now it was almost impossible to just reach out, make contact.

But in that room that day, he thought they'd done the right thing, despite the regret he sometimes felt. After all, who was going to be the one to suggest that the other person not move on from something like what they'd experienced? Who was going to ask the other to stay stuck? To drown.

Evan blew out a breath. It'd been a long time since he'd sat and just thought about all things Noelle. It still hurt. He hadn't even talked about Noelle with the therapist he'd begun seeing right after he'd come home, a retired forensic psychologist recommended by the Reno PD, who did consulting work as a profiler for them and taught classes at the university as well. Even though he'd been technically retired as a psychologist when Evan had first escaped from that abandoned building, he acted as an on-call therapist for the cops when needed and had agreed to see Evan. He'd been told by the cops who'd worked his case that Professor Vitucci was the best, and they hadn't been wrong. He'd helped Evan immensely. But there had been some things Evan couldn't talk about, even to him. Of all the sufferings, his complicated feelings for Noelle were almost the worst. And the one that hadn't ended when they'd gotten free. In some ways, it'd only become more painful.

There, in that dungeon, they'd been together. And as God as his witness, sometimes he yearned for the closeness they'd experienced in those cages. The bond they'd forged.

How sick was that? How twisted? Some inverse form of Stockholm syndrome he couldn't even begin to explain or justify.

But speaking of Professor Vitucci—psychologist, profiler, and all-around man of wisdom—it'd been a long time since he'd spoken to him. And he could use his insight.

CHAPTER
TWENTY-FOUR

"Evan," Professor Vitucci said on a smile, opening his office door wide and ushering him in.

Just the sight of the older man brought him much-needed calm. "Prof. It's great to see you." His home office looked basically the same, though Evan thought the couch was new, and maybe the area rug. He couldn't remember all the particulars of what the room had looked like the last time he'd been there years ago. That time was foggy. He'd been better, but he'd still been treading water. Stronger, even if his head was barely above the waves that rose unceasingly.

But though he didn't remember exactly what colors the area rug had been, he remembered the feeling of the room, and that remained unchanged. It still smelled woodsy and clean, and the same bookshelf heavily stuffed with books sat behind his desk.

Professor Vitucci looked virtually the same, too, though he had a bit more gray at his temples than he had before, and perhaps a few more lines fanned his eyes. But his smile was still open and warm, his demeanor relaxed. He'd put Evan immediately at ease eight years before, and he did so now. The professor sat down in his chair, and Evan took a seat on the couch facing him, putting his ankle on his knee as he sat back. "How have you been, Prof?"

"I'm supposed to be asking you that," he said with a smile. "Me, though? I've been great. This is the last semester I'll be working at the university. In a few months, I'll be retired for real."

"Why do I get the feeling your *retired for real* is still going to involve quite a bit of work?"

"Ah, you know me too well. Even after all this time. How's the PI business?"

"It's good. Better than good, actually. I'm finally at a place where I can pick and choose my jobs."

"No more jealous spouses?"

Evan laughed. "How'd you know I gave those cases up first?"

"Who wouldn't? It's disheartening to watch people betray each other."

He made a sound of agreement in his throat. "I do a lot of consulting work with the Reno PD now, actually. So I guess you and I are sort of coworkers."

When Evan had first started seeing him, the professor had told him he'd consulted on a case many years before where a troubled man who'd considered himself a game master had tormented the city for weeks. Evan found it comforting that the man had firsthand knowledge regarding the psychopathy of game-related crimes, if such a field existed, and also that nothing surprised Vitucci. He'd seen it all. Too much. Evan wondered how he maintained such calm, and even exuded it.

"You sound happy, Evan. Much more settled than you were when I last saw you. How long ago was that now?"

"Four years."

"Hard to believe. And how are you doing? Do you still have nightmares, or have those passed?"

"They've passed. I have one occasionally, but nothing regular. Nothing that makes me anxious to go to bed at night. You assured me that would be the case. Just a matter of time. And you were right."

"Most things are just a matter of time," he said. "It's very difficult to believe when you're in the midst of the pain."

He nodded. He'd found that to be true. Time didn't necessarily make the pain disappear entirely, but it sanded the sharp edges. It felt like now it was almost possible to run his fingers along it, to investigate the portions that still held splinters, that still had the potential to make him bleed. He played with the plastic end of his shoelace for a moment. The professor waited. He was good at sensing when someone was taking a moment to choose their words. "There's one thing that's still . . . difficult for me. Something that I wrestle with, I guess."

"What is that?"

He raised his eyes and met the empathetic gaze of the professor. "The girl," Evan said. "The girl who I was abducted with, who I escaped with . . ."

"Yes," the professor said. "The girl. What was her name?"

"Noelle."

"Ah, Noelle, yes. I never met her, but I remember most of what you told me about her. She helped you cope while you were there. She was instrumental in figuring out how to escape."

"Yes. Yes, she was."

"Are you still in contact with her?"

Evan shook his head. "It was painful . . . afterward . . ." He sighed. How to explain this?

"You became very attached while in captivity," the professor said, tilting his head as he studied Evan.

Evan nodded, grateful that the professor was as intuitive as ever. "We did. And afterward, it was like . . ." He moved his hand and lowered his foot to the floor. "It was like we were desperate to be together, but also desperate to be apart." Was that right? Sort of. "The desperation to be together was stronger." He frowned. "For me more than her. Maybe. But we both knew we needed to heal separately, I guess." He gave his head a small shake, frustrated. "I'm trying to verbalize what's only ever been a feeling. I don't know. I was wondering if it was a kind of Stockholm syndrome."

"Stockholm syndrome is a bond with one's captor. That happens too. But what you experienced is called shared trauma. Or unit cohesion, as it relates to war. And I don't believe it would be going out on a limb to say you survived a war of sorts, would you?"

Evan thought about that for a moment. The unrelenting fear, the isolation, the constant threat of physical harm, the helplessness. Yes, he supposed they had been to war. An atypical one, but a war all the same. "Yes," he said. "I would say that."

"Shared trauma bonds are very, very strong because for a time, they mean survival. Even brothers and sisters living under extreme abusive conditions experience this bond and find it difficult to leave it behind even when the abuser is no longer part of their lives. It complicates relationships in a very profound way. Sometimes that bond is even mistaken for deep love, but it's a love that feels desperate and possessive."

Evan sighed, taking his bottom lip between his teeth. "So it's not really love, then, even though it feels like it?"

"No one can tell you whether you love a person or whether what seems like love is solely a shared trauma bond. What I'm saying is that it would be more likely that the desperation you described was the latter." He sat forward slightly. "Unit cohesion serves an important purpose when you're at war, Evan," he said. "It's a necessary support system that makes it possible to survive more trauma. The trauma bond outside of war, however, serves no real purpose, as ongoing trauma is no longer a reality, nor should it be. I sense that you felt that. You and Noelle both."

"We did. We knew it was unhealthy. We just didn't know how to pack it up. We didn't know how to stop *feeling* it."

"And so you parted ways."

"Yeah."

"Perhaps for the best."

"Perhaps."

"But . . ."

Evan let out a laugh that was mostly breath. "But I wonder. Because sometimes I . . . miss her."

"Do you? Are you sure?"

"What do you mean?"

"I mean, did you get a chance to really know who she was during that time? Did she come to know you?"

He thought about that. "I'm not sure. Do you know someone more or less when you've been to hell with them? I have no idea what it'd be like to go to a movie with her. I don't know if she likes butter on her popcorn or if she prefers comedies to dramas, but I know that she's the bravest person I ever met and that she'd march straight into a fire rather than let someone else be burned."

The ghost of a smile floated over Professor Vitucci's face. "A person is a compilation of so many experiences and qualities," he said. "But, yes, perhaps you do know things about her that other people never have any occasion to learn about another, and good for them."

Yes, good for them. That was for sure.

"This has all been on my mind recently because I've been looking into some similar situations of people who were abducted and caged. I found a man in Texas who has a similar story."

The professor's dark brows raised. "I see."

"I think there's a high likelihood that what we experienced might still be going on. Or . . . it was anyway, as of a couple of years ago. I only have his testimony, and the police already looked into it but . . ."

The professor watched him for a moment, a look of concern in his eyes. "You have ways to access information others don't," he said. "So I understand why you'd be tempted to pick up the investigation. Just be careful," he cautioned.

"In what way?"

"That you don't immerse yourself in something that you need to be distancing yourself from. That you don't become stuck again."

Evan nodded. He'd thought the same thing. But how could he not at least try if there was the slightest chance that others out there were— or would be—victimized in the same horrific way? "I keep coming back to one thing," he said, thinking aloud now. It helped having someone to be a sounding board as he verbalized all the thoughts that had been rattling around in his head, disorganized and half-formed. "And that's that Noelle and I knew each other. Our fathers had a connection."

"Ah, yes. Remind me."

Evan did, summing up the affair his father had had with Noelle's mother, the stalking, his father accidentally killing her, and the court case.

"Yes," Professor Vitucci said, "it's coming back to me now. It is interesting. I believe I thought so at the time too. But the FBI didn't uncover anything that might have explained that connection."

"No, they didn't uncover much," he murmured. "But it's the origin story here, and I think it might be important."

"Ah, yes. Those tell a lot," the professor said. "If you can access them."

"It would help if I could ask Noelle some questions, especially now that she could look at things in hindsight, with clearer eyes," he mused aloud.

"But you're worried that those same feelings will resurface."

"Yeah. I guess I am." He paused. "Also, Noelle disappeared. I emailed her a few times years ago, but they got returned. I have no idea where she lives now." *Or if she's married. In a serious relationship.* Truth be told, that scared him. And it scared him that that scared him. *What a mess.*

"Well," Professor Vitucci said, "good thing you're not a private investigator or anything, because that would make it far too easy."

Evan laughed, and it felt good. Something shifted inside, feeling suddenly lighter. "True enough."

CHAPTER TWENTY-FIVE

Evan stepped from his car, looking around with some amount of awe. He felt like he'd arrived in a different world. Off to his left, just over a slatted walking bridge flanked by tall grass swishing in the slight breeze, the ocean cast off diamonds, sparkling in the sun. The call of a bird gliding up above caused Evan to raise his head and squint into the cloudless blue sky before looking back to the wooden sign announcing that he'd arrived at the right place: SWEETGRASS COTTAGES.

Where Noelle lived and worked.

His heart sped, and he took a deep breath of the salt-tinged air before shutting the door of his rental car and heading toward a brick walkway flanked by grand moss-draped trees that led to a plantation-style home.

Wow.

The website he'd looked at had been well done, but it didn't do justice to the beauty of this property in person.

The grounds were beautifully maintained, some sort of fragrant red flowers growing in beds along the porch and vining through the slats of the rails. He climbed the short set of steps, taking in the comfortable-looking wicker furniture—currently unoccupied—the hanging ferns, and the pots of cascading flowers. Underneath the eave, fans rotated slowly. Evan stepped to the vast mahogany door with a small gold sign next to it that read **RENTAL OFFICE**. With another flutter in his chest, he pulled the door open and stepped into the air-conditioned lobby.

"Hello, sir," a smiling blonde in a white blouse and navy shorts greeted, stepping behind the curved mahogany counter that sat in the middle of the foyer. There was a sweeping staircase behind her, with a velvet rope at the base that declared the upstairs private. "Will you be staying with us?" the young woman asked.

"Ah, no, actually. Well, maybe." He cleared his throat. "What I mean is, I'm here to see one of your employees. Noelle Meyer."

Her brows moved slightly, but her smile remained. "Noelle? Oh. Sure. Let me call her and tell her you're here. Your name?"

He hesitated, worried that she'd decline to see him. It was why he'd taken a flight here to South Carolina after he'd made the effort to locate her and find where she'd been living for the last seven years. He tried to convince himself it wasn't overkill that he hadn't just called her. He tried to convince himself that once he'd gotten it in his head to see her, he simply couldn't shrug off the yearning. The slight desperation he felt wasn't the same as it'd been. It was merely a want now. The need to see her. To make sure she was doing well. To reconnect in some small way, even if that simply meant getting some closure. But he couldn't force her to see him, even if it had taken him half a day to get here. "Evan Sinclair," he said.

The woman nodded, picking up the phone and dialing. After a minute, she set it down. "I'm sorry, she's not answering. She's probably making the evening rounds to the cottages and should be done in an hour or so. Do you want to wait?" She gestured to a small grouping of red upholstered furniture to her right.

He was far too antsy for that. "I think I'll take a walk to the shore and come back."

"Sure."

Evan left the house, descended the steps, and turned toward the shaded path, where he saw the side of a smaller building around the main house. The cottages? According to the website, there were ten cottages of various sizes and guest capacity, stretching out behind the main house, where the owner of the property still lived, a Mrs. Chantilly Calhoun.

Instead of heading to the shore, he took the path that led around the house, passing a sign that said COQUINA and had an arrow pointing toward a quaint bungalow that he could partially see through the foliage. Several paths lay before him, and he stopped, simply curious about the layout of the property.

He heard a little girl's voice saying something excitedly and then the sound of a woman responding. The child laughed, and then he heard the scamper of little feet as she ran down one of the paths nearby, her white dress flashing through the trees and bushes as she passed him.

Lured by the sound of that second voice, Evan moved through the trees, another larger cottage rising on his right. There were towels flung over the railing of that one and sand toys sitting on the porch. What a beautiful, serene place. Each of the cottages was tucked away among trees and foliage just off the meandering main path that he assumed stretched quite a way back.

He rounded a flowering bush, lush with pink blossoms, stopping as his heart rose in his throat and then dropped quickly. Noelle.

She was standing next to a cart with a long pull handle, jotting something on a small pad of paper. Evan stared. She was her but . . . a different person entirely. Her hair was swept up in a high ponytail; tendrils glinting with caramel had fallen out, framing her face and trailing over her neck. She was wearing a similar outfit to the woman who'd greeted him at the front desk, a white gauzy blouse and navy-blue shorts with white tennis shoes. Her skin was golden, cheeks flushed with the heat of the day, and a small smile curved her lips before she finished writing and stuck the pad and pencil in her pocket.

He couldn't speak. He was incapable of even moving.

She began to reach for the handle of the cart but stopped, her brow dipping right before she turned toward him, as though she'd sensed his presence.

She froze, eyes widening as they stared at each other across the span of space.

"Evan?" she breathed.

He stepped from the shade of the foliage, the sunlight falling over him as he moved toward her. "Hi," he said when he'd almost reached her.

Hi. What a stupid word. It didn't encompass even one of the hundred emotions he was feeling in that moment. She gave her head a slight shake, as though she didn't believe her own eyes, and when he'd made it to where she stood, she blinked before asking, "How . . . what are you doing here?"

"It's nice to see you." *Better, but still woefully inadequate.*

She let out a breath. "It's nice to see you too. It's just . . . unexpected. Wow. I . . ." She glanced back over her shoulder. "I . . . wow."

Hi. Wow. He almost laughed. Almost.

"I know you're working," he said. "And I'm sorry just to show up like this, but I'm here for a reason." He shifted awkwardly. God, this was weird. And after all these years. Without a phone call.

Her eyes widened again. "Is everything—"

"Yes. Everything is okay. For me, I mean. I just . . . well . . ." He rubbed the back of his neck. It was damp with sweat. He was still in the jeans and T-shirt he'd put on to travel and wasn't dressed for this muggy southern weather. He hadn't thought much of this through, he realized. Not the details anyway. He'd acted on his feelings, and so here he was, sweating in his inappropriate clothes and stammering through his explanation for being here. Showing up out of the blue, not just here in South Carolina but here to interrupt her life unexpectedly. "I actually need your help with something."

Dammit. That was not how he wanted to broach the subject, and he hadn't meant to say that so soon. He just didn't know what trivial niceties to use to make this less artless. He should have figured out what to say to her, but he hadn't. He'd been nervous, so here he was winging it, and it was all wrong. *I need your help with something.* God, that sounded stupid. Maybe it was stupid. Not just the words but even asking at all. He was suddenly second-guessing this whole thing. It was lovely here, serene, drenched in sunshine. And she was tanned and happy and peaceful looking and so beautiful it ripped his fucking heart out.

She was still staring at him, and he squinted up to the blue, blue sky and then looked back at her standing in front of a tropical-looking plant studded with tiny white flowers. "Man, the places we've been together." He wanted to cringe. Why had he said that? But she huffed out a small agreeable breath, his words seeming to bring her back from the momentary shock-stupor she'd been in. "You look great," he said.

"Thank you. So do you." She picked up the handle of the cart. "Walk with me?" She glanced back over her shoulder again. "I have a few more deliveries to make, and then we can talk."

"Okay. Great." He followed along as she turned down a path, pulling the wagon behind her.

"What do you do here?" he asked. He'd looked at the website, but staff hadn't been listed there, and so he had no idea what job she performed.

She glanced back at him, a smile gracing her lips but quickly fading. "Technically, I'm the owner's assistant," she said. "But I do a little bit of everything. Two of our employees went back to school last week, and so we're a bit short staffed." She reached into the wagon and took out a stack of white fluffy towels before turning toward a cottage they'd come to stand in front of. Noelle knocked on the door, and a woman answered, smiling as Noelle handed her the towels.

"Thanks," the woman called as Noelle turned with a wave.

"The owner's assistant," he repeated. "The owner being Chantilly Calhoun."

"The one and only," she said with a smile. "And you?" she asked as they continued along the path, turning and following another. Here and there were wooden signs that pointed toward each cottage, spelling out the names. LETTERED OLIVE, BANDED TULIP. And below each name was the picture of a seashell. "What are you doing now, Evan?"

Feeling like a moron, following you around at your job when what I really want to do is take you in my arms, hold you for hours, and then ask you questions that actually mean something. "Well, ah, you'll be surprised to know that I'm a private investigator."

She stopped and turned toward him. "You're kidding."

"Nope. I dropped out of Stanford and became a PI."

She tilted her head, a wisp of hair falling across her cheek. His hand itched to push it back. "I bet your dad loved that." She gave him the first genuine smile since he'd shown up here unannounced.

He smiled back. "He's still steaming mad," he admitted. He rubbed his hand over the back of his neck again. "But it's my life. I'm happy with my choices."

Their eyes locked for a few beats before she looked away, pulling her bottom lip between her teeth and glancing off through the trees. What did she keep looking for? Someone to rescue her? Or was she worried her boss would be unhappy with her chatting with him as she worked? "Well, that's good to hear," she said.

"Thanks."

He glanced at her hand as she leaned over the cart. She wasn't wearing a ring. His lungs expanded. He didn't want to admit how relieved he felt, but he did. He wouldn't think about *why*. He wouldn't.

She pulled a blue beach bag full of something out of the cart and carried it to the door of another cottage just through two tall trees. He heard Noelle and a woman exchange a few words, and then Noelle returned a minute later. "That's it," she said. "I have a few more things to do back at the house, and then I can meet you for a drink in an hour or so?" That worried look over her shoulder again confused him. "There's a place in town that has really good sweet-tea vodka. It's sort of a local favorite." She looked suddenly flustered. "I don't even know if you drink. Well, anyway, they have everything. Are you staying here, or are you flying home later today?"

"To tell you the truth, I hadn't really planned anything beyond today, Noelle."

She huffed out a chuckle, putting her hand to her forehead, her features scrunching. "God, Evan. This is just . . ."

"I know," he said. "I know. I'm . . . totally spinning here too. And I *expected* to see you."

It was surreal. They were two people who'd been to hell together, now standing in the dappled sunlight of an ancient tree under a clear summer sky. He couldn't remember the journey from there to here, and so each experience backed up to the other in his mind, making him feel slightly drugged and just a little delirious. A fever dream. A mixed-up impossibility.

"It's not just that," she murmured. "It's—"

"Mommy! Mommy!" came the childish voice he'd heard earlier, foliage rustling as the small patter of feet came toward them. He turned his head just as a little girl came down the path, running toward Noelle.

Her mother.

Oh.

Noelle was a mother.

"Can I go on a bike ride with Ewell to get ice cream?"

Evan blinked as Noelle turned toward the child, bending slightly so she could smooth her hair back. "Sure, honey. But change your shoes," she said, nodding down to her flip-flop-clad feet. "And wear your helmet. And tell Ewell only one scoop of ice cream this time, not three."

Evan's heart thumped in his chest.

Was Noelle married but didn't wear a ring? Or had she broken up with this child's father?

The little girl turned as Noelle stood straight, and Evan got the first glimpse of her full face. He swallowed, mouth going dry. Oh. *Oh.*

He took a step back, reaching for something, his palm finding the trunk of a tree.

"Who's that, Mommy?" the little girl asked.

"That's Evan," Noelle said, her voice soft as she watched Evan closely. "An old friend."

"Hi, Evan," the girl said with a grin. "I'm Callie." She was missing a front tooth. How old was he when he'd lost his front teeth? Six? Seven? Yes, right about that. *Oh God.*

He managed a smile, but he could feel that it trembled. "Hi, Callie. Nice to meet you."

"Bye, Mommy. Bye, Evan," she called as she skipped away, rounding the corner and disappearing through the greenery.

For several long moments Evan and Noelle simply stared at each other, eyes locked.

"Evan?" she finally whispered.

He lowered his hand from the tree, but he still wasn't sure he trusted his own knees not to buckle. "Is she . . ."

Noelle nodded slowly. "Yes, Evan, she's your daughter."

CHAPTER
TWENTY-SIX

Noelle stepped onto the beach where Evan was waiting for her and then approached him slowly, taking the opportunity to watch him without him knowing. A wave crashed, the water rushing forward and washing over his feet. He stood staring out to the horizon, where the sun was just beginning its fiery descent.

She still couldn't believe he was here, in this place where she'd often stood, especially in the beginning, staring out to the water as she thought of him and wondered how he was. He was as handsome as ever. Time hadn't changed that. But she hadn't remembered that their daughter looked as much like him as she did. Callie had simply become herself, and because Evan's face had been somewhat of a distant memory, she hadn't realized what a carbon copy she was. Minus her coloring, which was Noelle's. But the rest? All Evan. No wonder he'd taken one look at their child and known immediately who she was.

He must have heard her feet crunching in the sand as she drew closer, but he didn't turn, even when she came up right next to him. She followed his gaze to where the silhouette of a singular sailboat crossed in front of the glowing sun.

"It's peaceful here," he finally said. "I see why you made it home." The words were casual, but his voice sounded dull as though he was in a bit of shock. Of course he was. She couldn't blame him for that. She'd asked him to meet her on the beach so they could talk. She'd needed to let the rest of the staff know she was leaving for the day, and she'd hoped that a few minutes alone on the shore would help him get his bearings.

Instead of addressing the solitude of this private beach, she reached out, putting her hand on his forearm. "Evan—"

"Why?" He turned toward her, her hand falling away, the look on his face so tormented it ripped at her heart. "Why didn't you tell me? I had a right to know."

She released a breath, moving her eyes away from his and crossing her arms over her chest. "I'm sorry." She shook her head. "I don't even know how to explain it—"

"Try, Noelle. Because you at least owe me that."

She dropped her arms. He was right. She did. She just hadn't been at all prepared to do so. How could she have known when she woke up that morning that he'd show back up in her life? There was no script from which she might pull, because she'd never imagined this moment. All she had was the truth, in all its shades of gray. "I found out I was pregnant after I moved to South Carolina. I had rented a small apartment and was going to start job hunting . . ." She rubbed at her head as she cast her mind back to that time. She'd still been on such shaky emotional ground. But sitting on the shore each morning and watching the waves come in had begun ministering to her spirit right away. The decision she'd made after that night in San Francisco to move away, to start fresh, suddenly felt destined. She sensed that she was right where she should be.

Noelle sighed. "At first, I was almost in denial about the positive pregnancy test. I got the job at Sweetgrass. I loved it here, right from the beginning. Chantilly is . . . well . . ." She let out a small laugh that faded quickly. "She's a force. But she made me feel welcomed." *Loved.*

Noelle turned to him then, meeting his eyes. "I was going to email you so many times, Evan. I was." She glanced away. "But then . . . I would feel so afraid. Even more scared than I felt just knowing I was pregnant and alone. The thought of seeing you again . . . I don't know, it almost felt like . . ."

"Like you'd be traveling backward emotionally."

She nodded, her heart swelling. He'd been kind to provide that language for her when she was having a hard time finding it herself, and she appreciated it so much. Of course he'd understand that. Maybe he'd thought of her, too, now and again, and maybe he'd felt the same when he had. Maybe each time he pictured her, he saw her in that cage, just like that night in the hotel room. The night they'd made Callie.

"Yes. Only now, it wasn't only me I was thinking of. I was thinking of you, too, Evan. I really was. I thought about dragging you away from your life again—the one I hoped you were living well. What would it be like for you if you were just finding solid footing, and suddenly you'd have to figure out how to be a dad? We'd already decided that it was in both of our best interests to part ways. And I think we're probably both better for that," she finished softly.

His shoulders rose and fell, and he scratched his temple. He still looked confused and slightly angry. But mostly hurt. "Is she better off? Callie?"

It was a fair question and a complicated answer. "She's remarkable. She's smart and she's empathetic. She's happy, Evan." But she'd never known a father, and if she didn't miss that now, she would eventually.

"Who does she think her father is? Does she think he's some guy who just abandoned you? And her? Jesus, Noelle." He took a few steps, turning halfway away from her.

"I simply told her it didn't work out between her father and me. She's not even seven. She hasn't asked a lot of in-depth questions."

"And when she starts to? What then?"

"I don't know. Maybe I'd tell her the truth. I hadn't gotten that far."

He swore. It was mostly under his breath, but she caught it. He turned back to her so suddenly she almost took a step back. "You robbed me," he said. "You robbed me of her, of deciding whether or not I was capable of being a father. You took something else from me after all the things that had already been taken. And what really kills me more than anything is that of all people, of *all* people, Noelle, you should have known what that would do to me. That I'd already lost enough."

Regret washed through her, icy and bitter. God, when he put it that way, she felt so ashamed. She knew he had every right to feel the way he did and that his judgment of her was perfectly justified. And even still . . . she couldn't quite bring herself to say that she'd change it if she could. Her life wasn't perfect by any stretch. Sometimes she was lonely. And though she hadn't come up with any specific plan, sometimes she did worry about the questions Callie would ask when she got older and wasn't as easily distracted by ice cream and seashells and any of her other joyful pleasures. But Noelle was at peace. She felt healed. She could think about what had happened to her without breaking out in a cold sweat. She could catch sight of an ice pick or a length of rope or even a pair of red shoes without losing it. And she could set her thoughts and memories aside, if she preferred not to dwell there, even for a moment. *She* was in control. And it'd been a long, hard battle, but she'd won. So perhaps she'd been selfish. But maybe not, because healing meant that she was the mother Callie needed her to be.

"I'm sorry for hurting you," she told him. "I'm sorry for keeping her from you, and you from her. I can't go back, Evan. I can't change it."

He studied her for a second, finally sighing and giving his head a shake. "We were partners," he said. "Once, we were. We worked together during the most horrific circumstances imaginable. For God's sake, we would have been able to handle an accidental pregnancy together too." Despite the accusation in his words, his tone had softened, his anger obviously having faded, at least a little.

"Yes. Of course we would have managed. At the time . . . I decided we both needed more than just managing."

"You decided that without me."

"Yes, I did."

"That wasn't fair."

"I . . . I know."

"Do you?" She could see he'd asked it rhetorically, so she didn't answer. He squinted off behind her for a moment before meeting her gaze again. "I'd like to spend some time with her."

Her stomach squeezed. She felt momentarily defensive. But he hadn't threatened her. He'd merely asked to spend some time with his daughter. "Okay."

His eyes moved over her features before he gave a slight nod. "I won't demand anything of you, Noelle. I know you've been doing this on your own for a long time, and she's obviously living a good life. I just . . . well, I'd just like a chance to . . ."

"Yes," she said, rescuing him as he'd rescued her. He didn't know what to say either. He'd been even less prepared for this than her. "Of course. Tomorrow night the turtles make their journey to the shore. There's a big gathering on the beach. Callie's been looking forward to it for weeks."

"I'd love to be there." There was a bit of an awkward silence before he said, "I guess I'll get a hotel room nearby."

"We have a vacant cottage," Noelle said. "You're welcome to stay there."

"Okay. Yeah." He looked back over her shoulder again in the direction of the property. "That would be great."

She nodded. "And I know you're here for a reason," she said. "We can talk about that after Callie goes to bed tomorrow."

He ran his hand through his hair, her words causing a wrinkle to form between his brows. "Right. Yes. We'll talk then."

The sun dipped farther, and the last two people who'd been sitting on the beach a little way down the shore stood, packing up their things. "I should get home," Noelle said. Callie would be back from her bike ride by now, likely stuffed on ice cream. Getting her to bed would be a chore and a half. Despite the thought, her heart warmed, and she felt the pull toward her child. "Come with me," she said, turning toward the wooden bridge that connected the beach to Chantilly's property. "I'll show you to your cottage."

"Thanks," he said. "I'm pretty wiped."

She imagined he was. She'd just knocked him for a loop. And she was going to need tonight to find her footing once again, too, before hearing why he was here. What had made him decide to seek her out? She almost didn't want to know.

CHAPTER TWENTY-SEVEN

Cedro glanced over as the older man heaved into the metal toilet for the hundredth time. He groaned, wiping his mouth with his arm, and fell in a heap on the floor of his cage.

"You should be almost done," Cedro remarked casually. He'd watched his father detox before. Messy. Gross. The man in the cage next to him had been puking his guts up for the past three days. Or what Cedro thought were three days, if he could count on the schedule of the lights turning on and off to tell him when it was day and when it was night. Until that morning, the man had been crazed, ranting and sweating and plain out of his mind. Lucky break for him in some ways. In others, not so much. Because now, with a sane mind, he'd have to come to terms with where he was.

"If you've been wondering if the cage was part of your sickness, it wasn't," Cedro said. "The cage is real. And your stench is definitely real. I can smell you from over here."

"Shut the fuck up," the man slurred, rolling over and gripping his head.

"Make me."

The man pulled himself into a sitting position, gripping his bars and squinting over at Cedro. Cedro wasn't good at guessing ages. The guy looked *old* to him, but part of that was probably because he'd spent a week at death's doorstep. His eyes were sunken in, and though his hands were brown, his face was pale and was sorta green, and he had deep wrinkles that looked carved into his skin and a generous amount of gray in his short beard. Yes, he was at least oldish, and there was something just a little familiar about him.

"Who are you?" the man demanded, his voice scratchy.

"Cedro Leon."

"I didn't ask your name. Who are you?"

Cedro thought about that. Maybe the guy was asking because he was trying to figure out why he'd been snatched and locked in a cage with him in particular? Maybe it wasn't random like he'd thought? And maybe the guy hadn't barfed up every single one of his brain cells. "I'm nobody," he said. He didn't say it because he was sad or sorry about that. It was just true, and Cedro was a realist. He'd survived, so far anyway, in his life because he was honest, at least with himself. "I was crossing to the US. My brother's seventeen, and he's in Arizona. I was nabbed about an hour past the border." He'd been stung by a bee, or so he'd thought for a brief second. He'd quickly brought his hand to his neck to swat the insect, and that was the last thing he remembered. He'd woken in the dark, and at first he'd wondered if he'd been caught by border-patrol agents, but when the lights never came on and he realized that even when his eyes had had time to adjust to the dark, all remained pitch black, he knew something was very wrong. He'd felt around and realized he was caged. That's when he knew traffickers must have taken him. He'd panicked—yelled and kicked and gone a little crazy—but not for too long. He was where he was. Throwing a fit wasn't going to change it. At the first opportunity, he'd have to use his wits and his skills to get free.

What he hadn't at all expected was that they'd toss someone else in the cage next to him while he was sleeping and then turn on the lights.

"How old are you?" the stranger demanded.

"Fourteen," he said.

"Jesus fucking Christ," the man muttered, collapsing back down so that he was half-propped against the bars. "You didn't hire someone to bring you across?"

"You mean a coyote?" he asked, turning his head and making a spitting sound. He would have brought up some actual saliva, but he didn't think it smart to waste the moisture in his mouth. "Never," he said. "Animals." He knew what the coyotes did to those stupid enough to trust them.

The man just grunted. "So here you are. Too young and stupid to realize that whatever *this* is, you're probably better off than if you'd tried to cross that desert by yourself."

Cedro bristled. "What the hell do you know, you old used-up drunk?" His brother had crossed that desert and lived to tell about it, even though he was only a teenager like him. He'd written their mother when he'd arrived in Arizona and told them he was living in a migrant shelter and to follow his lead.

"Grim," the man said right before he went into a coughing fit.

"What's grim?" he asked once the man had gotten hold of himself.

"My name. Grimaldo. Friends call me Grim."

"You think we're friends?"

"Not even close." He coughed once more. It was rattly and loose. "I've seen you before, little pickpocketing thief," Grim said. "You stole something from me."

Cedro pulled in a silent breath, turning his head again and squinting over at the man's profile. *Oh.* It came to him then. He'd seen the man, too, in the small lawless border town he was from. Once. Only once. "You shot that dog," he said.

Grim turned his head, looking at him for a moment and then turning away again. "She was suffering," he rasped.

Yes, Cedro knew that. He'd seen the piece-of-shit car that hit her, watched from a doorway as it'd driven away, leaving the animal moaning and broken in the dirt road. Cedro hadn't known what to do, but he'd hated it, that moaning. He felt it inside himself like it was leaking through his pores. The man, *Grim*, had been in a building nearby. Cedro had tracked him as he exited the doorway and made his way toward the dog. He'd knelt down beside it, and then he'd taken a gun from the waistband of his jeans and he'd shot it in the head. That shot had rung in Cedro's ears long after the man had disappeared down the road.

He didn't remember stealing anything from him, though. "I didn't steal from you. I don't steal," he lied. "I sell vegetables from my mother's garden."

The man snorted. "A thief *and* a liar. A better liar than a thief, however. I'd like my property back."

Outrage rose in Cedro, even though what the man said was true. Maybe that was the part that made him so angry. This man thought he knew him. And he didn't. He didn't at all. "What is it you think I stole from you, pig?"

"A locket."

A locket. Oh. He remembered that locket. He'd gotten a pretty penny for it from the man who ran the migrant aid group near the border. He'd eaten regularly for the next month. It'd been a good month. Cedro didn't have many of those. "I don't know anything about any locket. You probably got drunk and lost it, pig."

Grim let out a chuff of laughter.

"Who are you, anyway?" Cedro asked. "And why are we here together? Who took us?"

"I have no fucking clue," Grim mumbled. "One of the gangs, I assume."

"What do they want with us?"

Grim glanced over, and his face looked like his name. "No clue," he mumbled again, but Cedro *was* a liar, after all, and he could spot another one.

"What do you do, other than roll around in your own vomit?" Cedro asked.

Another rattly cough. "A little bit of everything."

A little bit of everything. Which probably meant he took money from anyone who was desperate enough to pay an old drunk for his services. "Do you take people into the desert?" He refused to say *help*. Help was hardly ever what came to those who let someone else guide them out into that brutal place where even fewer laws existed than in the town where he lived.

"Sometimes," he said. "I help those who can pay for it."

"Help? Or *use?*"

"Look who's talking, pickpocket."

Cedro startled when the door directly in front of their cages slid open and a man walked through. He had a receding hairline and greasy black hair that fell past his shoulders. Cedro crawled quickly on his knees to the front of his cage. "Hey, mister. Let us out of here. Please. I don't have anything you want. I'm an orphan. No parents, not a dime to my name. I sell vegetables on the street, just enough to feed myself. Please."

The man gave him a slight smile, but it was cold, and it chilled Cedro so much that he let go of the bars and slunk back. "I am not authorized to make deals with you," the man said. His speech was clipped, and he had a slight accent that Cedro had never heard before. "You've been rented," he said.

Cedro's mouth went even drier than it already was. "Rented?" he croaked. He didn't look over at Grim, but he could tell by the still silence that he was watching this interaction closely, unmoving. "I . . . what do you mean?" But he thought he knew. *Oh, not this.* He'd done anything and everything not to have to do this. He'd stolen vegetables from others almost as poor as him and sat in the hot sun hour after hour to sell them on the street for nothing but change. He'd slept in alleyways, covered in trash so no one spotted him. He'd rooted through garbage for food. He'd picked pockets and sold what he'd stolen. He'd taken chances and barely survived. But he'd told himself he was doing okay because he hadn't resorted to making the trip to that squalid street where kids no older than him, and some younger, stared hollow eyed out of upstairs windows while old men entered through the doors below. "No," he said, more so for himself than because he thought he had any voice in this matter.

"You do have a choice, however," the man said, crossing one foot over the other and leaning on the corner of his cage.

"What? I'll do anything," he said. He hated to beg. He hated it. But in this case, he would do what he had to do.

The man jerked his head backward toward Grim's cage, a smile spreading over his lips. "Come with me, or I'll take his eye. Just one. He has two, after all."

From beside him, Cedro heard Grim release a long breath. "Ah, fuck me," the old drunk muttered.

CHAPTER
TWENTY-EIGHT

"Is that you, Noelle?" Chantilly called.

"It's me," she said, stepping into the massive bedroom suite and closing the door behind her. Chantilly wheeled out of the dressing room, a luxurious space that featured racks and racks of designer clothing, a marble-topped counter built to Chantilly's chair height in the middle that held her sizable collection of jewelry and accessories, and an entire wall of shoe racks that stored all her footwear, from the Louboutins to her pink feathered slippers.

Chantilly was seventy-five, and she still wore heels. Some might say the wheelchair made that possible, but Noelle knew the woman well enough to know she'd likely be wearing heels even if she'd had use of her legs.

"Well look at you," Chantilly said, her hands at her ear, head tilted as she put on an earring. "What's the occasion?"

Noelle smoothed her palms over her outfit. It wasn't overly formal at all—a cotton floral maxi sundress. But it was strapless and hugged her breasts, even if it was flared out from there, just grazing her ankles. "You know it's the turtle-hatching watch party tonight—"

"Yes, I'm well aware of the social events scheduled at Sweetgrass," she said, turning her chair and leaning toward a large gold filigree mirror on the wall and smoothing a platinum-blonde hair back into place. She turned, eyeing Noelle again, her gaze moving quickly over Noelle's hair—blow dried and curled in loose waves—to the makeup she'd spent fifteen minutes applying. Which meant thirteen minutes more than she usually spent on her face. She felt herself blushing under the older woman's knowing perusal. "What's unexpected is *you*." A twinkle came into her sea-green eyes. "And I'm wondering if it has anything to do with a certain guest who checked in to Atlantic Moon last night."

Noelle sank down onto the red velvet settee by the door. "You don't miss a beat, do you?"

"Not around here I don't," she said, the soft whir of her chair sounding as she moved toward Noelle and parked herself next to the settee. "Who is he?"

Noelle traced a button in the tufting. "He's Callie's father," she said softly, not meeting Chantilly's eyes.

"Oh *my*," Chantilly said, and in her peripheral vision, Noelle saw her bring her hand to the base of her throat in surprise. "Well, I didn't expect *that*." She felt the older woman's considering gaze on her. "And you're all gussied up for him, are you?"

She opened her mouth to deny it, but Chantilly had seen her almost every day for the past seven years, on regular workdays and on special occasions. She knew very well when Noelle was *gussied up* and when she wasn't. "I needed some confidence," she admitted.

"Well, getting gussied up will do that for a girl," she said, patting the underside of her swept-up hair. "Why is he here, and how did he take the news about Callie?"

"He was angry. And hurt. Mostly hurt, I think."

"I see."

"As far as why he's here, I don't know yet. He has something to discuss with me, apparently. I think it has to do with our past." Despite the warmth of the room, she shivered, wrapping her arms around herself and running her hands over her bare arms.

"Your past . . . ," Chantilly said.

Noelle nodded, swallowing. "I know I haven't told you all about that, Chantilly—"

"I looked it up," she said.

Noelle's head pivoted her way, her mouth falling open.

"Oh, don't look so surprised. You know very well I'm a nosy nelly." When Noelle only blinked at her, she went on. "You've grown into a poised, confident woman since you first arrived, so young and so timid, wearing a tiny baby bump. At first I wondered if you'd been abused," she said. "There was such a haunted look in your eyes. I thought it must be your daughter's father who'd hurt you so terribly. But then each time I mentioned him, though you were evasive and only told me he didn't know he had a child, your eyes filled with . . . what I thought might be love. And so I wondered . . ." She examined her perfectly manicured nails for a moment. "I went online. I read about the terrible crime committed against you so many years ago. I'd feared the child might belong to . . ." She waved her hand around as though the words were too terrible to utter aloud and should instead be brushed away. *One of the men who raped you.* "But the timing wasn't quite right. And so then I figured Callie's father was a man you met shortly afterward, when you were still recovering from what happened to you, too traumatized to settle down with anyone. Too afraid to love. Am I close?"

Too afraid to love. Maybe. But she thought the more apt description was that she'd really been incapable of love. Or a healthy form anyway. And more than that, she'd been especially incapable with Evan. She suddenly *wanted* to talk about all this with Tilly. She wanted to let her in on her fears, and regrets, and she wanted to hear her words of wisdom. They'd been close for many years, but she realized suddenly that she'd also kept her at a certain arm's distance, believing that Tilly would view her differently if she knew what she'd survived. "Oh, Tilly." She sighed. "I'm sorry. I should have told you. At first, I couldn't. And then . . . it became so easy to pretend I was *only* this new version of myself. I wanted you to know *her*, not that traumatized victim who'd been running away."

Chantilly reached out and put her hand over Noelle's where it rested on the settee. "I understand the desire to run away, my darling. You know I do." Yes. Noelle did know that. Chantilly had often referred to her monster of a husband. It was an open secret that he had abused her terribly, causing the injury that had put her in a wheelchair before he died. She'd inherited the beautiful property that had once belonged to the Calhouns, and she had turned it into a picturesque vacation spot for families. She'd never had one of her own, but now she was surrounded by them. "But," Tilly said, patting her hand, "you ran from him as well, didn't you?"

"I suppose," Noelle said. "In a manner of speaking. But he needed the distance too. We discussed it and we agreed. Later, when I found out I was pregnant, I made the decision to stick with that agreement."

"The terms had changed," Tilly noted.

"Yes. They had. I was wrong, I guess."

Tilly raised a perfectly arched brow. Noelle knew very well what it was in response to. *I guess.* "Does he want to know his daughter?"

"He wants to spend some time with her. I told him he could come along tonight."

"And then?"

Noelle let out a small laugh. "I have no idea. I'll hear the reason why he came here. And then I guess he'll go back to Reno, where he lives."

"I see." There was a short pause, and Noelle looked at Chantilly to see that she was considering her as she tapped a nail to her lips. "This dress," she said, her gaze moving down Noelle's body. "Are you sure it's only to inspire confidence?"

Noelle gave her a small eye roll, knowing what Chantilly was suggesting. "Yes. I mean, firstly, he's angry with me. Secondly, any connection we ever had is based on . . . very unhealthy things. And as if that isn't enough, he might be with someone for all I know. It didn't exactly come up."

"Ring?" she asked.

Noelle let out another small laugh. This woman was ridiculous, but she was so thankful for her. Her mother had been murdered when she was still a girl, and although she'd missed her over the years, she also knew she was very lucky to have both a friend and confidante in Tilly. A mother of sorts, but also a friend who she trusted implicitly. "No ring."

Tilly took in a breath, looking satisfied. "Tilly," Noelle warned. "Really. It's so much more complicated than that. Complicated doesn't even begin to cover it."

"Hmm," she hummed. "Okay, well, I'd like to say one more thing if I might." She took Noelle's hand again, leaning forward slightly. "I'm so very, very sorry for what happened to you, my darling. But mostly, I'm proud. What you did . . . escaping . . . *recovering* . . . from something so deeply *evil*. You are the strongest person I've ever known. Find happiness."

"I have found happiness."

"Find *more*. Go after it with gusto in whatever way you are able. You did not crawl out of that cage to live a timid life."

CHAPTER
TWENTY-NINE

Evan saw them immediately—the feminine figure he'd know any-where, still, even after all this time, holding the hand of the little girl. *His* little girl. The thought still made him dizzy. He'd spent the day attempting to organize his emotions, and he'd thought he had a handle on them, but one glance and the earthquake that had rolled under his feet when he'd first seen her was rumbling again, even if the magnitude was slightly less.

It was dark on the beach, but the moon was high and bright, and starlight was scattered across the sky. Noelle turned as he approached, and though he couldn't quite make out her expression, he thought by the way she held her shoulders she might be nervous. Once he'd read her so well. Now . . . "Hi," he said.

She gave him a small close-lipped smile. "Hi. How are you?"

"I'm fine. How are you?"

"Good. Thank you."

There was an awkward pause, and then they both laughed, Evan running his hand through his hair. "Let's start again. Hey, Noelle."

"Hey, Evan." She stepped aside to where Callie was looking in the other direction, out toward the ocean. "Callie, honey. You remember, Evan, right?"

Callie turned, giving him that same gap-toothed smile. "We met yesterday," she said. "Have you seen baby turtles hatch before?"

"I haven't," Evan said. "But it sounds pretty cool."

"It's very cool," Callie said. "Just wait!"

She took his hand in hers and led him the few steps to where they had a blanket spread out on the sand. Other people had spread out blankets as well or were sitting in beach chairs. The soft murmur of conversation filled the air, muted by the sound of the waves hitting the shore and the crickets singing from the seagrass behind them. The weather was warm, but there was a breeze off the ocean, and Evan couldn't remember experiencing a more beautiful night.

"They're why it's so dark down here, huh?" he asked Callie when they'd sat down, Noelle joining them and folding her legs to the side as she smoothed her dress.

"Yes," she said, and he smiled at the way her missing tooth gave her a slight lisp. "When the babies hatch, they go toward the moon. That's how they make it to the ocean. But if there are other bright lights, they get all confused and turned around."

"Ah," he said. "I've been confused and turned around before. I know how that feels."

Callie giggled. "Me too. Once, Miss Tilly bought me a swirly dress, and I twirled around so many times I didn't know where I was!"

Evan laughed. Noelle took a few water bottles from a small fabric cooler and handed one to him and one to Callie. "Miss Tilly is the owner, right? Chantilly?"

"Yes. She owns all of Sweetgrass. She's the boss of everyone, and my second-best friend after my mommy," Callie said.

"Ah. She must be pretty great then."

"She is. She rides in a wheelchair, and sometimes she sits me on her lap and we go super fast down the ramps!"

"Oh, Callie." Noelle laughed, but Evan heard the slight note of disapproval. He wondered if Noelle ever had to discipline Callie harshly.

He supposed she did. Callie was a child, after all, and even the most well-behaved children were naughty on occasion. He wondered if she ever felt lonely, or overwhelmed, or wished she had a partner to pick up some slack. He wondered if she ever wished that person were him.

But she'd never even told him Callie existed. And he was trying to understand and forgive, but he was presently having some trouble with that, especially now after seeing what a sweet, funny girl his daughter was and realizing how *much* he'd missed.

He made a point to tune back into what Callie was chattering about. He refused to get stuck in his own head and miss one more minute of her. "Before they made laws about the lights, the turtles would end up in swimming pools or even crushed under traffic," Callie said.

"That's terrible."

She nodded, turning her head and sucking in a breath. He looked in the same direction, and then he heard what must have drawn her attention. A very soft scuttling. "The nests," Noelle said, taking Callie's hand and standing. "They're over there." She pointed.

Evan stood, too, as did most of the others on the beach. He craned his neck, seeing movement on the sand.

"They're hatching!" Callie said, and Evan's lips tipped at the pure joy he heard in her voice.

A minute later, the first baby turtles came over the slight bank, moving in unison toward the water. Evan watched in wonder as the tiny creatures crawled over the sand, heading toward that bright orb hanging over the ocean. More followed, until it seemed that there were a hundred turtles all waddling as one. Single minded in their pursuit, doing exactly as nature intended them to do. There was something incredibly beautiful about it, and for some reason he couldn't even explain, a lump formed in his throat, remaining there until the last little creature met the tide, disappearing beneath the water.

"Okay," Noelle said, bending and beginning to collect their things. "Time to get you to bed, little miss."

"I'm not tired," Callie said, yawning.

Evan picked up the blanket, shaking it carefully so the sand didn't blow toward any of the other people also gathering their things and leaving the beach. He folded it and handed it to Noelle, who stuffed it in her large canvas bag. "Thanks. Will you come back with us, and we can have a drink on my patio?"

"Yeah. That'd be great. Thanks." They needed to talk. Not just about Callie, though something definitely needed to be worked out. He massaged his temple. How would visitation work? He was lost, and he still hadn't figured out a way through any of it. He didn't know if she might help figure something out that would give him some type of regular access to his daughter, or whether she was going to insist that they'd done fine without him thus far and be unwilling to let him play any sort of permanent role.

Would he push it?

He'd lost so much already.

But they were obviously doing pretty damn great on their own. Callie was a happy, well-adjusted kid who clearly loved her home. Who wouldn't love it here?

He sighed as they turned away from the water. He had no answers. "I guess we follow the others, huh?" he said. The moon had slipped behind a cloud and dimmed the night. He could barely see where he was stepping.

Callie took his hand in hers. It felt so small. So delicate. And he had this sudden urge to grasp it tightly, to refuse to let go. He took a deep breath and blew it out as they began to walk. "I used to get scared of the dark when I was littler," Callie told him, as though now she was fully grown and scared of nothing. He smiled down at her. He loved her voice and her chatty personality. "I wanted to sleep with the lights on all night. But my mommy reminded me of the turtles. She said that sometimes the dark is beautiful, and without it, we wouldn't see the moon."

~

"She put up a valiant fight," he said, exiting Callie's room and placing the book he'd read to her three times on the counter. "But in the end, she lost."

Noelle smiled, handing him a bottle of Corona with a sliver of lime stuck in the top. "I hope this is okay. If you don't drink, I have water, or juice. I don't keep soda in the house."

"This is great." He took a long sip of the cold beer.

"Do you want to sit on the patio? We'll feel the breeze off the ocean from out there."

"Sure."

He followed her to the sliding glass door next to the kitchen area and out onto a small garden patio featuring a round table with a green umbrella covering it and a few potted plants. It was surrounded by vegetation, but she was right, he could feel the breeze coming from the ocean, and the leaves rustled softly. They both took a seat at the table. "Your place is nice," he said, nodding his head back toward the cottage so she knew he meant the entirety of their home, not just the patio. He meant it. It was small but cozy. Noelle had decorated it mostly in shades of white and various blues.

What's your favorite color?

The color of that Easter egg dye that comes in those little kits from the grocery store.

"Thanks. It's messy," she said on a laugh. "But it's home."

He smiled. She'd made a good one for their daughter. Everywhere he'd looked, there was evidence that Callie was central in Noelle's life. A scooter leaning against the house next to the door, drawings covering the refrigerator, an organizer of children's craft supplies on the kitchen table, a wall full of photos of Noelle and Callie and some other people he didn't know. All this time, she'd existed and he'd never even known. That seemed so odd to him, like he should have been able to sense her somehow from across the country, a little girl standing by the ocean, a smile the same as his.

"Thank you," he said.

She tilted her head, giving him a confused look. "For what?"

"For keeping her. You must have thought about . . . other options."

She blinked at him, turning her head and looking out to the swaying leaves. He could see that she understood exactly what he meant. "I did. For at least a moment," she finally said. "But not much longer than that." She turned her gaze back to him, her brow dipping as though she was measuring her words. "When we were locked in those cages, I fought so hard to get free. To *live*. That instinct . . . to clutch at life, to hold on, is so strong, in all of us." She brought her hand to her stomach, as though remembering the tiny life that had once fluttered there, delicate, vulnerable. "That instinct must be there from the very beginning, I imagine." She smiled softly. "Like the turtles. An inborn instinct to survive, to head toward the light. Not everyone knows that, I guess. But we do." Her gaze washed over his face. He felt caught, unable to move until she looked away, back out into the night. "And so for me, just considering ending a life when I'd battled so hard for my own . . . I couldn't, Evan. To do so seemed to me like the most terrible of hypocrisies."

His heart jolted. He hadn't expected that. He'd thought that, now, he had more control over himself when it came to her. He'd thought he was angry. And he was. Sort of. "That makes sense," he said. "To me it makes perfect sense." Their eyes met, and she gave the smallest of nods, the confirmation that, yes, they both understood things that no one else might. At least not in such a personal way. Their decisions, all of them, were based on things other people couldn't possibly imagine.

Evan watched her as she again gazed out to the night, realizing that she was just as incredible as he'd remembered her to be. It was an epiphany, because for so long, he'd connected that feeling to the trauma bond Professor Vitucci had put into words for him. He'd doubted his own emotions surrounding Noelle. He'd believed them to be overblown and untrustworthy. And perhaps in some way or another that was true. But his opinion of her hadn't been based *solely* on what they'd experienced together, because that no longer controlled him and he still felt the same.

"And now, of course," she went on, her lips curving tenderly, "I couldn't imagine the world without her. What a terrible tragedy that would be."

"She's wonderful," he agreed.

"She is."

"Beautiful."

"That too."

They were both silent for a moment before Noelle spoke. "Evan, I know you might want to discuss . . . making plans . . . regarding Callie. Maybe visiting her or . . . well." She sighed. She was as lost as him. They'd been lost together before, and they'd helped each other through it. Maybe they could again, now that they both had clearer sight. The vestiges of his anger drained away. She hadn't been right to keep Callie from him, but he also understood why she had. Maybe if he'd been in her shoes, he'd have done the same.

At first, after they'd parted, he remembered wondering if she would call him or email him. He wanted it, God, he did, and yet . . . at the same time, whenever he opened his inbox and realized she hadn't, he breathed a small breath of relief. It'd been confusing as hell. She was so woven into his pain.

"I was thinking about staying for the next three or four days," he told her. "I hope you'll let me hang out with Callie a little bit. As much as you're comfortable with. And then we can talk about that before I go."

"That sounds good. Of course you can see Callie this week. And we'll figure something out."

He smiled. "Okay."

She smiled back. "Okay." Their eyes held, and she laughed, shaking her head and looking away. When she glanced back, her expression had become serious. "Now, tell me why you're here."

CHAPTER THIRTY

"I've been looking into what happened to us," he told her.

Her mouth opened slightly, but then she closed it, exhaling through her nose. She took a long drink from her beer and then placed it on the table. "I wondered," she said. "When you told me you'd become a private investigator, I wondered if it was because of what we'd been through."

"Partially. But I didn't choose it because I wanted to investigate our crime," he said. "It had already been investigated, and nothing helpful had been uncovered. The FBI never found anything, and neither did the PIs my dad hired. I didn't imagine I'd have much more luck than the Feds, who have access to all sorts of databases not available to me." He shook his head and took a sip from his bottle. "I chose the profession because I wanted to help other people find their own closure. I guess that aspect, especially, was appealing to me, considering we never found ours."

"I get that," she said. She did. Even hearing him say the words had made her heart constrict in understanding. They'd had to find their own form of closure, but in some ways, it would always be an open sore, because nothing could fill it entirely except true justice. True knowing of exactly what had happened to them, and *why*. She'd learned to live with the lack of answers, and there were lessons to be found there too. She'd discovered that the practice of *letting go* of that which was out of her control was a valuable one. But to assist others in attaining their justice must help Evan in his own acceptance. If she had been remotely interested in criminal justice, perhaps she'd have gone in that direction too.

"So if you didn't initially intend on looking into our crime, what happened that made you start digging?"

He gave a small shrug, and she regarded him for a moment, beautiful even in the dark. She knew that, though. She could have drawn the outline of his shadowy silhouette. It was imprinted in her brain, even after all these years. "Time," he finally said, answering her question. "An understanding of how the system works, police capabilities. I've formed relationships with officers over the years, made contacts at the Reno department. They're also able to access things I can't."

"I would think time would make it less likely there's anything to find."

"That can be true, but also, things resurface, other crimes happen that might be tied in. Connections are made. Cold cases are solved all the time. Especially if the crime is ongoing."

A slight chill made her cross her bare arms over her breasts. "Is that what you think?"

"Haven't you ever wondered about that?"

"I . . ." She closed her mouth, really considering the question. "I guess I try not to, because there's nothing I can do about it, but in the back of my mind . . . maybe." Maybe it'd lain there, unexplored. She'd put it away and labeled it *Torturous material. Handle with care.* Because she could think about that all day and night if she let herself. But who was that going to benefit? Certainly not her. And certainly not Callie.

She'd fought hard for her mental and emotional health. She wasn't going to hand it off so easily. Especially to something purposeless.

"I tried not to go there for a long time either. But I also . . . I don't know. I felt a responsibility, too, especially once I became involved with law enforcement and had the means. I asked a police officer I know at the department to keep her eyes open for any crimes across the country that even remotely resembled ours. A few weeks ago, she came up with something."

"What?" she breathed, her heart giving a sharp knock.

Noelle listened wide eyed as he told her about the Vietnam veteran he'd flown to Texas to interview. About him being locked in a cage, another man locked up in the same room. About the sick and horrific choices they were told to make. The torture. The terror. And, ultimately, the escape.

The police had doubted his story, especially when they found the building where he'd claimed to be kept devoid of any proof. She wondered if that would have been the case with the building where they'd been caged, too, if she hadn't set the place on fire.

Noelle let out a gust of air as he finished. She'd held her breath for much of his description, even though he'd made it as short and void of details as possible. She understood why he'd made the connection, though. She recognized the similarities too. They were hard to miss.

"Are you going to notify the FBI about that case?"

"The police didn't even notify the FBI. They investigated and deemed it the rantings of a drunk with mental health issues."

"But you believed him."

"I did. I looked in his eyes, and I believed him."

She played with the label on the beer, considering grabbing another. But she had to work in the morning, so she'd stick to one. She offered Evan another, though, but he declined. "I didn't just come here to put that case I described in your head, Noelle. I came because of something else. I'm hoping you can help me with it. I thought about calling you, at first . . . that's exactly what I planned on doing. But the more I thought about it, the more it seemed weirder somehow to call you on the phone than to come in person and ask for your help."

She got that too. And as much as she'd felt unprepared to disclose the fact that they had a daughter she'd never told him about, she was somehow also glad that he'd unintentionally ambushed her. If he'd called, she'd either have had to choose to directly lie to him about her life, about Callie, or if she had decided to tell him, she'd have had to live with the fear of his reaction before she did. No, it was better that he'd surprised her. She hadn't feared it, because it'd been sprung on her. And he was still here, still asking for her help, even after realizing he'd been denied his child for over six years. "What do you need help with?"

"I've always come back to the fact that we knew each other. We have a connection through our fathers. I can't believe that wasn't known by whoever abducted us."

She nodded. They'd talked about that way back when. Before their escape . . . *before we learned to speak in code.*

"I agree," she said. "Didn't we wonder if it was what made things more interesting?"

"Yes," he said. "But if we were chosen purposefully for that connection, then someone knew about it."

Right. This all sounded familiar. They'd picked all these possibilities apart long ago. "We have no proof of any of that, just our suspicions," she said.

"I looked into your father."

Her gaze shot to him, and she saw that he was watching her. "*My* dad. My dad is dead." She heard the resentment in her tone and took in a breath, letting it out slowly.

"It's not because I suspected him of wrongdoing. I just thought knowing more about him might trigger something I already knew about my own father. Maybe I could make even more of a connection. And I asked that contact at the Reno PD to pull anything on him she found interesting."

Noelle shifted in her seat. She felt irrationally bitter and worked to tamp that down. It was funny that it was still her gut reaction to defend her father when it came to a Sinclair. Even if that Sinclair had turned out to be a decent human being and was the father of her child. "Did she find anything?" she asked, attempting to sound casual.

"She did. Your father filed a missing person report right before you were reported missing."

What? She frowned. "On whom?"

"A man by the name of Dow Maginn."

It took a moment for the name to penetrate her memories. "Dow? He went missing?"

"Not only that, but he was later found murdered, the gunshot victim of an apparent mugging."

"I didn't know." She gave her head a small shake. "He was my dad's friend. I think we sent him an invitation to the memorial, but Paula took care of all of that. If the invite got returned, she probably just tossed it. Or if she asked me, which I don't remember, I probably figured he'd moved or his shop went out of business. The guy wasn't necessarily the most stable person. I remember him being a heavy drinker when he was at our house. He and my dad would watch a game, and he'd pass out on our couch." She frowned again. "When I . . . came home, I had no reason to look into his whereabouts. I'm honestly surprised my dad even noticed he was missing. They were friends, but from what I recall, there were periods of time where Dow didn't come around for months. That was just him."

Evan tapped his fingers on the edge of the table. "What else do you remember about him? He owned a computer repair shop, right?"

She nodded, casting her mind back. It'd been so long since she'd seen Dow Maginn, or any of her father's old friends, mostly tradesmen who often worked together on jobs or recommended each other to those looking to have work done. She'd barely remembered his name when Evan said it, or that he existed at all. He was a nice enough guy, but he was her *dad's* friend. She hadn't missed his presence in her life. "Yeah. He did work with computers." She remembered something. "He might have been into some low-level hacking," she said. "I think I remember hearing him brag that he'd changed the amount he paid for his electric bill or something. I remember wondering if he could change my math grade in the school computer."

Evan tilted his head, running his hand over his jaw. "Hacking the electric company? That doesn't sound low level."

"No, maybe not."

They sat there for another minute, Evan's tapping becoming quicker, as though keeping tempo with his speeding thoughts. "Computer hacking," he repeated. "Noelle, you do realize that if we were being watched, there'd have to be a person, or people, on the other side of a screen?"

She stared at him in the low light. "Are you suggesting that Dow . . . had something to do with what happened to us?"

"I have no evidence of that. But it's odd, right?"

She massaged her head. *Maybe. Maybe not.* It was all too much. "I don't know what to think."

Evan sighed, running his palms over his thighs. "You're tired. And I know you have work tomorrow. I should go. If you think on it, though, and anything comes to you that might help regarding Dow Maginn, will you let me know?"

"I will," she said, standing, Evan following suit. She grabbed the empty bottles, and they went into the house. She set the bottles on the counter, and they walked toward the front door.

Evan glanced toward Callie's room as they passed the hallway. When they got to the door, he turned toward her. "Will you let me know . . ."

She nodded. "I'll call and let you know her schedule tomorrow to see what works. She loves to go on bike rides. Especially if it involves ice cream." She smiled, feeling sort of awkward and shy for some reason. "Maybe you'd like to take her on one. Sweetgrass rents bikes. I could have one delivered to you."

"I'd love that," he said, the words spilling out quickly as though he was eager to cement the plans before she withdrew them. She wasn't going to do that, though. Now that he knew about his daughter, she wasn't going to keep her from him.

"Great. Have a good night, Evan." She pulled the door open, and he stepped through, turning again.

"Thanks for tonight," he said. "Not just for letting me tag along . . . spend time with you and Callie, but for listening to what I had to say about my own investigation. I know it's not easy dredging all that up. You could have refused to talk about it."

She leaned her head against the side of the door. "It's not easy," she admitted. "But if there's something I can help with, I will. Just . . . be careful, Evan, about getting dragged back under."

He nodded, understanding in his expression. He'd obviously thought about the same thing. "I will. Good night."

"Good night." She closed the door, engaging the locks and walking slowly toward her bedroom. There were so many emotions swirling through her. Relief, tentative happiness. Hope that positive things would come from Evan's presence in Callie's life. But she also felt concerned . . . on edge . . . anxious . . . a tremble of fear racing through her system with the worry that Evan—with her assistance—might have new avenues to follow regarding the crime they'd survived. And the deeper worry that following them might be like opening a Pandora's box that couldn't be closed.

~

A couple of days later, Noelle stood at the window, watching as Callie sprinted down the beach, her red sundress flying out behind her, arms raised, as the kite she was holding rose high into the sky. Evan ran next to her, jogging leisurely but easily keeping pace, his head raised to the sky as well. She couldn't hear them from where she was, but she could tell they were laughing, and it made her smile.

"He's a natural, it seems," Chantilly said, the whir of her wheelchair announcing her presence even before she spoke.

"He is," she said. A natural father. It made her happy. And it made her ashamed. He'd accused her of robbing him, and she had. But she'd robbed Callie too. She saw that now.

"Hindsight is twenty-twenty, my love," Chantilly said. Noelle glanced at her, her platinum updo as shiny and elegant as always, makeup flawless, her silvery-blue pantsuit perfectly pressed. She was a vision, and Noelle was often startled by her loveliness. She'd come to expect it. There was something about her that simply glowed. Noelle had remarked on it once, and the old woman had told her that if she glowed, it was because she was living her second chance, the life she'd never dreamed she'd have, and it made her shine from the inside.

Noelle had thought about that later and realized that she was living her second chance too. But she didn't glow. Not like Chantilly.

Because you were given no closure, a small voice whispered. *And because of it, you haven't ever truly left it in the past. It casts a shadow. Not so much that you haven't moved on. Not so much that you haven't found peace. But it's there, and it dulls your light. Even a little.*

Okay, but what was she supposed to do about that? She'd formed her life around that unfortunate fact because there was nothing she could do.

Not then. But now?

Noelle sighed. "Yes," she agreed. "I can see clearly that I should have told him about Callie. But he's here now, and he seems to have forgiven me. Or at least he's willing to put his resentment aside. He wants to have a relationship with her."

"Are you going to tell her he's her father?"

"Yes. Yes, when the time is right." He'd been in South Carolina for three days, and Noelle could already see the bond they were forming. Of course, Callie was an openhearted girl who loved easily. But she and Evan clicked in a way she hadn't seen Callie click with anyone else.

Perhaps she recognized herself in him. Maybe their shared DNA called to them both. The same shared DNA that Leonard Sinclair had passed on. But she refused to think about that. About *him*. "He's started a new investigation of the crime we survived together," she said.

"Oh. Oh, I see. Is there still something to investigate?"

"He seems to think so."

Callie stretched her arms high, the kite caught in a gust of wind, and Evan reached over, taking the strings from her and commandeering the swooping fabric. He ran in a wide circle, obviously pretending to be the one controlled by the kite, and Callie fell to the ground, her head tilted back as she clutched her stomach in fits of joyful giggles.

Noelle couldn't hear them, but she could feel them between her own ribs, like the phantom kicks she'd felt even after Callie had vacated her body. She breathed out a laugh.

"What are you going to do?" When she glanced at Chantilly, she saw that the old woman was watching Evan and Callie frolic on the beach, and she, too, was smiling.

"I don't know," Noelle said. "His investigation led to questions about one of my father's friends. And . . . I just keep thinking about the planners my dad always used."

"Planners?"

"Yes, you know, the three-ring calendar books? He always had one. Even when he got a cell phone, he liked to write things down. It's where he kept all the information about his scheduled jobs, appointments, et cetera. He even used it as a diary sometimes, you know, writing notes or memories in the margins. I packed all his stuff away in storage before I sold his house." There had been no money to pocket from the sale. She'd been lucky the housing market was good and she could pay off the second mortgage. But she'd kept those planners, among other things that were valuable to her. "And I keep wondering if that planner might . . . I don't know. Offer something small." Or maybe it'd just be painful and heartbreaking to read through the things her father was doing in his final days. Painful and unnecessary.

"Maybe it's time you clean that storage container out anyway," Chantilly said. "The last time you took a few days off was to deliver a baby. You haven't taken a vacation in seven years," she scolded.

"This *is* a vacation." She turned slightly, sweeping her arm around the beautifully elegant room with a view of the ocean to the beach itself, sun sitting high in the sky, where her daughter gleefully flew a kite.

"I'm glad you think so. But, Noelle, darling, perhaps it's time that you go put your father to rest completely. Clean out his things and say goodbye, for real this time. And if there's any chance, even the smallest one, of finding something that will help solve your crime, you must. Otherwise, they might still be out there, putting people in the same cage you once inhabited."

Chantilly's words hit Noelle like a cold gust of air, and she shivered. That was the difference, perhaps, between those who were able to find their shine without also being given closure. They were able to move on because they didn't have to worry for the unknown souls out there who might be similarly victimized because no one had ever been brought to justice.

And now Evan was presenting her with an opportunity to do her part in turning over every last stone. How could she refuse if she ever hoped to truly shine?

She leaned down and wrapped her arms around Tilly, kissing her on her velvety cheek, breathing in the lovely scent of Chanel No. 9. "I love you," she said.

"I love you, too, darling girl."

An hour later, when she stepped onto the sand, she bent, removing her sandals, and carried them in her hand as she walked toward where Evan was standing, watching Callie with the kite nearby. The wind had died down now, and Callie controlled the kite easily, her neck bent back as she watched it glide through the air.

Surprised pleasure danced over his expression when he turned her way. "Hi." He pulled his phone from his pocket and looked down at it, obviously checking to see if the time had slipped away from him.

"I got off early," she said in explanation. She'd told him she'd meet them at the beach at five, and it was only four.

"Oh. Great. You can take a turn next," he said, grinning and nodding his head toward Callie.

She smiled, but it quickly slipped. He turned more fully toward her. "What is it?"

She stretched her toes in the sand, stalling. She was frightened, she realized. She had made her decision, and yet, saying the words to him, making the commitment, had fear gripping her. Was she really about to do this willingly? "Paula's coming to stay with Callie for a couple of weeks," she said.

"Paula?" He looked confused.

She bobbed her head. "You remember Paula, right?"

"Yes, of course."

"Paula is a children's book editor, so she can work from anywhere. Two weeks, that's all I have. I put my father's belongings in a storage locker when I sold his house. He was good at recording things, sort of obsessive about it, actually. And . . . well, I made my reservations. I'm going to come with you. To Reno. Back to Reno."

Evan's brows lifted in surprise. "That's . . . wow, that's great. Thank you. Thank you, Noelle."

She gave a decisive nod. She hadn't mentioned the fact that Paula had been more than willing to stay with Callie but had expressed hesitation about Noelle spending time with Evan for any reason, much less to delve into the past. Noelle was nervous, too, but she also felt an inexplicable resolve. It was time to lay the past to rest, at least as far as she was able.

CHAPTER
THIRTY-ONE

Grim waited, breath halted as the kid decided the fate of his eye. Grim had often received compliments about his eyes. His wife had told him they were what she first noticed about him. If there was anything about him that was considered attractive, even now, he thought he could say somewhat objectively that it was his eyes. Interesting that the twinge of fear at how they might go about removing said eye also carried with it a measure of vanity. He almost laughed. The things you could learn about yourself under circumstances you never imagined.

The kid was staring at him, his eyes wide with fear. But his expression was also somewhat lax, like he was either in shock or seeing something in his mind's eye. The bloody extraction of Grim's eyeball, most likely.

"I'll go with you," the kid said softly, turning his gaze to the greasy-looking man wearing black jeans and a leather jacket that was cut like a blazer. *What the hell?* Grim pulled himself up, leaning forward, his nose through the bars. The man used a key to open the lock on the top of Cedro's cage and then lowered the door on the front. He stood back so Cedro could exit, a Taser held at his side.

"Wait," Grim called as the kid started following the man out the open door. "Wait!" he called again. But the man ignored him. Clearly, it wasn't Grim's choice whether he kept his eye or not. It'd been Cedro's, and he'd made it. *Why?*

"Stupid kid," he muttered as the door shut. Grim slid back down to the floor of his cage. He still felt like hell but better than he had since he'd woken in the dark, begging like an animal. He hadn't begged for his life. He'd begged for some alcohol. Of course, he hadn't gotten any, and his body had rebelled. He'd thought he'd die a time or two and hoped he would. That was surely coming, only he figured now it was going to be even more painful than it would have been if he'd died of the DTs. "Just my fuckin' luck."

Grim had heard about something like this from the men who dealt in drugs and humans crossing the border. Word was, there was some kind of game being played by rich elites who got their rocks off doing sick shit to caged humans. Humans who'd never be missed. Throwaways like the kid.

Like you. Nobodies who have nobody.

The smugglers and traffickers—the cartels—all wanted a piece of it, obviously. Where there was money, there was always the desire—at least by some—to partake. But from what Grim had heard, this game was more exclusive than the likes of even the biggest drug kingpin. Grim had only half listened to the murmurings. Even for someone like him, who had seen depravity the likes of which most people didn't think existed, he thought the stories about this game were overblown and unlikely.

Apparently, he'd been wrong. Or maybe he'd been too drunk too often over the past few years to pay attention like he should have. He ran a hand over his gnarled beard. He could smell the vomit stuck to it, and it made him want to vomit again. If he hadn't needed to drink the water he'd been given so badly, he would have used at least some of it to clean himself up. *Goddamn it, what was happening to the kid right that second?*

The kid. Cedro. The one who'd stolen his locket. He'd seen him around town. He looked like a dirty little urchin, even if he was a teenager, but the boy was quick and stealthy, Grim would give him that. It hadn't been hard to steal from Grim himself, as he'd been three sheets to the wind when the kid had taken his locket. But he'd watched him swipe things off others, and he was good. Good enough that he hadn't been dragged over to Calle Miguel and turned into a prostitute. Or killed for the organs inside his body that many considered the most valuable part of him. Yet.

Though this might be part of that. Or worse. So apparently their luck had run out. He didn't care personally . . . much. After all, he'd been killing himself slowly. This would get it over with in a hurry, even if there was some pain in the process. But he was surprised to find that he cared about the kid dying this way. He'd thought he was beyond caring about anyone or anything.

It felt like hours before the boy came back. Grim had allowed himself to drift off. Sleeping was the only time he wasn't actively suffering, and he knew his body needed it if he was going to get through the last part of this detox he'd been forced to endure. He sat up as the kid was pushed back into his cage, coming to sit against the bars as he stared stoically ahead, expression blank. He'd seen that look before. Too many times to count. He'd also seen those unmistakable hand-size bruises on the jaws of young boys. The split lips from being forced apart. *Fuck.* "I could have lived without an eye," he said.

"Shut up."

"Make me."

Cedro's gaze whipped in his direction, a small spark lighting in his eyes. Grim let out a slow breath. Okay, not gone, just temporarily extinguished.

"Why'd you do it?" Grim asked. "You shouldn't have."

The kid was silent for so long Grim thought he was going to ignore him. Finally, he asked, "The day you shot that dog . . . you said something over her. Like . . . a prayer or something. What'd you say?"

Grim paused. He hardly remembered that day. But he probed his memory. He owed the kid at least that. He'd heard the dog's moans before he'd seen it. Someone had left it lying in the street. Suffering. He knelt down next to it and stroked its fur and . . . "I said the prayer of Saint Michael."

Cedro let out a slow breath as though he was relieved in some way. As though Grim's answer had satisfied two questions instead of the one he'd asked out loud. "My mother used to say that prayer," he told Grim.

Ah. His mother. Was that why he'd sacrificed himself to save Grim's eye? Because he'd thought he'd heard him say the same prayer his mother had once said? Grim didn't pretend to understand that. Nothing about this horror show made sense.

"You know you're gonna get yourself killed if you keep stealing from dangerous men," he said as much to change the subject as to needle the kid a little so he'd produce some bluster. He'd need to know it was still possible.

"The only men with wealth are the dangerous ones," Cedro told him, lifting his chin. "What choice do I have?"

Grim shrugged. *True enough.* There were no tourists in their town. The regular folk were dirt poor. He wouldn't argue the point because the kid was right. "Your English is good," he noted.

"My mother taught me and my brother," he said. "She wanted us to go to the USA."

Grim turned at the clanking sound that indicated the roll and cup of water were arriving. He moved to the back of his cage. He was so fucking thirsty.

The small door in the wall opened, and he reached for the food and the water. He saw Cedro doing the same next to him. Grim was surprised to see that his roll was on a tray this time, whereas before it'd arrived on nothing. He pulled it forward, lifting the white napkin that sat next to the roll, his heart giving a jolt at what he saw lying beneath it. A paper poppy, the red-orange tissue delicate, the stem made of a pipe cleaner wrapped in green floral tape. He ran his finger along the stem, encountering a series of very small bumps. They almost felt like—

"I got some candies," Cedro said from next to him. Grim looked over to see Cedro holding up two red-and-white-striped peppermint candies in clear plastic wrappers.

What the hell is this?

He ran his fingers along the stem one more time. "What do peppermints mean to you, Cedro?" Grim asked.

"Mean to me?"

"Yeah."

Cedro looked confused. "My dad used to bring them home sometimes," he said.

His dad. Okay.

"Why do you ask? What does that flower mean to you?" He pointed at what had been delivered to Grim.

"Nothing," he said. "Just something pretty, I guess." He bent the stem around one of the upper bars, decorating his cage. He didn't tell Cedro that Poppy had been his nickname for his daughter, and someone wanted him to think about her. Someone was sending a message. *Why?* And who?

CHAPTER THIRTY-TWO

The door to the storage locker let out a high-pitched squeal as it rolled upward, revealing the contents Noelle had hastily unloaded with Paula and Paula's parents eight years before. She took a deep breath of the still night air before stepping into the small musty space piled with furniture and boxes.

"Where should we start?" Evan asked from behind her.

She dragged a finger over a cardboard box, disturbing the layers of dust. She'd considered telling Evan she wanted to do this alone. But when she really thought about it, she realized she *didn't* want to do this alone. She wanted him with her. Once, she'd all but been turned inside out in his presence. He knew the all of her, and vice versa. It seemed that comfort level hadn't quite faded as much as she'd imagined, because she found she wasn't the least bit concerned with showing her emotions in front of him. It felt like second nature. Interesting. Slightly concerning. But true.

"His organizer would have been with the things I cleaned out from his bedside table. Most of the boxes are labeled." He hadn't had an office, nor had he needed one. His equipment and tools had been stored in his truck. Paula had very kindly listed those things for sale, including his vehicle, and sent her a check from the proceeds. She'd used the money to pay off the last of her father's bills and the rest to fund her relocation to South Carolina. The other more personal items, including some furniture, Noelle had moved here, intending to go through it all one day, possibly keeping some of the pieces that reminded her of her mother. That had never happened, and she'd instead continued to make the seventy-nine-dollar-a-month payment that kept her from being where she was right that second.

It hurt. Being surrounded by these things. Memories came hard and fast as she glanced around at the recliner her dad had fallen asleep in so many nights, now covered in a sheet, to the box labeled *Dishes* that she knew contained the blue-and-white-flowered set her mother had picked out and she had eaten on all her childhood.

There were photos here, too, her parents' wedding album, school pictures of her through the years. It was odd, because things didn't hold people inside them, but in a way they also *did*, because Noelle didn't think she'd have had a flash of her mother's tender smile or the sleeveless yellow top she'd worn as she'd placed a bandage on her knee if she hadn't glimpsed the old pink scooter her dad had kept in the garage even after Noelle was far too big for it. Objects conjured memories, and that was a gift, she supposed. But also sadness, not only because of the stirred emotion, but because she wondered how many items she'd tossed that carried the ability to evoke a memory that now she could never get back. Letting go was painful, deeply so.

How many times had Paula offered to clear this space out for her? To toss the contents, or donate it, or whatever Noelle wanted? But Noelle had consistently said no. It was in another state and inaccessible to her unless she boarded a plane to get to it, but still . . . she never could bring herself to imagine it . . . gone.

She suddenly understood why people were hoarders. Those who had lost so much already were scared to death of losing more. And so they held on, no matter the terrible clutter and filth it created.

But she wasn't here to diagnose the reason for other people's mental health disorders, and she needed to stop her mind from wandering so far and wide. She was on a mission.

Evan was crouched behind a pile of boxes, craning his neck as he looked for the place where she'd jotted a note about the contents with a Sharpie. "It looks like this is all kitchen stuff," he said. "Even though the bed is over here." He nodded to the wooden headboard leaning against the wall.

She looked at the boxes he was shifting around. The tape had peeled off the tops and was hanging loosely so that a few of them were gaping open. She frowned, glad they were kitchen items and not things that couldn't be cleaned or that bugs or moisture might ruin.

Like journal paper.

She looked around, trying to remember unloading these items from Paula's dad's truck. She pressed her lips together, casting her mind back before walking to two boxes piled one on top of the other. She leaned around them. "Here," she said, picking up the box on top and setting it on the floor and then leaning down and picking up the one beneath it. A cloud of dust wafted into the air, and she coughed as she averted her head.

She turned toward Evan, and he took it from her. It was heavy, and she knew that was because there were books inside. But his papers should be in there, too, including his collection of organizers. He'd kept them all, years' worth.

"Check inside," she said. "Make sure that's the right one."

Evan took his keys from his pocket, using one to slice down the middle of the tape, and then Noelle stepped forward, opening the flaps to peer inside. *Yes.* Just as she'd thought, there was his collection of organizers, her mother's books piled just beneath them. "That's it," she breathed, and she could hear the emotion in her voice. She hadn't tried to hide it.

"Are you okay?"

She nodded. "Yes. Let's get that back to the hotel, and we can go through it there."

Evan hefted the box up and then gave her a tilt of his chin. "Let's go."

~

The hotel where she was staying in downtown Reno was just a few miles from where Evan lived in the Virginia Lake area. He'd offered to let her stay with him, but she didn't think that was a great idea on several levels. Mostly, though, because she needed clarity of mind while she was traveling back in time to that last week before she'd been abducted and her father had died of a heart attack she'd always imagined had been brought on by the intense stress and heartache of finding out she was missing.

She couldn't help feeling partially responsible, though rationally she knew that was untrue and unfair to herself.

She'd loved her father fully. She'd grieved him deeply. She missed him still.

He would have loved Callie with all his heart.

Evan set the box of items on the desk by the window as she came up beside him. "How about I pour us a drink while you start going through that? What would you like?" he asked, walking to the mini fridge in the open cabinet that housed the television as well.

"Something strong," she murmured, pulling out the first leather-bound organizer and checking the date. That one was older than the one she was looking for, and so she pulled out the next one, and the next, beginning to organize them by year. Her father had never been consistent in the type of book he used. Some of them were leather bound, some had cardboard covers with various designs—a desert, a close-up of a leaf, the Reno skyline—and others were covered in plain-colored plastic.

Evan held a drink out to her. "Rum and Coke," he said. She took it and clinked her glass to his. "To answers," he said, holding her gaze, his expression grim.

"To truth," she added. He gave a short nod, and they both took a sip before Noelle set hers down and pulled out another planner, and then another. "Here it is," she breathed, holding up the maroon leather-bound book from eight years before.

She brought it with her as she sat down on the edge of the bed, and Evan joined her, though he kept an arm's distance, letting her page through her father's calendar by herself first. She appreciated that, swallowing as she took in his precise handwriting, the one that had been inside her birthday cards and on her notes to the teacher and a hundred other things. She knew his writing as well as she knew her own.

She paged to two weeks before she was taken, moving her finger over the squares and reading his jotted notes.

"Look at this," she murmured, pointing to a note in the margin. Evan leaned in.

"Dow, shop two fifteen," he read. He frowned at her. "Is that an appointment? He met him at his shop a little over a week before you went missing, then?"

"Sounds like it," Noelle said. "And a week before Dow was killed."

"Did you ever know your dad to meet Dow at his place of business?"

"No, but I don't know that I would have had any reason to know that. Dow and my dad worked on a few jobs over the years. I do know that once my dad installed some big lighting system that involved computerization, and he consulted Dow on it. I don't remember where, or who hired him, but I remember my dad was excited about the job." She remembered because it was one of the first times she'd seen his eyes light up over anything since her mom died. He seemed enthusiastic about the project, but she also remembered him saying it paid well. And they'd needed the money. Desperately. They'd been buried under debt. The job had ended, and he'd gone back to mostly sulky and silent, but for a moment, he'd been his old self. Yes, she remembered.

She flipped backward, seeing the name of an insurance company and an arrow running through the days of that week. She thought he might have been installing the electric system in the new build of a regional office. They definitely wouldn't have required a computerized lighting system or anything out of the ordinary. So why meet with Dow at his shop? She had no guess. But it could have been any number of perfectly normal, uninteresting reasons that had nothing to do with anything relevant to them.

Noelle paged forward through that week, past the meeting with Dow. "Look," she breathed, her eyes going over her father's note at the bottom of the page. It looked atypically messy, as though his hand had been unsteady when he'd written it. "Dow. Not a robbery. Murder? Police?"

"Your father thought Dow was murdered," Evan said, lifting his head. She raised hers, too, taking in his worried expression. Yet despite that, there was a tempered excitement shining in his eyes. They were onto . . . *something*. But what?

"Apparently he did," she said. "But what made him think that? Other than just a hunch?"

"I don't know. He also put *not a robbery*. But it was a robbery. Or at least, his personal items were missing from his body. Your father had some reason to believe robbery was not the motive? Also, why put *police* with a question mark? Did he think the police had something to do with it, or was he questioning whether he should go to the police?"

"He'd already done that, though," she said. "He'd reported Dow missing the day before."

"True," Evan said, pulling his bottom lip between his teeth and tapping his hand on his thigh. "So was he considering going to the police about additional information he had?"

"Maybe. But that's pure speculation at this point." She thought about it for a minute. "My father, though . . . he was a good man, Evan. If he had information regarding a crime committed against his friend, he wouldn't have questioned going to the police." Their eyes met and held, and she knew what they were both thinking. Her father had gone to the ends of the earth—at least as far as he was able—to bring justice to his wife. He'd ultimately failed, and it had ruined him. Why *wouldn't* he try to help the police solve his friend's murder if he was in possession of information that would do just that?

"Did Dow have any relatives or friends who might be willing to answer a few questions?"

She cast her eyes to the side. "I think I remember him mentioning a sister. But I never met her."

"I'll look into that," Evan said.

"Okay." Feeling troubled, Noelle turned the page. The week she'd gone missing. She had the insane urge to slam the book shut, as though opening it to that particular day could conjure malevolent spirits who might shuttle them both back to that moment and make them relive it once more. She reached out, grabbing the drink she'd left on the desk and taking one long sip before placing it on the floor at her feet.

Evan picked up his drink from the floor and took a long swallow. *That week.* It lived and it breathed. It took up physical space in her mind somehow, a place where her cells still quivered, and she figured his did as well. How could it not? "I went missing this day," she said, tapping March fourteenth. "But he didn't know it yet. Paula is the one who called to let him know she was worried. She's the one who called the police." There were no notes regarding her disappearance or what he'd been experiencing that day. But he'd obviously been sick with worry, so much so that it brought on a massive heart attack and he'd dropped right on his living room rug. Paula had found him later that day when his calls had gone unanswered. She'd had a hunch something was wrong and used the key they kept hidden on the porch to go inside. He was already cold by that point. There was no chance of saving him.

"André Baudelaire," Evan read after flipping a page back. Noelle found the place where her father had written the name, followed by a phone number. Evan picked up his phone from the bed and quickly did a search as Noelle took another sip of her drink. "Purveyor of antiques, collectibles, and fine jewelry," Evan read. "He's still in business. His shop is in MidTown."

"What would my father have been doing at an antique shop?" Noelle mused aloud.

"Not a collector?"

She let out a mostly humorless laugh. "Did you see what was in his storage container? Not even close."

"Selling something?"

She chewed at the inside of her cheek briefly. "Anything he had of any value he sold after my mom died." She didn't have to tell him why. He already knew. Even the gorgeous antique ring that had once belonged to her mother's grandmother was gone. It'd been sold to pay for the lawyer's fees that came from suing Evan's father for wrongful death. And losing.

"Well, we can stop in to see Mr. Baudelaire tomorrow, too, if you're game."

She turned the page of her father's calendar, her chest constricting as the pages grew empty. She sighed, shut it, and placed it aside as she picked up her drink and drained the last of it. Something about those last few weeks was . . . off. Maybe it was part feeling, but it was also that he'd seemed to be meeting with people he didn't ordinarily meet with. So . . . yes. "I'm game," she confirmed.

She set her glass down and lay back on the bed. Evan did the same, falling next to her, their feet on the floor as they stared at the ceiling. She didn't look at him, but she felt his warmth. It was a little odd to be with him in a hotel room. Not only because she'd never imagined any circumstances where she would be, but also because the last time they were in one together . . . they'd made Callie.

A different kind of warmth spread through her, brought on by the alcohol, she figured. But also because of him. She turned her head to find he was already staring at her. "Oh," she said. "Hi." Then she giggled, and it sounded so unlike her that she giggled again. He was smiling, too, and as their gazes caught, they both went serious.

"Hi," he said.

She turned away first, biting her lip. *Not a good idea.* She was still attracted to him. But she'd felt that physical attraction in South Carolina, too, and sort of taken it in stride. Who *wouldn't* be attracted to Evan Sinclair? Plus, it'd been a long, long time since she'd been with a man. She was probably just a little buzzed and a lot desperate. She nearly giggled again but swallowed it down. What she hadn't expected was the yearning that was solely for him. Evan. That deep-down emptiness that somehow still carried his name. She'd felt it blossom to life almost the moment she'd laid eyes on him again. Worse still, she saw something similar in his eyes too. This time, however, it felt less . . . grasping, she supposed was a good enough word. Less all encompassing. Less dysfunctional. Which was good. But that had been achieved over long years and much distance. They couldn't go back and do something that would make it hard to separate again.

Hard to parent Callie and work out some schedule that they were both satisfied with.

"God, I think I'm getting drunk," she said, rubbing her temple and sitting up.

"Lightweight." He pulled himself up too.

"Guilty." She laughed.

Evan stood, obviously reading correctly that she needed some space. "I should go. How about I pick you up for breakfast tomorrow at nine, and we'll head to the antique dealer? See if he remembers anything?"

"Sure. That sounds good." As unlikely as that was. It'd been almost a decade. Who knew if her father had dealt with a person who was still employed there, or still alive, for that matter. And if he or she was, how slim a chance was it that they'd remember someone who came to the shop so long ago?

She walked Evan to the door and pulled it open. "Thanks for coming with me to the storage place," she said. "I appreciated that."

"I'm the one who's grateful you're here," he said. "Thank you, Noelle."

She nodded, giving him a small smile. "See you in the morning."

CHAPTER
THIRTY-THREE

The next morning, Evan pulled on his seat belt and then allowed his eyes to linger as Noelle was focused on belting herself in too. She was so casually beautiful in jeans and a navy tank top, hair in a loose braid, little makeup. And all he could think as he looked at her was that he itched to take her back up to the hotel room and spend a few hours in bed. God help him; he didn't want to want that, but he did. She was sexy as hell to him, which was sort of an epiphany. He'd half convinced himself that those feelings were all mired in that unhealthy bond Professor Vitucci had talked about, and so to find that he still felt that intensity, minus any current trauma, sent him for a loop. But he shut that thought down. There was no way Noelle would participate in some brief affair, and truth be told, the thought of that left a bad taste in his mouth too. They shared a child. It would be foolhardy to complicate the amicable rapport they'd managed to find despite . . . everything. And that word encompassed a whole hell of a lot.

He'd watched her at breakfast as she'd spoken about Callie, telling him about their FaceTime call from the night before. Her whole face lit up when she talked about their daughter, and it made him smile. They were going to have to discuss what things would look like regarding Callie moving forward, and he was grateful Noelle seemed open to that, but for now, the leads they'd obtained from her father's notebook took priority.

Not Callie, not yet. She was safe and happy in South Carolina. And definitely not taking an afternoon to figure out whether they were still as combustible in bed as they'd once been—not that she necessarily had any interest in that whatsoever. After all these years, they might have a small break. Maybe. And that was the focus here and the purpose of her trip.

"Do you have an office?" Noelle asked when he'd pulled away from the curb, breaking him from his turbulent thoughts. "Or do you work from home?"

"I rent a space that's somewhat close to the shop we're going to. I used to work solely from home, but it's never a great idea to invite clients to the place you live. Especially if they end up being disgruntled *former* clients."

She laughed softly, turning his way. "Have many of those?"

He shrugged, shooting her a smile. "Not since I stopped dealing with cheating spouses."

She laughed but then gave a dramatic cringe. "You used to stake out hotel rooms, trying to get a money shot through the drapes?"

"Luckily, that particular scenario never played out. But let me say this—people do really tawdry things when they're sneaking around. And they don't always bother with a hotel room."

"*Tawdry.* Oh, I bet." She grinned.

They chatted a little about his job and the police departments he worked with, and it was easy and comfortable. He realized they'd never really interacted like this, and he enjoyed the hell out of it. He enjoyed *her.* He'd forgotten how much. Although maybe he'd never had a chance to figure that out, as they'd spent the majority of their time getting to know each other under horrendous circumstances, and then there had been suffering in the aftermath. It was hard to fully enjoy someone—or anything, for that matter—when you were struggling to put the pieces of yourself back together. She was funny and quick and laughed easily. He supposed this side of her had always existed. And if she'd lost it completely for a time, she'd obviously taken it back.

"That's it there," he murmured, pulling into one of the street parking spots a few doors down from the sign for **BAUDELAIRE'S FINE ANTIQUES.**

They got out of the car and began walking toward the storefront. It was a warm day, but the awnings provided shade. There were large planters of tropical flowers on each corner, and people strolled the street, window-shopping.

Baudelaire's display featured several large pieces of furniture, and though Evan knew virtually nothing about antiques, he knew luxury when he saw it. He'd lived among it all his life. These were obviously items that had come from very wealthy homes.

The bell over the door jingled softly as they entered, inhaling the scents of old leather and furniture oil. "Do you know anything about antiques?" Evan asked, leaning into Noelle, whose head was turning this way and that as she took in the myriad items: furniture, linens, paintings, china, and an L-shaped glass jewelry case in the middle of the dim store.

"A little," she said. "Chantilly has several pieces handed down through her husband's family. Chantilly didn't have a good relationship with them. Or her husband, for that matter," she said cryptically. "But Chantilly says beautiful things should be appreciated, and so she kept them all."

He'd like to hear more about Chantilly and this deceased husband of hers, but that was for another time.

"May I help you?"

They looked up, and a tall, thin, middle-aged man was approaching. He was wearing a slight smile on his face and had a rather large strawberry birthmark at his hairline.

"Yes," Evan said, stepping forward and extending his hand. "I'm Evan Sinclair, and this is Noelle Meyer."

The man took his hand and gave it a shake, his grip much more robust than his appearance. "Gervais Baudelaire."

Evan retrieved a business card and handed it to the man. "We're looking for André Baudelaire."

Gervais looked down at Evan's business card. "A private investigator?"

"Yes. My . . . partner and I are investigating a cold case, and his name came up."

"He's my father," Gervais said, a crease forming between his brows. "He's here in our office. Would you like to speak with him?"

"That would be great."

Gervais gave a nod, tucking Evan's business card in his vest pocket and then turning and disappearing through the doorway near the back from which he'd emerged. He heard him climbing a set of steps that must go to their business office overhead.

"It can't be," Noelle said. Her voice sounded hoarse, breathy, and Evan spun around·to see her leaning over the jewelry case as she peered at something inside.

He walked to where she stood. "What is it?"

"It's my mother's wedding ring."

"What?" Evan leaned over, looking below where her finger tapped on the glass. It was a platinum band featuring filigree detailing, a large stone in the center, and two stones flanking the sides. It was delicate and beautiful and looked very expensive and very old. "It belonged to my great-grandmother. I . . . is this why my father came here?"

Movement caught Evan's eye, and he straightened, watching as an older man walked from the back of the shop, a pleasant smile on his face. "Mr. Baudelaire?" Evan asked.

"Yes. Good morning, Mr. Sinclair, Ms. Meyer." He shook Evan's hand and then Noelle's. "My son tells me you're investigating a cold case. May I ask what case it is?" He had a subtle French accent, as though he'd been in America for many years but still retained the bare hint of his mother tongue. Next to him, Evan noticed Noelle wrap her arms around herself as though chilled.

"Yes. A man named Dow Maginn was the murder victim of an apparent mugging gone wrong eight years ago. We have new information that he may have been specifically targeted." A little bit of a stretch but true enough, and he didn't want it to sound like they were questioning him over a few scrawled notes in an old calendar and a hunch. Which was basically the case but may not have inspired the man to offer any information he might have. "But first, Mr. Baudelaire, may I ask you about a ring in your case? My partner, Noelle, believes she recognizes it, and it may tie into the case I just mentioned and the reason we're here."

The older man glanced at the display case. "Of course," he said, walking around it to the other side, where he could open the lock and the sliding portion of the glass that allowed access. "Which one?"

Noelle pointed down at the ring from the top, and André Baudelaire removed the ring carefully, placing it on the top of the case.

Noelle picked it up, eyes wide as she brought it closer to her face, lips parted as she turned the piece of jewelry this way and that. "It was my mother's," she confirmed. "Look, her grandmother's initials are carved inside. They're faded, but you can still see them."

"Your mother's grandmother?" Mr. Baudelaire asked. "How fascinating."

She placed the ring down, her hand hovering over it for a moment as though it'd been hard to let it go. "Yes. Mr. Baudelaire, my father believed his friend Dow Maginn was murdered. He wrote the name of your shop down in his calendar the day before Dow was killed. We're trying to figure out if there was any connection, as my father has since passed away."

Mr. Baudelaire frowned. "Oh, I'm sorry." He picked up the ring, studying it in much the same way Noelle just had. "This lovely piece, yes. The interesting thing is I only took it out of the safe about a year ago. I'm surprised it hasn't sold yet but expect that it will sooner than later. Some romantic young man sophisticated enough to recognize timeless beauty and understated class when he sees it. And one who has a fiancée who prefers the unique over the ordinary." He smiled, a subtle tipping of his lips, before he placed it delicately back in the case and slid it shut. "Your father did not want to part with it. In fact, he asked if I might consider more of a pawn-like deal than an outright sale. I don't do that, and I told him so. But . . . he seemed so desperate. So . . . distraught. It's why I still remember him." He rubbed his clean-shaven chin absently, as though trying to recall the specifics of the interaction from so many years ago. "He took the deal I offered. No promises. But . . . I put the ring away anyhow, believing he'd be back to buy it. It got lost in my safe, I suppose. I have quite a collection in there. But styles are cyclical. Platinum, gold, round cut, colored diamonds, you get the idea. I buy for beauty, and for a certain je ne sais quoi." A smile floated over his lips. "But I display for the current trends and what will sell."

"Then we got very lucky," Evan said. What were the odds that her great-grandmother's ring had sat in a safe, forgotten, until only a year before Noelle had walked through the door of this shop and recognized it? And that it hadn't been purchased during that time?

"Is there anything else you can tell us about my father? Did he say why he was selling the piece? You said he seemed desperate. Did he say why?" Noelle asked.

Mr. Baudelaire shook his head. *Of course not. No such luck.* "He needed money in a hurry, I assume. I can't think of another reason. But if there was one, he didn't provide it to me."

Noelle gave the ring one last look. Evan saw the longing in her eyes. It was being sold for over fifteen thousand dollars, however, and it appeared to Evan, who knew very little about antique jewelry, that it was well worth the price if the stone had been properly appraised. And if the longevity of his business spoke to Mr. Baudelaire doing things by the book, then it most definitely had been. What it came down to, though, was that he doubted Noelle had that kind of money. She lived in a small cottage and had been raising a daughter alone. If he'd still had access to the Sinclair fortune, he would have written a check right that moment and gifted it to her. As it stood, he only had his PI salary and a trust that may or may not still be his when he turned thirty. If his father's dissatisfaction with his life's choices were any indication, he wasn't going to count on it.

"We appreciate your time, sir," Evan said, pulling a card out of his wallet, even though he'd already given one to his son. "If you think of anything else about your transaction with Mr. Meyer, no matter how small or seemingly inconsequential, will you give me a call?"

"Certainly."

The door tinkled again as they stepped outside. They walked in silence down the block, and he pulled the door of his car open so she could climb inside. He got in the driver's seat, turning the ignition and blasting the AC but not pulling away from the curb.

"What are you thinking?" he asked.

"I didn't know my father still had that ring," she said. "I never asked him, but . . . I just assumed it went the way of the other items he sold to pay off bills." *Bills associated with his lawyer's fees and court costs from suing my father and losing.* She didn't say it, but she didn't have to. A small knot formed in his gut. He didn't feel guilty . . . exactly. But the reminder that what had happened between their fathers would always be between them made him feel sort of mad and sort of sad, and God, he wished he could snap his fingers and make it go away. But he couldn't.

He'd have snapped his fingers and made a *lot* go away if he could.

"So he hadn't sold it, even though at the time he'd very much needed the money. But then he did sell it eight years ago."

She nodded. "Mr. Baudelaire's assessment had to be correct. He needed money badly. But *why*? What made him even more desperate for money than he'd been after my mother died? Because from what I witnessed, that was level-ten desperation."

"I'd say an even higher level of desperation made sense if he knew you were missing. Maybe he'd think he needed ransom money or something like that. But he didn't know you'd been abducted at the time he sold the ring. No one did."

She sighed, adjusting the vent so the air blew more directly at her face, lifting the tendrils escaping from her braid. "It had to be something to do with Dow, then," she said. She chewed at her lip for a moment. "I'm not saying Dow wasn't a decent guy and a longtime friend, but . . . I don't know, I don't see my dad *desperate* about him being potentially missing. For one, like I said, you couldn't exactly set your watch by the guy, and for two, they just weren't *that* close. And it was only a couple of days until the police found his body anyway. My father would not have panicked over two or even three days. Hell, I can't even imagine him panicking over Dow not returning his calls for a few weeks."

No, it didn't make sense. Evan tapped on the steering wheel, thinking. "Okay. Is it possible that Dow's disappearance had something to do with yours?"

She seemed to think about that for a minute. "If it did, why didn't he call to check on me? There were no voice mails on my phone later. I hoped there would be . . . just to hear his voice at that time would have been . . ." She sighed, leaving the rest of that thought unspoken. "But he hadn't called my work, either, to find out if I'd been showing up. And Paula said that when she called him he sounded horror stricken. From what we can piece together, time wise, he *died* very soon after that phone call. I've even wondered if the news itself was what caused his heart attack."

Evan rubbed the back of his neck. There was *something* here, within all this Dow-ring-selling-Paula's-phone-call confusion, but what, he couldn't begin to say. There simply weren't enough pieces. He thought for a minute. "Wait, the money," he said. "Considering the price of the ring and a markup, André Baudelaire had to have paid him at least ten thousand dollars. There must be a record of it in his bank account. Maybe it also shows where it went. Would you have access to old bank records?"

She frowned. "There was nothing like that in his account when I closed it. He didn't even have enough for a cemetery marker. Paula's family paid for that, and for the memorial service too. I paid them back later from the sale of some of his things. He was dead broke when he died. But maybe there's another box of receipts or bank statements or something in storage. He had a laptop. I think it was one Dow refurbished and then sold to him for cheap. I don't remember packing that away, but I wasn't in the best of spaces at the time. My memory is hazy on some things."

And overly sharp on others. Yeah, he related. "Okay." He put the car in gear and looked over his shoulder before pulling onto the road. "I forgot to mention I found Dow's sister online last night and made a call. She said she could meet with us tomorrow after work."

Noelle nodded, looking out the window distractedly. "Okay. I'll make another trip to the storage container later and look for the bank statements."

"Do you want me to come with you?"

"No, thank you. I think this time I'd like to go alone. But I'll call you as soon as I'm done."

He nodded, though he wanted to press the matter. But she'd been doing things on her own for a long time now, and he didn't want to act overbearing. The problem was, he'd started thinking of her as a partner again. They just *worked*. They had from the get-go. And that reminder made his mind wander. To other ways they might work as a team. Those thoughts scared him, because he had no reason to believe she'd even entertain the idea. He'd let her go once for a similar reason. And it had hurt like hell. His instinct was to shun any avoidable hurt ever again, especially because he didn't function well with a broken heart, and Noelle Meyer was the only one capable of giving him one.

CHAPTER THIRTY-FOUR

The next day, Noelle removed a pair of sunglasses from her bag and slid them on her face before turning to Evan in the driver's seat. "I found a couple boxes last night of what looks like paperwork. There was a file full of job quotes at the top and a stack of other things. I brought them back to my room. I'll start going through some of it later tonight or tomorrow."

Evan glanced at her as he pulled onto the highway. "Okay, great," he said. They were headed to see Dow's sister, a woman named Louise whom Noelle had never met. She knew Dow had referred to her at least once or twice; she just couldn't remember anything specific that he'd said. But apparently, she'd been willing to meet with them, and perhaps she'd have something to add to what they already knew. Something had been going on with her dad in the week before she went missing. She didn't know what, but she had a suspicion whatever it was had, at least in part, contributed to his sudden heart attack.

"Did you locate his laptop?" Evan asked.

"No. And I spent a good hour going through the boxes. I did a decent job labeling them, so once I got them spread out, it was easier to see what was what. I made a pile that I plan to donate and put a few things aside I'd like to ship to South Carolina."

He glanced at her, and she could see in the dip of his brow as his eyes quickly moved across her features that he was looking for what might be emotional upset in her expression. She did feel slightly emotional but not necessarily in a bad way. She'd shed a few tears as she'd looked at specific items in the boxes, and though she'd wanted Evan with her the first time she'd gone there, she was glad she'd spent some time alone among her father's things the second time around. It had been cathartic, and she felt cleansed in a way she hadn't before.

She'd also spoken to her father, asking him if he needed to tell her something and, if so, to please lead the way. She wasn't certain such a thing was possible, but it sure couldn't hurt to try. At the time of their escape, she hadn't known her father was dead. But maybe he'd lent a hand then too. *Somehow.* She liked to think so because it meant he was *there*, leading them out of that fiery hellscape.

Louise Cook lived in a ground floor apartment in a somewhat ratty-looking building in East Reno. Evan lifted the knocker and gave it two swift taps. A dog started howling in another apartment across the way, and they both looked over their shoulders but then back to Louise's door as they heard shuffling on the other side. The door was pulled open, and a woman in her sixties stood there in a blue velvet housecoat and slippers, wearing a bandanna on her head. There didn't appear to be any hair beneath the head covering, and Noelle wondered if the woman was going through cancer treatment.

"Louise?" she asked, offering her hand.

The woman shook it as she nodded. "Noelle Meyer. You look like your dad through the eyes," she said, turning her attention to Evan. He introduced himself, too, and she stood back so they could enter.

"Did you know my father well?" Noelle asked as they followed her to a set of couches a few feet away. She and Evan sat down on one, and Louise took the one across from them, pulling her housecoat down over her knees before reaching forward and shuffling a stack of mail into a pile and turning it over. She wasn't quick enough, however, that

Noelle didn't notice the large red *Past Due* marks on what looked like medical bills.

"I only met him once or twice. Dow recommended him for a job back when I was married and we'd just bought a house. It ended up having some electrical issues, and your dad fixed them. It's been a long time, but a flash of his face came back when I looked at you. Funny the things your brain files away without you even knowing. He was a nice man."

"He was," she said, her heart giving a small thump. She cleared her throat. "Actually, my dad is part of the reason we're here." She glanced at Evan quickly. "I don't know if you read about what happened to me—"

"I did," she said, and Noelle was grateful she'd cut in, saving her from describing any portion of what they'd been through. "I was really sorry to hear what happened to you. I can't begin to imagine. They never caught the guy who done that, huh?"

Guy. More like guys. "No. But, um, we've recently found some new leads, and part of what we found involves your brother."

A slew of wrinkles appeared on Louise's forehead, and she tugged lightly at her bandanna. "Oh? What is it?"

"I know the police believed the motive in your brother's murder was a straight robbery, but my father seemed to think differently. There are a few notes in a calendar he kept, and while they don't give any more information than that, it's clear he believed it was more than what met the eye."

Louise's frown deepened. "Oh . . . I see. The police didn't ever find who it was that robbed him, but yes, they seemed to think it was just a 'wrong place, wrong time' situation. Dow's bad luck." She let out a sigh and tugged at her bandanna again. "Truth be told, Dow generally made his own bad luck. He was always so damn *smart*, growing up. Things just came to him, especially computers. Our dad flipped when he came home one day and my brother had taken his whole damn computer apart, chips here, circuit boards there, and I don't even know if I'm using the right terms, but you get the picture. Anyway, Dow says, 'Don't worry, Dad. I just wanted to see how it worked. I'm putting it back together now.' And damn if he didn't do just that and powered it up like it was brand new." She shook her head, her eyes unfocused. "Damnedest thing." She sighed again. "Unfortunately, he preferred to tinker and code than do anything that brought in much money. He had a shop, and he fixed other people's computers, but he could have done that in his sleep. If he'd have had an ounce of ambition, that man could have gotten a job with NASA or the CIA or . . . whatever." She gave a short laugh. "He futzed around, and he drank a lot. And then he got himself killed in an alley by some meth head who wanted whatever petty cash he mighta had in his wallet." She shook her head again. "I don't know why your dad might have thought it was anything other than that. But if it was, I don't have a clue as to why anyone would want to kill my brother."

They were all silent for a moment as Louise tugged on her bandanna, Evan obviously going over what Louise had said. After a moment, he leaned forward. "Louise, Noelle seems to remember Dow telling a story about hacking into the electric company. It may have been a joke, but do you have any idea if he ever did that sort of thing?"

"Hacking?" She raised her brows, the hair sparse and thin. "If he did, he never told me about it. But my ex-husband was a bailiff. He was real serious about law and order." She let out a small huff of breath that made Noelle believe that Louise was being sarcastic in some way Noelle didn't have enough information to understand. "And Dow didn't like him anyway. He didn't come around a lot while I was married to him."

"Did you clean out his shop after his death?" Evan asked.

"Nah. I called another computer repair shop, who came in and made an offer on some different parts and whatnot. The rest I paid to have hauled away to the dump. When all was said and done, I pretty much broke even."

"My father had a laptop that seems to be missing," Noelle said. "Do you happen to know if the other computer repair shop might have taken it if my father left it at Dow's shop?"

"There were three or four computers Dow was working on, but they belonged to customers. I contacted those people, and they came and picked them up. They were all spoken for."

Noelle ran her hands over her thighs, then rested them on her knees. What Louise had offered hadn't really advanced their case, but she couldn't think of anything else to ask her. She glanced over at Evan, who was pulling a card out of his wallet, which meant he'd obviously come to the same conclusion. He set the card on her coffee table. "Here's my number in case you think of anything else."

"Oh, wait," Louise said, standing. "I do have a small box of his things in the extra bedroom." She tapped her fingers on her chin momentarily. "He'd been living with some woman friend on her couch, apparently, after some roommate situation or another went bust. When she heard about Dow, she brought the stuff he'd left at her place to me. It looked like a bunch of junk, but I wasn't really in a place to go through it at the time either. I only remember it even exists because I saw it when I moved to this apartment nine months ago. Follow me."

She turned and led them down a short hall to a room on the left, then pushed the door open and stepped inside. It looked like she was using it solely for storage. There was no bed or any other furniture, just piles of boxes, plastic bins, and household odds and ends. Noelle and Evan remained just outside the room, as there was really no space for them to stand inside.

"Do you remember her name?" Evan asked as Louise rummaged through some things. "The woman who dropped off his things?"

She stood straight, squinting for a moment. "No. No memory at all of her name."

They waited as she went back to moving this and that aside, murmuring to herself and forming a path to the far wall, where she bent, retrieving a cardboard box, the flaps tucked closed, the name *Dow* scrawled on the side.

Interesting to think that if they moved forward in the investigation, it might be thanks to the contents of several dusty cardboard boxes belonging to her father and his friend.

Louise handed it to Evan. "Thanks," he said. "We'll look through it and return it afterward."

"Don't bother returning it," she said. "Just toss whatever isn't useful. Lord knows I don't need something else to store." She sighed. "I suppose it's just one less thing my daughter will have to get rid of once I'm gone."

～

"Oh wow, that's good," Noelle said around a mouthful of Thai noodles. They'd stopped on the way to Evan's house at a restaurant he said was one of his local favorites and gotten dinner to go. Now they were sitting at his dining table, cartons and bags spread out around them as they ate off paper plates. "I feel like I haven't eaten adult food in far too long."

Evan wiped his mouth, picking up his beer and taking a sip before setting it down. A smile played around his lips. "Adult food?"

She shrugged. "Well, at least anything that has a spice rating over negative three."

He laughed. "Callie's not a fan of spice, huh?"

She smiled. "Not yet. I should probably introduce her to more variety, but there's a kitchen right on site, and she's got the cooks wrapped around her finger. They're more than happy to make all her favorites all the time, notably spaghetti and meatballs. It's far too convenient to let them take care of dinner many a night."

He watched her for a minute. "You work hard."

"I do, but I like my job."

He nodded but seemed slightly troubled, the way she noticed he did each time she spoke about her job, or her life, or South Carolina. And she knew why. They were going to have to address it sooner or later, especially because she only had a week and a half left in town. They'd uncovered a few unusual things that caused more questions, but so far nothing that indicated they'd break the case wide open. They had beer in hand, so why not now? "About Callie . . . ," she started.

He stilled slightly, fork halfway to his mouth.

She took a quick swig from her beer bottle, her eyes sweeping his apartment. His place was small and had an open layout, and the only rooms she couldn't see fully were the bedroom behind a closed door next to the kitchen and the entirety of a powder room to the right of that. It was clean and neat and featured the basics as far as furniture. But he clearly hadn't done much to decorate or add any form of personal touch. It was the quintessential bachelor pad. "You said you'd like to work out an agreement as far as seeing her. But . . . I imagine when it comes to some cases, you can work from anywhere, right?"

"Some," he said. "Not all. But I can arrange my own work schedule in advance."

She nodded, a quick dip of her chin. "We'll have to tell her first, of course, that you're her father. I think she'll take it well. She already likes you, and . . . she longs for male attention." His eyes shuttered momentarily, and she wondered if he was considering whether there had been other men in her life. She'd dated a few, but no one who'd become serious. But Noelle had mostly been referring to the men who worked at Sweetgrass and had taken her little girl under their wings. She basked in their attention, and it made Noelle feel guilty. She knew very well what it was like to have a male look at you with love. Her own father's pride in her had meant everything. She'd blossomed under it. She'd felt the terrible loss of it twice, once when he'd been too consumed with the grief over her mother's death and then again when she'd come home from experiencing horror and he hadn't been there.

"I'd like to be there when you tell her."

She thought about that. "Okay. Yes, she'll have questions. It will be good if you can answer the ones she has for you." God, her heart was beating fast just verbalizing all this. It made her realize that she'd have to prepare. She'd have to explain things to Callie in a way that she could understand. And they'd have to figure out what to tell her about what they'd experienced together and what to leave out that was far above her maturity level. Which was quite a bit. So, yes, they'd have to coordinate their stories. Her heart rate slowed slightly. He'd be on board with that. He'd be fair and agreeable. She didn't have to worry that he wouldn't be.

"Maybe I can accompany you when—"

A knock on the door made him pause, his head turning toward the sound. She looked over her shoulder to where the front door was.

Evan stood, dropped his napkin on the table, walked to the door, and looked through the peephole. She thought he stilled slightly, even though she could only see him from the back. But his pause seemed overly long, like he was trying to figure out whether to open the door or not, before his shoulders dropped and he flipped the lock and pulled the door open. "Aria," he said.

Oh. A woman. Now she understood his discomfort.

"Hey." She heard the smile in the woman's voice. "Sorry I didn't call, but I think you'll be happy about why I'm here."

He stepped back so she could enter. The woman wearing a police uniform stepped inside, her smile faltering as she looked at Noelle sitting at the dining table, a beer in hand. She glanced quickly at Evan and then back to Noelle. "I'm sorry. I didn't realize you had company."

"Aria Dixon, this is Noelle Meyer," he said.

Understanding came into Aria's face as she stepped forward. Noelle stood, meeting her in the living room area and holding out her hand. "Hi, Aria."

"Hi, Noelle," Aria said, her gaze moving over Noelle's features and then doing a quick assessing sweep of her body. She saw discomfort

261

in her eyes and noticed that her cheeks were flushed. And she heard familiarity in the way Aria said her name. This must be the contact at the police department that Evan had mentioned.

She was young and very pretty in a sweet and wholesome way, and when Noelle glanced at her hand, she saw that she wasn't wearing a ring. If Evan *wasn't* involved with her, she'd have been surprised. And, damn, but she hadn't expected that hot sweep of jealousy that flashed through her, making her feel itchy and insecure. She hadn't expected to feel the very *opposite* of wholesome, the way she had after she'd exited that cage. She'd thought she left that feeling behind years ago.

Clearly Aria Dixon was displeased by her presence, but still, she smiled, and despite the discomfort in it, it looked sincere. "Evan's spoken of you. It's nice to meet you," she said.

Noelle nodded, feeling even more off balance. If Evan had spoken of her, it was clearly regarding their past. He was looking into the case, and Aria was helping him dig, and so naturally, he would have had to confide in her about their experience. It had been a long time since she'd been around people who knew the details of what she'd been through when she was still a teenager, and it made her feel exposed and vulnerable. For a brief moment, it made her feel like the shy, ostracized girl she'd once been, standing in the presence of this strong, well-put-together woman. This uncomplicated, beautiful, *available* woman. This cop. "It's nice to meet you, too," she murmured.

The moment grew more awkward as they all looked between each other, Evan seeming to come into the present as he took a step forward. "Aria, would you like a drink?"

"No, no. It's been a long day. I'm headed home. I'm sorry to bother you. Noelle, again, nice to meet you." She turned and walked back out the open door, and Evan met Noelle's eyes, a spark of guilt in his. He released a breath, looked as if he was considering saying something, but then turned and went after Aria.

Unsure whether or not to shut his front door behind him, Noelle stood there, watching as he jogged to where she was walking down the path toward the street. He touched her arm, and she stopped, turning and saying something that made him stick his hands in his pockets and look like a chastised little boy.

Words floated to Noelle, and she was able to string together that Aria felt used. He'd asked her to provide information for him to find a way to reunite with Noelle, "the woman who makes your voice get all wobbly every time you say her name, while I wait around like a pathetic puppy." Noelle grimaced. Aria's voice had risen, allowing Noelle to hear the entirety of that sentence. She stepped away from the door. Nothing about what Aria was saying was true, of course, but the woman obviously felt scorned. Which meant that they were either involved or had been.

Maybe she should leave. But then she'd have to walk past them to do so.

Evan and Aria exchanged a few more words that appeared terse, and then Aria pulled something out of the bag she had on her shoulder, shoving it at him. He really had no choice but to take it, stepping back with the force of her handoff. Then she turned, holding up her key fob and clicking it. A red SUV parked at the curb flashed its lights.

Evan stood there for a moment looking torn, but then he turned, making his way slowly back to Noelle. "If you want to go after her, Evan—"

"I don't." He came inside and closed the door behind him. He set the folder down on the table and sat back down, running a hand through his hair, leaving it sticking up in the front. She had a sudden, brief flash of the way his hair had looked in that cage. Overgrown, greasy. Messy in a similar yet different way than it was now. She dropped into her seat. "Sorry about that awkwardness," he said.

"You don't owe me an apology." She folded her napkin over, and then folded it again. "You have a life. Relationships. And I don't want to make anyone feel uncomfortable. If she got the wrong impression, you should go fix it."

"Should I?"

She raised her eyes, her hand stilling where she was fiddling with the napkin. "Should you what?"

"Set her straight on what's going on with us?"

"Going on with us? There's nothing going on with us."

"No?"

"No. We're investigating the crime we both lived through. What do you mean?"

A muscle in his jaw tightened. "Jesus, Noelle. Are we going to dance around this? You used to be more honest than that."

She let out a short humorless laugh that communicated her sudden offense. Clearly, this was coming from whatever had just happened with Aria, but she didn't fully understand it. Sure, she felt the tension in the air when they locked eyes. And, yes, she was attracted to him, who wouldn't be? But so what? "I'm not dancing around anything," she insisted. "Some things should just be left alone. We already decided that."

"Things change."

"What changed?"

"Well, we have a daughter, for one."

"Yes, and we were just trying to figure that out."

His nostrils flared slightly. "Don't you think we should try to figure out what's between us too? Still?"

"Figure out what's between us? We already figured that out. Long ago. And it isn't good for anyone."

"Like I said, things change, Noelle. It's been seven years since we decided that. We're reinvestigating the crime we were victims of because new information came to light. Don't you think it might be worth reinvestigating *us* too?"

"No," she said, standing, the chair tipping backward and falling to the floor. "Stop it. What is this?" He stood, too, and she turned away. He came up behind her, and she halted as though his body were a magnet keeping her from pulling away. He put his hands on her upper arms and gently turned her to face him. "There's even more reason now than there was then not to revisit *us*, Evan," she said. She couldn't stand it. Even talking about it hurt and made her remember exactly what it had felt like in the months after she'd left the hotel room that day, even before she'd found out she was pregnant. In a way, her pregnancy had helped mitigate the terrible grief of their separation because though she knew it was in both their best interests not to be together, she had a small part of him with her. Always. And it was enough. More than that.

Her daughter was the very air she breathed. She was the living embodiment of what could never be but *was*. The most beautiful paradox. Callie. She turned her face, lowering her chin. "It's good that you're seeing someone else, Evan. She should be your priority, not me."

"I'm not seeing her." He swore, stepping away. She felt relieved. And bereft.

"Sleeping with her, whatever. It's good. It's healthy. You don't have to explain anything to me."

She met his gaze and saw the anger there, the frustration. God, where had this come from? And why had it flared like this? It must mean that he had kept it tamped down and Aria showing up like that had set it off. "And you, Noelle? What about you? Are you having *healthy* sex with someone? A few someones, maybe?" His eyes flashed. She saw the anger, but she also saw the hurt. "Did it help?" he asked, taking a step toward her again. They were close once more, and still she couldn't move away. *You can, Noelle. You don't want to. Evan's right. You used to be more honest.* "That day in the hotel room? I've wondered. I've wondered a lot, actually. Did it help you loosen up? Were you able to enjoy yourself with other men because of me?"

"Stop it," she said, and even she heard the tears that threatened in the sogginess of her voice.

"Why? You get to use me and not let me know if it was worth it?"

His words were sharp. They made her bleed inside. "God, Evan. It wasn't like that. You know it wasn't. Don't make it ugly." What they'd experienced together that day . . . it had hurt, and it had helped. And she held it in her heart as one of the most beautiful days she'd ever lived.

He let out a harsh breath, fisting his hair in his hands and stepping away. He turned, his shoulders curling forward, and she heard him swear under his breath. For a moment they both stood there, Noelle frozen as she watched his back rise and fall. After a minute, he turned toward her, his eyes speaking regret before his mouth did. "I'm sorry. God, what are we doing?"

"Did you really feel used?" she asked. Because she had to know. He'd been victimized, too, and if he'd walked away that day feeling worse rather than better, she was going to have a hard time forgiving herself.

"No," he said. "No, I didn't feel used. I'm sorry I said that. I spoke out of anger." He looked away for a moment, his forehead smoothing out as he took in a big inhale of air. "I felt sad," he said. "And I second-guessed myself. I felt . . . God, so conflicted. I felt almost relieved, and I also wondered if I should have fought harder. For us."

She understood that. Her feelings had been so terribly conflicted too. They still were. She supposed they always would be. Which was the point she'd been making, and now he was making it too. "We'll always be confusing together," she said. "Our emotions will always be volatile. And we'll flare on a dime. It took less than a week to reaffirm that fact."

His gaze moved slowly over her features, searching for what, she didn't know. He looked away, frowning. It didn't seem he'd found whatever he was looking for.

He closed his eyes and squeezed the bridge of his nose for a moment. "Listen, we figured out once how to set things aside to best work together. I know we can do it again. I hope you'll stay."

"I didn't say I was considering walking away. I'm committed to helping for these two weeks. Something was going on with my dad, and I'd like to know what. So . . . yes. Let's set all that aside. Nothing good comes from it." She held out her arm, and though he hesitated, he finally grasped her hand, giving it a quick shake.

"What do you say we go through Dow's box?" he said. "And then I'll drive you back to your hotel?"

"Deal." She offered him a small smile. "Partner."

He let out a breathy laugh. "Partner."

Evan cleared the table while she grabbed the box from where he'd set it by the door when they'd come in. She put it on the cleared table, where only their half-drunk beers now remained. She wasn't in the mood to drink any more, though. Truth be told, she was exhausted. She'd look through this old junk, and then when she got back to her room, she'd take a hot shower, call Callie to say good night, and fall into bed.

Evan unfolded the box flaps, tucked inside one another, and pushed them back. There were a few pieces of clothing on the top that she picked up and set aside, doing the same with a folded towel and a pair of slippers that looked unworn. Underneath that was a stack of fiction books, mostly spy thrillers, it looked like. She had trouble picturing Dow as much of a reader, but apparently, he had a few more layers than she'd imagined. Or maybe the female friend he'd been staying with had purchased them for him to make him more literary. She handed them to Evan, who flipped through one, stirring up some dust and then coughing. She laughed softly, pulling out a canvas bag at the bottom. It looked mostly empty, squished down by the things that had been on top of it.

She unzipped the bag, pulling back slightly in anticipation of a musty smell and then letting out a small gasp when she saw what was inside.

Cash.

She pulled it out, meeting Evan's eyes. "How much?" he asked.

She dropped it on the table, spreading it out and then estimating. "About ten grand."

"The money your dad got for the sale of your mom's wedding ring."

He'd given it to Dow. But why? For what? Dow had stuffed it in a bag and stowed it at a friend's house. And then he'd been killed before he was able to do anything with it.

CHAPTER
THIRTY-FIVE

The knock at her hotel-room door the next morning startled her slightly just as she was finishing securing the rubber band in her hair. She knew it was Evan, though, and so she walked to the door and pulled it open. "Morning," he greeted, pushing off the doorframe where he'd been leaning.

"Good morning to you. Sleep well?"

"Like a baby."

She almost rolled her eyes but resisted. She was annoyed, though, mostly because *she'd* slept like crap. Tossing and turning, her mind veering from questions about her father, her mother's ring, the money they'd found in Dow's old possessions to Evan and the argument they'd had. She'd also done her fair share of picturing the pretty woman named Aria wrapped around Evan like a pretzel. She rubbed her forehead. What was actually wrong with her?

"Just kidding," he said as she shut the door and turned. "I slept like crap."

She let out a laugh, shaking her head. "Good. So did I."

He had a file held under his arm, and he tossed it on the desk before taking the few steps to the bed and sitting on the edge. She'd pulled the sheets up, but it was still mussed and freshly slept in, and dammit, they'd agreed to set all talk of *them* aside. She'd vowed to set all thoughts of them aside as well. So why, ever since they'd had a fight about it, did the tension seem to vibrate even higher? Why did the sight of him sitting on a bed make her feel flushed and dizzy?

"What's that?" she asked, her arm flying jerkily toward the desk where he'd put the folder.

"It's the file Aria brought over last night."

"Oh." God, she'd forgotten to even ask about that, and he hadn't looked inside it after they'd discovered the cash in Dow's things. They'd spent time talking through why he might have had it, not coming to any conclusions that made a whole lot of sense. She'd been exhausted, though, and so they'd agreed to pick things up in the morning after a full night's rest, crappy though it turned out to be.

"Remember the man named Lars Knauer I told you about? The case that started my digging?"

"Yeah. Aria found that one, right?"

"She did. And now she found another one."

"Jeez, she's the MVP of this case. Did you call and thank her?" she asked as she picked the file up. She almost cringed. She wanted to kick herself. Why had she said that? And it'd sounded snotty too.

When he didn't answer, Noelle glanced up to see him looking at her, his lips tipped very slightly. "I doubt she wants to hear from me just now. But I will." He stood from the bed, walking toward her. "Listen, I know you didn't ask, but I'm not involved with her. I was, a year ago. For a very short time. I decided it was a bad idea and ended it, okay? She obviously had hoped to take up where we'd left off, and she felt slighted and used by your presence in my house."

"She shouldn't have."

"You made that clear."

His tone conveyed his irritation, and she looked down, opening the file in her hands, avoiding the conversation altogether. "So this case . . ." Her gaze ran over the particulars.

Evan reached forward and closed the folder. "Hey," she protested.

"Her name is Tallulah Marsh. She's a prostitute. Are you up for an overnight trip?"

Her mouth opened and then shut. *Overnight trip?*

He reached in his back pocket and pulled out two folded pieces of paper. She took them, unfolding the top one and reading. "It's a boarding pass to Las Vegas in my name."

"It takes less than an hour to get there. I took a chance that you'd be up for it."

"I mean . . . sure. If you think it'll be worthwhile."

"I have no idea, but I thought it was worth the ninety-nine-dollar airfare and thirty-nine-dollar rooms. Who knows, we might even win big on one of the slots." He grinned, and she couldn't help the chuckle that bubbled up.

"Okay, well, big spender, it sounds like an adventure at least." She handed the papers back to him, and he stuck them in his pocket. "Let me pack an overnight bag while you go down to the restaurant in the lobby and get me a coffee."

"Yes, ma'am."

She grinned as she shut the door behind him, wondering what had happened to the cautious, well-planned single mother that she normally was. And why it was so easy to get swept up in Evan Sinclair's vortex.

~

The bar smelled like musty carpet, sour beer, and old cigarette smoke. Evan drew back slightly as the door swung shut behind them, obviously enjoying the stench about as much as she did. She would have laughed, but that might have meant she'd inhale more air than she had to, so she held that back.

The bartender, a dead-eyed man with sparse, slicked-back hair, looked up slowly from the glass he was wiping out as they approached. "What can I getcha?" His voice was as flat as his expression.

"Hi. We're looking for a woman named Tallulah Marsh. Her roommate said we might find her here," Evan said.

Evan had told her he'd called Tallulah that morning, and she'd agreed to meet with them and given Evan her address. But when they'd shown up there, her roommate, a twitchy bleached blonde with sores on her face, had told them that Tallulah had gone to this musty hole-in-the-wall.

Without turning his head, the bartender pointed his finger to the back of the bar, where the tables disappeared into gloomy darkness, the high backs concealing anything they might have been able to see from where they stood. "Thanks," Evan muttered. She felt like they were in some strange underworld, sort of like the bar from *Star Wars*, the movies she'd once watched with her dad. She fully expected that when they rounded the corner of the first booth, there would be an alarming alien.

Her assumption wasn't totally off.

"Tallulah Marsh?" Evan asked. The older woman raised her eyes, which had to be a feat, considering her eyelashes were about two inches long and heavily studded with rhinestones. She even managed to bat them at Evan.

"That's me, handsome. Looking for a date?" she asked, shooting Noelle a grin. "Couples are extra."

The woman grinned again, and despite her overdone makeup and white-blonde hair heavily streaked with pink, her cheeky smile was warm and made Noelle want to smile back.

"I'm Evan Sinclair. We spoke on the phone this morning."

"Yes. You sounded like a dream on the phone, and you look like one too." She gave him a wink. "You said you had questions."

"I do. We do." He gestured to Noelle. "This is Noelle Meyer. We wanted to ask you about a police report you filed a few years ago."

Her expression faltered. She glanced between them and nodded. "For a price, I'll give you just about anything," she said.

A price.

Evan reached for his wallet and took out the bills he had inside. It looked like a couple hundred dollars. Well, there went their slot machine fund. "Is that enough?" he asked.

She picked it up, taking her time counting it out, and then stuffed it in the front of her shiny pink jumpsuit. From where Noelle was standing, she could see that the shorts or skirt or whatever it was ended at the very tops of her thighs, and tall white boots hit just below it.

"Have a seat," Tallulah invited.

Noelle scooted in first and steeled her spine not to give in to the instinct to investigate what she might be about to sit down on. The inside corner of the rounded booth was so murky, it was like hurling herself into a terrible-smelling void. No telling what she'd encounter. Tallulah was watching her, one brow raised, lips tipped slightly. She had the feeling she'd passed some test Tallulah had just given. Good. Maybe she'd be more likely to open up to them if she didn't see them as prissy and afraid of dark corners. She had a feeling Tallulah's life was full of them.

Of course, she didn't know that they'd wallowed in their own filth—and that of other strangers, too, though she hardly wanted to bring that to mind—for over a month once and lived to tell the tale.

Evan slid in next to her, his thigh pressing against hers. The interior of the booth smelled like old vomit and bleach and something sweet, but she didn't think it smelled like a dead body, and so things could be a lot worse. "I'm a private investigator in Reno," Evan said. "I've been looking into what I believe is a series of crimes, not only because I believe they might be ongoing, but because we"—he gestured between himself and Noelle—"were victims of the group of criminals orchestrating these crimes."

"You were locked in cages like animals?" Tallulah asked.

"Yes," Noelle said. "And asked to make sick choices between hurting the other person or being hurt ourselves."

Tallulah watched Noelle for a moment from beneath the curtain of her jewel-studded lashes. "Yeah, that's what they did to me," she finally said.

"We read your police report," Evan told her. "They didn't take your claim seriously."

"Listen, good-lookin', I'm a prostitute with a drug past and an arrest record as long as my lashes." She offered a smirk, batting said lashes, but her smile quickly faded. "They never take women like me seriously. They told me I needed to get off the streets and stop going home with perverts. True enough, right? Like I'm gonna disagree? Maybe you got a real nice penthouse and a bag of cash I could live off of for a few years. Get me off the street? I asked the cop." She leaned in, her bangles clicking on the chipped brown or gray or dark-green tabletop as she laced her hands in front of herself. "But this wasn't some weird pervert. And believe me, I've had my share of those. One guy I went home with when I first got started in the business locked me in his basement for a week and took advantage six ways to Sunday. That's another story altogether, right? But this was different. This was . . . organized, I guess."

Evan and Noelle looked at each other, and Evan nodded at Tallulah. "Yes, ours too." He told her the basics of what had happened to them, waking in darkness, caged, asked to sacrifice the other in various ways. He made it brief. Which was good so he wouldn't potentially lead her story, but he also obviously wanted Tallulah to trust him and be honest about what had happened to her. Noelle knew just by watching him that he was good at his job. Naturally empathetic. Easy to open up to. And it was clear to Noelle that Tallulah had good reason not to trust those who'd listened to her story before. Or half listened anyway.

"Wow," Tallulah said once he'd wrapped up, her eyes moving between them. "You escaped. You burned that shit to the ground." She looked vaguely impressed, raising her hand and leaning around the booth before yelling, "Stan, a round back here."

They waited a minute as Stan shuffled their way, coming to stand at the head of the table.

"The usual," Tallulah said, setting her gaze on Noelle and raising her arched brows higher.

"Vodka tonic," Noelle answered the unspoken question, even though she wasn't really in the drinking mood, and it was still before 2:00 p.m. But if Tallulah wanted to share a round, they should probably share a round.

Stan turned his empty gaze to Evan, who ordered a beer on draft.

"I got out, too," Tallulah said. "Not in such a badass way, but I did."

"I think if you got out at all, you're allowed to claim badass status," Noelle said.

Tallulah tipped her chin.

"We'd love to hear about how you got out," Noelle said. "But first, who was in there with you?"

"Another dried-up old prostitute," Tallulah said, and despite the insult, there was obvious affection in her voice, and a heavy dose of sadness. "Iris. Real name, too, just like mine. Some people don't believe my name is really Tallulah, but it is. Tallulah and Iris, we said. Iris and Tallulah. Sounds like one of those froufrou clothing lines for babies who don't ever play in dirt. Poor things." She looked away, but Noelle saw the brief flash of grief. She was pretty sure that expression had not been in response to the poor germ-insulated babies but rather to the mention of Iris.

Another prostitute.

Interesting.

"What happened to Iris?" she asked.

"She didn't make it out," Tallulah said. "They shot her in the back. She was behind me. Right behind me. We were almost to the door. Old bat was slow as molasses." She put her face in her hands for a moment before sitting upright, expression grieved as her shoulders raised and lowered.

Stan arrived at the table with their drinks on a tray, and Noelle was grateful for the timing and that it gave Tallulah a chance to compose herself.

Tallulah picked up her drink and took a long sip through the straw. "Anyway, I was injured, but I made it out. They didn't come after me. I was surprised, to be honest, but grateful too. The police went back the next day, and there was nothing there. Not a sign. They made it disappear in twenty-four hours. They said I must have the location wrong. There were no cages, no body of an old sweet prostitute with a heart as big as the moon." That flash of pain again. "Nothing," she said. "Not a damn thing."

God, she couldn't even consider what it would have felt like to leave without Evan. Everything—everything—about her life would be different. Noelle was intimately aware of the friendship and connection forged, and grieved for Tallulah. "How'd you manage to get out of the cages?" Noelle asked softly.

Her eyes brightened, heavy lashes bobbing. "I used my wits," Tallulah said. "I engaged the guy with the key. I was always good with sweet talk. My gramps used to call me a silver-tongued devil, said I could sell ice cubes in a snowstorm." She laughed. "I mighta done big things. Better things. But then drugs came along, and well . . ." She shrugged, and though Noelle could see she'd once been beautiful, time and poor choices had taken a toll. At least she still managed to be colorful, even if she was doing it in the back corner of a musty bar.

"So you engaged the jailer . . . ," Evan said.

Tallulah nodded, taking another long sip of her drink and then looking off behind Evan into the gloom. "Yeah. I might not have even tried if I didn't keep getting these gifts with my meals that reminded me of who my gramps had seen me as." She looked at Evan, and her whole face seemed brighter. "It was almost like Gramps himself was sending me signs from above somehow, you know? *You got this, Lulabug,* I heard him saying. *Remember who you are.* And I did. For a little while anyway. I did."

CHAPTER THIRTY-SIX

Evan dropped his duffel bag on the bed and walked to the window and then pulled the heavy curtain aside. The window was tinted, and so although it was midafternoon, it looked like it was early evening. Par for the course in a gambling town, where it was in the casinos' favor to trick people's bodies into thinking it was perpetual night. Perpetual party hour.

"So what do you think?" Noelle asked from behind him. He turned from the window, watching her for a moment as she sat down on the bed, opening a bottle of water and taking a swig.

"I think Tallulah experienced the same thing we did."

"If she's not making it up."

"The police thought she was."

She screwed the top back on the bottle, her expression thoughtful. "Evan, is it possible that the man you spoke with in prison, and/or Tallulah Marsh, read about what happened to us and used the details from our crime to fake their own?"

"To what end?"

"I don't know. Maybe they were involved in something they were trying to cover up."

"But both of them went to the police on their own. They weren't arrested or even questioned for something else. I can't think of a motive for faking their story. Especially since nothing ever came of it."

"True," she said. "But people fake crimes for different reasons. Just because nothing came from it doesn't mean there wasn't intention . . . to get attention or . . . who knows. People do weird things all the time for reasons that are hard to understand."

He walked to the desk across from the bed and turned the chair toward her before sitting down. "But both of them? I had the same thought about Lars, even though my instinct was that he was telling the truth. But we have two people now who are telling similar stories."

She nodded, biting at her lip, her eyes meeting his. Something moved between them, a current that made the hairs on his arms stand up. They needed to stop meeting in hotel rooms like this. The thought almost made him laugh. *Pretend she's your business partner, nothing more.*

Right. *You used to be more honest, too, Evan.*

"Did you get the feeling Tallulah was lying?" he asked, forcing his attention back to the conversation at hand.

"No." She sighed. "But now we have two people who might have been victimized by the same people, or group or whatever, as we were, and we still have nothing to go on. The police checked out the locations, and even if they missed something in both cases, so much time has passed that even if we could persuade the local authorities to reexamine the scene, any evidence would be totally destroyed by now."

"The weird thing is," he said, "the police didn't believe Lars or Tallulah because of who they are. Their stories were easily dismissed. But we were different. We were noticed. The news showed up. Articles were written. If some sort of *choosing* was done, why choose two people who would be high profile?"

"Especially you," she said softly. He didn't deny it. As the son of Leonard Sinclair, Evan's abduction was never going to fly under any radar.

"Maybe they didn't mean to," she said. "Maybe they didn't know who we were. Or who you were."

"But again, our connection."

"Yes. You're right, it's off," she said on a sigh.

He sighed too. He felt her frustration. "We need to find someone else. We need to build more of a pattern."

"Well, I doubt Aria's going to be so gung ho to dig through reports for you now," she said. There was a note of bitterness in her tone the same way there had been that morning, and it made a well of hope open within him. She was jealous. At least a little. She uncapped the bottle again and took another sip.

"Probably not," he agreed, suppressing the smile that threatened. "Any more thoughts about why your dad might have sold your mom's ring and given the money to Dow?" he asked, changing the subject, since they'd run out of ideas on the current one.

"I racked my brain last night," she said, massaging her temple. "It had to be for something extremely important to my dad. Of all the money problems he had, all the bill collectors that called our house, he held on to that ring through it all. I didn't even know, but he did. I just can't imagine what he let it go for. Nothing makes sense."

"Like I said before, the only thing that makes sense is if he let it go for you," Evan said. "You would have been important enough for him to sell your mother's ring."

"I agree. It's the only thing that makes sense to me too. But I wasn't missing yet. And if he'd been somehow told in advance that I would be and was . . . I don't know, trying to pay someone off to stop it from happening, he'd have let me know in some way. He'd have warned me or hidden me or *something*. At the very least, he would have called me."

Yes. But there was some thread of truth floating around their attempts to understand. It was like he felt it, but he just couldn't connect it to the part that would then link it to something else until the trail led them to all the answers. It was frustrating as hell, because it wasn't like they had nothing. They just didn't have enough. Not yet anyway. "Hey," he said. "Since we're here, what do you say we change and go check out the strip? It might help us clear our minds. Sometimes ideas end up coming to me about a case when I put my brain on search and then go off to do something else." He smiled. But it was true. It'd helped before.

She ran her finger over the label on the water bottle for a minute, finally nodding. "Do you mind if I lie down for a little bit? I slept awful last night. I'd like a shower, and then I'll meet you in the lobby?"

He stood, holding out his hand. She took it, and he pulled her to her feet. "Sounds good. I'll see you in a couple hours."

"I'll be ready to win the biggest jackpot in town." She laughed over her shoulder as she opened the door.

"You're here with me," he called to her. "You already did." The door shut, but he heard her laugh from the hall outside.

CHAPTER
THIRTY-SEVEN

Grim moaned as he sat up, his head swimming. But after a moment, the world cleared, and for the first time in a damn long time, there was no pounding in his brain.

He still remained caged, however.

He would have preferred an aching head.

The kid was already up. He heard him using the toilet and turned away to give him what privacy he could as he brought one arm over his chest, stretching it, and then doing the same with the other one.

The paper poppy caught his eye, and he wondered again who had sent it and what the point was of reminding him of the daughter he'd loved and lost, the little girl who had been murdered because of him.

There was the whooshing sound of the toilet flushing, Cedro's waste being sucked into some container below wherever they were being held captive. Was this whole setup designed in a way that could be easily disassembled once he and Cedro were dead? DNA washed away, carted away, swept away.

How easy it would be to dispose of their bodies. Just drop them off somewhere in the unforgiving desert and leave them for vultures. If their bones were ever found, which was unlikely at best, the kid would be thought to have made the poor decision to cross the desert in search of a better life, Grim illegally transporting him.

What ripe pickings monsters had. So *many* throwaways to choose from. He looked at that handmade flower again. Poppy hadn't been a throwaway. Neither had her mother. Not to him.

He used the toilet, flushing just as he heard the clunk of the trays being delivered. He crawled on his knees to the end of his cage and took the tray from inside the shaft where it'd been lowered. There was another white napkin on this tray, and when he lifted it, there was a prayer card below. Grim picked it up, looking at the picture of the blessed mother on the front and then turning it over. On the back was the "Our Father" prayer in Spanish. What the fuck was this? Was someone mocking him?

He read it and then flipped it back over, running his finger over the art. *Oh.* Yes. There. Those small bumps.

"What do you have?" Cedro asked.

"A prayer card," Grim murmured. "Did you get anything?"

"The same," he said, holding his up.

"Can I see it?" Grim asked.

Cedro hesitated, clearly considering whether it was something he should guard from Grim. But then he shrugged, obviously deciding that in their situation, a prayer card was of little value, if any at all, setting it on the floor and flicking it across to Grim.

Grim picked it up. The picture on the front was the same, but instead of "Our Father," the prayer on the back was the Hail Mary. Grim read through that one, too, and then used his finger to feel the small bumps hidden within the artwork on the front.

His heart was beating swiftly, pumping blood through his veins. Making him feel alive in a way he hadn't in a very, very long time.

Grim ate the roll and drank the Styrofoam cup of water. He saw Cedro doing the same from his peripheral vision. He sat down, stretching his legs as far as they would go in the narrower direction of the crate he was in.

"Who was in that locket?" Cedro asked after a few minutes.

Grim considered not answering, but again, hell, the kid had sacrificed for him. And by the expression on his face when he'd returned, he'd paid a hefty price. "My daughter," he said.

"What's her name?"

"Penelope." *I called her Poppy.* Who had known that? "And she's dead. She died five years ago."

The kid considered him. "Is that why you're drinking yourself to death?"

He let out a surprised chuckle that ended in a sigh. Direct. But not wrong. He'd been drinking heavily before that too. But it'd definitely increased after that. "Yeah," he admitted. "Most of it anyway."

"What's the rest?"

That I was responsible. That I've seen too much evil to care much about life anymore. All these things were true, but he didn't exactly know how to express them, especially to a fourteen-year-old kid. The fact that he was acknowledging them to himself was frankly surprising the hell out of him. "I guess I don't have a lot to live for, kid," he said.

"Kid," Cedro scoffed. He pointed his finger at him. "Listen, I didn't save your eye so you could go and kill yourself once we get out of here," he said, a clear note of anger in his voice.

Grim almost laughed but held it back. *When we get out of here.* So the kid had a pipe dream. Or he didn't get what this was about. The chances of them escaping this were close to nil. He turned his head and then nodded to the candies sitting in the corner of Cedro's cage. "You didn't eat your peppermints."

Cedro shrugged. "I'm saving them."

"For what?"

Before the kid could answer, the door slid open, both of them turning toward the same man who'd come into the room the day before. Only this time, he headed straight for Grim's cage. "You've been rented."

Fuck. *Fuck.* "Fuck you."

The man barked out a laugh. "You have a choice of course."

"Fuck you," Grim repeated. This time the man didn't laugh.

"Come with me, or I take his tongue."

His tongue. He didn't look at Cedro. He didn't want to see the look on the kid's face. "Show me the way," he said to the man. The man looked vaguely disappointed but took the key from his pocket and opened the lock on the top of Grim's cage, inaccessible and blocked by a square piece of metal. The front folded down, and Grim walked out, half hunched over. He came to his full height once he'd exited, stretching his back.

The man waited for Grim to walk in front of him, holding the Taser, ready to shoot Grim should he make any sudden moves. He didn't glance at Cedro as he shuffled past his cage.

"Open the door," the man told Grim once they'd walked along a long hallway and turned down another, eventually ending up at a door.

Grim's mouth was dry, his heart beating swiftly. He opened the door, his breath stalling at what he saw, his brain attempting to make sense of what this was.

It was a treadmill.

A *treadmill.*

And behind it and on each side were wide pits of burning coals, surrounded by what looked like electric fencing.

"One hour," the man said, barely suppressed glee in his tone. "You run for one hour."

One *hour?* Grim stared in mute horror. He'd just spent the week puking up his guts and then sitting or lying in a cage. He didn't think he could run for ten minutes, much less an hour. And when he fell off, he'd fall into . . . a pit of fire with no escape.

"There's still time to change your mind," the guard offered. "His tongue, or you run."

CHAPTER THIRTY-EIGHT

Noelle shut the heavy drapes in her room and fell asleep for a good two hours before waking up and taking a long, hot shower. She dressed in the outfit she'd brought to go to dinner, a black minidress with slightly puffed sleeves and some lace detailing on the body. It was sort of casual and sort of not, and she'd bought it for a cocktail party at Sweetgrass three years before and hadn't worn it since. She really had no idea why she'd packed it to go to Reno other than that she didn't know exactly what their investigation would entail and she wanted to be prepared. Little did she know she'd be wearing it on what was essentially a date with Evan in Vegas. Not a *romantic* date but a date between business associates who needed to clear their minds for a few hours with some bright-light distraction. What had he said? Put your mind on search. She didn't know if there was some specific process to that, so she simply whispered the word *Search* and went about getting ready.

Evan knocked on her door when he said he would, giving her a sweeping glance, appreciation in his gaze that she didn't want to admit thrilled her. They ate dinner at a steak house on the strip, a dim restaurant with red velvet booths and black-and-white photographs on the walls of all the celebrities and sports stars and politicians who had once dined there. Noelle ordered some fruity drink on the menu that came in a gargantuan glass with maraschino cherries and plastic swords and paper umbrellas and a wedge of pineapple at the top. It made Evan laugh when she picked up the heavy goblet and took a sip, and he shot a picture with his cell phone to send Callie.

And, God, it felt good, and it felt weird. And maybe every interaction she ever had with this man from now until the end would feel slightly surreal, because they'd been trapped in cages together, for Christ's sake, and now they were sitting in a restaurant, laughing and drinking cocktails as big as their heads.

How could those two worlds both exist simultaneously on one planet?

And yet . . . they did.

After dinner, they walked along the strip to another, larger casino, Noelle dazzled by all the lights and the sounds. She'd grown up in a casino town, but that had never been part of her world. Having lived in a working-class neighborhood, she'd never done the touristy things, and later . . . never had the opportunity to party. She'd never felt safe enough. She'd lost so much by such a young age, and the only thing she could focus on was surviving week by week. Sometimes day by day. And then finding out she was pregnant . . . well, that changed everything.

A cocktail waitress brought them watered-down drinks as they sat at the slot machines and fed them tokens and came within a few dollars of losing every cent they'd set aside to gamble with, which wasn't much. But she considered it money well spent, and she could tell by the smile on his face that he did too. She couldn't remember the last time she'd had so much fun. She'd needed it, and she hadn't even known. She allowed herself to feel young and dauntless, just for a little while. She looked at Evan sitting on the short stool next to her, casually putting their last few tokens into the machine. "Thanks for tonight," she said.

He looked over, and her breath halted. He was so gorgeous, and he looked so happy too. So . . . *carefree.* The lights behind him flashed and blinked, creating a colorful halo, startling her. She'd gotten a small glimpse of his unreserved happiness when he'd been flying a kite with Callie, but it hadn't looked like this. Because he hadn't been fully uninhibited then. It was as if he'd been testing his fatherhood status, overcome by the shock of it, nervous perhaps, about what the future looked like.

Maybe before they'd been locked in those cages, unlike Noelle, he'd often been carefree. He'd come from a wealthy family with status, he'd been popular all his life, guys had wanted to be him, and girls had swarmed him in school. Yes, she supposed he'd lived many happy days, but she'd never been a party to it, not like she was now, and she felt frozen in the ray of his joy. *Beautiful.* His eyes softened as he stared at her. "My pleasure," he said.

He pulled the lever, and they lost the last bit of their money, both doubling over and laughing. She wasn't sure what was funny exactly. It just was. Maybe it was that their luck had apparently run out. She was okay with that, though, if running out of luck in this instance meant they weren't going to be tycoons. Once, they'd received all the luck they needed just when they needed it, and that's why they were here now, laughing in the face of loss. Because they *could.* What a wonderful thing to lose and be able to say *no big deal.*

They walked through the casino, people-watching. Noelle's thoughts swirled, the lights and the sounds and the competing noise causing her to go deeper into her own mind. Everywhere gamblers were betting. Some winning, most not. What was the draw that so many had to taking a risk, by pulling a lever, or tossing a pair of dice, or laying down a hand of cards? Was it that brief moment of soaring hope that was so addictive, even if it was almost guaranteed to crash?

They walked on, Noelle's mind continuing to wander. Words and phrases Tallulah Marsh had said kept popping forward, and she swore she could see them, written in a glittery pink the same as the woman's outfit, flashing like the rhinestones on her lashes. *It was like someone knew me.*

Who? Who had known her? And hadn't Noelle felt the same?

A slot machine on her right caught her attention, the cartoon animals grinning wildly. A bear, a moose, a rabbit.

Little rabbit.

He'd called her *little rabbit* because she'd called herself that first. She reached for the conversation from the room she'd spent eight years trying to forget. She was floating somewhere between here and there, the surrounding chaos making her feel like she was in a dream. Her hand in Evan's as he led her along. Safe.

The man with the very slight accent—or maybe *accents*—had given her the graphite from the pencil. She was certain that's why he'd made the request that he had. Not because he'd wanted a picture drawn by her. That was subterfuge. He'd known she would understand its possibility. He'd emphasized the word *break*, which had made her remember it. And then he'd uttered, *You're so* hot. And it'd seemed odd because it was. He'd been offering her clues. *Break. Pencil. Hot. Fire. Oh.*

She stumbled slightly, catching herself. "Hey, are you okay?" Evan asked, stopping and turning toward her.

"Yes. I'm fine. Can we go back to the room?"

"Yeah. Of course. We're basically penniless anyway." He laughed. He didn't care. He was a PI who lived in a nondescript apartment after he'd been surrounded by luxury, and all that had obviously meant nothing to him because he'd given it up to pursue his own dream, a career where he brought justice to others but one that might never result in great wealth.

She thought back to that conversation they'd had so long ago in the café in San Francisco when he'd told her he wasn't happy at Stanford. He'd felt himself heading toward the exact life his father led and said that it felt like a death sentence. And so he'd changed paths, despite the fact that it must have been difficult. Evan had never taken the more predictable route because it was easier and expected of him. He'd forged his own way. He valued things far beyond money and power. His life was the proof of that.

You're wonderful, Evan Sinclair.

They made their way through the casino and then out onto the street where the weather was still and warm. Desert air.

Like Reno. *Like Mexico, where you limped over the cracked earth.* She grabbed Evan's hand again, taking the initiative, whereas before he had been the one to take hers, and he looked over at her, seeming surprised. But then he gripped her tightly, and they walked the rest of the way to their hotel.

"Hold on, just a second," she said, sitting on one of the lounge chairs next to the pool as they walked through the open area. She slid off her heels, giving a short laugh. She rarely wore them, and they'd given her blisters that she was only noticing now.

Evan sat on the lounge chair next to her and lay back. She looked over her shoulder as she massaged her foot, giving him a slight smile and then lying back too. The stars above were so clear, so bright. He reached out and took her hand, and she remembered the moment they'd lain like this in the desert, bloody and broken and staring at these very same stars. *Gemini. The twins.* She wanted to laugh and she wanted to cry and she wanted to clench her eyes shut, but she couldn't. She'd just begun to see.

"Do you . . . want a drink in my room?" Evan asked as they both sat up. "Or just a water . . . we could order room service, too, if you're hungry. Maybe dessert?"

He was nervous, and it made her smile. "Water would be good. I . . . I think I remembered something . . . maybe."

Ten minutes later, the elevator dinged, and they got off on their floor and then walked the short distance around the corner to Evan's room. He unlocked the door, and they both went inside, where she kicked off her heels again and sat on the desk chair, bringing her other foot up and massaging that one.

That man had massaged her too. He'd touched her. He'd let his hands linger wherever he'd wanted. He'd brought her pleasure that had also hurt.

She started to shut her eyes, to shake her head and block it out, but then stopped, squeezing her foot to keep herself there. In that room of horrors.

"All those things we received, Evan . . . the graphite from the pencil, the rose petals . . . some of them were random . . . gifts . . . but some of them were not."

He pulled two waters from the mini fridge and handed one to her. "Yes. I agree. It was like someone was trying to help us."

Okay, great. She didn't have to convince him of that. She nodded. "Yes, so from what we know, many people were watching us."

"Yes," he said. "Because it was a sort of game. Sickos who put us in cages to see what we'd do. For the pure thrill of it. Like a coliseum of sorts."

Coliseum. Like the Roman Colosseum, where kings had watched slaves fight for their lives for the pure entertainment of it. A chill made her lift her shoulders and then drop them. "Yes, so there would have to be money involved, right?"

"Always follow the money," he murmured. "So they—whoever those sickos were—watched us from a live feed that showed everything. They'd pay to watch. It was a digital coliseum, and they were the crowd in the stands."

She pictured all those dull-eyed gamblers they'd walked past in the casino. "Yes. But what if they didn't just watch. What if they were also given the choice to . . . bet."

That seemed to surprise Evan. "On what? On the choices we'd make from the ones given?"

She nodded.

"And then some of them rented us for purposes of sex or violence," he said.

289

"Yes. But other victims, who were maybe not so 'rentable,' for lack of a better term, were placed in different situations."

"But the purpose was always to see how much another person would be willing to suffer in order not to be the cause of someone else's."

"Twisted," she whispered. "But on paper, interesting."

"Too bad it wasn't just on paper."

"Too bad."

"Okay, so which of the watchers sent us the random gifts? Like the butter or the peanuts."

"Maybe the renters sent food gifts as sort of a demented way to say thank you. Maybe it brought them some sick sort of glee to see us eating it. Maybe some of them were trying to keep us healthy-ish so the game would continue."

"And the other gifts? The ones that weren't random?"

"They—or maybe just he or she, but I think more likely a he—were supplying us with items that might help us escape. That *did* help us escape."

"Like the pencil. That you used to start a fire." He paused. "The million-dollar question is, How would someone guess you'd even know how to do that?"

"Maybe he knew I was the daughter of an electrician. I knew how to start a fire in an electrical outlet because I'd followed my dad around on jobs since I was a kid."

He scratched his jaw. "I mean, I wouldn't have known how to do that. A pencil, or the uses for what's inside it, would have flown right over my head."

"Right. It was personal. He'd researched us."

Evan appeared slightly dubious, and so she bit her lip, trying to think of the right way to clarify this. For a moment there in the casino, it had clicked in her mind, and she didn't think she was explaining it adequately enough, or maybe it was just that in her mind, the thought had been braided together with the *feeling*, and she had no way to convey that part.

"What about you?" she said. "You were given that mallet. I'd guess it was approved by whoever oversaw that kind of thing because it was presented as a musical instrument to go along with our singing. But that wasn't the true intention of the sender. And you knew it wasn't. Maybe the person who sent it knew you'd smash your hand to get it through the bars."

He paused as though he'd already considered her being sent a tool that would allow her to start a fire but hadn't considered what he'd been sent. And how he'd used it. "How could he know that, though? How could anyone?"

"It was the first thing that was threatened," she said quietly. "I saved your fingers in exchange for my virginity."

He turned away, but not before she saw the deep pain in his eyes.

"It hurts you, even now," she said.

"Jesus, of course it does."

"Someone saw that. They gambled on you crushing the bones in your hand. And they were right."

"Okay." His voice was choked. "Okay." He was quiet for several moments, as though weighing that possibility, letting it sink in. "A part of me relished it," he finally said. An admittance. One she could tell was difficult for him to utter. "I felt so damn guilty for what you'd paid with for my fingers. I almost enjoyed each blow." Unconsciously, he extended his fingers and then curled them in a fist.

Oh God. "Evan—" she said, her voice breathy.

"I know. I know I didn't need to feel that way, but I did. Sometimes I still do." He turned back toward her, uncapping the water and taking a long swig. "So what you're saying is someone bet on me breaking my own hand?"

She watched him for a moment but took his cue to keep going. Keep looking at this. "Yes, but I don't think it was a singular bet. I think it was one link in a . . . string." She paused as she looked down for a moment, her mind zipping through each stage of their escape, and then she raised her head. "Maybe that was it, one of the bets was whether we'd escape. Whether or not we'd manage to get free."

He was quiet for a moment as he appeared to think that over. "So us getting free was always a possibility?"

"Probably a very remote one. The only reason we did is that we were sent an array of the exact things we needed to get past one barrier and move on to the next."

"Damn." He gave his head a small shake and raised his brows. She could see by his expression just what he thought, and she agreed—it was a lot, and her brain hurt too. "I mean, there would have to be rules, right? Like you couldn't just send a gun on our food tray? Whoever helped us—whoever made that bet—would have to strategize and plan and then hope we'd *get* it without being told."

"Yes. Which would mean our entire escape was choreographed, in a way."

"Who, though? What type of person could do that? But wouldn't call for help for us?"

He crossed his arms over his chest, leaning his shoulder on the cabinet that held the television. She chewed at the inside of her cheek for a moment, trying to see the entire picture of what they were discussing. It was difficult, though. They were assuming quite a lot, and the rest of it sounded too unbelievable to be true. But they had to brainstorm. What else did they have?

"Evan," she said after a moment. "I have to tell you about this man."

"What man?"

"One of the men who rented me."

She saw him tense, but he took his time answering, taking a long drink of water and using the back of his index finger to wipe his bottom lip slowly. "We said we were never going to talk about that."

"We never said that."

"It was understood, Noelle."

She tipped her head, conceding the point. "It was. Yes. But now?"

He pushed off the armoire, pacing toward the wall. "Now what?" he asked when he'd turned back to where she sat.

"Why honor that understanding? We kept secrets then out of self-preservation. But now . . . don't you think it will help to talk about some of what happened in that second-floor room? Maybe not all of it but . . . we don't have anything to be ashamed of, Evan. We were victims, you know that."

He didn't say anything. She saw the churning emotion in his expression, and she wanted to go to him, but she didn't. She sensed by his stance that he'd push her away. "One stands out," she said. "One man stands out. And I think there's a possibility that he's the one who sent the items we needed. He's the one who requested that I write him a note or draw him a picture with the pencil that I broke to extract the graphite. He led me toward that conclusion even before I was given the tool." *Break . . . You're so* hot. "I picked up on his clues because he used a form of the language we'd been speaking, very subtly murmuring some words and emphasizing others. The blindfold helped because it made my sense of hearing that much more sensitive, but mostly I was primed to listen in a specific way because of our secret language."

"Do you think he knew what we'd been doing?"

"Maybe. But if he did, he didn't use it to expose us. He used it to help us." She took in a deep breath. "But it wasn't only that. It's like . . . he knew me. He played me like a fiddle. And thank God, but how?" Her eyes were cast to the side now, and she stared behind Evan, unseeing, thinking aloud as much for herself as for him. "I think he sent the rose petals and the fingernail trimmers and probably the mallet too."

He stared at her, his expression so troubled. She saw the light of curiosity, and she knew he thought she might be onto something. It made the pain of the recollection worth it. She was pulling forth these awful memories for a reason. He took the few steps to her, and he reached out his hand. Without thinking at all, she grasped it, and he pulled her to her feet and led her to the small sofa near the window.

They both sat down, facing each other. "What else do you remember about this man?" he asked gently.

She pulled in a deep breath and let it out slowly. "He didn't wear a mask, or at least he said he didn't. But he had me blindfolded, so I never saw him. But his voice . . . he sounded older, maybe late fifties or early sixties. He called me *little rabbit*," she murmured. She closed her eyes, bringing him forth, not able to help the grimace that took over her features. She didn't hide it. She didn't need to, not from Evan. "He was . . . cultured. I could tell that. He had a slight accent, very slight. It was odd, though, because it seemed to almost . . . move between different ones and only linger in certain words."

"Different accents?"

"Yes. I don't know how to explain it. But in any case, it'd been a long time since he'd spoken exclusively in whatever language, or languages, he'd once used."

"Like that man who owned the antique shop that we spoke with."

"Yes . . . but Mr. Baudelaire's accent was very obviously French, and only French. I recognized it. I'd heard that language before. It was easy to identify his accent."

"Do you think you might recognize the other man's accent if we played some recordings of people speaking in different languages?"

She opened her eyes and gave her head a slight shake. "I don't know. Probably not. I can't even bring it forth now. The FBI had me describe what I could of the men from that room, other than their faces, which were masked, and I couldn't describe that man's accent then either. Just that he had a very slight one. But I didn't listen to recordings."

"Maybe we should try that. When we get back to Reno," he said.

"Maybe." Although she didn't know how that would help. What if she listened to hundreds of recordings and thought she recognized his accent as Turkish or Swedish or somewhere else she'd never been? What did they do with that?

"What else?" he prodded gently. Their knees were touching, and his nearness made her feel slightly nervous but mostly comforted.

"He talked about jewels." She squinted her eyes, trying to cast her vision back, turning on lights in the place she'd tried so hard to black out. "He told a story about a man who collected women and draped them in jewels."

"Collected?"

"I think he meant abducted. Stole. He said something that related the situation to us."

"Okay." His voice held a deeper note of curiosity now, and it spurred her on.

"I think he told me that a pregnancy occurred with one of these women, and twins were born, a boy and a girl. And he mentioned a ball that turned into a massacre."

He blinked, reaching out and taking her hands in his. "Noelle, all of that might be something to look up. Certainly if there was a massacre of some sort, it would be in the news. So would women reported missing . . . maybe there was even an arrest of someone who now is free, someone we can investigate."

"Or maybe it was all a load of crap." She paused. "I gave that information to the FBI, too, and they told me at the time that there was nothing in police databases that matched that type of crime."

He deflated slightly. "Maybe they weren't looking for the right things. Or maybe no one ever got caught."

"Maybe." She drew her shoulders up. She'd been the one who'd pushed this conversation, and she'd been eager to speak about it, to get it out. But it'd taken a lot out of her, too, and she suddenly felt the exhaustion that came with the weight of the memories from that upstairs room. The men who'd raped her, the way she'd bled, the way it'd hurt, how revolting she'd felt attempting to clean herself with her underwear and then putting them back on—the way the remembered pain hit her sometimes when she least expected it. *My God, it was so unspeakably disgusting.* She leaned back, depleted. Who had that man been, and how had he known her so objectively?

"We should go to bed," Evan said. "And talk more in the morning, or when something else comes to one of us."

She nodded, meeting his gaze. He was searching for something in her face, so she averted her eyes. She knew what he was looking for, and he'd find it if she didn't turn away. She wanted him too. She felt vulnerable and sad, and she wanted him the way she always wanted him when she felt alone in the dark. Noelle stood. "Thank you for tonight," she said. "I know it didn't exactly end as fun as it started off."

He stood too. "It's okay. You didn't really make this trip for fun. I enjoyed tonight." He looked briefly shy, boyish. "And maybe we have another something to follow when we get back."

He walked her to the door and then stood watching as she let herself into her room. She was exhausted, physically, mentally, and emotionally, and yet after she'd sent Paula a quick text and climbed into bed, she spent a long time staring at the ceiling, restless and sleepless and swearing she could feel Evan's heat emanating from the wall next door.

CHAPTER
THIRTY-NINE

Noelle looked around at Evan's office. It was small, and he obviously hadn't put a lick of design thought into it, but it was oozing potential. There was exposed brick along the far back wall, the ceiling was high and had black-painted exposed ductwork, and there were two extremely tall windows looking out onto the street that let in a ton of natural light. It had a good vibe, even if it desperately needed a throw rug and a few pieces of art.

"The typical shady PI digs?" he asked.

She laughed. "No, actually, Sherlock, I was just thinking the opposite. You need something much more dreary with less character if you're going to uphold the shady PI role."

He grinned. "Have a seat." She took a few steps to the plastic chair on the other side of his wooden desk with the black leather inset. The desk was cool. The chairs looked like he'd picked them up at the local Walmart. She sat down on the cheap plastic and crossed her legs.

Evan took the seat across from her and pulled out a file. They'd arrived back in Reno the afternoon before, and she'd spent the rest of the day cleaning out the remainder of the items in the storage container. She'd scheduled a pickup with a local secondhand store that had taken the large items of furniture she didn't want. She'd considered keeping her dad's recliner, but there was no practical way to get it to South Carolina, and she didn't have room for it in her cottage anyway.

She did keep one of her mother's plates, though not the entire set. She would put it on a stand on her bookcase when she got home. And she found the box of photographs she'd been looking for and took that too. The bright spot had been calling Callie and telling her that she had photos to share with her when she got home. Photos of when Noelle was a little girl. Callie had giggled with delight, and the sweet, innocent sound had given Noelle a much-needed boost.

After returning the key to the rental office, she got her deposit back and thought, *That's it.* The job had been necessary, but it was also another goodbye—a *final* goodbye—and she'd been exhausted when it was done. That, in combination with the poor night of sleep she'd gotten the night before, had her in bed by nine and out cold by ten after.

She'd needed it.

Evan, apparently, had spent the rest of the day doing online research into anything that might have connected to the story the man with the slight accent had told her so long ago.

Jewels.

Abducted women.

Twins.

A potential massacre.

Like the FBI, he hadn't found any specific crimes that matched perfectly, but he told her he did have some possibilities, and so she'd met him in his office.

"What did you find?"

He opened the folder, and she could see that it was a short pile of printouts. "I have to believe that if the part of the story about abducted women is true, the man who committed the crime was never caught. Or even charged. Maybe he killed them and then died himself, and his crimes were never discovered."

"Even a massacre?"

He shrugged. "Maybe it was a small massacre."

She gave him a look that was the melding of a smile and a grimace. "Hmm. Okay. Well, that doesn't help us."

"No, but I did find a few things that might be of interest. I narrowed my search to specific dates, which made it a little easier."

He handed her the printouts, and she took them, scanning the page at the top of the pile. She moved that one to the back and read the second one. Each page was a series of articles from different locations about local missing women who were never found. She pulled the third page forward and read that one. "Slovakia?" she said. "You went worldwide?"

"Where I could," he said. "Because of the accent."

"Good thinking," she murmured, looking quickly through the rest of the stack. It was pretty depressing to know that a basic internet search pulled forth so many missing women.

"I still need to do some digging," he said. "But it'll take more time. As it relates to other countries, there's not a lot in English, so I pulled what I could for now. That's just my initial find."

Noelle moved back to the one from Slovakia, reading quickly through the headlines for that one. Several young girls had gone missing. Children under twelve. *There was once a man who collected things, very fine things. Jewels. Rubies. Emeralds. Diamonds. And he draped them on the women he stole.* No, if she was going to take the man who'd told her the story at his word, then this didn't exactly fit.

She flipped the page, reading brief snapshots of crimes from the Netherlands that weren't quite right either. There was the headline from an article near the bottom of that page that interested her, and she read the small portion that Evan had printed out and compiled on the one page. "Do you have the entirety of this article printed out?" she asked, tapping her finger on the one she meant.

He craned his head slightly and then nodded. "Hold on." He had another folder on the other side of his desk, and he pulled that one out, going through the larger stack. She liked how he'd compiled snippets for each geographical location onto one page. It made it much easier to get an idea of what she was thumbing through. A few of them she'd been able to dismiss right away, as the timing didn't quite work as far as the age of the man she thought they were dealing with.

She scanned the page he'd handed her. "Local authorities looked into a man in Brussels named Dedryck Van Daele, the heir to Van Daele Diamonds, a major diamond-mining company." She looked up. "Diamonds?" Jewels. *He draped them in jewels* . . .

Evan nodded. "I remembered you mentioned jewels and thought that might be an interesting link."

She read through a few more paragraphs. "So they looked into this man named Dedryck because a few young women went missing in the area where he lived, and one of those women—a waitress in town—told her friend that Dedryck had invited her to a party a few nights before she disappeared." She frowned. "That's all the evidence they had? That sounds kind of weak."

"I guess the local authorities thought so, too, because I didn't find any more information about the police looking at him for the other disappearances that followed."

"Did Dedryck have children? Specifically twins?"

"No," Evan said. "At least none that he claimed at the time. I actually can't find any more information on him after that one article. The family business is no longer in operation."

"Hmm." That was interesting too. There was no one available to carry on the family dynasty? Or had it failed financially? Was it worth looking into? "Dedryck would be . . . what, in his eighties?" she asked. "Did you look for a record of his death?"

"I did, but none exists. So either I didn't look hard enough or he's still alive but living and working somewhere else."

"Odd."

"I thought so too. But again, it might not be connected to the man who told you that story."

She sighed, setting the papers on his desk. "Even so, these crimes aren't even related to ours. They may or may not have something to do with some man I barely remember who told me a story that might be a lie." And if he'd told it to her for some other purpose, she had no idea what that might be. She let out a short laugh that held more frustration than humor. "I feel like we're wading into the weeds, Evan." And potentially about to trip down rabbit holes.

He ran a hand over his face. He looked as frustrated as she felt. And tired too. He was the one who'd stayed up half the night downloading files about missing women near and far.

"And I'm running out of time," she said softly. "I have less than a week before I'm scheduled to go home. I cleared out my dad's storage locker. I can't just hang around town. I need to get back to my life. I need to get back to Callie."

"You promised two weeks."

"That's up in five days."

"We've made progress, though."

"Not enough." She looked toward the window momentarily. "Listen, with your approval, I'm going to give that money to Louise." They'd discussed the money they found among Dow's things briefly on the plane to Vegas but hadn't come to any conclusions. Noelle knew she could have made a reasonable claim to it, considering it had almost certainly been the money her dad had been paid for her mother's ring. But he'd also apparently given it to Dow for reasons unknown. Noelle didn't feel right keeping it. And if the past-due medical bills she'd spotted on Louise's coffee table were any indication, the woman could use it.

"Are you sure?" Evan asked. "We could use it to buy your mom's ring back."

She shook her head, even while a buzz of yearning vibrated under her ribs. She wanted that ring. But . . . what did it matter? It wasn't like it had good memories attached to it, for her or for her father. Her mother had cheated on him and been shot because of the affair that led to her being where she shouldn't have been. "No. I'd rather give it to Louise."

He gave a small shrug. "I'm fine with that. It's your call."

"Meet for dinner?" she asked.

He paused, looking like he wanted to say something, but either he changed his mind or the right words didn't form. Instead, he simply nodded. "Do you like Indian food?"

"I love Indian food."

"Great. I'll text you with the name of a great little place near your hotel." She could see that he was both frustrated and slightly sad, and she wished she could change that, but she couldn't.

"Sounds good." She gathered her things, and he walked her to the door where they said goodbye. When she got down to the street, she looked up at his window to see him standing there, hands in his pockets as he stared down at her.

~

Noelle had run some errands and stopped in a couple of shops, looking for the perfect gifts for Callie, Paula, and Chantilly. She had dropped her purchases back at her hotel room and had picked up the cash in the duffel bag she'd left in the safe in the closet and was heading to Louise's house.

It was interesting being back in Reno. She'd held some amount of fear inside about returning to the place where so many personal tragedies had occurred to her. But she was surprised to find that everywhere she turned, there were good memories too. And while they didn't cancel out the bad ones, they helped dispel the anxiety she'd felt about being back in her hometown. Another victory, some more closure. And she was grateful.

Her phone rang as she was walking through the hotel lobby, and she pulled it from her purse, smiling to see that it was a FaceTime call from Callie.

"Hi, Sugar Plum." Her daughter's lovely face filled the screen and made her smile.

"Hi, Mommy!"

"How's my girl?"

"Good! Me and Paula went shell hunting, and I found the biggest one ever! I put it on my shelf." She turned the camera around for a moment so Noelle could see the large shell sitting among her books and other favorite items.

"You made sure it wasn't still someone's home, right?" she asked on a laugh.

"Yes," she said, turning the camera back around as she rolled her eyes. But then she grinned. "I miss you, Mommy."

"I miss you, too, baby girl. But I'll be home soon." She turned the corner, heading to where she'd parked her car. She didn't mention possibly coming home early, because she hadn't even checked to make sure there was a flight just yet. She'd do that tonight, after dinner.

"Paula wants to talk to you, Mommy."

"Okay. I love you, Callie. I'll talk to you in the morning, okay?"

"Okay, Mommy. I love you too."

Callie handed the phone to a smiling Paula, who was obviously making food at the counter as she spoke on the phone.

"How's it going there?" Noelle asked.

"Great! Callie and I have been all over town. She's showing me the best bike trails and candy shops."

Noelle laughed, clicking her key fob and then opening the door of her rental car and tossing the duffel bag onto the passenger seat before getting in. "I bet. Watch that one. She has her mother's sweet tooth."

"Oh, I'm aware." Paula smiled, but then her face went serious. She glanced over her shoulder and then moved to the other side of the kitchen. "How are . . . things?"

Noelle put the key in the ignition and turned the AC on but then sat back in her seat without buckling yet. "Hard," she admitted.

"Complicated." She squinted out the window for a moment and then looked back at Paula's concerned face. "We've discovered a few things that are odd, but nothing that leads anywhere specific."

Paula gave her a sympathetic look. "You'd have regretted it if you didn't try at all, though."

"I know. You're right. Anyway," she said, pulling her buckle across her body. "I might be coming home a little earlier than scheduled. I'll let you know."

"Take as long as you need. This is a vacation for me. Your daughter is a joy."

"Thanks, Paula. I owe you."

"You never owe me." She blew Noelle a kiss, and Noelle blew one back, and then they said goodbye, and Noelle disconnected the call before pulling out into traffic.

It took less than ten minutes to make the drive to Louise's apartment. Noelle smelled rain in the air as she got out of her car and looked up at the sky. It was pewter and deep gray, with beams of silvery light shining through the clouds. She never missed an opportunity to take in something beautiful, and she did that now, staring at that heavenly sky for a moment before putting the strap of the duffel bag over her shoulder and walking to Louise's door.

When the older woman answered her knock, her face registered surprise. "Oh. Hi. Did you forget to ask me a question?"

"No. We found something in your brother's things, and I wanted to return it to you."

"Something?"

"Money," she said, thrusting the bag toward her.

Louise frowned, blinking in confusion before she unzipped the bag and peeked inside. She sucked in a small breath. "This is—"

"Over ten thousand dollars. My dad apparently paid Dow for a job in cash, so, um, it's yours." Noelle gave her a smile. "I wish you the best, Louise."

She started to head back to her car when Louise called her name. Noelle turned, tilting her head to the side in question.

"Hold on one sec," the woman said, pulling at the scarf on her head the way she'd done before and then turning and disappearing for a minute. Noelle took the few steps back to her door, and Louise reappeared, holding something out to her. An iPad. "I'm sorry," she said. "I wasn't totally honest. This was in Dow's things. It was near the top of the box, and I found it when I moved. I even charged it a week and a half ago so I could wipe it and then sell it. I just hadn't gotten around to it yet." She looked momentarily embarrassed. Noelle pulled in a breath, reaching for the electronic device. "Sorry," Louise said. "I really needed the money."

Noelle shook her head. "Don't be. I understand. I'll . . . I'll look at this, and then I'll return it. You can still sell it if you want to."

Louise shook her head and nodded to the duffel bag she'd placed on the floor near the door. Tears filled her eyes, and she tugged on her scarf again. "No. Keep it. Do whatever you want. His code was our dog Scout's birthday, oh four eleven. Stupid man loved the hell out of that dog. Still cried when he talked about him until . . . well, until the last time I saw him. For someone so technical, he sure did pick an easy password, but that was Dow for you. Brilliant and stupid as hell. Anyway, I hope there's something on it that will help. Thank you for that." Again, she nodded toward the duffel bag. "You have no idea how much it will help."

Noelle walked to her car in a slight daze. Well, that was the last thing she'd expected. An iPad. Not a phone, which would have given her more hope of finding something. For all she knew, Dow had used this to download books to further impress that female friend. And yet even so, her heart sped up with excited hope. Anticipation of what might be on it.

She got in her car and cranked up the air and then turned on the iPad. It still had 10 percent charge. She let out a long slow breath as she typed in the code Louise had given her. The programs and apps popped up on the small screen, and Noelle opened the photos. There were only a handful, and at first, she didn't comprehend what they were. When she did, her eyes widened, and she almost dropped the device. "Oh my God," she breathed. She couldn't search much more right then, as anything else would require a wireless connection. She set the iPad on the passenger seat, and with shaking hands, she gripped the steering wheel. *Was this the link they'd been looking for?*

CHAPTER FORTY

Cedro let out a small yelp as the door slid open. He'd been drifting into a disturbing dream, and the sound had pulled him quickly from slumber. He watched as two guards entered this time, the man who had taken him out of there and the one who stood guard in the other room. One was holding Grim under his shoulders, and the other was carrying his feet. Cedro's pulse jumped, and he stared as they carted him over to his cage, tossed him inside, and then brought the door up and secured it.

Cedro waited for the men to leave before hurrying to the far side of his cage. "Hey! Hey! Are you alive?" he called. Panic rose in his throat. He didn't want to be alone. *Please don't be dead.*

Grim lay on the floor of his cage. He was soaking wet, and his skin was bright red. As Cedro stared, trying to see if he had injuries anywhere, the old man started *laughing*. It was soft at first, but then it rose. Cedro blinked. Had he gone insane? What had happened to him to drive him out of his mind? Grim wrapped his arms around his waist, turning onto his side and howling with laughter.

"What's wrong with you?" Cedro yelled. He wished he had something to throw at the man. His laughter was confusing and scary.

As if the older man had read his mind even while he was having fits of laughter, the sounds grew softer, the laughs turning to gulps and then to shallow breaths. He groaned, removing his arms from his waist and then turning onto his stomach, his cheek against the cold cement floor.

For several minutes, he simply breathed that way, drops of moisture rolling down his cheek. Was he soaked in . . . sweat? What had they made him do? "I thought you were dead," Cedro said.

"Almost," Grim remarked, peeling himself off the floor and rising slowly until he was sitting, slumped against the bars. "But not quite."

Cedro felt steaming mad, and he wasn't even sure why. He made a sound of disgust in his throat. *How could the old man laugh if they'd done to him what they did to me?* "If you wanted to die, why didn't you, pig?"

Grim smiled, and there was something almost gentle about it. "That's a good question." He sighed, then let out another small laugh that faded quickly. Cedro wasn't going to ask what was funny. Whatever had happened in that room down the hall had made him sweat buckets and made him laugh, but Cedro didn't want to know, because then he might have to tell Grim what had happened to him, and he couldn't do that.

Cedro glanced over at the two peppermint candies. He could throw the candies at Grim, but he'd probably miss with all those bars in the way, and even if they hit him, they wouldn't hurt at all. Plus, he wanted them. He didn't know why he was saving them; he just was. They reminded him of his father, some of the only good memories he had. His father had told him to eat them slowly, they could be a choking hazard . . .

Cedro turned his head to see Grim picking up the two prayer cards they'd both received, fanning himself with them for a moment, his expression thoughtful. "You know your prayers, don't you, Cedro? Your mother taught them to you, didn't she?"

Cedro made a grunting sound in his throat and swallowed down the emotion that the mention of his mother brought. Yes, he knew his prayers. He said them sometimes before he fell asleep, not because he was asking anyone for help but because they made him feel less alone.

"Good," Grim said, and something came into the man's eyes that Cedro didn't know how to describe. For a moment, the old man, drenched in sweat and barely sitting up in his cage, looked *fierce*. "Pray with me, Cedro," he said.

CHAPTER
FORTY-ONE

Noelle hardly remembered the trip to Evan's apartment, almost surprised she'd been able to guide herself there in a stupor of shock. She grabbed the iPad and her purse and then climbed out of her car and rushed toward his door.

It only took him a minute to answer her knock, his brow lowering when he saw her. "Noelle. Hey, I thought we were meeting for—are you okay?"

She thrust the iPad toward him. "I took the money to Louise, and she gave me this. It was Dow's. She was going to wipe it and sell it." She stepped inside, and he shut the door behind her.

"Have you looked at it?"

"Just the photos." She opened the iPad and then brought the photos up, handing him the device. She didn't know exactly what they meant. Her brain felt fuzzy, and she was having trouble connecting the dots between *this* and everything else they'd found.

Evan took it, his frown increasing as he scrolled through the handful of pictures. "These are pictures of . . . the gym where I used to go." He looked up at her. "The gym I was taken from."

"I thought so," she said. He'd never told her the name of the gym where he'd been snatched, but she'd recognized it as one that used to be—and perhaps still was—about ten minutes from their high school. All the jocks had used it. "What does it mean?" she asked.

Evan had opened something else on the screen, and his eyes widened as he looked at it. "He wrote the name and address of the gym in the notes app," he said. "And my name too."

She let out a breath. Okay, well, if they'd been wondering if there was a definite connection between Evan and the photos, they didn't need to guess anymore. Had Dow come upon information that Evan would be snatched and was gathering evidence? Was it why he was killed? Had he gone to her father because what he'd found involved the son of the man her father had once sued? Had her father learned something, too, and feared the same people who killed Dow were after him? Her mind veered from one question to the next.

Evan tapped on something else, and then paused, rotating the screen, and then rotating it again.

"What?" she asked.

He turned the iPad toward her. "This photo here. It's blurry and looks like a picture of a picture." He bit at his lip, appearing troubled.

She took the iPad from him and turned it in the same way he had, trying to make heads or tails of it. "It looks like the corner of a couch and the corner of a screen." It was an odd photo. It almost looked like someone had dropped a camera and it snapped a photo on the way down or like someone had been trying to take a photo secretively. She brought the iPad closer, squinting. "Can you see what's on the screen? You can see a portion of a website. Or maybe it's a whole website, but it's a strange one." It was weird because it wasn't the name of a business or anything recognizable. It looked like a string of numbers and letters, separated by slashes and dashes. She reached for her phone and realized that in her haste, she'd left it in her car.

"What's your wireless password?"

He gave it to her, and she typed it into the settings and then pulled up a search engine. She went back and forth, entering the website address from the picture a few numbers at a time. It was a long enough string that she couldn't remember it in its entirety. "Damn," she murmured when it told her the site didn't exist.

"Noelle."

She looked up, surprised by the grim expression he was wearing. "What is it?"

He rubbed his finger under his bottom lip for a moment. "What if . . . what if that was the website viewers used to watch us? To . . . send gifts . . . to rent us and whatever else was available as part of a sick game we were unknowingly playing?"

She frowned, blinking. She'd just been wondering at Dow's possible knowledge of Evan's abduction. But to have direct proof of people being caged and tortured? She shook her head. They had questioned the fact that Dow was a hacker, and maybe he'd come upon something because of those skills, but . . . "If Dow had hacked into the actual game, he would have called the police, whether he saw me or you or anyone. Any decent person would."

He shook his head. "The date on the notes app is from less than a week before I was abducted." His eyes speared her, and she blinked, looking away.

"What are you saying?" she asked. But she thought she knew. And it was too horrible to comprehend.

"I went missing from the gym in those photographs, the one listed by name and address in the notes app. The one where I had a physical therapy appointment scheduled for that day and that time. Someone knew I'd be there. Someone set me up to be taken. To be caged."

Her mind swirled. He was suggesting Dow didn't just know about his possible abduction but had been involved in it. Had set him up. "Dow would have no reason to do that. Dow didn't even know who you—"

"The date on the notes app is also the same day your father had an appointment at his shop," Evan said softly.

311

She gave a jolt as the further implication of what he was saying hit her. "No. No way. Are you blaming my father for this?" she asked, her voice incredulous with the shock she felt zipping down her limbs. "You think my father had his hacker friend break into this site and set you up to be part of this sick, nasty game as what? As what, Evan? Revenge against your father?"

"What else makes sense?" His voice was calm but wary. He was looking at her like he knew his suggestion was likely to make her explode in anger. And yet she also saw the resolve in his eyes. What he was saying made sense to him. But it didn't to her. *No.*

"*Anything* else makes sense," she gritted, attempting desperately to keep her cool even while her blood was boiling.

He let out a whoosh of breath, dragging his hand through his hair. She caught sight of the white scars on his knuckle, and they served to cool her ire. The moment he'd caused the terrible injury that had resulted in those scars flashed in her mind . . . the pure grit it had taken to keep *going* in the face of excruciating pain. For a greater purpose. As a punishment he didn't deserve. For her.

"Listen," he said. "He might have had second thoughts. Maybe he regretted it. Maybe that's why he sold the ring and gave the money to Dow to try to . . . I don't know, fix it somehow. But Dow *didn't* fix it. Instead, maybe he wasn't robbed but killed by whoever's site he hacked."

She shook her head. "That's all too wild. It's speculation. And it doesn't even make sense. My father would never do that. He wouldn't." She turned away, hugging herself.

"Are you sure?" Evan asked, coming up behind her and turning her back toward him. "My father ruined his life, Noelle. You even said it yourself. What better way to get back at him than to have his son murdered by monsters?"

"But your father wouldn't even know," she said, her voice weak. "You'd just go missing, and he'd wonder where you were." She tipped her chin, looking into his eyes, searching them, something dark slithering through her mind. He closed his eyes briefly, looking pained as though he'd heard the hiss of that slimy thing. "Unless your father . . ." Her voice was a mere whisper now.

"Unless my father is one of the men who watched," Evan said, his voice breaking on the last word. He cleared his throat, though, and she could see he was gathering himself. "Unless the photo of that website was taken at my home," he went on, his voice stronger now. "That looks like the color of the couch we used to have in our basement theater room. That camel-colored leather . . . it was unique."

She gasped out a sound of horror, bringing her hand up to cover her mouth. The couch. He'd recognized the couch. *Oh God.* She felt like she might throw up. She grimaced, shaking her head. She tried to work out the timeline, but her mind wouldn't cooperate. There had to be some detail that would make all this speculation impossible. But she couldn't think clearly enough to figure out what that was.

She shook her head again. "No, no, none of this is true. God, I can't even think this about my father! He's dead and gone and can't defend himself. I won't even entertain ideas like this about him."

"But you'll entertain them about my father? You don't have trouble believing he could do something evil and demented." He didn't sound angry or surprised. Which made her all the more livid. Because he was right. She had *no* trouble believing his father was capable of evil. The man had been enemy number one in her house as long as she could remember. She felt that way because it was how her father had felt, and she'd carried on that legacy because it was all she had to give him. It was up to her to keep his hatred alive. And, oh *God*, she was confused and angry, and she wanted to drop to her knees and cry.

But more than that, she wanted to fall into his arms. He saw it in her eyes, she knew he did, and he stepped closer, making himself available. She turned away. She wouldn't allow this need to take hold. She'd already made that clear.

"Stop turning away from me, Noelle, for Christ's sake. I can see that you need me. And I need you too. Okay, guess what? We thought we were enemies once and discovered we weren't. And maybe those initial feelings *were* born from sickness and trauma. Who the fuck cares? Does it really matter? Does it make them less real? I'm sick to death of deconstructing it. It's been seven fucking years, Noelle. How long do we need to test the theory that we only want each other because of the suffering we experienced together?"

She was shaking, and tears burned the backs of her eyes. She wouldn't look at him. She couldn't.

"Or maybe the real problem," he went on, his voice scratchy now with emotion, "the thing you really can't get past, even after all this time, is that my father killed your mother, and I'm a Sinclair. No matter what, that will never change. We agreed not to talk about it back then, we agreed that we had less of a chance to escape as enemies. And so we put it aside, out of necessity. But that necessity ceased to exist once we were free, didn't it? We never discussed it, Noelle, and maybe we need to now, because you've never let it go. *Look at me.*" She did. She lifted her eyes to his face. She owed him that much. "Does it fester inside? If you had acknowledged me as Callie's father, she'd be a Sinclair too. By blood, she is. Which is it, Noelle? Are you afraid that we'll *take* from you again like we did before? Or is it that when you look at me, when you look at our daughter, you wonder what your mother would think? How your father would feel? Does loving me seem like the deepest betrayal you could possibly commit?"

She let out a sob, but she didn't break eye contact. "Sometimes both." The whispered words eked from her lips like poison. She was afraid, and she was ashamed. It was awful, and it was true. He was right—her fear and her guilt had festered—and because she'd allowed it, part of her had rotted too. The admission had actual weight, because when it dropped from her lips, her shoulders curled forward, and she felt like she might fall to the floor.

He stepped forward, taking her in his arms, and she leaned against him. "I love you, Noelle. I would do anything to protect you. And our daughter. Haven't I proved that? Haven't I?" A moan made its way up her throat. He was solid and warm, and yes, he'd *always* protected her with everything he had to give. He'd always stepped toward her when perhaps he should have stepped away. She'd just confided her deepest, most shameful secret. She hadn't even ever verbalized it for herself. But he had, because he knew her and loved her anyway. His father had used the legal system once to take from them—not just her mother's life but her father's dignity, his trust, their happiness, their future. But Evan would never do that. She didn't deserve him. She didn't want to be that person, so irrational and so unfair. No one was responsible for the sins of their father, least of all Evan, who had only ever been good to her.

And, really, maybe he had reason to hate her too. Him being a Sinclair was part of the reason she'd kept Callie from him, and he should at least hate her for that, but he didn't. Was it possible her own father, the man she'd loved and trusted, had somehow arranged for him to be put in a cage and tortured for something he did not do?

It was all sick. So *much* sickness. So much depravity. And she suddenly realized that, amid all the muck, they might be the *only* thing that wasn't. She'd gotten it all wrong. So backward. In some small way, she'd started becoming what their fathers were, whether she'd known the extent of their perversion or not. Noelle and Evan were a rejection of all the sickness and disease that had come before them. Of all the lies, *they* were the truth. Or they could be. And somehow, deep inside, she knew they must celebrate that if they were going to continue forward. Because it was the only thing that would offer the strength they'd need. If hate was darkness, then their love would be the light.

"I'm sorry," she breathed. "Oh God, I'm so sorry."

He took another step toward her. "There's nothing to be sorry about."

"There is. There is. I've loved you all these years, Evan. I love you. I do." The truth. And it set her free from a different kind of cage.

He let out a groan that was filled with relief, and when he leaned in to kiss her, she didn't only let him, she met him halfway. They were like an explosion, like a galaxy melting, like the hottest fire that ever burned. They stumbled toward the couch, their lips never parting, tongues entwined, every atom in her body trembling with the singular need she'd held at bay for so, so long. Maybe it was so good because they'd known the depths of despair together. Maybe each joining would forever be a celebration that . . . they. Were. Not. *There.* Was that so bad? To rejoice? To be joyful in each other's presence, a constant exalting of the fact that they both were free of the chains they'd once worn? Free to love. Free to feel pleasure. No bars between them, not even air.

CHAPTER
FORTY-TWO

Silvery morning light seeped around the blinds. Evan felt her stir and then watched her lashes flutter before she opened her eyes just a crack.

"Good morning," he said, leaning forward and kissing her shoulder.

Her smile was gentle, innocent, maybe even slightly shy. Her eyes moved over his face, and he saw the moment she remembered everything that had happened just prior to the kiss that led them here. He'd held her afterward, and she'd fallen quickly asleep, likely needing the escape of slumber after the shock of what they'd discovered on Dow's iPad and all the awful implications. She released a breath, lowering her gaze. "I'm so sorry," she said again. "I'm so, so sorry."

He reached out and moved her hair away from her face so he could see her better. He sighed. She was sorry for her loyalty, the trait that had in some ways kept bars between them long after they'd run through the desert together toward a partial freedom. She was sorry for hurting him and for the guilt she carried for wanting him, the sworn enemy of the people she'd loved most in the world. For the fact that the person she'd given her loyalty to might be partially responsible for the hell he had been through. He'd worked out the timeline in his head as the sun had risen, casting light over her skin, the woman he loved and always would. She was beautiful, and she was so torn in so many different directions. They'd seen each other's souls, and maybe once you'd seen a soul, it belonged to you in some profound way that could be felt but not explained. He *knew* her. He understood every facet. She was imperfect, but so was he. She was fearful and extraordinarily brave. She was scarred inside, but she was *his*. It had been true then, and it was true now. It would be his greatest truth for the remainder of his days, and he would not deny it again.

"Water?" he asked, kissing her shoulder once more.

She nodded, propping herself on her elbow. "Yes, please."

He got out of bed, completely unfazed by his nudity. She'd seen all of him, physical and otherwise. He grabbed two water bottles from his fridge and then returned to the bedroom, where she'd piled pillows behind herself and pulled the sheet up over her breasts. He felt a buzz in his groin and briefly considered pulling the sheet from her body and burying himself in her softness again, but they had important things to talk about that shouldn't wait, not if they were going to break the curse of their fathers, and it was imperative that they did, because they had a child now too.

He handed her one of the water bottles, and they both uncapped theirs and took a drink. He set his on the nightstand and then pulled on the boxer shorts that were lying on the floor. Clothing would help keep his thoughts focused.

"How?" she asked. "My father . . . Dow . . . all of it. How did it happen?"

He got back into bed, propping his own pillows up against the headboard and turning toward her, glad she was on the same track as him. Grateful she was willing to accept the probability that her father had been involved in their abduction, no matter how much it had to be killing her.

"I've been trying to work it out," he said. "I've been going over some possibilities while you slept, and there's something missing."

"What?"

"Well. My dad did ruin your father's life. Your father hated him, he blamed him. But that had been true for many years. What set him off? What happened to make him do something so drastic?"

"So evil," Noelle murmured, the trace of grief floating over her features. He wouldn't try to placate her and tell her it was not. They'd both lived it, and honesty was vital here if they were going to get to the heart of the truth.

Yes, then, evil. What had made her father do something so incredibly evil?

"I didn't see my dad a lot in the week before I was taken," she said. "But he did seem off. I worried that he was sinking back into depression. But he seemed antsy too. I don't know. My dad went through mood swings, and he had for years. He'd seen a therapist for a while, and it'd seemed to help." She paused, looking troubled. "I wish I would have suggested he make an appointment, but . . . well, the way he was acting wasn't abnormal, so mostly I hoped it would pass as it had before and just tried to stay busy. I *was* busy. But . . . yes, to . . . set you up to be tortured, he had to have come upon something new. It broke him. It bent his mind, and it made him do something appalling."

Evan agreed that it had to be something new. The man had lived with his wife's death, the knowledge of her betrayal, and the outcome of the trial that followed for many years. From what Evan understood, he'd just been getting his life back on track . . . was working regularly and managing his debt. His daughter was thriving in school. She hadn't gone missing yet. So what happened? And if Evan himself had been the target, how and why had someone determined that Noelle be caged too? And with him? He knew they were missing something.

Noelle was chewing at the inside of her cheek. "What about that photo of the weird website from what could be your home theater room?" she asked.

He didn't have the photo in front of him, but he conjured it then. It had reminded him of the camel-colored leather, but . . . it was the smallest corner. As evidence, it was pretty shaky. But if it *was* their home theater, and if the website *had* been part of what they'd experienced, and if it *was* his father watching it when the photo had been taken, then maybe that's what led her father to become aware of the whole thing. Those were a lot of maybes and too many ifs. "You think my dad might have been viewing that site and your dad found out?" Evan asked.

"Well, maybe. But first . . . if it was your home in that photo, where did it come from? And how did my dad know your father was involved in anything like that?" She paused briefly. "Could Dow have sneaked in and taken it?"

"Based on what? Also, security's pretty tight at the Sinclair manor." It was a good question, though. "Dow did have the photo, so if he didn't take it, then your father must have found it and given it to him," Evan said.

"And then he used the information from the computer to hack into some dark internet site."

They were both quiet as they digested that. "Okay, so where did my dad get it?"

"Could your mother have taken it?"

She blinked.

"There was a photo on your mother's camera. She had it in her purse that night, and the police took it. The photo came out in court that proved your mother's affair with my father."

She let out a breath, briefly closing her eyes. "You think that could be a photo she took on another occasion? From what I know, there was only one photo. But it spoke volumes, apparently."

Yes. From what he'd heard whispered around his house by the staff, it was a photo of his father's private parts. Parts that had been proved to be his by a mole or some other identifiable attribute. It was all so humiliating and sleazy. No wonder Noelle's father had nearly lost his mind.

"Maybe there were more from that original batch. Maybe the others told a different story."

Her eyes widened briefly. "What do you mean?"

"I don't know," he said. The last thing he wanted to do was give her hope that things had been different than the trial made them out to be. Because, truthfully, any other potential photos might tell a story that was *worse* than the one that had been told, not better.

He thought her mind had traveled along a similar path by the worried frown on her face. "My mother's books," she said.

"Her books? From that box?"

She nodded. "Now that I think about it, it's sort of weird that they're in there. I'd put my mom's favorite books on my bookshelf after she died." She scratched her head. "I can't remember if they were missing from my bookshelf when I packed up the house, but . . . that whole period is blurry. But if they had been on my shelf, they would have been packed up with my other belongings, and I'd have taken them to South Carolina. Instead, they were in a box with my father's things. Including the organizer he'd been using until the day he died."

"What would he have been doing with your mother's books in the days before his death?"

"I don't know. But I think we should go back to my room and go through them more thoroughly." Despite the certainty in her eyes, he also saw the fear. Since last night, so much of what she thought she'd known had been set ablaze. And they were about to walk farther into the fire.

They'd come out of a burning inferno once before, however, and they could do it again. He knew they could.

He took her hand in his and kissed her knuckle. "Together," he said. "Let's go."

~

Evan watched as Noelle tore open the tape on the box that she'd already secured in preparation for shipping and then unfolded the flaps. He saw her swallow as she lifted the things from the top, setting them aside. Her father's things. Her mother's books were at the bottom of the box, and she took them out, laying all six of them on the bed and sitting down.

Evan followed suit, picking up the copy of *Little Women* and thumbing through it. He held the front and back of the hardcover and tipped it before he gave it a small shake in case something fell out from between the pages that he'd missed. Nothing.

He picked up the second book near his thigh, beginning to do the same when Noelle pulled in a breath. He looked up, and she turned the book in her hands toward him. The inside was cut out to form a small hidden compartment.

"Oh shit," he said, dropping the book in his hands. "What's in it?"

Noelle, wide eyed, laid the book on the bed and took the piece of paper out that was on top, unfolding it. Evan saw that her hands were shaking.

Her eyes moved over the paper, and she looked up at him, her expression set in confusion. "It's a travel itinerary," she said. "To Hawaii."

"Hawaii?"

She nodded, reading over the paper again and then handing it to Evan. He took it and skimmed it, confirming that it was travel plans. It looked like her mother had been planning a trip to Hawaii.

"It was my dad's dream to go there," she said distractedly.

"Was your mom planning a trip for them?"

"I mean . . . it was about to be their anniversary. But . . . Evan, if she was having an affair, why plan a romantic trip to the place my dad had always dreamed of going?"

He had no answer for that. "What else is in there?"

Noelle had been staring off behind him for a second, obviously attempting to work out that puzzle. At his question, she gave her head a small shake and then removed a folded envelope from the small compartment and unfolded it. She pulled out a short stack of photos. "Oh my God," she breathed, dropping them like they'd burned her skin.

Evan picked one up, bringing it closer to his face. His own hand was shaking too. That was definitely his home theater, the way it had looked many years ago, when he was a teenager. Before and after Noelle's mother was shot. Bile moved up his throat at what became clear. He wanted to shut his eyes, to throw away the horrific evidence of what had been caught on film.

The photo was from behind the couch, near the doorway, he estimated. A man could be seen sitting in front of the screen, his hand on his genitals. A small portion of the screen showed in the upper corner. The edge of a cage and what looked like something unidentifiably bloody behind the bars. "Oh Jesus," he gasped, dropping the photo as well.

It was his father. He was sure of it. The photo had been taken from behind. It had to have been Noelle's mother who'd taken it. There was no intimacy happening. His father hadn't known she was there.

CHAPTER
FORTY-THREE

The Sinclair estate was far more massive than she'd pictured it. And she'd pictured it often, because she'd imagined her mother's death again and again. She'd seen her as the news articles and live reports had described her: a vindictive, jilted lover, obsessed with the man who had recently broken her heart.

It hadn't made sense as far as the woman Noelle had known her to be, even though the story had never wavered.

Evan took her hand, leading her through the back gate that had required a code typed into its lock. The same way their cages had required a numerical code so long ago. She shoved that memory aside. Her nervous system was already clashing and clanging. She hardly needed to create more anxiety.

Evan released a breath when the gate clicked open, apparently relieved that the security code hadn't been changed. He'd told her he hadn't been to the house in months and security was changed semiregularly, so they'd gotten lucky. Whatever else Evan's father considered his son, a threat wasn't one of them.

Noelle's head turned in each direction as they made their way through the manicured gardens, hurrying around a corner when they saw the back of a gardener, a pair of shears in his hand as he clipped at a bush.

"Are you sure your dad's out of town?" she whispered as they walked along a pathway beneath the eave of the house.

"He was yesterday," Evan said. "He texted me from New York. He's been there for a week."

Her speeding heart rate decreased slightly. New York was across the country. That made her feel a little more secure, whereas even the gun tucked into a holster at Evan's waist had not. On the chance that Mr. Sinclair did see them on the security cameras she didn't have to assume were everywhere on this property—she could see one placed at the corner of the roof, and there'd been another one on the gate—he couldn't do much about it. He could call the police, she supposed, but Evan was his son and could easily come up with a reason for being here. She, however, was a different story, and she tried her best to stay slightly behind Evan, hiding her face from view of any cameras.

But what she really hoped was that the man was in some meeting on the fortieth floor of a skyscraper and would be none the wiser.

Evan typed another code into a keypad next to a pair of french doors, and those clicked open too. Noelle followed him inside, stepping into a luxurious home office with floor-to-ceiling mahogany bookshelves that featured a library ladder that she could see moved on a rail around the entirety of the room, a gargantuan wood desk, and oil paintings she could only assume were originals, lit by gallery lights.

If she wasn't so damn nervous and upset, she'd have taken a moment to appreciate the room. As it was, she felt a lump of bile in her throat and swallowed it down heavily. This was the room from which Leonard Sinclair had stepped, raising his gun and shooting her mother on the path they'd just walked.

There was a photo of the man himself above a marble fireplace. She stared, her heart thumping swiftly. He was smiling, his teeth white and capped. He was tanned, and though he was no longer in the prime of his life—physically speaking anyway—he was still very attractive. Noelle could admit that, even though to her he was a demon. She saw Evan in him—kind, protective, loving Evan—and it made her feel disoriented and confused. It made her feel like there might be some good in the man smiling down at her. But, no, Evan was not in *him*. And the only part of this man recognizable in Evan was his genetics.

Evan went directly to the large desk, pulled out the high-backed black leather chair, and opened the drawer on the right. She came to stand next to him as he riffled through the files, exhaling a breath of frustration before turning the other way and going through the drawer on the left.

After a moment he shut that one too. "Nothing here," he said, pushing backward on the chair and getting up. She followed him to the other side of the room, where he stepped up to a bookshelf and pulled one of the titles halfway out. "I used to hide in that cabinet over there when I was a little boy," he said, nodding his head backward and then walking to another book on a different shelf and pulling that one halfway out too. "I'd spy on him through the crack. I wanted to know what my father did in here instead of paying attention to me." He turned to yet another shelf and pulled a third book halfway out and finally one more near the bottom. Noelle heard a small click, and then one of the shelves began to swing outward. "He never even knew I was here," Evan murmured.

In front of them was a secret room. "Wow," she said. Evan clicked on a light inside the door, and they both went in. There were file cabinets to their left, a table in the middle of the room, and a large oil painting on the far wall.

Evan moved directly to one of the built-in wooden file cabinets and pulled open the top drawer. Noelle thought she heard a noise and turned back, peering out into the office. Nothing. She released a breath. She tiptoed quickly across the room and turned the lock on the french doors that led to the garden. She didn't know where the second door led, but she locked that one too and then returned to the hidden room.

"She worked for him," Evan said. Noelle turned and hurried to his side, where he was looking down at a piece of paper he'd pulled from a file.

"What?" she breathed. He handed her what she could see was a contract. "Oh my God," she murmured, bringing the hand not holding the piece of paper to her mouth. "He hired her to do housecleaning work."

Evan shut his eyes momentarily and nodded as Noelle tried to make sense of everything they'd learned. He pointed at the date. "It was summer. I never saw her here because I was with my mom. She took a job and didn't tell your dad because—"

"She wanted to surprise him with a trip to Hawaii for their anniversary," Noelle said. *Oh God.* She'd have *had* to take an extra job. *A secret job.* They did fine at that point, but nowhere near fine enough to afford a Hawaiian vacation. She felt a sob rising in her chest again and tried desperately to hold it back. They needed answers. She could lose it later. "Do you think they really had an affair?"

"I don't know," Evan said. "But probably not. My father covered up the fact that he employed her. He must have paid her in cash. The only reason to lie about that was to distort her reason for being in his home. He made her sound like a jilted lover, when she was really just doing housecleaning."

"To try to explain her sneaking around his property? And therefore . . . justify him shooting her."

Evan looked about as ill as she felt. "Yes. The photos we, and your father, found show what she'd first walked in on. My father sexually aroused as he watched something awful. Something that looked very real to your mother, though maybe she questioned it. Maybe she came back to see if she could get more proof that it wasn't just a horror movie he was watching."

She nodded. "The pictures she'd already printed were also grainy and unclear. Because she'd come up behind him unsuspectingly and was nervous. She needed photos that were more convincing."

"But he discovered her," Evan said.

"And shot her—on purpose—before she could leave with the proof or tell anyone else."

"Yes," Evan said. She heard the horror in his voice too. Their emotions were unraveling right along with the truth. "If she got shot outside, maybe he was the one who surprised her and not the other way around. Maybe he took her camera and destroyed that film. Maybe he even went so far as to take a suggestive photo of himself and put that new roll of film in there."

"But he didn't know that she had more pictures at home, hidden in one of her books," she said. "Photos that my father would find years and years later."

She was barely holding back a scream. Her father had been ruined by the thought of his wife having an affair. Because it hadn't made sense.

Because it hadn't been true.

Noelle felt sadness and rage and injustice rise up inside her the same way it must have done for him. It'd festered like an open sore, made worse by the fact that her mother's death had become a media sensation. Her father had been laughed at, cringed over. And yet he'd loved his wife unendingly, a love that came to feel like a humiliating curse. It'd wrecked him. Noelle had watched it happen in real time. Little had he known then that there was something dark and malignant beneath the story that was a lie.

She felt weak. She took a few steps back, leaning against the edge of the table for support.

She pictured her father the moment he found the itinerary and the photos and understood the terrible truth, or at least part of it. He must have taken them to Dow, and when he broke into the site, they realized that whatever reason she'd been at the Sinclair home, it wasn't because she was stalking her lover. She'd seen something. She'd snapped photos. It was the reason she was murdered. He'd been stripped of his life and, more cruelly, his trust in the woman who had owned his heart. And left with nothing. He'd trusted in the justice system once before and been screwed, and so this time, instead of turning to the police, he'd taken matters into his own hands, part of his soul so twisted he'd done the unthinkable and set his sights on an innocent in retribution for what had been done to him.

How long had he stewed, allowing the open wound to become a gaping sore that he fell into, melding with the rot? Becoming it. Morphing into the very monster he despised.

Planning his revenge.

Her eyes lifted to Evan as he watched her. His wheels were turning, too, as the picture became clear. He turned away, folding the contract and putting it in his back pocket. The drawer closed with a small click. "We should try to find the files from the case," Evan said, his voice scratchy. He cleared his throat as he moved to another drawer. "His lawyer might have returned them—"

"It doesn't matter," she said. "The case presented was all lies. They must have known, but even if they didn't, they looked the other way." Uninterested in the truth. Only there for the money. "There's nothing to be done. Trying your father again would be double jeopardy."

She clamped a hand over her mouth. It was all too much. Too much. Evan stepped forward, wrapping his arms around her, whispering calming words against her hair.

Us, she reminded herself. *We are the cure. We are the answer to the sickness that wants to spread.*

He stepped back after a moment, their pained eyes meeting. "My dad," he said. "He wasn't surprised by your presence in that motel room that day in Mexico." He blew out a breath, looking over her shoulder, back in time. "His reactions . . . have always felt off."

She drifted back there for a moment, pictured the bandage around his broken hand, that shower where'd they'd tried so desperately to cleanse their souls, making do with their bodies, the furniture piled in front of the door, the way his father had looked at her with hatred. But Evan was right, no surprise. "Maybe you told him on the phone that I was there with you," she said. She'd been in the shower when he'd called his dad.

He frowned. "Maybe, but I don't think so. Also . . . he seemed to know about my hand. He told me he'd get a surgeon. How did he know it wasn't burned or . . . just needed a cast." He massaged his temples. "And he didn't call the police. He came there himself. He explained it later by saying he didn't trust anyone, and I didn't, either, so I accepted that."

"What are you thinking?"

"I don't know. But maybe . . . he didn't call the police because he knew the rules. He knew once we got out of there, we were free. Bets were paid, and the cleanup crew went to work. We'd won, and no one would come after us."

She felt full body shivers, but she steeled her spine and tried her best to clear her mind, to think. She wished she could help, but *everything* seemed off that day. "It all feels . . . distorted. I don't trust my own memories. But, yes, your father did seem to know more than he should have."

"Because he'd watched us."

She looked away. There seemed to be some evidence to suggest he'd watched whatever game they'd been a part of at some point, but to watch *them*? And not *do something*? Even for a monster, it didn't make sense. Her mind snagged on something. "The rope," she murmured.

"The rope?"

"Yes, the one I was sent. It didn't fit at the time. What was it for?"

"Are you thinking my dad sent it? For what reason?"

"Maybe he was giving me the opportunity to hang myself. Maybe he thought if I did, you'd be free." A twisted kindness? Or merely a plea to end the game for his son? *Hang yourself. End this.*

Evan looked like he was going to be ill. He turned and jerkily started opening more drawers, pulling out file folders and loose papers, giving them a brief glance and tossing them on the floor. "Evan—" She stepped forward and put her hand on his arm, but he shrugged her off.

"There must be something here," he said. His voice sounded the way it had when they'd been in those cages. Parched. Broken. There was too much horror being tossed at them to begin to comprehend. His dad had watched them. Watched his own son suffer. Be brutalized. Wither away. Be humiliated.

She understood that he needed to throw things, and if he wanted to throw his father's files—hell, if he wanted to pick up the cabinets themselves and toss them at the walls—she had no reason in the world to stop him. Hell, she'd even join him. She pulled a drawer all the way out and let it crash to the floor, spilling its contents.

Evan had gone over to the oil painting on the wall and was pulling it open like a small door. Ah, so there was a compartment behind it. She started stepping over the spilled contents of the drawer when something caught her eye. She bent, picking up a piece of paper with writing on it that definitely wasn't English.

"Evan, look," she said, and he turned his head. He was holding what appeared to be a necklace case, and he brought it with him as he walked over to her.

"I don't know what this is," she said, handing him the paper, "but look." She tapped the spot at the bottom that held an address.

He looked up, meeting her eyes. "Brussels?"

She nodded. "That story you printed. The diamond-mining company. The missing women. They were from Brussels."

"What is this, though?"

"I don't know. It looks like some formal document. We'd have to try to translate it. But there's a name on it."

"Fontane Lejeune."

"Have you ever heard that name?"

"No. The man from that article who'd been questioned was named Dedryck Van Daele."

Noelle frowned. Still, that was odd. She heard another small noise from outside in the office and tiptoed quietly to the door, peering out again. No one. And the doors were locked. *There's probably a full staff in this house. You're only hearing them. Relax.*

When she turned back toward Evan, he'd opened the top of the box in his hands. She approached him, looking at what he was holding. A red gem sparkled up at them, the large stone resting at the end of a delicate silver chain. It looked very old and very expensive. "A ruby?" she asked.

"I don't know," he said. "But it's from a jewelry store in Belgium. What the hell is going on?"

"I have no idea," she said. She pulled in a breath. "But we need to find out what the connection to Belgium is."

He held up the jewelry box. "You know who we can ask about this?"

"Yes," she said. She knew just who he was talking about—André Baudelaire, purveyor of antiques, collectibles, and fine jewelry. Evan stepped over the mess they'd left, leaving the compartment exposed. It had been empty, except for the necklace. And then they both exited the small hidden room where Leonard Sinclair stored his secrets.

A few of them at least.

CHAPTER
FORTY-FOUR

Evan drove, his mind filtering through what they'd just discovered as Noelle used a search engine on her phone to look up the name Fontane Lejeune. Unfortunately, all the hits she got were in Dutch.

"He might have been the son of a judge," she said. "There's a photo from the early sixties of a man named Sevrin Lejeune being sworn in to office. The boy in the photo is named Fontane."

He glanced over at her to see a troubled frown on her face. "What is it?" he asked.

"He looks like Callie."

"Let me see," he said, coming to a stop at a light and taking the phone. There were three children in the photo, and Noelle didn't have to point out which one was Fontane. He did look like Callie. He looked like boyhood pictures of Evan himself.

He looked like his father.

Evan swallowed, handing the phone back to Noelle as the light turned green. The little boy was his father.

He didn't understand that. He'd never heard the name Lejeune in his life. Why would his father move from Belgium and change his name?

He parked down the street from André Baudelaire's antique shop, taking Noelle's hand after they'd both exited the vehicle and hurrying toward the black awning with the gold lettering.

Evan pulled the door open, and Noelle went in first. The same scent greeted him as the first time he'd been in the shop, and there was something comforting about it, and something spooky. Again, it brought to mind some attic full of a grandmother's treasures. Not that he'd ever known either of his own grandmothers. His mother's mother had died when he was two, and he'd been told his father's had died before he was born.

But he suddenly wondered about that.

Wondered if she was alive and well and living somewhere in Brussels.

When they entered the shop, Mr. Baudelaire himself was wrapping what looked like a crystal champagne flute in a piece of tissue paper at the counter. The old man glanced up, a look of surprise lighting his face. "I had a feeling you'd be back for that ring." He smiled, placing the glass carefully inside a padded box in front of him as they stepped toward the counter.

"No." Noelle smiled. "Actually, we're here to ask you another question. Sorry to take more of your time. I'm sure you're very busy."

The old man pushed the box full of items wrapped in the same tissue paper as the flute to the side next to several more boxes just like it and rested his palms on the L-shaped glass counter. "It's not a problem. Most of my clientele shops online now. My son, Gervais, is in charge of all that. He's quite good with photography and computers, while I'm useless with technology. Sometimes I feel more like I operate a shipping business these days than anything. These flutes, for instance"—he nodded to the open box of wrapped items, next to the already sealed boxes—"are going out momentarily, and they will grace the tabletops of a local formal event that will be attended by very important men, or so I hear. Nineteenth-century Baccarat crystal." He glanced at the boxes again, his gaze almost loving. "The best on earth. Available to a certain clientele with the means and the appreciation for such rare beauty." He seemed to come back to himself. "Oh goodness, there I go blathering on again and holding you up. My point is, consultations with actual humans are a pleasure, so ask away."

"Thank you," Noelle said, pulling the jewelry box from her purse and laying it on the counter.

Mr. Baudelaire looked curiously between him and Noelle and then down to the box. "This company was in Belgium," he said. "The logo is very recognizable."

"Oh. You've heard of it?" Evan asked.

"It's world renowned. Their pieces are known for the high quality of their gems and Van Daele diamonds," he said. "They're not in business anymore, but when they were, they catered only to the wealthiest clientele. That's still true, only now their pieces are collectibles."

"Van Daele diamonds," Evan murmured, shooting a look at Noelle. There it was, that link.

"Yes," Mr. Baudelaire said, glancing up momentarily. "The two companies worked hand in hand. Van Daele is no longer in business either. There was rumor at the time of the closing that the heir to the company had brought some trouble upon himself."

"What kind of trouble?" Evan asked.

Mr. Baudelaire tapped a finger on his lips. "Hmm, from what I recall, a party got quite out of hand and even turned bloody."

"Bloody?" Noelle asked, blinking.

"Mmm," Baudelaire hummed. "So it was said. I even heard whisperings that it was a massacre. I can't imagine that was true, however, or certainly the police would have made an arrest or two." His face did something funny, but Noelle didn't know the man well enough to guess what it meant. *Massacre.* It was the same word that man from the second-floor room had used in his story. A chill made her draw her arms toward her body. "But in any case," Baudelaire went on, "the business folded. I suppose the family has . . . moved on to other pursuits. When they closed their doors, many other businesses in the area linked to them did as well. I suppose they all relied on each other in various ways. Anyway, I'm eager to see what you've brought me."

"We're not selling," Evan told the older man. "I'd just like some basic information. I'm willing to pay for it."

"Nonsense. I'm happy to provide my expertise." The man reached forward and opened the box, leaning back slightly as the necklace was revealed. "Oh my." He stared for a moment, and Evan saw the delight in his eyes.

"Is it a ruby?" Noelle asked.

Mr. Baudelaire reached in a drawer beneath the counter and removed a magnifying glass. He put it up to his eye and leaned forward, studying the gem. "Oh my," he breathed again. "Just as I thought. Not a ruby, a diamond. An exceedingly rare red diamond."

"A red diamond?" Evan asked. He hadn't even known such a thing existed.

"Mmm," Mr. Baudelaire hummed, his magnifying glass still aimed at the necklace. Evan thought he saw the man's hand tremble slightly. Age, perhaps. Or maybe the rarity of the item he was inspecting. "A gorgeous piece," he said. "A shame the clasp is broken, but that could be easily repaired. It's sized for a very slender neck, perhaps that of a child or a young girl."

A strange shiver went down Evan's spine, and he couldn't even say why. Except . . . who would have a child wear a red diamond necklace? That seemed . . . very odd.

"I'd estimate it would take in several million dollars at auction," the jeweler said.

"Jesus," Evan murmured. His father owned many items worth a lot of money. Property, cars, a private jet. He regularly gave his wives expensive pieces of jewelry that they then took with them once the inevitable divorce came to pass, farewell gifts that stood in for anything else, as airtight prenuptials had been signed. But Evan had a gut feeling this wasn't just some expensive item his father had purchased for no reason and held on to. No, this was meaningful. This was from the same place his father was apparently from. A past he'd lied about.

"The interesting thing," Mr. Baudelaire said, closing the box, "is that this isn't the only red diamond in Reno. And from what I recall, the other one has the exact same filigree surrounding the stone. Or very similar." He pushed the box toward Noelle with one finger, his mouth turning down as though he were saying a sad goodbye.

"What do you mean?" Evan asked. "Where's the other one?"

The bell over the door rang, and Evan looked over his shoulder to see a deliveryman. "Five minutes and I'll have these ready," Baudelaire said, nodding to the boxes next to him. The man tipped his chin and linked his hands in front of himself as he waited. Evan turned back to Baudelaire, eager to hear what he'd been about to say.

"A few years ago, I was at a Christmas party. One of those social events put on by some organization asking for money for their charity. A hospital, maybe . . ." Mr. Baudelaire turned and bent toward a drawer under the counter. He pulled out a magazine and started paging through it. Evan shot Noelle a look. She stared back, her eyes widening as they waited to see where the hell this was going. "A man stood next to me as we waited for our drink order. When he put his hand on the bar, I noticed his ring. I remarked on it, and he told me it was a ruby. Curious, because I could clearly see it was not. It is my business, after all. But he turned away quickly. He seemed eager to depart. That moment many years ago ate at me. I wondered if I should have found him and corrected him. I'd hate to think someone was unknowingly undervaluing something they possessed and perhaps treating it accordingly. But the interaction was odd. A few months ago, I came upon an article, and I recognized the man I'd spoken to . . . ah, yes." He put the magazine down on the counter in front of them and pointed to a picture attached to an article.

Both Evan and Noelle leaned forward, looking at the photo announcing the retirement of a beloved professor at the University of Nevada.

Evan knew him immediately.

"That's the name of my father's therapist," Noelle said, confusion in her tone as she brought her index finger to the headline.

Evan's head whipped in her direction. "Professor Vitucci? He's my therapist," he said.

"What?" she asked, her brows knitting. "I don't understand."

Neither did he. What the hell was going on?

CHAPTER
FORTY-FIVE

Noelle took in the set of Evan's jaw and the way he gripped the steering wheel. If he'd been tense and confused before, he was even more so now. So was she. He took his hand off the wheel as he drove, stretching it for a moment and then returning it to where it'd been. "Professor Vitucci came highly recommended by the officers involved in our case," he told her. "They'd worked with the man. They knew him."

She thought back to the time right after they'd escaped—the questioning, the interviews, the bright lights, and the somber looks. Yes, Noelle thought she remembered the police offering to give her a recommendation for a therapist too. She'd immediately turned them down, too overwhelmed to consider talking to another stranger at that point.

"Is it possible he was recommended to your father as well?" Evan asked. "He also worked with the police when your mother died. This might be a simple coincidence based on our connection to the Reno PD."

"Maybe," she murmured.

Evan had told her a little more about his experience with Armand Vitucci after they'd left Baudelaire's shop and begun the drive to the professor's home office, the one Evan had often gone to for sessions. She still had no idea what to expect. Her father had clearly liked the man enough to go to him off and on for several years, but other than that, he hadn't dispensed any other information, and she hadn't asked because it'd seemed like a personal relationship that wasn't necessarily her business. Evan seemed perplexed in general, and specifically about why the professor would have a rare red diamond with the same filigree matching the one they'd found in his father's safe, but he also seemed intent on defending the man. She could tell by the way he spoke of him that Evan highly respected him.

They'd also discussed briefly what Mr. Baudelaire had said about the Van Daele diamond company and rumors of a massacre. More links between the man who had originally told her the story about the king and his court, Brussels, and some supposed massacre that may or may not have really happened were forming. She sensed the answers that would make it all clear were close but just out of reach.

Forty-five minutes after they'd left the antique shop, they exited Evan's car and began walking toward a lovely ranch-style home with stone exterior. Noelle glanced over her shoulder as they approached. She was jumpy and out of sorts, and she knew by the grip of Evan's hand that he was too.

They paused at the front door that was open a few inches. Alarm rose inside Noelle. It felt like an invitation but also some odd threat she couldn't explain. "Is that normal?" Noelle whispered, gesturing to the cracked door.

Evan shook his head, pushing it open with two fingers. "Professor Vitucci?" he called. No answer. He gripped her hand harder as they stepped inside the open foyer, and Evan called his name again.

"Back here," came a distant male voice.

Evan nodded to her, and they moved toward the back of the house where the voice had come from.

They passed an open powder room and a short hall that led to what Noelle assumed were bedrooms. A scent met her nose, drifting from the direction of the room where they'd almost arrived. A cologne. *Distinct. Layered.* Her heart lurched.

"Evan—" She pulled on his arm as they stepped through the open doorway, a large desk in front of them, where a man sat in a leather chair turned toward the wall of bookshelves.

From her peripheral vision, she could see Evan look at her questioningly, but she could not take her eyes from the man in the chair, turning slowly toward them. An eternity and an instant passed before he faced them fully.

"Hello, little rabbit," he said, a smile tilting his lips. Noelle let out a tiny gasp. Sitting before them was the man from the photo Baudelaire had shown them.

And he spoke in the voice from her nightmares. *The voice from that room.*

He was black haired, with a generous amount of gray at his temples. *Dashing* came to her muddled mind. Noelle gripped Evan's hand and moved her other to his biceps, where she held on tightly too. *Vitucci?* Her father's and Evan's therapist was the man who'd . . . rented her? The one who'd given them the tools to escape their cages?

Vitucci turned his attention to Evan. "Evan. Hello. Very nice to see you."

"What the hell is going on?" Evan asked. Though she couldn't take her eyes from the older man, she felt Evan move slightly and assumed he was going for his gun.

Vitucci smiled again, his gaze moving to the place where Evan was surely removing the firearm. "Don't be rash, Evan. I'm not planning on harming either of you. I'm quite fond of you, actually."

"You expected us. How?"

"Baudelaire." He nodded toward the couch near the wall. "Please have a seat. This is going to take a few minutes. And you'll have a much better shot from there, should you need to fire at me."

They both hesitated together, but then Evan pulled her slightly, and she followed him to the couch, and both sat down. She was grateful. Her legs were shaking, and she felt better with a wall to her back rather than an open doorway.

"Baudelaire told a little white lie," Vitucci said after turning his chair so he faced them, lacing his hands on the desk as though to put them at greater ease. It worked. "He doesn't enjoy lying, but he's loyal. He raised me after I barely survived the massacre that happened in the house of horrors I grew up in, otherwise known as the Van Daele manor. My mother was the woman I told you about, little rabbit, whose throat was slit on the ballroom floor. She was hired help there, without family, no real skills to speak of. A throwaway. A nobody. Van Daele and his friends debased her at their parties. They captured her if she tried to run. They broke her eventually, so that she begged them for the drugs they provided. She anticipated her cage for the reward of escape. An appalling paradox, no?" His lips tilted, but the upper half of his face remained stoic.

"I worked there, too," he went on. "In the kitchen. In the garden, wherever I was needed. I stole their jewels and their books. I learned to read, and I learned to plot."

Their jewels. House of horrors I grew up in. So it *had* been his story. And the massacre wasn't merely rumor, the way Baudelaire had framed it. She remembered how the man sitting in front of her had whispered, murmuring soft and low against her ear, moving subtly through different accents she hadn't been able to quite identify. He was using a very slight one now, practically imperceptible, but she thought she recognized the cadence as purely Italian. That would make sense, with a name like Vitucci. Then again, nothing about this man seemed to make sense. *Who are you really?*

Her mind pulled forth the other things he'd said in that room so many years ago. *They had only each other.* They. The twins. A boy and a girl. His sister? Her gaze moved to his pinkie finger, where a flash of red glinted in the light. A red diamond. One of two. Just like the children themselves, who wore matching gems to signify their ownership by gluttons. "You. You were one of the twins in the story you told me in that room," Noelle said. She felt Evan go more rigid beside her.

"Correct, little rabbit. But it was not a story. It was my life. She was my life. Her name was Celesse." A note of something she'd almost call longing had come into his voice, but with his next words, it was gone. "I protected her when I could. I offered myself in exchange for her if there was interest. Sometimes there was. Sometimes there was not." He paused, his pinkie tapping lightly against the desk very momentarily. "As a boy, living in that house, I had survived—and helped my mother and sister survive—by reading not only books but people. By collecting. Personality clues. Habits. Fears and motivations. That's what being a good therapist or profiler is about too. You put all those collected clues together, like a puzzle. If you've collected enough pieces, it forms a picture."

"You could have used those qualities for good," Evan gritted.

"I did use them for good. Perhaps someday you'll come to agree."

"No, you became one of the monsters you claim to hate."

"Yes, but it's the only way to take such monsters down."

"How?"

Vitucci didn't answer him; he only smiled and went on with his story. "That night . . . they thought I'd died along with the rest, but a kind man who worked at the mortuary noticed I was in fact not quite dead after all. He understood who the men who ruled that city were. His own family had been victimized by their power. His betters, or so they thought themselves, were covering up the scene of the crime, and it gave him the opportunity to secret me away to a doctor in Italy. Vitucci. He healed me, and he gave me his name, as he had an in with the medical clerks in his village. He was a very old man, however, and so he sent me to his cousin in France to be raised. Baudelaire took me under his wing. He educated me. He raised me as a son. He helped me trace the bastards who thought they'd killed me, along with my mother and sister, here to Reno, Nevada, in the United States of America."

He paused and looked between them. "They'd hidden themselves behind false names and new companies. It took years before I recognized one of them on the news, a man named Fontane, who was being sued for wrongful death. He'd changed his name to Leonard Sinclair. But I'd known him as the son of a judge who had guaranteed court cases were always ruled in his friends' favor. That judge was one of the originals. Although who knows if that's the correct term. It's hard to say where anything begins. All I know is that their games have evolved over the decades in both numbers and depravity. What may have begun as a little nonconsensual fun with the hired help has grown into a multibillion-dollar, highly technical organization focused on perverse blood sport. It's stunning what can happen when certain appetites are insatiable and money is no object."

Noelle sucked in a breath. She was overwhelmed, a low hum of static competing with her thoughts, but even so, she registered his comment and knew there was another ingredient that made that type of victimization possible. She'd called it evil because she had no other word. All she knew was that not everyone with unlimited amounts of money and opportunity committed atrocities. She leaned into Evan, taking comfort from his closeness.

Vitucci sighed. "In any case, when I saw Fontane, I knew Van Daele and his cohorts were here after all. They must be. Where there was one, there were more. Rich men and their sons so bored by their lives of wealth and privilege that they only found thrill and meaning in collecting humans and degrading them. Still so rich, so insulated. But I knew evil did not simply fall away from men like them. The craving only grew stronger."

Evil, yes. So he agreed. But wasn't he evil too? She was so confused. Heartbroken. Empty. But they had to know the rest. The truth was going to help them heal. No more questions. No more lies. "What happened that night?" Noelle asked. "Why did they leave their country?"

That slight pinkie flutter again. "The night of their annual ball. The one that turned so bloody? Their privilege happened. Their egos happened. Their gluttony spilled over. Those men made all the rules, they always had. One big club of influence and power. They kidnapped women they didn't think anyone would miss. They held them against their wills. Occasionally, they killed them in one way or another. Sometimes for sport, sometimes by accident, a few times simply because they became inconvenient. I watched as their lust for power grew. The viciousness that had once been enough no longer satisfied. They became greedier, more twisted. However, everything changed that night. They went too far. They not only murdered one nobody as a result of their entertainment, or even two. They hacked up fourteen people with table cutlery and carving knives. It was quite the scene. I still see it sometimes when I close my eyes. But what once was a nightmare is now my motivation. Anyway, even with their vast network of contacts, if a cover-up was going to have any chance of succeeding, they had to close their companies, take their assets, and disappear. And the irony of it all was that I'd chosen that night for our escape. So many drugs. So much revelry. It seemed like the perfect opportunity. It almost was."

Evan made a sound of disgust in his throat that also held the hint of a sob. "If you were so smart, why didn't your escape plan work? Why didn't you save your mother and your sister?"

"Because neither were brave enough to follow through. They weren't like you. They'd lived a life of victimhood. They didn't know how to be anything different, even when presented the chance. I tried to force them, but in the end, I watched them both die, and I almost did as well."

"Maybe that would have been better."

"I think not," Vitucci said. "In any case, those men made sure all the bodies disappeared. My mother's and sister's bodies were burned,

I imagine. Why would it matter? Who would miss them? Perhaps it's why I derive such intense pleasure from watching others make their escape, finding the courage to follow through where my beloveds did not. I help those who can be helped. I'm quite good at it. However, I can only assist the ones who are committed to some decency, even amid terror. The others . . . well, perhaps they don't deserve to be saved anyway." He turned slightly in his chair, and it let out a quiet squeak. She felt Evan's muscles tense from beside her. "So that's my origin story," he said, looking at Evan. "We agreed they were important, did we not? Sometimes they are everything."

Noelle was beginning to be able to think more clearly, her mind following along with what he was saying. Forming a picture of where this man had come from, of who he was, attempting to merge him with the vague outline of the man from her memory.

"You watched us in those cages, and you did nothing to help," Evan said.

"On the contrary. I did everything to help. And here you are."

"We were tortured!" Evan yelled. "We almost died!" His sudden shout had startled Noelle, but it had also bolstered her anger and therefore her bravery. She sat taller.

Vitucci's eyes flickered to her, and she saw the minute tug of one side of his lips before his gaze returned to Evan. *You profiled us. And Tallulah. And the man Evan visited in prison. And perhaps others too. You knew just what made us tick. You guessed our limitations and our strengths. And you were right.*

"I understand your anger and your hurt," Vitucci said. "I won't attempt to disavow you of either. I had a greater goal than you, and maybe at some point, you'll see the bigger picture. For now, what I can say is that I did not know where you were. No one but a select few did. There are levels upon levels upon levels. I had only one way to rescue you and the others. Help you rescue yourselves."

"You could have notified the police, you sick fuck," Evan said. "You had *proof.*"

Vitucci let out a short breath. "The police? The FBI? Some of them are players. Did they help you, Evan? Did they *solve* the crime? No, of course not. Because they were not meant to. Your own father greased the wheels that drove the investigation straight into a ditch. You have no idea how deep this goes. All the money and all the blackmail. There is one chance, Evan. Only one."

One chance? One chance for what? And how? What was he saying? That if he'd notified the police, they'd either be unable to find the location on the screen or, worse, they'd cover it up? And how would they identify any of the men who'd done this anyway? They'd worn masks. She felt sick, dizzy.

Vitucci glanced at his watch as if he had somewhere to be.

"The only place you're going is prison, Vitucci," Evan said.

The older man gave Evan a small smile. "I'm prepared," he said. He nodded down to his desk. "If you would, Evan. There's something for Noelle in that top drawer. But first, I'd like to see her diamond, please."

Her diamond.

Evan hesitated but then stood, removed the jewelry box from his pocket, walked the few steps to the desk, and placed it down. As Vitucci took it, Evan leaned toward the desk from the side, his gaze held on the older man before he slid the drawer open and removed a manila envelope and a laptop. Noelle let out a small gasp. Was that . . .

"It's your father's computer," Vitucci said as he opened the jewelry box and gazed down at its contents. Noelle thought she heard him exhale or perhaps sigh before he closed the box and focused on her again. "And in that envelope, you will find the photos I took from his house. The best of the shots your mother managed to get and the way in which Dow Maginn was able to access their server. Or at least the one they used at that time. They have, of course, beefed up security since then." His mouth moved into a smile.

Evan handed Noelle the computer and the envelope, and she took them, setting them on her lap and placing her hands over them. So many questions were tumbling through her mind about her father and Dow she hardly knew where to begin.

"Your father and I shared the same enemy, Noelle, though of course he never knew that," Vitucci said, obviously reading her confusion. "I made a point to have one of the officers who worked on his case offer my services at a highly discounted rate at the time of the trial against Evan's father. Your father was deeply distraught, as you know, and he took me up on it."

Evan let out a whoosh of breath. "You did the same for me," he said. "You swooped in to *help*, when you really wanted information."

"And a connection, yes. But I helped you emotionally, too, Evan, did I not?"

Evan looked away, appearing so incredibly torn. This man *had* helped him; Evan had told her as much.

"What did you want with my father back then, at the time of the trial?" she asked, saving Evan from having to admit that, yes, this man had helped him. She remembered that moan suddenly, the confession he'd torn from her despite her best efforts.

"I wanted to know about anything that might not have been in the court transcripts," Vitucci answered. "I wanted to know about your mother, about any small thing that might help me take my enemies down."

"But you didn't get that," she said.

"Not at the time, no. But I was the one who'd originally sent your father to Baudelaire when he'd expressed his deep sadness at having to sell some family heirlooms to pay his debts. Baudelaire paid him far more than they were worth. I'm certain it's why he returned to him years later to sell the final item he'd kept—your mother's ring. Baudelaire noticed that he seemed . . . unwell. Desperate. He needed a priest, truth be told. But Baudelaire bought his bauble, and then he called me and suggested I reach out."

"For therapy."

"A yearly check-in, I told him, and he didn't question it. Maybe, to him, it seemed serendipitous. He was having a nervous breakdown. He asked me about medication. I suggested we talk first. He was driving when I called him. I told him to pull over and compose himself and then come straight here. I'd heard that Fontane's son, Evan, had gone missing. Could that possibly be related to Mr. Meyer's deeply agitated state? The timing was interesting. Anyway," he looked at Noelle. "Your father said he'd gotten involved in something he couldn't get out of. Something online. He'd had his friend hack a site where they hurt people. That's when I knew it involved *them*. I *knew*. But that's all he would say."

The words pierced her heart even though she and Evan had already figured out that her father had been responsible for Evan's abduction. But to have it confirmed seared her soul. Her father had set Evan up as a victim in one of their brutal games. "You didn't know about the games then," she said. "When my father told you he'd discovered something . . . you hoped it would lead to Evan's father, to . . . Fontane . . . and the others. It was a stroke of luck, your chance to avenge your mother's and sister's deaths."

"Very good, little rabbit. But I wouldn't attribute it to luck. I'd positioned myself well. But it was my chance, yes. I'd waited a long, long time. They'd moved their lust for blood sport here, and I had finally been presented with an *in*."

Evan released a breath. "Did you kill Dow Maginn?"

"Of course. You had been abducted," he said to Evan. "Mr. Meyer saw you in the cage and immediately regretted what he had done. His hatred had gotten the best of him. He sold that ring hoping he could buy your freedom, but, of course, that's not the way the game is played. And even if it was, ten thousand dollars is petty cash to those men.

Mind you, I only pieced all those details together later. I see you're not shocked, which means you've deduced some of it too."

Noelle nodded, even while tears burned the backs of her eyes.

"Fontane logged in and expected to see a stranger in a cage at the start of another game and instead saw his own son. He went to the big bosses, or the midlevel bosses, you might say. The originals are highly insulated and only emerge once a year. They told him the game was already started, bets had been made, money put on the line. They were even angry he had the audacity to assume who ruled the game. Fontane's father was long dead, and he had been nothing but a mere boy when they'd immigrated to the United States. I imagine the fact that he'd gotten himself embroiled in a high-profile investigation and trial didn't ingratiate him to those men. No, Evan was staying, his captivity was underway, and the first days of darkness while the players placed their initial bets had commenced. Some captives screamed and begged during that time, chewed at their hair, banged their heads. All things that helped players determine how much money they'd first put on the line. How could they admit to these men that a mistake had been made? That a *nobody* had hacked in and put them all at risk? Trust in the system would be gravely compromised, and to play such a game, trust in the system is paramount. The players wondered, of course, at the contestant who was chosen, the son of a player. But that, too, turned out to be a boon, as it was assumed to be payback for some transgression. And so it acted as a warning and naturally helped tighten internal security. As some reconciliation to your father, however, they did allow him a request: to match Evan with the contestant of his choice. Fontane chose Noelle."

She brought her hand to her mouth, holding back her tears. *Oh God, oh God. It was the very definition of evil.*

Her head swam, her muscles ached from holding them so tight. And the only reason she wasn't slumping over with the weight of her grief was because Evan was holding her up. His solid body. The love and support she could feel emanating from him.

Of all the crushing horrors she'd experienced, the knowledge of what her father had done almost broke her. Instead of reporting what he'd found, he had Dow put Evan's name in as the next contestant. Change a name. And an abduction location. The low-level muscle who'd nabbed Evan would have no clue. They were simply following the orders they'd been given, and as far as they knew, the abduction had gone smoothly. The players would only find out that something had gone awry when they logged in to play.

Had it been simple for Dow to hack their site? Was it easy for someone who'd once hacked the electric company? Or had he found it a challenge? Either way, he'd been successful. She closed her eyes, visions swimming before her. Her father seeing Evan on screen, trying desperately to reach Dow, hocking the only thing he had of value to try and bail Evan out of that cage if possible, to have some financial leverage to fix what he'd done, and then dying of a heart attack when he found out that his own daughter was there too. Because of him. Because of what his actions had led to.

An eye for an eye.

Two men so bent on revenge that they sacrificed the other's child.

"Why did you have to kill Dow?" she asked. Her voice sounded monotone. Was she going into shock? Maybe. But the emotional numbness was a blessing.

Vitucci sighed. "I needed the computer he'd logged in on, and so I paid him a visit. Afterward, I couldn't risk that Dow would give my name to the police or perhaps go to them to confess what he'd done. I killed him, yes, but the organization would have done much, much worse. You two don't have to imagine the ways in which they might have exacted revenge once they located the man who hacked their elaborate game."

A chill went down Noelle's spine. No, she didn't have to imagine. But she also didn't want to think that this man had done Dow a favor by swiftly taking his life.

"When your father had a heart attack, I went to his home and took his laptop and the photos. And when I understood exactly what the situation was, I paid a visit to the man who would be the sponsor I needed to play—Fontane. They don't just let any old chump join in, after all." He smiled, and it appeared as serene as his other smiles.

"A sponsor?" Evan asked. "My father? But why? He vouched for you because you had evidence against him?"

"No. He vouched for me because I'd done him a favor in the past and I had an in with the Reno PD and plenty of access. I'd hidden evidence in the case against Noelle's father. I'd let him pay me off."

"What?" Noelle breathed. "I thought you were helping my father. Why? Why would you hide evidence for . . . Fontane?"

"I was helping myself, Noelle."

"But . . . if you had evidence against him, you could have used it to have him arrested."

"I could have, but exposing Fontane would have meant exposing myself. And I had a bigger goal in mind."

She thought she might scream. A game. It was all a game, and he was playing a different one, but he was playing one nonetheless.

"I explained to Fontane how I'd come upon the information about the game in a session with Mr. Meyer," Vitucci went on. "I told him I'd not only take a payout as I'd done before but that I'd like to play. It had appealed to me. By that time, Dow and Mr. Meyer were both dead anyway. All cleaned up. Or so they thought. And so it came to be that I was there to help you both free yourselves, just another compromised player in their vast web."

Evan raked a hand through his hair. "How do we find these fucking monsters?" he asked. "All of them. I have friends on the police force—"

"I do as well, Evan. Didn't you hear me? *I'm* your friend on the police force. And yet, I've done so many favors over the years to prove my false loyalty. I've made files disappear, hid evidence. All toward an ultimate end, but even so." He shrugged. "If I have trust issues as far as the authorities are concerned, you'll kindly understand why." The professor glanced at his watch one more time and then signaled to a remote sitting on his desk. "If you could do me one final favor, Evan."

Again, Evan hesitated, but then rose, walking to the desk and leaning in. He picked up the remote. "There," Vitucci said, pressing some buttons on the open laptop sitting on the side of his desk and then nodding to a television screen on the opposite wall from where they sat. "Turn it on, please."

Evan looked at Noelle. She imagined her eyes were as wide and shocked as his. He gave her the slightest of nods, and her breath released. They were together. They could handle anything. *Partners.*

Evan pointed the remote at the TV and pressed the On button, and the screen blinked to life. For a beat, Noelle didn't comprehend what she was looking at. She leaned closer as Evan swore under his breath. Both of them stood, walking together toward the screen until they were directly in front of it, as though it beckoned in some silent way. It was a room. And in it were two cages, one containing a young boy, and the other an older man. Noelle stared, her mouth falling open, a wail rising in her throat as she tried desperately to swallow it down.

"An orphaned pickpocket, living off his will alone in a town run by criminals," Vitucci said. Her eyes moved to the young, skinny boy. He was just a kid. A sob choked her, and she let out a stuttered breath. "And an ex–border guard who ignored the pleas of the woman he fell in love with in that sad, poverty-stricken town, who asked him to bring her across the border. He followed the law back then, and so she took matters into her own hands and was killed when she attempted to cross with their daughter. He blames himself. He tries to make amends by living solely outside the law now and drinking himself to death. For her." Noelle looked at the older man, who was wrapping a piece of fabric around his bloody wrist. He had no hand. *Oh God.*

Their gazes hung on the screen for several minutes as they took in every staggering detail. At the top were two names: Trigger and Goliath. They obviously referred to the two people in the cages. A wave of nausea overtook her. They had named them, like circus animals. She gulped down the sickness, feeling faint.

It was too much to comprehend and grotesquely familiar. *What were our game names? How did you monsters refer to us?* She let out a strangled cry, turning toward Evan. Evan wrapped his arms around her, letting out a sound that was both anguish and fury. The feed was live, streaming from Vitucci's computer. Those two people were there in cages right that very moment. Evan let go of her, whipping in the other direction, to face Vitucci. She turned as well, bringing her hands to her mouth.

Vitucci was gone.

Her gaze moved to his desk. So was the jewelry box holding his sister's diamond.

CHAPTER
FORTY-SIX

Caspar paused to straighten his bow tie before using the flat of his hand to knock on the rusted steel door. It was pulled open by a young expressionless gentleman. "Invitation, sir?"

Caspar removed the coveted printed card stock from his inner coat pocket and wordlessly handed it to the greeter, who took a long moment to inspect it before handing it back. He recognized the man. He was the lackey who'd shot that old prostitute in the back when she was so close to freedom. The man gestured Caspar to spread his arms and then patted him down once he'd done so. "Have a lovely evening, sir."

"I intend to," he murmured, stepping through the metal detector, into a wide-open space that was mostly concrete. He had no idea where he was. He'd been picked up at a designated spot and then blindfolded and driven here. Wherever *here* was. Somewhere in Reno, that's all he knew. Obviously, the originals hadn't wanted to travel far.

He pulled in a slow breath before moving toward the arched doorway from which the sounds of organ music and conversation flowed. He'd waited eight long years for this night. To be in the same place with all these players. He'd sacrificed; he'd given up opportunities to enact small forms of revenge, because he wanted them *all*, not just one. What good did it do to smack a cockroach, or even a few, when the rest would just come scuttling back once the lights went out?

Oh yes, he had a mission here tonight, but first . . . first he would savor this for a moment. He exhaled slowly.

He had finally proved his loyalty and earned their trust. Or perhaps they were planning to kill him. He'd won the game so many times, after all. The other players had grown irritated. And suspicious. He hadn't cheated—he'd played by their rules. He'd won using his wits alone, and with the help of the contestants, but even so, and though there had been few "winners" overall, he'd caught wind of the displeasure of the others. They preferred to possess the victories. All of them. Watching those they considered so much lower than themselves walk away—or run away, as the case always was—was a bitter pill to swallow. Why should men like them swallow anything bitter at all?

The thought made him smile and spurred him forward toward the celebration beyond.

He'd told Evan and Noelle how he'd spent his life collecting clues about people. It'd helped him survive once. Then it'd allowed him to provide insightful therapy to his patients and interesting lessons to his students and even to help the police solve crimes. He'd thought of himself not just as *a* collector, but *the* Collector. A persona. Because it'd allowed him to separate himself from the helpless boy he'd once been, the one who'd been used and victimized. The one who'd watched his mother bleed out on the floor as his sister was hacked to death. Yes, he'd gone by several names, in his own mind and on the lips of others. But tonight . . . tonight he was Caspar again. But this time, he was not helpless. He was not the broken boy who'd barely escaped with his life, and his pockets filled with the gems he'd stolen over the years. The ones that, later, Baudelaire had helped him sell. The ones that had made him rich.

He stepped into the room. Bach's Fugue in G Minor swelled, laughter rose, and the splashing sound of the champagne fountain at the center tinkled pleasantly. Despite the plain walls and concrete floor, there were riches here, the unequalled luxury men like these enjoyed surrounding themselves with, from all corners of the earth. French and Irish crystal, German dinnerware, silk tablecloths from Myanmar, English roses, and Japanese orchids. The world was their playground, and for them, nothing was unavailable. He knew these men well enough to know they'd destroy it all with gusto by the end of the evening. What spoke of your own power even more strongly than possession?

Destruction. True kings not only invaded. They pillaged too.

He could see by their coloring that the six women in cages hanging above the party were from places both near and distant as well. The king and his court had learned, after all. Abducting people from one singular geographical location eventually became problematic.

They'd destroy them as well. Tradition and all.

Caspar glanced up to see a young girl with tangled black hair. She peered down at him with half-open, drugged eyes. She was naked, her hands bound and a gag in her mouth. The jewels she was draped in sparkled in the reflected light.

Ah, a nod to where it'd all begun. How nostalgic these beasts could be.

The combination of beauty and violence. It was their ambrosia, and they devoured it. It was what gluttons did.

They'd done so for decades, gathering in numbers, making it more unlikely that they'd ever be stopped. And each act of depravity made them more and more desensitized. And so they created a bloody game where the outcome was never quite certain, and it added to the thrill because it hinged on the wills of their victims, one of the only things they could not control, in a world where everything else was predictably theirs for the taking.

He glanced away from the girl. *Hold tight,* he thought. *If I've played my cards right, you might have a savior.* Of course, it would be up to her too. No one could save you if you weren't brave enough to save yourself. He'd learned that well.

He was here to avenge it.

Speaking of vengeance, there was old Dedryck, the king. The one who'd started it all. My, but he had aged, and quite poorly, despite his vast wealth. He looked like a withered corpse in a wheelchair, his tuxedo hanging on his bony frame and a blanket draped over his lap. His back was hunched, but his sparsely haired head was raised, and he was staring at Caspar, his beady eyes trained directly on him. Could the old man even see him from that far away? It seemed so.

A server approached with a tray of flutes filled with pale-golden champagne. He bowed slightly, extending the tray. His disguise was impeccable; even Caspar barely recognized him. Caspar noted that he had done an impressive job covering his birthmark as well. It was undetectable. "Sir?" the server asked, his pinkie finger making the most minute movement toward one of the glasses. Caspar picked up the flute. How lovely. Baccarat, if he wasn't mistaken. The server moved away.

"Mr. Vitucci." Caspar turned, responding effortlessly to the moniker. He'd been living under it for longer than he had not, after all.

A man approached him, clapping him on the back as he let out a deep laugh. "Nice touch," he said, nodding to the tissue paper poppy pinned to Caspar's jacket. "Ironic." The man grinned, and so did Caspar.

"Indeed," Caspar agreed.

A woman in a cage near the back of the room screamed through her gag, the sound muted, her weak plea only met with laughter from the men below.

A nobody to them. Less than that. They chose people who could be easily dismissed. No one would miss them should they disappear. No one would listen to them if they told their story. And these men made sure nothing checked out. Few lived, anyway, so who cared if there were a handful of scattered crazies with a similar story too outrageous to believe? Certainly not the police. They'd made sure of that.

"I don't think tonight's your night, Vitucci," the man said softly, leaning toward him, his rotund belly preceding him and bumping Caspar's. "One of them has lost a hand."

"Hmm," Caspar hummed disinterestedly, taking a long sip of his champagne. He wondered if this was the old man who'd taken Noelle's virginity so many years ago. That man had had this same physique. The man tipped his own flute back, guzzling it in one gulp. *There you go, you disgusting hog. Bottoms up.*

The server passed by, presenting another full tray of champagne. Caspar drained his glass and took another, as did the old man. "It's almost a shame that things look so bleak for them," the man said.

Caspar smiled. "Almost," he said. The man ambled away. Caspar looked around. Everywhere here there were bankers and politicians, members of various agencies, and high-powered attorneys. The amount of money they represented was in the billions. They could buy their way out of anything.

Or so they believed.

But they had missed something. Eventually they always did, because they thought themselves invincible.

The man who now called himself Leonard Sinclair was standing at Dedryck's side, watching him from across the room. Caspar raised his glass to Leonard—*Fontane*, the spoiled son of a judge and the man he'd once watched rape his sister and tear the necklace from her throat as Caspar had been bound and helpless. He'd taken to the debauchery quite easily, as Caspar remembered. Fontane still didn't recognize him, not only because they believed him dead, but because Caspar had been a nobody when he'd known him before, invisible to men such as him. Caspar had guessed correctly that Fontane had kept his sister's diamond, the one Caspar assumed the bastard took out now and again to remind himself how untouchable he was.

Fontane raised his glass in return. Caspar knew very well what the man was cheering to. He hoped Vitucci would be dead by the end of the night. And perhaps his hope was well founded. But there was much Fontane did not yet know.

The room dimmed slightly, a hush falling over the party as the screens around the room blinked to life. The final act had arrived.

CHAPTER
FORTY-SEVEN

Grim hissed out a breath, pain radiating up his arm as he used his teeth to tie off the makeshift bandage he'd fashioned from the sleeve of his shirt.

His head swam at the sight of the blunt end of his arm. His fucking hand was gone. *You made it out of that room alive, though. It's only a hand. And your right one at that.* His father had beat him each time he used his left hand to write, convinced that it meant Grim was stupid. He'd minded him at home but defied him at school and once he had moved out of his house. *Take that, you mean ole fucker. Noncompliance pays off in the end,* he thought, barely suppressing a manic laugh.

He hadn't left Cedro. That was the point. Tears tracked down the kid's face, and he swiped at them, trying to hide the fact that he was crying. He wasn't so hardened that he didn't still have the ability to cry. And Grim was glad for that. Grim knew what it was like not to feel. It was no way to live. Hence the fact that he'd been on a suicide mission prior to being abducted.

He supposed some would consider it an irony that he was currently fighting so hard to live.

"Cedro," he said, and Cedro turned his head, his eyes held to his, obviously trying hard not to look at Grim's wrapped stump, blood seeping through the gray fabric. He'd lost a lot of blood in the last few hours. It was now or never. They'd been given all the tools. He'd received the messages sent by the unknown person. He didn't know if they were tricks or lies, but they had to try. He raised his left hand and did the sign of the cross. Cedro let out a slow breath but then tipped his chin. He'd understood the sign.

Grim lay down, attempting to sleep. They would need rest for what was to come. His phantom hand throbbed with agony, and a bead of sweat rolled down his cheek. He felt hot and clammy. His eyes found the poppy twisted around a bar of his cage, and he pictured his daughter, the vision of her face becoming clearer the longer he focused. He hadn't allowed himself to picture her for so long, and now he saw her in every corner of his small cell, in the room where they tortured him, and in Cedro's eyes as he looked at him from across their divide.

Poppy.

If we get out of here, I'm going to try to adopt you, Cedro. And your brother. Why not? They needed someone. Why not him? *Why the hell not? Do something good with what you might have left of your miserable life, Grim. Something that makes up for your failures.* The thought gave him hope, something tangible to shoot for. A goal and a dream. Two things he barely remembered.

He slept, he supposed. He wasn't sure. But he became aware of the door opening and the same man entering their room. Grim pulled himself up, meeting Cedro's eyes as the man came to stand before Cedro's cage. "You've been rented."

Here we go. He didn't look at Cedro for risk of throwing him off in any way. The kid started to cry, but this time his cries were manufactured. Big gulping sobs as he sputtered and begged. "Exit or I tase you," the man told him.

Cedro hung his head, his shoulders shaking as he cried for another moment. "Wait," he said, reaching back and grabbing his last peppermint. "Please."

The man looked slightly confused but then smiled slowly. "Sure," he said. "A last supper. Enjoy."

Cedro curled his shoulders forward and crawled on his knees slowly to the front of the cage while the man stepped back. Cedro stood and unwrapped the candy slowly, placing it in his mouth and sighing. The man jerked his head, and Cedro began to walk but then suddenly stopped short, bringing his hands to his throat.

Grim moved to the front of his cage. "Cedro!"

The man with the Taser had taken another step back as Cedro began flailing, his face turning beet red now as he brought his hands to his throat once more.

"Jesus, he's choking. Help him!" Grim called. "Beat him on the back!"

The guard hesitated but then stepped forward, using his fist to beat Cedro's back over and over.

Grim didn't even notice when Cedro picked the key from his pocket. For a moment, he doubted if he had. But then Cedro drew in a big gasping breath, lowering his hands and drawing his shoulders back. There were tears streaking down his red-tinged skin. He drew in another breath, and then another, turning his foot slightly in the sign they'd agreed on through their prayer language.

Grim wanted to weep. He almost did, a sob of pride filling his throat so full he had to work to swallow it down. *That's it. That's my brave boy. Good job, Cedro.*

He took another breath, straightening and steeling his spine. One step down, many more to go.

The man gave one final knock on Cedro's back and began to step away when Cedro spun and raised his hand high above his head, rage blooming in his young face as he swept his hand downward toward the guard's artery.

One chance, you only have one chance, Cedro.

CHAPTER
FORTY-EIGHT

Even with his muscles tensed, pride shimmered in Caspar's chest as he watched the dance he'd choreographed over so many weeks. He hadn't anticipated one of his dancers being without a hand, and yet even so, they performed beautifully. The room had stilled, the sounds of old Dedryck's wheezes easily heard in the piqued silence.

"Well, I'll be damned," he heard a man utter.

You certainly will be.

Grim, the man who'd once fathered a girl named Penelope and called her Poppy, burst from his cage after Cedro unlocked it and the grated door fell forward. The particulars of each game were different. The cages unique. The rooms unexpected. It had kept Caspar on his toes. Cedro stepped over the guard lying in a pool of his own blood on the floor. His aim had been pure perfection. The sharpened tin whistle lodged directly and deeply in his artery before Cedro dragged it downward, tearing it open. He'd needed to get close to use it, and he'd figured out just how. The guard had bled out in seconds. *Perfect,* Caspar thought. *A few more steps and you'll be free of that room.*

The murmurs were rising now, the excitement and disbelief moving through the crowd of men as they watched Cedro and Grim jimmy the door that was locked from the outside. Caspar stood still, his back pressed to the wall as he watched the partners succeed in turning the lock, run from the room, and then sprint down the hallway. A guard gave chase, shooting at the men as they zigzagged, avoiding the bullets. Grim said something that sounded like "Pivot," and they both turned together, rushing the surprised guard. They fought the gunman, Grim one handed, both emaciated, working together as though they'd trained to do so. The chatter in the room was growing louder now, men downing their drinks and reaching for more as the entertainment played out. Some drank in celebration; they'd bet well. And others scowled as they tipped back the alcohol, draining their glass in one long guzzle.

The odds had just turned heavily in the favor of those who had bet that the two contestants would escape.

Grim and Cedro had overwhelmed the guard and taken his firearm. Cedro stood over him and fired once, the second shot producing nothing. The gun had only contained five bullets. There were rules for everything. In any case, Cedro's one shot had been enough. The guard lay dead, or dying, on the ground. Cedro threw the empty weapon, and they turned again, heading toward the exit.

Caspar could see on the screen that they'd almost reached the door. How much hope must be rising in their chests? *Almost there. Almost free.*

He had a moment of worry, just one, but then a few lines of static rolled across the screen before the picture blinked off and then immediately blinked back to life. Only now what was on the screen was *them*. Sounds of shock rolled through the crowd, and a man next to him suddenly cringed, bringing his hands to his throat as he began to choke.

Another man in front of Caspar did the same, and in less than ten seconds, a whole slew of men were gasping and writhing on the floor as they foamed at the mouth. He caught the eye of the server with the covered birthmark, Gervais Baudelaire, his brother for all intents and purposes, and gave him the smallest of smiles.

Caspar hadn't had the pleasure of seeing Grim and Cedro burst through the door of the building they'd been kept in, but he took a brief moment to picture it, inhaling a deep breath of the freedom they were experiencing right that moment. *Run. Run. Take this experience, and let it make you better. Stronger. Like Evan and Noelle.*

He'd sent the matching red diamonds to Baudelaire through a courier. He should be receiving them right about now. He'd know what to do with them without Caspar spelling it out—spread the wealth as he saw fit to those who had possessed enough innate decency to sacrifice themselves for a stranger. How rare the quality was that inspired such a choice. As rare as the two red diamonds that would help them live easier lives.

More men were falling now from the poison that had laced the inside of the glasses delivered a mere hour before. They gripped their throats, their faces turning a hideous shade of purple. A terrible death. One not nearly terrible enough.

But it would do.

The caged women were screaming and shaking their bars. Someone must have flipped the switch that lowered them, because they began to descend. *Shit.*

"Caspar!" Gervais yelled just in time for him to turn and duck, narrowly avoiding the steak knife Fontane swung at him despite the fact he was obviously dying. Green foam ran from his mouth, and his eyes were so bugged out they looked like they might pop. The sound of Caspar's name caused Fontane's already strained eyes to impossibly widen even more, and threw him off enough that Caspar was able to easily grab the knife from him. He brought his fist back, smashing it into Fontane's face, the man grunting in pain as blood spurted from his nose. Caspar punched him over and over and over again until he was driven back against a table laden with all manner of delicacies and carving knives that would now go to waste. He leaned in and whispered two words in Fontane's ear. "For Evan." And then he dragged the blade across his throat and watched the life in his eyes extinguish. There was poison on

Fontane's tongue, but the real poison had dripped into his soul. His son would not carry his twisted legacy. It dried up here, with him.

The noise around Caspar was growing louder, a chorus of misery and death. The sound of demons floundering. He wanted to watch it until the end. But the women in the cages needed help. "Get them out and then leave," he said as Gervais approached.

"I'll come back for you," Gervais said.

"No," Caspar answered. "It's too risky. We talked about this."

"You'll meet us, though, right? You'll be there?"

"Help them, brother," Caspar said, squeezing his shoulder.

Gervais paused. He'd known him much of his life. He sensed what Caspar was not telling him. "Help them," he said again, meeting his eyes and giving him a nod.

The cages had reached the floor, and a couple of the women were moaning and slamming their shoulders against the bars, begging to be set free. Gervais's gaze lingered on Caspar for only a moment longer before he turned, heading toward the nearest cage. The final task to free the innocents.

This night would not end as that one had.

CHAPTER
FORTY-NINE

Noelle was barely controlling the sobs that had been racking her body as she'd watched the two men escape their cages, killing the guard who gave chase, just as she and Evan had done. Beside her, Evan watched, still and silent, his arm wrapped around her body, gaze trained on the screen.

Evan had called Aria, and Noelle could hear the sirens approaching now. But what could they do from there? Watch in helpless horror along with them? They had no idea where the two men were. They were free, though. Safe. Noelle knew from experience. They had won the game.

And they also had no idea of the location where naked, caged women were hanging from the rafters and a horde of men in tuxedos had collapsed on the floor, their hands gripping their throats as though they'd been poisoned.

Evan continued to hold his phone to the screen, his hands trembling as he filmed what was going on. They didn't know if the live stream of what they were watching would be saved somewhere once it was over or whether it would be gone forever, so they made sure to capture it. Made sure that they could provide still shots of every man in there, both struggling on the floor or dead. *Insurance.* These were the men who had caged them, the ones who paid to victimize and torture them and many others. No cover-up would be possible. What had happened in the dark would be brought to the light. They'd make sure of it.

Evan continued to film the screen even when the police arrived, swarming the residence, and then they watched as a man in a server's uniform picked one lock after another with some tool Noelle could not see well enough to identify. He freed the naked women in the cages, untied them, and removed their gags, as the men behind them continued to vomit and seize and then grow still, one after the next. The server kept his face directed away from the camera so she couldn't see him as he let the women out of their cages, and then together, they all stumbled toward the exit, the man pulling what looked like red velvet tablecloths off the tables and tossing them to the women.

"Six people, five wrapped in bright red," Aria was saying into her radio to the police helicopters she'd dispatched. "They left a building. They're running. Within a five-mile radius of this address." They had to be, Noelle prayed. Vitucci had only left an hour before. Whatever building he was in wasn't far.

Noelle turned her face into Evan's shoulder, crying quietly. So much death, so much sickness. Somehow, inside, even though she didn't know all the particulars, she knew that this was the final battle. And yet, even so, despair flowed through her along with the rage. She lifted her head and made herself watch them die. Rome was falling, and she had to bear witness.

She had to know that evil eventually ended. The visions in front of her were horrifying, but they were also a complicated form of justice, and watching it unfold was going to help her heal, help her unravel her grief.

It. Was. Over. She glanced up at Evan to see his eyes trained on the screen, too, and despite her raging emotions, the one that glowed brightest was her love for him. And she vowed with everything in her to keep that glow front and center, no matter the darkness that threatened to descend in the wake of this horror.

We leave here whole.
We leave here together.

Her gaze moved back to Vitucci as he walked slowly through the dozens of bodies, maneuvering around some, stepping on the throats of others, pausing and leaning closer to a few faces before their bodies went still. She had the notion he'd wanted those particular men to see his face in their final moments.

She watched the man who had staged this moment and so many others. She wondered what his real name was, the man who was some strange and elusive mixture of evil and goodness, revenge and righteousness. Both a sociopath and a savior. She knew suddenly and clearly that the event she was watching would go down in history, as would he. She wondered if he'd be called a villain or a hero. Even she wasn't sure, and he'd helped save her life and that of the man she loved standing beside her.

Sirens began wailing in the distance. A limping Vitucci approached the old man in the wheelchair slowly. He was the only one not on the floor. Whatever poison had been administered, the old man hadn't consumed any.

Vitucci slowly wrapped his hands around the frail man's neck and leaned closer, whispering something in his ear. The man began to shake but not with fear. With rage. His eyes bugged out, a hellish wail coming from his mouth, and his clawlike hands raised as he uselessly attempted to fight back. The sounds of helicopters could be heard in the background now too. Vitucci leaned back, the old man's face going a deep shade of red as he squeezed. The old man stared up at Vitucci, still defiant even as death's shadowy figure swooped nearer. "Caspar," he wheezed.

"That's right," Vitucci said. And then he squeezed and squeezed, the man's face going from red to purple to near black as Vitucci brought his face so close to his that their noses nearly touched. Still, Noelle did not look away, even as Vitucci finally let go with a gusting exhale, and what had been the old man tipped from its wheelchair and fell to the floor in a heap of flesh and bones.

Vitucci turned, the expression on his face victorious but somehow shocked as well. He stumbled as though he was having trouble finding his footing and let his head fall forward for several long moments, his shoulders rising and falling. The room was silent now; the last of the death throes were complete.

Vitucci reached for a glass sitting on a table next to him. Noelle blinked as his gaze met hers over the screen, and she sucked in a breath, certain he knew she was watching him. Certain he was looking straight at her. He raised the glass and toasted the camera, and then, without any hesitation, he brought it to his lips and threw it back, swallowing every drop. Then he reached for another and another, downing them both before falling to his knees, one word whispering from his lips, too silent to hear. But Noelle watched his mouth and was certain he'd uttered "Celesse."

EPILOGUE

Noelle squinted out over the ocean as the waves crashed on the shore, rushing toward her and then falling away. Overhead, the clouds were clearing, shafts of sunlight streaming through the gloom. The storm that had raged through the night had passed. What was it about the morning after that made the world feel cleansed? It was a smell. It was a feeling.

"Mommy!" Callie called from a few feet up the beach, her hair lifting in the wind. "Look!" She held up a shell of some kind and then put it in her pocket. Noelle smiled at her daughter's unceasing joy at finding a shell when shells were so plentiful where they lived. *Never lose that, baby girl. Never take anything wonderful for granted, no matter how much of it you have.*

A figure caught her eye, stepping off the walking bridge and onto the sand. Evan. Her heart galloped and then soared, her breath catching with happy surprise.

"Evan!" Callie shouted as he drew closer. Their little girl ran in his direction, her short legs pumping. Evan's laugh was caught by the wind and delivered straight to her. She laughed, too, as he swooped Callie into his arms and spun her around. Her heart squeezed tightly. That sight. *Oh, thank you God for that sight.*

Evan set Callie down and took her hand, and Noelle waited, watching as they walked together toward her. "Well this is a surprise," she said, her lips trembling as she tried not to smile, tried desperately not to fly into his arms the same way Callie had. He hadn't told her he was coming. She'd flown home from Reno three days before, and he'd stayed to assist the police as they began unraveling the crime that had rocked the entire globe and to sort some of his father's affairs. They'd both been in shock when they'd said goodbye, knowing she had to get home to their daughter, both desperate for that, even while it was important that Evan stay.

There hadn't been time for plans, or even for more than a few uttered words. *I love you. Kiss her for me. We'll talk soon.*

Evan squinted out to the ocean for a second, a playful smile tilting his lips. "Do you figure there's much of a need for a PI here in town?"

Her heart flipped, and she couldn't help the tiny laugh that bubbled up her throat. He was moving here? She blinked tears from her eyes, his softening as he stared so lovingly at her. A few feet from them, Callie had become entranced with yet another shell that she'd spied and run to collect. She was holding it up now, her gaze moving over the details of that particular one.

"There's always need for a PI. I can solve a few mysteries for you right off the bat, though."

He grinned, a ray of sun hitting his eyes so that she could practically see right through them, the blue deep and endless. "Yeah? Like what?"

"At least one cup of coffee before I'm conversational. Preferably two, but definitely one."

"I appreciate the heads-up."

"I'll do anything after a salted caramel crème brûlée."

"Anything?"

She confirmed with a nod.

A brow shot up, and he pretended to search for something in his pockets. "That one's very important. I think I should write it down."

She laughed. He was here. He was *here*, and for a moment she let all the horror they'd experienced fall away and she was only hope. Only wild, beautiful, healing hope. She let it wash through her, the sunlight after the storm.

"Come on, sweetheart," she called to Callie, linking arms with Evan as they turned toward Sweetgrass. Callie ran ahead of them, skipping and singing one of their favorite nursery rhymes. Noelle could see Tilly sitting on the porch. She couldn't wait to introduce Evan to her. They were going to love each other.

"Can we figure out when to tell her?" he asked, his eyes on Callie.

Noelle pulled him closer, laying her head on his shoulder as they walked. "Yes. Let's get you settled and her used to you being here, and then we'll sit down and tell her." Noelle couldn't wait. She couldn't wait to be a family, to share the ups and the downs and the boring. God, she couldn't wait to share the beautiful boring.

They had a lot to talk about; she'd have to prepare herself for the emotional impact of the updates he surely had. All she knew at this point was the good news that Cedro Leon and Grimaldo Zamora were safe with Cedro's brother in Arizona and that Grimaldo had already expressed interest in becoming their sponsor, and that the women who had been freed from cages were being cared for, their families contacted. The handful of men who had survived the poison were in custody, except for one lone server, the man who had seemed to be helping Vitucci or . . . Caspar. He hadn't been recognizable to her or to Evan, and Noelle had a feeling he'd remain unidentified, and strangely, the thought didn't distress her. Whoever he was, and whatever conflicting feelings she had about Caspar, that man had been there to assist in taking down evil.

Yes, there was so much more to learn about the monsters who'd victimized so many. And all that was important. But so was this. A few moments of blessed peace. Of only them.

He stopped, and she did too. "Oh," he said, reaching in his back pocket. She watched to see Callie run across the bridge, raising her arm toward Miss Tilly, who waved her forward. When Noelle looked back at Evan, she saw that he'd removed a jewelry box. "This isn't what you think," he told her. "Yet. Because I've got better plans for that."

She laughed softly. Okay, so he wasn't proposing. She was glad, because she wanted at least a little time to process all they'd been through so she could focus solely on the future. Again that wild hope billowed inside. She glanced up to see that Callie had made it to Tilly. "What is it?"

He opened the box, and she inhaled a breath. "My mom's ring."

"Baudelaire sent it to me," he said. "It came in the mail anonymously. But it had to be him. Who else?"

She stared down at it for a moment, thinking about that before picking up the beautiful, delicate piece of jewelry, the one her mom had once worn.

She slipped it on her right hand.

"For now, a promise," Evan said, their eyes meeting. A promise. That they'd love hard, that they'd always be honest, that they'd try their very best to be a living embodiment of the victory that had risen from the ashes of evil. *Love.*

"A promise," she repeated. They were good at keeping those.

They turned, fingers linked, and headed toward the house. Whole. Together.

ACKNOWLEDGMENTS

As with all stories, this one was a journey. Thank you to so many who walked it with me.

To Kimberly Brower, who is a force of nature. I have no idea how you do all that you do, but I'm so grateful that you throw me into the mix.

To Marion Archer, for your wisdom and deep sensitivity.

To Charlotte Herscher, who challenges me in ways that help me grow and is a true pleasure to work with even when asking me to rewrite large sections of my first draft. I'd work with you a hundred times over! And thank you to Maria Gomez and the rest of the Amazon team, who make the process run so smoothly and (seemingly) effortlessly.

To my readers. Thank you for your enthusiasm and kindness, for making me want to strive to do better each time, and for constantly showing up. My appreciation is endless.

To all the book bloggers, Instagrammers, and BookTokers: I am humbled that so many of you have turned your creativity and passion in my direction.

To my husband, thank you for being so damn good at keeping promises. I love you.

TURN THE PAGE TO SEE A PREVIEW OF MIA SHERIDAN'S BOOK *BAD MOTHER*!

CHAPTER ONE

Reno, Nevada, the one place on earth she'd vowed never to return to. Unfortunately, that pledge had blown up in her face, an outcome that was an iffy mix of fate and her own emotionally charged decision-making.

Would you change it? Sienna asked herself for the hundredth time.

And for the hundredth time, she still wasn't certain of the answer.

Only . . . yes, yes, she was sure of the answer. She'd do it again if given the choice. She just hadn't anticipated the choice leading her here.

The cloudless desert sky—vivid blue and endless—stretched above as she pulled open the door to the police department before stepping into the blessed relief of the air-conditioned building.

"May I help you?" the woman at the front desk asked on a smile.

Sienna smiled back, though not quite as widely. "Sienna Walker here to see Sergeant Dahlen."

"Oh, hi! You're the new detective from New York, right? I'm Chelle Lopez. Nice to meet you. What do you think of Reno so far?"

"Hi, Chelle. Nice to meet you too. And I'm actually from Reno. Originally, I mean."

A look of surprise lit Chelle's round face. "Oh, well then, welcome home."

Sienna schooled her expression, even while a knot twisted in her stomach at Chelle's words, and she watched as the woman picked up the phone and let Sergeant Dahlen know she was there.

"She'll be out in just a minute."

"Great, thanks," Sienna said as Chelle picked up another call. Soon she was laughing at something the person on the other end said and lowering her voice as she chatted on what was obviously a personal call.

Sienna had barely taken a seat when a very tall, striking woman in her fifties with white-blonde hair in a spiky pixie cut entered the lobby, her eyes focused on her. "Sienna Walker?"

She stood. "Yes. Sergeant Dahlen? Nice to meet you in person."

The older woman, who was wearing a black pantsuit, a black shirt, and red high heels, moved toward her and shook her hand quickly as Sienna lifted her chin, attempting to see eye to eye with the woman and failing. "You can follow me this way."

Sergeant Dahlen led her through the station, buzzing with the midday activity of a busy police force, her long legs causing Sienna to have to hurry to keep up. They entered an office, and Sergeant Dahlen closed the door behind them. She gestured to a chair in front of her desk, and they both took a seat as she picked up her phone and asked someone to come to her office. Sienna did a quick sweep of the room, which was completely devoid of clutter and appeared as squared away as the woman who inhabited it.

She replaced the phone in its cradle, leaned back, and crossed her legs as she perused Sienna. "Your captain, Darrin Crewson, and I are both army veterans."

"Yes, he told me, ma'am."

"Ingrid." She paused, her eyes narrowing very slightly. "There's nothing I wouldn't do for my fellow brothers and sisters in arms."

Sienna nodded, her nerves tingling. "Yes, and vice versa, Darrin said." If an icicle morphed into a person, Sergeant Dahlen is what it would look like, Sienna thought. Lovely in a cold, sharp way.

Sergeant Dahlen—Ingrid—lifted her chin as though reading Sienna's thoughts and agreeing. "Even so, I don't need nor want a troublemaking renegade causing me headaches and unnecessary paperwork. I hate unnecessary paperwork."

"No, ma'am. I don't intend to cause this department—er, especially you—any trouble. What happened in New York was a . . . unique situation. I won't let it happen again." Her tone sounded weak, even to herself. She straightened her back, attempting to convey the message of strength with her posture where her voice had failed. Sienna had a strong feeling Sergeant Dahlen had a low threshold for weaklings.

The older woman studied Sienna for another moment, and she resisted the urge to squirm. If that was the look the detective sergeant used when she was interrogating a suspect, the department must have an insanely high solve rate. Anyone would crack under that glacial gaze. Her eyes moved to the window, and Sienna let out a silent breath. "We have a major staffing shortage right now in the Reno PD, so when Darrin requested the transfer, that made things a little easier on our end." Sienna resisted a flinch. "But," the sergeant went on, "Darrin also told me you're a damn good detective when you're not going off half-cocked and that any department would be lucky to have you."

Thank you, Darrin. For that and a dozen other kindnesses. "I'm going to do my best to live up to that generous description, Sergeant."

"See that you do."

Sienna turned at the sudden rap on the glass of the door, and a dark-haired woman opened it and peeked her head in. "Come on in, Kat," Ingrid said.

The woman named Kat came in, taking a seat next to Sienna. She had her hair pulled back in a tight bun, and her lips were red and full. She reminded Sienna of a Bond girl in a pantsuit, if a Bond girl would ever be seen in a pantsuit, fashionable and well fitted though Kat's was. "Katerina Kozlov, this is Sienna Walker, your new partner."

Kat turned, assessing her very directly but not unkindly. "Well, thank God the percentage of testosterone in this place just reduced another fraction." She leaned in slightly. "Ingrid being the biggest supplier of said testosterone." She shot a grin at the older woman, whose eyebrows rose slightly but who seemed otherwise unamused. Sienna fought the smile that would make it appear she was laughing at her boss's expense on the first day of a new job.

Kat held out her hand. "Welcome to homicide," her new partner said. "Call me Kat."

Sienna shook. "Hi, Kat, nice to meet you."

"All right, now that the niceties are out of the way, why don't you show Sienna to her desk and get her acquainted with the layout."

Kat stood. "Come on, partner. I'll show you the most important room in this building—the one where we keep the coffee."

Sienna thanked Sergeant Dahlen and then followed her new partner out the door.

The coffee lounge was small but adequate, featuring a corner kitchen area and a table off to the side, where no one currently sat. Kat picked up a paper cup and held it up to Sienna, her brows rising in question.

"Sure, thanks," Sienna said. Kat poured two cups of coffee and handed one to Sienna before turning and leaning against the Formica counter. "So what'd you do?" she asked.

Sienna let out a small, surprised laugh, then swallowed a sip of weak coffee. She hadn't expected the direct question right off the bat, though she knew well that rumors spread quickly among cops. "I neglected to follow orders."

Kat looked mildly disappointed. "Insubordination? Damn, I was hoping you had an affair with the chief or something juicy."

Sienna let out a chuckle that died a quick death. If only. "Well, it was a little more complicated but not very juicy. The orders I disregarded came down from the mayor."

Kat's eyebrows rose. "Ah." She was obviously considering that nugget of information. "So they did you a favor and shuffled you out of town before the mayor could demand you resign or be fired."

"They obviously don't call you Detective for nothing."

Kat smiled, nodding to the door and tossing her cup in the garbage. "Let me show you to your desk. We're going to be spending a lot of time together. If you decide you feel like telling me the details of that story, you won't have to travel far."

She followed Kat to their work area, the only privacy a flimsy partition, with two standard-issue metal desks just like the one she'd had in New York. She pulled open a drawer, expecting the squeak that followed. The familiar piece of furniture felt like one of the only things in her life that hadn't changed. Welcome to Reno PD, Sienna.

~

Sienna was surprised that the trailer park looked slightly less squalid than she remembered. Maybe it was due to the wash of golden light from the setting sun softening the ramshackle trailers and patchy grass. Or maybe it was because her memory had exaggerated the seediness of this place. Or maybe it was because at some point, someone had come along and tried to rejuvenate Paradise Estates Mobile Home Park—a true misnomer if ever there was one—and somewhat succeeded, even if minimally.

Perhaps a mixture of all those things.

In any case, here it sat, in front of her, the layout the same, though the girl she'd been, the one who'd grown up here, felt different in every way. Even though she was sitting in her car, staring out the window, she had a strange sense of imbalance as she looked down the rows toward the lot where she'd once lived, as though the world had shifted subtly beneath her.

Why were you pulled here? She'd found herself driving in this direction after meeting with her new boss and partner, without even really deciding to do so, almost as if by muscle memory alone.

The heart is a muscle too. Yes, and maybe that was the one she'd been using. She'd been raised in this trailer park. She'd left for school every morning from here, until the day she'd graduated high school. She'd had some of her happiest moments in this place and some of her worst.

She'd fallen in love here. Her chest squeezed as she turned her head to the right, gazing down the row where his trailer sat. Of course, it wasn't his anymore. Or his mother Mirabelle's. Someone else lived there now, she was sure. He had made it big. And though it had turned out she didn't know as much about him as she'd once believed, she knew in her heart of hearts that the first thing he would have done with the money he earned was to buy his mother a home. A real home, not housing made of plastic walls that swayed in any moderately strong wind.

At the thought of Mirabelle, she felt a pinching sensation under her breastbone and unconsciously brought her hand up to massage away the pain. She missed her. Still. She'd been the only real mother Sienna had ever known, her own an alcohol-drenched shell of a woman who had been generally unaware of Sienna's existence. The woman who had passed on her green eyes and her golden-blonde hair to Sienna and—thankfully—not much else had died five years before. When Sienna had learned the news, she'd felt little more than a passing sadness that might accompany the knowledge that any wasted life had ended.

She'd sent her father a check to help with the cremation costs and made a donation in her mother's name to a local charity that helped drug and alcohol addicts find recovery. It was enough closure for her. And while her father had very promptly cashed the check, she hadn't spoken to him since.

She'd left this mobile home park eleven years before without saying goodbye to either of her parents. The ache in her heart had only been for Mirabelle. At the time, that particular ache had been drowned out by a greater one, though, and it was only in the aftermath that she had realized her grief had layers.

She stared, unseeing, in the direction of what had once been her home. Her mind cast back.

~

Mirabelle pulled the door of the trailer open, wiping her hands on a dish towel. "Sienna? What's wrong, sweet girl?"

Sienna let out a quiet sob, allowing Mirabelle to usher her into the trailer, where she led her to the plaid sofa and sat her down. Mirabelle took a seat next to her, turning so they were knee to knee, and took Sienna's hands in hers, squeezing gently. Lemons and lilies met her nose, and the scent served as comfort before Mirabelle had even uttered a word. She took a deep, shaky breath. "I got invited to Amybeth Horton's birthday party, and my dad said he'd bring home some money so I could buy her a present, but he didn't, and now I can't go." Truth be told, her father hadn't necessarily forgotten. He'd likely never intended to at all or even thought twice about her request after she'd made it. He'd come home drunk that afternoon, and she hadn't "reminded" him, as it was best to steer clear entirely when he'd been drinking. He was mean in general, and liquor only enhanced that attribute. Sienna's face screwed up, the disappointment of having looked so forward to something, having been included, and then being let down—again—by her parents bringing all her misery to the surface. She couldn't go without a gift, though. That would be humiliating. The other girls Amybeth hung around weren't rich by any stretch, but they had more than Sienna's family. In every conceivable way.

Sienna wished she weren't so hyperaware of that, but she was four-teen, no kid anymore, and it was just her personality. She noticed every-thing. She always had. Not like Gavin, who was perpetually happy go lucky and didn't seem to care what anyone thought. He was observant, too, when he wanted to be, but his observations didn't seem to con-stantly hurt him in some way or another the way hers did.

Gavin wasn't currently at home. She knew that, and it was the only reason she'd come. She didn't want him to see her cry, but she'd needed a mother. She'd needed Mirabelle.

Mirabelle frowned, wiping Sienna's cheek with her thumb when a tear spilled from her eye. "Oh, darling. I'm so sorry." An expression flitted over her pretty face, part sadness, part anger, but then she set her lips together, tilting her head as she thought. "When is the party?"

"Today," Sienna said, taking a deep breath as the sharpness of the misery lessened. She still felt disappointed, but she was here, in Mirabelle's neat and orderly trailer, being listened to as though her pain mattered. She'd only come to her for comfort. She knew Mirabelle didn't have a lot of money either. She worked as the assistant to a magician named Argus, a kindhearted Greek man who called Sienna "Siennoulla" and brought homemade baklava to Mirabelle sometimes in a white box with a black ribbon, which Sienna and Gavin gorged themselves on until their stomachs were stuffed and their lips were coated in honey. Their show wasn't that popular, though, and barely paid the bills. But Argus said that the joy it brought to their audiences was worth far more than riches.

Sienna knew that to be a little white lie since he let Gavin, who was amazing at cards, play online poker under his name and split the profits, a fact they kept from Mirabelle. Sienna didn't like keeping secrets from Mirabelle, but she also knew that the extra money Argus told her had come from ticket sales and put into her earnings lessened Mirabelle's stress and allowed them to pay all their bills, even if there wasn't much left over at the end of the month.

Sienna was old enough now to know that the tricks they performed were just that, but she couldn't help watching them practice with pure delight in her heart and a gasp on her lips when an act went just right.

There was something enchanting and beautiful about the choreography alone when it came to a perfectly executed show.

"Today . . . ," Mirabelle repeated. Sienna opened her mouth to speak, but Mirabelle grabbed her hand and pulled her to her feet. "Come with me. I have an idea."

"An idea? Mirabelle . . ." Mirabelle pulled her into her bedroom at the back of the trailer. She let go of Sienna's hand and stepped up to a dresser next to the door. This room smelled even more strongly of lily of the valley, and her bed featured a quilt of yellow roses. Mirabelle opened the top drawer of the dresser and pulled out a small wooden box. She opened it and reached inside, and Sienna noticed a stack of photos, but Mirabelle covered them with her hand before Sienna had a chance to see who they were of. Her family? Mirabelle didn't ever talk about her family. She didn't have any pictures hung—except of Gavin—and she and Gavin never had any relatives over for holidays or anything else, but maybe she'd had a falling-out with them.

Sienna wanted to ask, but she also didn't want to invade Mirabelle's privacy.

Mirabelle brought something out of the box and held it up. Sienna blinked. It was a beautiful, delicate silver bracelet with pale-purple stones. "Do you think your friend would like this?"

Sienna's gaze flew to Mirabelle's. "Like it? Oh yes, but I couldn't—"

"You can, and you will." Mirabelle took Sienna's hand and pressed the bracelet into it. Without letting go of her closed fist, Mirabelle looked down, seeming to be considering what she was about to say. "I know I haven't spoken of Gavin's father," she started haltingly, meeting Sienna's curious gaze, "but he was not a nice man, Sienna. He was violent and cruel, and so I took Gavin and I left him."

"Oh," Sienna breathed. "I'm so sorry," she said, her voice small.

But Mirabelle smiled. "Don't be sorry, love. I'm not. Our life is better without him." But something shifted slightly in her expression, as though she wasn't entirely sure of what she said.

"And . . . and you have Argus," Sienna said, wanting to make the haunted look in Mirabelle's eyes disappear.

Mirabelle's worried frown transformed into a gentle smile. "Yes. Yes, I have Argus."

Mirabelle let go of her hand, and Sienna opened it, the bracelet catching the light and sparkling up at her. "It's not an expensive piece," Mirabelle said, her words rushed. "But more than that, it has . . . difficult memories attached to it. I should have given it away long ago." She stared at it, appearing troubled for a few moments before seeming to catch herself, her smile brightening. "It must be fate that I kept it and that it should belong to Amybeth. Let it make new memories. Good ones."

Sienna considered it doubtfully. It was lovely. And Amybeth was kind. Sienna would love to gift it to her, but she wasn't certain she should allow Mirabelle to give her something that—despite her words—looked valuable.

But if it was, wouldn't she have sold it by now? There were several times she'd seen Mirabelle wringing her hands, a worried frown on her face as she'd gone through her bills. "I—"

"Oh! And I have a box that will be perfect for it too." She grinned, pulling Sienna into a hug. "Say yes, Sienna, and you go to that party and have the time of your life. Nothing would make me happier."

Sienna smiled back, love and gratitude gripping her so that she could hardly breathe. "Okay, Mirabelle. Thank you. Thank you so much."

~

A little boy caught Sienna's attention, breaking her from the recollection that had tears burning the backs of her eyes. God, it'd been a long time since she'd let herself get so fully immersed in a memory. The child ran from the side of one of the trailers and ducked behind a tree, holding his hand over his mouth as though to keep himself from laughing out loud as three other children turned the same corner he had, each ducking behind a tree or the side of a porch. They were playing hide-and-go-seek. Mirabelle had never let them play that particular game. It'd made her nervous, she'd said, that one of them would hide somewhere and get trapped. And she'd looked genuinely distraught when she'd said it, so Sienna and Gavin had obeyed. At least while she was home. Sienna's lips tipped slightly, and she swallowed her emotion down as she watched the innocent game play out, the "finder" making the others howl with glee as he located them. These kids were young still. They lived and played with optimistic joy. They weren't old enough yet to realize that others would look down on them for where they came from. They weren't self-conscious of their secondhand clothes or their parents' broken-down car that would likely backfire in the carpool lane and make others nearby dive for the bushes in fear that a lunatic was firing a weapon into the crowd.

Sienna's smile melted as she reminded herself she'd be better served to stop projecting her own insecurities and cringe-inducing memories onto these children. Maybe they'd be strong enough not to define themselves by where they came from. Maybe their parents—though poor—gave a damn about them. Maybe they have mothers like Mirabelle and not like my own.

She made a pained sound of frustration in the back of her throat, turning the key in the ignition and starting her car. She didn't have time for this right now, nor was it helpful. Why she had come here, she really had no clue, other than maybe to prove to herself she could. So, fine, now she had seen it, faced it, survived it, and she could go on with her life, knowing that though it now sat closer, it still had no real power over her. It was only a place. It did not live and breathe.

She turned her car, stomping on the gas so that her tires spun, and a billow of dust exploded in a grainy cloud behind her.

If it doesn't live and breathe, then why are you racing away as though it might find a way to chase you? But she pushed the whisper down, knowing there was no good answer.

ABOUT THE AUTHOR

Mia Sheridan is a *New York Times*, *USA Today*, and *Wall Street Journal* bestselling author. Mia lives in Cincinnati, Ohio, with her husband. They have four children here on earth and one in heaven. Other romantic suspense novels include *Bad Mother*, *Where the Blame Lies*, and *Where the Truth Lives*.

Find Mia online at https://miasheridan.com and on Twitter (@MSheridanAuthor), Instagram (@MiaSheridanAuthor), and Facebook (https://www.facebook.com/miasheridanauthor).